The Man Who Changed Colors

By Bill Fletcher, Jr.

Critical Acclaim

"Bill Fletcher is a truth seeker and a truth teller – even when he's writing fiction. Not unlike Bill, his character David Gomes is willing to put his life and career in peril to expose the truth. A thrilling read!"
–Tavis Smiley, Broadcaster and *New York Times* Bestselling Author

"A fascinating tale of murder and intrigue in a small New England town, and the dogged reporter who pursues the truth, only to discover an underground web of fascist thugs, part of the hidden blowback on U.S. soil from Africa's long struggle against Western colonialism."
–Juan González, cohost of *Democracy Now* and author of *Harvest of Empire: A History of Latinos in America.*

"Fletcher keeps us glued to this novel of complex international politics, abuse of government powers, corruption and twisted justice."
–Cindy Domingo, writer and international solidarity activist.

"Only Bill could deliver the compelling nuances of this political crime novel. This book will have you eager to learn more not just about David but about the history of the tense relationships of Cape Verdeans, Portuguese and African Americans through liberation, colonization, and fascism."
–Denise Perry, cofounder & Executive Director of BOLD

"Fletcher's protagonist assiduously unravels a mystery, taking us on a stimulating journey across time and national borders in the process. An irresistible read, a political education and curiosity teaser all at the same time."
–Barbara Ransby, professor, writer, activist and author of the award-winning *Ella Baker and the Black Freedom Movement*

"Penetrating and beautifully written. The exploration of deep and vexing moral questions pertaining to labor relations, race, ethnicity, class, immigration, and gender is profoundly captivating. A true gem for the Cape Verdean community and beyond and a great gift to the labor movement."
—Ricardo Rosa

"His characters, while shaped by powerful social forces, are three-dimensional human beings, with their strengths and passions, foibles and limitations (like us!). When you join them on this journey, you will have difficulty putting this book down until you are finished. And then, I suspect, you will join me in waiting for Fletcher's next book."
—Peter Rachleff, co-author *By These Hands: Portraits from the Factory Floor*

"The Man Who Changed Colors pulls you in and takes you on a journey of twists, turns and reveals in this illuminating mystery. A fine addition in the tradition of hardboiled stories reflecting the flaws and gains of the working class, and that which continues to divide us."
—Gary Phillips, author of *One-Shot Harry*

"This intriguing mystery once again has journalist David Gomes caught up in a Cape Cod labyrinth of murder-or-not, brutal worker exploitation and union politics, post-colonial legacies, issues of race and racial identity, and love under stress. Brother Fletcher has penned a remarkable page-turner about a vital Cape Verdean diaspora, and a really beautiful love story. I can't wait for the film, and I'm already figuring out who the stars should be."
—Bill Gallegos, former executive director of Communities for a Better Environment, *The Nation* **magazine Editorial Board**

"A suspenseful story for shipyard workers and newspaper reporters. It's even more meaningful if you know the Cape,

Boston, and New Bedford. Fletcher's approach to the racial issues is especially masterful. A good read from many perspectives."
–Brigid O'Farrell, author of *She Was One of Us: Eleanor Roosevelt and the American Worker*

"If you know Bill Fletcher, you saw flashes of his life experiences throughout The Man Who Changed Colors. Racism in labor, immigration contradictions, class struggle, Star Trek—it's all there, mixed in with intrigue and murder. Bill has proven that he is as masterful in the art of fiction as he is with political commentary."
–Jamala Rogers, author of *Ferguson is America: Roots of Rebellion*

"Much like Walter Mosley did in creating his crime-solving protagonist Easy Rawlings as he navigates the color lines in postwar LA, Bill Fletcher brings us a murder mystery through the eyes of investigative reporter David Gomes. Fletcher leans on his vast knowledge of both labor history and the revolutionary struggle of Cabo Verde to introduce readers to a fascinating and often overlooked convergence of cultures on the shores of Cape Cod."
–Sean Gonsalves, reporter, researcher and Cape Verdean author

"Beginning with two crimes scenes 26 years apart, Fletcher leads readers through a story whose pace accelerates with every chapter as reporter David Gomes investigates a shipyard accident in 1978. The investigation takes the reader into the different communities on Cape Cod. Fletcher has done an excellent job weaving a tapestry with nuance across ethnicities and within ethnicities. He creates characters representing a range of émigrés whose backgrounds are not well known to most readers."
–Steve Pitts, Emeritus Associate Chair, UC Berkeley Labor Center

"Bill Fletcher Jr. has a remarkable skill in depicting the time and place, the full flavor of the Massachusetts Cape and Islands in 1970s– not unlike that of Robert Parker, but with a keener eye for the intricacies of class and racial struggle. In his effort to solve the murder of Alberto Pires, investigative reporter David Gomes, bears witness to the dizzying complexities, despairing absurdities, and infinite possibilities of contemporary American life."
–R. A. Judy, Professor of Critical and Cultural Studies

"Using the backdrop of Cape Cod's complex stew of race and class dynamics, Bill Fletcher weaves an intense and finely wrought mystery that is somehow smart, eminently readable, and deeply nuanced. A thoroughly satisfying read."
–Makani Themba, Writer, Activist

"The Man Who Changed Colors weaves its murders with a lush tangle of threads: racism, workplace safety, union struggles, the precarious state of community newspapers, gangsters who worked for fascists in Portugal and Greece, and, of course,
love. You won't be able to put it down."
–Ellen Bravo, co-author *Standing Up*

"A death occurs at the shipyard and [journalist] Gomes suspects it's much more than a presumed accident. As the story unspools with layers of intrigue and danger, Gomes' investigative skills and determination are vividly highlighted, and Fletcher captures this intensity as he graphically details the various workplaces, the landscape, and most rewardingly the language and disposition of the individuals as they interact in this engrossing murder mystery."
–Herb Boyd, *Institute of the Black World*

Library of Congress Cataloging-in-Publication Data:

Fletcher, Bill Jr.

The Man Who Changed Colors

1. Cape Verde —Fiction 2. Immigration 3. Mystery story
4. Investigative journalism 5. Racism 6. Cape Cod 7. Bill
Fletcher, Jr.

Cover art by Anna Usacheva

Cover design by Matthew Tallon

Book design by Matthew Tallon

Set in Palatino.

Published by Hardball Press, Brooklyn, New York
ISBN: 979-8-9850979-6-2

www.hardballpress.com

To Danny Glover, who pushed me to enter the realm of fiction.

PREFACE

March 2004, Mattapoisett, MA

Spring was coming and the ground was softening. At the construction site it was especially muddy. The construction crew was laying the foundation for a new housing development. Not far from Route 195, it was a great location for people with money who wanted to be close enough to Boston, New Bedford, and Providence, but distant enough to enjoy a bucolic life.

The place overall felt and smelled like a swamp, which is what the land had been. In some places the mud came up to the knees.

Near what was to become the sidewalk and half in the street, another set of workers were gathered, some drinking coffee, all walking around to stay warm, all wearing two layers of clothes to fight the cold. They were members of the Laborers Union, at the site to protest non-union construction being carried out by the non-union side of a company that had a Janus face—one side of the company had collective bargaining agreements with unions, the other side (using a different name) was entirely non-union.

Dozens of union members were beginning to assemble an informational picket line, pulling their signs from a van when a voice cried out from somewhere on the site, getting everyone's attention.

"Hey, Jerry! Come here quick!" yelled one of the non-union construction workers.

Foreman Jerry Walker jogged over to Art Agapov, the worker who yelled. Agapov, a thirty-something Russian immigrant, tall with gaunt features, black hair streaked with gray, and dark eyes, had been digging one of the foundations.

"Take a look at this, Jerry," Agapov said with a slight Russian accent, pointing towards the ground.

Peeking out of the hole that Agapov had been digging was what looked like the top of a skull. Throwing down his shovel, Agapov said, "I'm not messin' with that."

******

When the State Police cruisers approached, sirens blaring, the union protesters were not sure what to make of the situation. They only saw a group of the workers gathering. The protesters assumed that the police had arrived to break up the gathering and prepared for a confrontation.

The officers jumped out of their cruisers and rushed onto the construction site, ignoring the protesters. Jerry approached the officers and took them over to the hole where the skull had been found. The union protesters stopped their marching and stared in disbelief at the discussion between the police and the foreman. Too far away to hear what was being said, the protesters could tell that something was very, very wrong.

"I wonder what they're talkin' about," one of the protesters said to his buddy. Nobody in the union knew.

Minutes later a full crime scene team pulled onto the scene. The team taped the surrounding area around the hole and began carefully digging around the skull, like archaeologists at the site of an ancient civilization. The crime scene team took their time uncovering more and more skeletal remains of a body, their outfits getting muddier by the moment,

State Police Officer Hanley turned from the site to look at Jerry. "Well, Mister Walker, the bad news is, this site is going to be temporarily closed. We not only have to figure out about these remains, but we need to do some checking to see whether there are others. You know—"

"Hey, Hanley, sorry to cut you off," called one of the crime scene personnel, removing her gloves to rub her nose. "It looks like we have another body in here. And there is something else...some junk that I won't be able to identify until we clean this place up."

Hanley looked at Jerry and shrugged his shoulders. Jerry pointed his right index finger at his head like a pistol and pulled the imaginary trigger. He walked off to give the crew the bad news, they would have some unexpected free time today...and maybe tomorrow as well. *Free of work and free of earning money*, he thought as he walked to the site's trailer.

******

The 6 pm news had just come on. Sitting by himself, as he did most nights, Rodrigo Coval grabbed a beer while he watched the day's events unfold.

"The remains of two people have been found in an unmarked grave in Mattapoisett along with what appears to be an antique clock. There are no indications of the identity of the bodies. The police on the scene have told this news reporter it appears that the bodies had been there for a very long time."

Try twenty-five years, thought Coval, while he sat in his favorite chair, listening to the reporter. *Twenty-five fuckin' years of nightmares.*

Coval stood up and looked at his beer belly for a moment—remembering a once muscular, firm body. He turned the television off, walked over to the window of his small, undecorated one-bedroom apartment in Buzzards Bay, Massachusetts, and stood there looking out at nothing, sipping his beer.

His former boss, Carlos Souza, had given his final order: take out two people who had created unnecessary problems for their organization. Coval, a loyal soldier, did as he was asked. He tricked the couple into believing that Souza needed them both for a new operation.

Taking them to a deserted lot in Mattapoisett—more of a

swamp than anything else—he forced them out of the car, then had them dig their own graves. They dug through the muddy ground, pleading the whole time for their lives. Coval just listened… patiently, as the couple continued to dig.

Coval shot the woman first, silencing her annoying voice. He then turned toward his cousin. The cousin did not beg, he just asked if Coval truly understood what he was getting ready to do. The cousin talked about his loyalty to the organization and the sacrifices he had made.

All at once Coval's cousin stopped talking. He looked at Coval with a peaceful expression on his face, his whole body seeming to relax, as if the tension had evaporated.

When his cousin lowered his eyes, Coval raised the pistol and put a bullet into the silent man's head. After all, thought Coval, a soldier must do what a soldier must do. Besides, his cousin had been greedy and stupid. He should have known better. For the woman, good riddance, Coval had always despised her. He never understood what his cousin was doing with the nigger slut, anyway.

When Coval returned to headquarters to report in, he was stunned to find there was no building, just a smoldering wreck. He had no idea what had happened. *What the fuck?*

Coval waited each day for the police to arrive to arrest him for the two murders, but it never happened. He drifted through life, his best friends gone, the organization, extinct. Yet he could not seem to move on. In his dreams—his nightmares—he was regularly visited by his cousin, who always seemed to ask the same question, with a deadly pale, blank face.

"*Why?*"

Coval stood in his apartment, returning his gaze to the world outside his window, wondering whether he would now, finally, be able to sleep peacefully. Maybe he would finally be arrested?

Maybe he had not been as careful as he thought? Maybe they would find him?

Coval turned away from the window and walked into his kitchen, opening one of the doors to a cabinet and pulling down a bottle of *Johnnie Walker Red*. He filled a shot glass and drank it in one gulp, feeling the warmth—and burning—all the way down... like the burning of hell.

A tear rolled down his face.

1

Alberto Pires returned to his position on the starboard side of the liquefied natural gas tanker under construction. Already covered in sweat, he had just taken his 9 am break. It was one of those Massachusetts summer days where the heat and the humidity were off the charts, even this early in the morning. Like most welders in the shipyard, Pires had gotten used to the heat and humidity. Hated it but gotten used to it.

Pires climbed through the partially completed hatch to enter the compartment where he and his partner, Alice Love, had been working. Looking around, he realized that he was alone, Alice gone on break. Slowly he climbed up the ladder fifteen feet to get to his position on the wooden planks resting on metal stiffeners. He sat on the upturned can he used while welding or when taking a break.

Pires took a quick look at Alice's position and the can on which she had been sitting. Her electric arc welding line, holder and shield were lying next to her can. Damn, he hated working with women, even women as gorgeous as Alice. The shipyard was no place for them, and he could not believe—at least until he'd met Alice—that women could make good welders. But sure enough, she was not just good, she was great. Even with half the men in the shipyard hitting on her, she ignored them and kept working. Maybe she was *uma lesbica?* He did not know.

Pires felt his undershirt clinging to his soaked body. He hated this work, but at least he had a job. When Pires arrived in Massachusetts from Portugal the welding job was the only work

14

he could find. It did not help to remember that once he had been a big man. An important man. But wasn't that the story for so many immigrants?

Pires pulled his mask over his mouth and nose, making sure to cover his mustache and short beard to protect them from the fumes and dirt. He refitted the ear plugs, muffling the sounds around him, and donned his helmet. The hammering and drilling had picked up in tempo as more of the workers returned from morning break. The smell from the welding wasn't too bad in his compartment because there were only the two of them, and there was a blower making a sound like a persistent moaning, constantly pushing the smoke out of their hole.

He stood up, attached the welding rod to the holder and locked it into position, then pulled his shield down, closing the visor and looking through the darkened lens. In the darkness he struck the arc, watching it glowing golden, creating what looked like lava. The lava turned into a welding bead which he lay horizontally across the top of the compartment.

He heard a noise below, not stopping to check but assuming that Alice was returning to her position. He felt the vibration of someone climbing the ladder and then heard someone—probably Alice—climbing up to their position.

He kept welding, focused on the bead and the golden, molten metal being put into place.

With the welding rod burned down to about an inch, Pires stopped, lifted his shield and disconnected the remnant of the rod from the holder, throwing the remnant down.

He turned around, expecting to see Alice, but there was no one there.

Curious, Pires, standing nearly six feet tall, rose and walked over to the ladder situated against the planks. He leaned over to take a look, but lost his balance and fell forward. Suddenly everything went black.

2

A relaxed David Gomes approached the offices of the *Cape & Islands Gazette* early in the morning. His wife, Pamela Peters, was at Boston University for her graduate program in fine arts, leaving David at home in Hyannis, alone most of the week. Most mornings when he found himself looking at her picture on his side of the bed, it was just easier to get into the office and keep focused rather than fixate on not being with the love of his life.

At 8:15 am the offices were officially closed, so David used his keys to enter the *CIG* building off of Main Street in Hyannis. "Building" might have been a stretch. The structure was a nicely refurbished, two-story house. The paper's owner, Jacqueline Reynaud, lived on the second floor, while the first floor and finished basement were used by the paper. As the paper had grown over the last several years, so had the need for space, leading to an expansion into the former parking lot. This allowed for a new conference room and additional office space. The success of the paper led Jacqueline to wonder whether she needed to vacate the second floor and find other accommodations or purchase another building for the paper.

David, close to six feet, brown skin with a short, well-groomed Afro, carried his beige sports jacket over his shoulder, a pen held behind his right ear and his work folder under his arm. As he unlocked the door and stepped inside, a chime went off, but no other sound emerged from the dark front office. Though the door was locked, the alarm was off, meaning either someone had screwed up, or there was another early riser already at work.

Gomes stood for a moment looking at the vacant receptionist desk. He really missed Susan O'Hara, the long-time receptionist and all-round troubleshooter who had occupied that space for years. O'Hara had recently departed, deciding that she had, indeed, left her heart in San Francisco and needed to settle there to be with the love of *her* life. O'Hara had been the heart of the operation, impossible to replace.

Jacqueline had hired a young Black woman named Marcia Blake as the new receptionist and administrative assistant. Blake was good but not yet on the scale of O'Hara, a probably unfair comparison given O'Hara's length of service. Gomes thought of Blake as a refugee from Boston. As soon as she could, she decided to up and leave the city, her family, and try a new life. She had good administrative skills for someone in her early 20's but was not exactly warm and fuzzy.

Yes, she was quite professional, but there seemed to be something missing; a wall that kept the world at a distance. It showed in little things, like rarely smiling and never laughing, and bigger things, such as keeping her private life private and never inquiring into anyone else's life.

"Bonjour, monsieur Gomes."

Startled, Gomes almost bumped into his Quebecois boss and owner of *CIG*, Jacqueline Reynaud.

"Bonjour, yourself, Jacqueline! What brings you downstairs this early?" he asked, turning towards her.

Jacqueline was standing at the entry way to the main work area holding a steaming cup of coffee. With dark features and a skin coloring that seemed more Mediterranean than Quebecois, she wore a nicely pressed, fitted jean skirt and a summery light blue blouse. To some she would be thought of as dressed casually for work, but Jacqueline always had a level of dignity and charisma that made anything she wore seem stylish and appropriate.

"As with you, I suppose, I had a number of things that I wanted to get done," Jacqueline responded, leaving David wondering, as he often did, about Jacqueline's social life.

"David, if you have a moment, I would like to chat with you before everyone gets here."

Gomes asked whether he could get some coffee before they chatted. Jacqueline agreed, telling him to meet her in the conference room.

Gomes entered the conference room, having dropped off his jacket and folder at his desk, and took a seat opposite Jacqueline. He loved the new conference room, it felt spacious due to the tall windows and wonderful natural light. A long, wooden meeting table with space for ten chairs and a wall-long bookcase gave the room a certain elegance.

"David, in the last few weeks there have been three separate developments, all unexpected. But these developments come on top of a problem that I have hesitated to discuss with you: the paper is facing financial...challenges. Before you ask, no we are *not* on the verge of collapse. But it feels more like a person slowly bleeding out."

"But Jacqueline." Gomes put his coffee aside and leaned over the table. "I thought that we've been doing well. I mean, we expanded...our circulation is up, and we renovated the office," closing his remarks while gesturing around the conference room.

"Advertisements are down and our costs continue to rise. While our financial situation...evolved...there have been important... developments." She stopped for a moment to look directly at Gomes while she took a sip of her coffee.

"The first is that a group of newspapers in southern Massachusetts have started discussing a possible merger. They have approached us to join in these discussions, with everyone understanding that no commitments are to be made at this point."

Jacqueline finished her coffee and wiped her mouth lightly with a paper napkin.

"The second development is that we have been approached by the *Boston Outlook* about what they call a 'change in our relationship.' They have not been clear as to what that change may be, but they seem to be interested in exploring a number of possibilities, including absorbing us."

As Gomes opened his mouth to ask a question, Jacqueline held up her finger to stop him.

"Which then, my David, leads to the third development. I have been approached by good friends in Quebec. With the PQ. You know, the Parti Quebecois. There are amazing opportunities that have opened in government and within the party. I am being asked to consider various roles."

"Are you ready to *leave* all of this, Jacqueline?" David retreated into his chair, stunned, his voice low and cautious.

Reynaud sat silently for a moment.

They both looked up when they heard the door chime. Into the office walked Marcia Blake, who proceeded to the reception area.

"Damn, *everyone* is here early!" Gomes noted, bringing a smile to Reynaud's face.

Jacqueline's smile slowly evaporated as she returned to the discussion. She did not answer Gomes' question, but started talking through the different options. Gomes listened carefully, his face blank, thinking to himself that something was not being said but not sure what it was.

He was trying to ask his original question again about whether she was willing to give this all up when the phone in the conference room rang. Gomes, closest, picked it up.

"David," Marcia Blake said, "I'm sorry to bother you and Jacqueline, but I have a Doctor Maeda on the phone asking for you. She said that it was important. It has to do with a shipyard worker getting killed."

19

3

As Gomes drove his Toyota Corolla down Route 28 towards Falmouth, he wondered how this Dr. Maeda had gotten his name and why she had picked him, of all people, to call about the death of a shipyard worker. He kept looking back and forth between the paper with the address Dr. Maeda had given him and the addresses of the buildings on Route 28 while working to avoid the on-coming traffic. He finally saw the building on his left, the "Grant Professional Building" it advertised. Gomes made a left turn and found a parking space in a small lot.

The Grant Professional Building was nothing exceptional, brown brick with white lettering naming it, just two floors, probably built in the late 1960s. When he entered the building he found the directory. "Dr. Nancy Maeda, GP: Room 204." Before turning away, he looked at the directory closely and saw at the same room number, "Falmouth Family Practice." There were other names on the directory, including other medical and dental practices, none of which he recognized.

Though there was an elevator, Gomes walked to the second floor and looked for room 204. He heard a door close and saw in front of him an older man, probably in his 60s, with brown, thinning hair, pale skin, bushy eyebrows and a gray beard. Gomes smiled at the man, but the man only stared at Gomes suspiciously as they passed each other, not shifting his eyes. *Even on the Cape,* Gomes thought, familiar with a certain look he frequently received when he appeared on the scene with his brown skin. No matter

20

how often it happened, it caught Gomes by surprise.

Entering room 204, Gomes saw a twenty-something brown haired woman sitting in a reception space to the right of a closed door. Her reception area was behind a wall, with open space to communicate with visitors. The room was painted off-white and there were several photographs on the wall displaying nature scenes, not photos that someone would have picked up at some 5 & 10 store, but instead, very professional.

"May I help you, sir?" the young woman asked, remaining seated, a blank expression on her face.

"Good morning. David Gomes to see Doctor Maeda," Gomes responded, smiling at the receptionist.

"One moment, sir," she said, picking up the phone. Gomes overheard the receptionist announce his arrival in a low voice.

"Mister Gomes, please come on back, make a left and go to the first door on your right."

Gomes approached the door in the reception area, heard a buzzer and a click, and then felt the door unlock. He entered and proceeded down a short hall, noticing several offices on the right and left.

Entering the first office as instructed, he immediately locked eyes with an Asian woman sitting at her desk wearing a white doctor's coat, eyeglasses resting on the top of her head. She put down some papers in front of her and quickly stood up as Gomes entered.

"Mister Gomes, thank you for meeting with me so quickly. As you may have guessed, I'm Nancy Maeda," she said formally, with a smile, curiously dropping her title. "Please have a seat."

As Gomes sat down he looked around, checking out his surroundings. He removed the pen from his ear and opened his notepad. Again, he noted, very professional-looking photos, this time a mix of nature, objects and people. On her desk, a black and

21

white photo of a family, well-dressed, standing in front of what looked like a shack.

Dr. Maeda looked about 5'6" to Gomes. Brown hair tied up in a bun. Her complexion was a very light brown and, though smiling and welcoming, she seemed slightly uncomfortable.

"Doctor Maeda, you mentioned on the phone the death of a shipyard worker. I was very curious, so I drove down here, but you said the death was in Quincy and my paper basically covers the Cape and Islands. Sometimes we cover things over in New Bedford. Not to be funny, but why call me?" Gomes offered this with a smile so that Maeda was not offended by his question.

"Mister Gomes, what do you know about shipyards?"

Gomes, surprised by the directness and content of the question, rubbed his short beard.

"Not a whole hell of a lot, to be honest, Doctor Maeda. I mean, I guess you'd say that I know the basics, but that's it."

Maeda nodded her head slightly.

"Shipbuilding is the second most dangerous industry in the country, after mining, Mister Gomes. Does that surprise you?"

Gomes nodded and encouraged her to continue.

"There's all manner of dangers in shipyards, whether from the materials that they use, such as asbestos—at least on the older ships. But also, the fumes and dust. The noise is intense and can ruin the eardrums of the workers. And the ever-present danger of something falling on a worker or a worker falling on something."

Maeda stopped speaking for a moment, looking flustered.

"Forgive me, Mister Gomes, for being impolite. Can I offer you something to drink? Tea, coffee, iced-tea, lemonade or just some water?"

"Iced-tea sounds great, Doctor, with a little sugar in it, please."

Maeda stood up and left the room. Gomes sat there looking at the pictures on her wall. He shifted in his chair to look again at the family picture on Dr. Maeda's desk. There was something about it; something about the look in the eyes of those in the photo, that drew him in. A dignity mixed with sadness.

"That's my family, Mister Gomes," Dr. Maeda said as she walked back into the office with two glasses of iced tea, handing him one.

"*Poston*," she said with emphasis as she walked over to her seat. "The concentration camp where my family was placed during World War Two. The baby in the picture is me. I don't have a memory of it, and my family didn't want to discuss it after we were released. We were placed on an Indian Reservation, Mister Gomes, over the objections of the Tribal Council!"

Despite the intensity of Maeda's words, there was a surprising lack of emotion behind them. Her eyes seemed to tell all. Gomes shook his head with a combination of understanding, empathy, and anger.

Maeda took her seat and sipped some of the iced tea, then shifted gears away from the discussion about her family.

"Mister Gomes, last week—as I told you on the phone—a welder named Alberto Pires at the Quincy shipyard fell to his death. About a week or so prior to that, another welder fell a reported twenty feet and was nearly killed. How he survived is anyone's guess. About a week prior to *his* fall, another worker fell only about ten feet and was killed.

"I've been affiliated with a group called the Massachusetts Coalition for Occupational Safety and Health, otherwise known as MASSCOSH. You may have heard of it. That may seem curious to you, Mister Gomes, given that I am in a family practice, but for years I've been concerned about health and safety in the workplace. A doctor friend of mine in Cambridge encouraged me to get involved, so I did.

"Mister Gomes, I need you to write a story about what's

23

happening in the shipyards. You can look at the Quincy yard, but there are other yards in the area, including East Boston, Quonset Point in Rhode Island, and several other places. Quincy is hiring a lot of people from different parts of Massachusetts, and these deaths—and injuries—highlight the dangers of this industry. Dangers that can and should be addressed by these companies!"

Maeda's voice and tone had strengthened with emotion as she spoke. She was leaning forward towards Gomes with her final words, surprising him with their passion.

"Doctor, I understand what you're saying, but this sort of story goes beyond my jurisdiction, so to speak. Wouldn't this be a better story for the *Boston Globe*, or *Boston Outlook* or whatever the Quincy paper is? I mean, we're pretty much a small-town paper?"

Gomes caught himself sitting forward and slowly eased back in his chair. Maeda looked over at a picture on her wall of a mountain top, then returned her gaze towards Gomes.

"Mister Gomes, we've tried some of the bigger papers, and we also tried in Quincy. No one seems to be interested in our story, though we've gotten the pat on the head telling us that they'll be looking into it. We also went to some radio stations. No luck."

"Why?"

"Not sure whether the story is not sexy enough or whether the media fears these shipbuilding companies. In either case, we're at your doorstep." She stopped for a moment and then leaned toward Gomes. "You have a reputation for integrity. I've read your work over the years, your stories in connection with the murder of that Osterville contractor back in 1970 were riveting. We think that you can do justice to this story."

Gomes had a flashback hearing the reference to the T. J. Smith story. He shook with a chill in hearing Dr. Maeda's reference, thinking about the attention that he received at the time with his investigation. He also thought about how that moment of attention seemed to vanish so quickly.

"But there *is* another reason, Mister Gomes. This *is* a Cape Cod story," she said, snapping Gomes back to attention. "The deceased, Mister Pires, lived right here on the Cape. In fact, he lived in Hyannis."

Oh, boy, Gomes thought, moving his hand across his forehead. *Looks like I've been hooked like bluefish off Popponessett Beach.*

4

Gomes sat at his desk looking at the address of the late Alberto Pires. He knew the street; it was not far from Hathaway's Pond, heading out of Hyannis. He used to go to the Pond when he was a kid.

Though his eyes were focused on the address, Gomes was lost in thought as he reflected on his conversation with Dr. Maeda. She had informed him that she was approached by a caucus of activists at the shipyard who wanted help exposing the health and safety dangers at the yard. They told her about the Pires case and other examples of injuries and deaths. Maeda wanted something done and was frustrated that the media seemed to care not one bit about what was unfolding. Gomes mulled over whether he had received his marching orders.

The phone rang.

"This is Gomes."

"Hey gorgeous, anyone hitting on you today?" His wife Pamela Peters asked with a chuckle in her voice and a smile that Gomes could see in his mind's eye.

"Hey yourself, sweetness. How's Boston University treating you today?"

They spoke for a few minutes about her graduate teaching assignments, research, as well as photography, all the time Gomes gazing at her picture on his desk. She was expanding into film and video, though her first love was photography. *And, damn was she beautiful,* he thought to himself.

"Plans for the weekend, good looking?" Pam asked.

"Nothing that can't be moved around," he responded, putting

his feet up on the corner of his desk and leaning back in his chair to look at the ceiling.

"Excellent. I've got some studying that I have to do one day, but the other day is going to be for you and me to go play. You pick it."

"We'll figure that out when you get home on Friday. By the way, I had a meeting with this doctor today about the death of a welder at the Quincy shipyard. Are there some folks at BU that might have some research on shipyards?"

"I'll have to check I—"

Pam stopped abruptly. Gomes could hear her speaking with someone in the background.

"Listen, David, I'll have to get back to you, a student just came in with a problem I've got to deal with. I'll check on shipyards. See you soon, lover."

Gomes hung up and removed his feet from the desk, re-centering himself on his chair just as Jacqueline approached.

"Good afternoon, boss," he said with a grin.

"How did your meeting go with the doctor?" Jacqueline responded. She seemed distracted, her eyes looking between some papers she was carrying, Gomes and the floor.

"Interesting, Jacqueline. The doctor wants me to look into a story about the dangers of working in shipyards. A Cape Verdean immigrant just got killed there. Fell about fifteen feet."

Gomes could tell that she was only half listening. Something in her eyes: a far-away look.

"Keep me posted. I don't want a research paper," she said brusquely. "If you are free, I want to finish up the conversation we started this morning."

Gomes tucked a pen behind his ear and stood up. Rather than head to the conference room, they took the private stairs up to her apartment, where she often had confidential discussions, though now much less the case since the construction of the conference room.

The apartment had two-bedrooms, one bathroom, a kitchen and dining area, the latter connected to a small living room. Jacqueline used one of the bedrooms as a guestroom and office, when she needed to concentrate. Paintings and prints decorated the walls and the windows provided excellent lighting. Though this building was on the edge of 'downtown' Hyannis, the trees behind the office made it feel private.

Jacqueline stepped into her apartment and went to her refrigerator, pulling out a pitcher of iced coffee. She looked over her shoulder and asked Gomes whether he wanted any. He gratefully accepted it, listening as she dropped ice cubes into glasses, then poured the iced coffee. She turned to the dining table where Gomes was sitting, handed him a glass and sat down.

"Excellent!" he said regarding the iced coffee, and he meant it, drinking half the glass in one gulp.

"David," she started, looking back and forth between Gomes and the glass of coffee, "I am pulled in different directions about what to do with the paper and, I suppose, what I want to do with my life. The financial crunch is real, but it is not the only thing. I came to realize that there was nothing holding me here any longer and, I suppose things didn't work out on some fronts the way I had hoped."

She took a sip and looked at David with a deep, penetrating gaze; the sort of gaze where you feel someone is looking into your soul.

David looked at his shoes and then looked up, suddenly catching Jacqueline's eye. He cleared his throat.

"So, one way or another, you're saying that you *are* leaving?"

"The future has not been written, David, so I'm not sure. I want you involved in the decisions about the future of the paper, and that includes whether you believe there are things we need to do which can address our financial situation."

She finished her coffee and placed the glass down.

"You can count on me, Jacqueline," he said, also finishing his coffee, choosing not to explore any of the subtext to this discussion. When he and Pamela reconnected, his relationship with Jacqueline had changed, as was inevitable. Though he and Jacqueline were able to work together well, there was still an edge; a kind of smoldering discomfort, as if something was missing. Whatever it was, the vibe was surfacing in this discussion.

"Bien," she offered with little emotion, handing over a folder containing various papers.

"Inside the folder," she said, pointing towards it, "are exploratory memos about possible scenarios for the future. The papers with the red clip are from the southern Massachusetts papers. The papers with the black clip are from the *Outlook*. This is all completely confidential, of course, and I do not want any discussion with the staff or any of our friends about this. Of course," she added, looking down for a quick moment, "you may discuss this with Pamela."

Gomes took the folder and glanced at the papers.

"We have our first meeting with the southern Massachusetts papers next Friday. The *Outlook* is sending one of its editors here the following Tuesday. No promises and no commitments. Just a discussion."

Gomes put the papers back in the folder and rose, thanking Jacqueline for her confidence in him but feeling a queasy sense in the pit of his stomach. It seemed as if his course in life was about to sail into uncharted waters.

5

Late the following day Gomes drove his Corolla to the home of the late Alberto Pires. The day had been uneventful. Most of it involved reviewing the memos that Jacqueline shared with him about future scenarios. He tried to put aside his own wish that *CIG* remain independent. There were real stresses and strains on all small papers. Even competing with the *Cape Cod Times* was a challenge, despite how well *CIG* was doing. There were grounds to contemplate a very different future.

The group of southern Massachusetts papers that were considering a merger did not make sense to Gomes. He felt there was a lack of vision. The exploratory inquiry from the *Outlook* was more interesting. It looked as if they were open to various scenarios regarding the future relationship with *CIG*.

And then there was his own future. As much as he loved *CIG* and loved working for Jacqueline, Gomes had to admit he was becoming restless. Yes, he had his moments, but it was becoming increasingly clear that there were things he wanted to do that he could not accomplish while at *CIG*.

Gomes snapped back to reality when he saw the name on a mailbox: *LOPES*. That was the name, but the house was hidden behind foliage. Gomes couldn't see where to park, so he made a right turn into the driveway and entered another world.

There was a lush, green canopy over most of the yard, with light breaking through the trees at different points. With his window open Gomes could hear the sounds of birds in the trees and the sound of an occasional animal running in the grass. The driveway led to a light brown, single floor house.

Seemingly out of nowhere, a man appeared. Gomes figured he must be Tommy Lopes, the cousin of Pires that Dr. Maeda had mentioned. Gomes had called Lopes the day before and arranged to drop by. On the phone, the man sounded suspicious, but curious. Lopes looked like a bouncer. He was tall, a good six feet plus. Brown skin the same color as Gomes, a black beard, short cut hair in an Afro style. He was dressed in blue overalls and a white t-shirt, making Gomes think of an auto mechanic. He stood near the driveway watching Gomes approach.

"Mister Lopes, I presume?" Gomes asked after shutting off the car and getting out, trying to sound friendly.

"Yeah, I'm Tommy Lopes," he responded in a voice that was completely incongruent with his appearance. It was soft and almost melodic. Though Lopes looked threatening, there was nothing in his voice to indicate such an intent.

"Mister Lopes, I'm Gomes, from the paper. Thanks so much for agreeing to meet with me."

"Come on in, Mister Gomes," Lopes responded as he turned to walk towards the entrance.

The house was nothing to write home about. It reminded Gomes of a barracks. Upon entering Gomes found himself in a living room. A hallway went past a kitchen; Gomes assumed the doors off the hallway were for a bathroom and bedrooms. The living room doubled as a dining room.

The first thing that struck Gomes was that the house was very clean. The furniture was not the most modern, but it was not archaic. It was clean and functional.

"Pull up a rock, Mister Gomes. Want some lemonade or something stronger?" Lopes asked.

"Sure, that would be nice, Mister Lopes. Lemonade works for me."

31

Lopes disappeared, returning a few minutes later with two full glasses, which both men attacked immediately.

"Nothing like good lemonade on a hot day," his host said after taking a long and deep sip from his glass. "So, before we get started, I appreciate the '*Mister* Lopes' stuff, but you can call me 'Lopes.' Everyone else does."

"That's a deal, as long as you call me either 'David' or 'Gomes.'"

They nodded at each other and raised their glasses in salute.

"Alright, *Lopes*, as I told you on the phone, I'm doing a story about the dangers facing workers at shipyards. I'm going to focus on your cousin, Alberto. I'm starting with you because...well, it seems to me that we should begin at the beginning."

Lopes sat for a moment nursing his lemonade. He put it down on the table, keeping a piece of ice in his mouth while he seemed to think.

"Well, Gomes, this may be a bit of a disappointment but I'm not sure what I can tell you. I didn't really know him." Lopes spit the piece of ice back into the glass.

Gomes was surprised by the statement, raising his eyebrows, but said nothing.

"Here's the story, Gomes. So, like one day I get this call from my Aunt Rosa who lives in New Bedford. Rosa Macedo's her name. So, she tells me that we have this distant cousin from the islands who's been living in the Azores a couple of years and got a job here in America. You know, at the Quincy shipyard. For some reason the company decided to hire Cape Verdeans and Al worked up some sort of deal and got a job.

"So, Aunt Rosa says to me, she says, 'look, Tommy, the guy needs a place to stay, can you put him up for a while?' So, I says 'yeah,' and the next thing I know the guy shows up. Been with me since. Maybe about two years."

Lopes took a sip of the lemonade, the story apparently over.

"He came here and stayed with you. Tell me about him. Who were his friends?"

"*Friends?*" Lopes gave his guest a questioning look, as if Gomes had asked for the answer to the ultimate question of the universe. "As far as I could tell, I was Al's best and possibly only real friend. Yeah, he was in a carpool to work, and I guess you could say that they were all friends, but it wasn't like he hung out with them. Maybe on Fridays after work they would have a beer, but that's about it."

Lopes sipped his lemonade.

"Alright, then. What about a girlfriend?"

Lopes raised his eyebrows and shook his head. "Al was a strange one, Gomes. Yeah, he'd see women, but—and I mean this—he'd only go out with married women! Seriously. And he never brought them back here."

"Why? Did you have a rule about that or something?"

"No way!!" Lopes said with a strong laugh. "I've brought ladies by here and Al knew that he could, too. No, let's just say that Al had his own rules. One seemed to be that he would not bring a woman home. A second was that he would only date married women. He didn't talk much about it, but my read is that he didn't want commitments. Having affairs made it much easier for him."

"Were any of those relationships serious?"

Lopes shook his head no.

"Nah, not at all. He'd see someone for a while then move on to someone else. I saw him with a couple of women, but he never went out of his way to introduce me to anyone."

"So, this may sound like a strange question but, what was he like?"

Lopes sat silently for a moment, eyes unfocused.

"Let me show you," he finally said, standing up and signaling with his right hand for Gomes to follow him.

Gomes followed Lopes through the house toward the back, looking into rooms along the hall. One was a bathroom and the other two were bedrooms. At the end of the hall was a door to the outside. Lopes opened it and then pushed open a storm door, holding it open for Gomes.

"You want to know what he was like? Take a look." Lopes pointed with his right index finger.

Gomes looked and saw a fabulous garden. There were flowers, fruits and vegetables in neatly ordered rows, and a greenhouse at the back of the house.

"You want to know about Al? This was Al. He loved to garden, and he was damned good. Every day from when the weather started to warm up until the ground froze in the fall, he'd be out here. After work and on weekends he spent all his time here. During the winter he'd be in the greenhouse.

"The guy would cook the vegetables, and some of the fruit… and brother, he was a good cook…and he'd sell the flowers, fruits and vegetables to make a little cash. But I think that he'd have done this gardening regardless."

Gomes stood looking at the garden, envisioning Pires on his knees working the land. He suddenly realized something.

"Lopes, you have a picture of your cousin? I just realized I've never seen what he looked like."

"Nah, no picture…wait a second!" he said, snapping his fingers, "I do have *one* picture. Not a great one. Come on back to the house."

They walked back in, wiped their feet off, and stopped at the second door on the left. Lopes opened the door (it had been ajar) and walked in. Gomes stood outside while Lopes walked around looking for something. This gave Gomes a chance to glance at the accommodations.

The room was spartan. There was a small bed, likely more

comfortable than a cot, but not much more. A desk with a notepad and a pen on it, but nothing else. A dresser, on top of which sat deodorant, aftershave, keys, some change and a small closet. Hanging on the wall was a cross with a Europeanized Jesus. There was no Bible. In fact, there were no books. There were a couple of magazines, one of which was *Playboy*. Not the sort of place that would make one feel as if they were home.

Lopes picked up something on top of the dresser.

"Here you go, Gomes. Not a great picture, but it gives you an idea of his looks."

Gomes looked at the identification badge from the shipyard. It was a crude color photo of Pires. Looking like a mug shot—like most ID badges —was a picture of a Black guy in his 30's. Skin a little darker than Gomes'. Hair, about the length of Lopes. Eyes staring at the camera. What looked like a scar above his left eye. No mustache. No beard. No smile.

"Mind if I keep this for a while, Lopes? I'd like to use it in the story."

"No problem, Gomes. Just get it back to me eventually. I'd like to, you know, have something to remember the guy with," Lopes said with a sigh.

"Thanks, Lopes. Listen, can I get the number for your aunt? I'd like to speak with her if you don't mind."

Lopes walked over to the desk and wrote the number down on the pad laying there. He handed it to Gomes with a sad look on his face.

"He was a decent guy, Gomes. He should've lived to a nice old age." Lopes shook his head. "Man, I don't know what to do with his stuff. It's here and I don't know what to do with it."

Gomes nodded his head with understanding, all the while thinking about those eyes in the badge's photo, staring with no hint of a smile.

6

Sitting at his desk, Gomes looked at a list of names to contact regarding the Pires death. Rosa Macedo, Pires' aunt, was at the top of the list. She thought that Gomes should speak with the president of the shipbuilders union at the Quincy shipyard. There was also one of the welding department's shop stewards. There was the welder who fell a week prior to Pires' death, and there was this caucus of dissidents called "Shipyard Workers United" that was pressuring for progressive change in the way the union operated. Maeda had a good relationship with the caucus and she offered to provide Gomes with introductions.

Gomes set out to make phone calls and arrange appointments. He was worried that this would be challenging, since it was now August and a lot of people took time off to go on vacations. But he had no choice.

Over the course of the next two days, Gomes set up appointments. Rosa Macedo was evasive, but he was finally able to pin her down, though she claimed to have little to say. The union contacts were straightforward. The president of the union and the shop steward agreed to meet with him, though the union president was less than enthusiastic, quickly getting off the phone. The caucus leader, eager to meet, invited him to a leadership meeting. The company, on the other hand, flat out rejected his request for an interview.

******

Rosa Macedo's home was off of Route 195 in Fairhaven, a town to the east of New Bedford, a couple of blocks off of Route 6.

Macedo's home was a small single-family house, with two floors and a slanted roof. The color was a dull white and, though an older home, appeared to be in good condition. To the right of the house was a driveway that led toward the backyard, but Gomes could not tell whether there was a garage in back. He pulled up in front of the house late in the afternoon and walked up the short, five-step landing to the front door to ring the doorbell.

The woman who came to the door was not Gomes' idea of the aunt Lopes mentioned. Gomes assumed that she would be an older woman. In a technical sense, Macedo was. Lopes was in his 30s, Rosa Macedo was in her early 40s. She looked about 5' 6", with a very light brown complexion, almost yellow. Straightened brown hair, shoulder length and wearing an attractive plum colored dress covering a very attractive figure, she appeared to have just come home from work. Gomes realized he'd need to adjust his thinking about "aunts" from now on!

"Mister Gomes, I guess?" she asked, opening the door and looking harried. "Come in, come in. I'm on the phone, I'll be off in a second." She walked around a corner deeper into the house.

Gomes entered the house and took a quick look around. To his right was the living room, which was immediately striking in how well it was put together, like an exhibit area in a museum. Macedo was standing in that room holding a phone with an exceptionally long chord.

To his left was a dining room connected to a kitchen. Directly in front of him was a closet door, and to the right, a staircase.

"Listen, Agostinho, I told you, I left the papers in your in-box on your desk!" Macedo was almost yelling into the phone, looking completely exasperated, as if the person with whom she was speaking was an idiot. "Yes, and you may have lifted it out along with something else so, *please,* look at your desk. Yes, that's right. Hmm…okay, great! You found it. I told you it was there. Listen, boss, I have a visitor here, so I have to sign off and I'll speak with you tomorrow. Yeah…no problem. Bye."

Macedo hung the phone up more carefully than she probably would have had Gomes not been standing there. She looked up at Gomes.

"Well now, Mister Gomes, I apologize for that. I work as the executive secretary at a law firm in New Bedford. We do landlord-tenant work, some unemployment compensation work, as well as workers' compensation," she offered, using the gender-neutral term that had increasingly replaced the older term, 'workmen's compensation.' "My boss has a habit of losing things and then blaming everyone else. I'm sorry for that." She took a breath and smiled for the first time. "Can I get you something to drink? It's a hot day and probably a hot drive down here from the Cape."

Gomes accepted her offer of iced tea and she left the room to get it. Gomes took the opportunity to examine the room. It felt like a nautical exhibit. There were sea charts from the coastal area around New Bedford encased in glass. There were pictures of various 20th century sailing vessels of vastly different types. Sitting on a desk was a small Portuguese flag next to an equally small US flag. Interestingly, there was no flag for the now independent Guinea-Bissau & Cape Verde. On the same desk was what looked like a gold-plated nautical clock and barometer with a wooden base. Gomes could not make out the language written on a gold strip in the base. The look and the craftsmanship grabbed his attention. He pulled out his 35 mm SLR camera and took a photo of it. He then started photographing the rest of the room.

"You like my living room?" Macedo asked, with equal amounts of suspicion and pride as she entered the room with the iced tea.

"Miz Macedo, this is a striking room! It really feels like a museum. You must love the sea!" He turned away from the items and refocused on her.

"It's '*Missus*' Macedo, Mister Gomes and, yes, I do love the sea. My father was a seaman and my mother was a seaman's wife, as well as having worked in the mills. My brother and I grew up hearing everything about the sea and my father's voyages."

Macedo sat in a chair near the entrance to the living room; Gomes settled on a chair near the desk and pulled out a notepad. As he did so, Macedo crossed her legs and lit a cigarette, seeming a bit uneasy.

"So, Mister Gomes, as I said on the phone, I barely knew Al," she opened, jumping right in. "A relative asked me to help him out. I made some inquiries, and then I got him settled over at Tommy's place in Hyannis. In the couple of years he's been in the States I guess I've seen him maybe…twice."

She blew out some smoke and looked at Gomes defiantly as the smoke curled around her head. Gomes found himself thinking she would make a good actress for a cigarette commercial. Those dark eyebrows.

Gomes sat for a second thinking. Macedo had made a point of saying that she was "Mrs." but there was no indication of another occupant in the house, though he saw the wedding band on her finger. It was also unclear what was making her either uneasy or restless.

"You said your father was a seaman, Missus Macedo. All of his life?"

Macedo seemed perplexed by the question, inhaling more smoke and shaking her head.

"He sailed on freighters, Mister Gomes, and during the War— during World War Two—he was in the Merchant Marine. He mainly worked in the engine room. He was never home, Mister Gomes, but when he was home, he was all there, filled with stories and always bringing gifts." She was visibly relaxing, taking one more puff of the cigarette and then putting it out in the ashtray next to her on a small table.

"What about your mother? You said that she was a 'seaman's wife' and that she also worked in the mills."

"Yes, Mister Gomes," she said, shaking her head for no obvious reason. "She was left raising me and my brother and she did her best. She worked in this textile factory in New Bedford, sometimes part-time, sometimes full-time, depending on many things. The place has long since closed, and my mother is…well, she died some years ago."

Gomes was masterful at keeping someone talking. In this case he had Macedo talking about her family history, what she loved and hated about the New Bedford area, and ultimately about her husband who, one day decided to up and leave, not to be heard from again, though she believed he was in Chicago.

Gomes asked her about various items in the living room, including the clock and barometer.

"A friend gave that to me. It's beautiful, isn't it?"

"Yes, Missus Macedo, it is. Someone must love you a lot! I don't recognize the language on it. It's not Portuguese, I can tell that."

Macedo chuckled. "No, Mister Gomes, it is definitely *not* Portuguese. It's Greek."

The two of them kept chatting until Gomes realized it was starting to get late.

"So, Missus Macedo, going full circle, this huge family of yours is in Cape Verde, Portugal, and the US of A, correct?"

Macedo was caught by surprise. Gomes noticed her suddenly sitting up straight, almost at attention, crossing and uncrossing her legs, and pulling out another cigarette to light.

"Yes, Mister Gomes, quite a big family. Al, for some reason, lived a couple of years in the Azores and then decided to come to America for work. I don't know whether he intended to go back to Cape Verde or Portugal or just stay here."

Realizing he was getting very little from Macedo, he asked if she would agree to have her picture taken. At first, she balked, but Gomes threw on the charm and was able to convince her to be photographed in different parts of the room. As he took the snaps he thought, *this is one hell of a unique room.*

The phone rang.

Macedo answered it. Gomes watched as she seemed to almost change her appearance while speaking. She chuckled, lowered her voice, and then said something, but Gomes could only make out the word "soon". Smiling, she glanced briefly at Gomes, though Gomes knew the smile was not for him, then she hung up.

"If that's all that you need, Mister Gomes, I'm going to offer you a farewell. I have to meet a friend for dinner. I hope you understand."

Macedo's forced smile ended the conversation. Gomes said his good-byes, left a business card in case she could think of anything else, and headed back to his car.

7

"This whole thing seems a bit screwy, Pam," Gomes said as he sat at the dining table soaking up the last of the spaghetti sauce with a piece of garlic bread.

Pamela Peters, Gomes' long-time friend, partner and now wife, was finished with school for the remainder of the summer and back at home with David. She was so much more relaxed being home. And they could now have serious eye-to-eye conversations rather than relying on the telephone.

"No one seems to know this guy; not even his family!"

Pamela and David had rekindled their relationship after a break of several years. They never stopped loving each other, but when Pamela took a job in New York—and when David could not get himself to fully commit to Pam—they decided they needed time away from one another. That need for space changed when David ran into Pam at a conference and they started talking…and could not stop. It was not long before they decided that they needed and wanted each other, so marriage was the next step.

Gomes would tell everyone—including Pamela—that she was the most unusual person he had ever met. Of mixed Wampanoag and African American descent, she had very dark skin and dark, wavy hair. Her hazel eyes would light up a room. But Pamela was more than gorgeous. She was an incredible listener and very wise. She provided Gomes with the best advice and they operated like partners, in large part because they were best friends. Gomes would tell those closest to him that when Pamela would talk, he would feel as if she was massaging his brain with invisible fingers.

"I'm not sure that's very unusual," Pam said, looking at David with those wonderful, slightly slanted eyes. "Immigrants have come to the States for years, including from Cape Verde, barely knowing relatives that vouched for them. This just seems like another example."

David felt that this conversation was probably unfair to Pam, since she had only recently arrived home and was still decompressing from her Master's in Fine Arts program. An expert photographer, Pam wanted to get a terminal degree and add teaching to her credentials. And here he was hitting her with this work problem.

"Alright, maybe I'm overthinking this. Switching gears, what do you think about this situation with the future of *CIG*?"

As Pam stood up to begin clearing the table, David went over to the sink to wash the dishes.

"I'm sort of stunned to hear that there's a financial problem. I mean I know that there are challenges facing many small-town papers, but you haven't mentioned anything to me."

"That's because she never mentioned one word about it until this conversation."

Gomes was washing the dishes, listening to the water come through the faucet. Pam continued drying the dishes. Both seemed lost in thought.

"What did Jacqueline mean that things had not worked out the way that she had hoped, David?" Pamela asked, staring at the dish she was drying, catching Gomes by surprise with her question.

David followed suit, looking at the dishes carefully while he washed them, inspecting for any bit of grime.

"At first I thought that maybe she was referring to the paper, but I think that it really came down to her social life," he responded carefully. That was the truth, though he knew that it was not the whole truth.

The Man Who Changed Colours

Pam kept drying the dishes, saying, "Jacqueline is a beautiful, smart, and engaging woman. I've never understood why she has not had a steady relationship. I mean, I didn't see her for a number of years, so what do I know? But I got the impression, from time to time, that she was waiting for something. Or maybe someone. Do you know what I mean?"

Out of the corner of his eye he saw that Pamela had stopped and was looking directly at him.

"Yeah, Pam, I do," his "I do" being all he was prepared to say about the matter. "But what do you think about the situation?"

"I'd start in a different place." She returned to the dishes with renewed energy level. "There are really two different issues here. One is the paper's financial situation and whether there are ways to stop the bleeding. But then there's something else. I think, given the invitation from her Quebecois friends, she's trying to decide what to do with the paper. What would *she* like to see happen, regardless of whether she returns to Quebec?"

"I agree," said David, setting another plate in the drying rack.

"If the only matter is going back to Montreal, she could just sell the paper and not think about it. But if she's really trying to think about the paper's future, she needs to come up with her own vision. You know what I mean? I can't come up with the vision and neither can you, my love." She put her arm around Gomes and gave him a sweet kiss on the cheek.

"Understood, great wise one!" he said, at which point Pamela spanked him lovingly.

"Don't start what you can't finish, Pamela," Gomes said, laughing.

Looking sensuous, she leaned close to his left ear: "What makes you think I can't finish?"

All right, then, Gomes thought.

8

It was a Monday morning, with Labor Day fast approaching. The mood on the Cape was already beginning to shift as vacationers were leaving or seizing the final moments for playtime before the transition into fall, the dramatic slowdown of the pace of life, and a return to what many year-round Cape residents thought of as normality.

Gomes showed up to the office later than usual because of work that he had been doing over the weekend. He did not punch a time card and Jacqueline was very supportive of flexible work schedules. As she would regularly say, *"My principal concern is that the work is done on time and with high quality."* The staff took her at her word and, as a result, a good relationship existed over the years, even with a few bumps.

Gomes walked through the doors of *CIG* around 10:30 am and greeted the receptionist, Marcia Blake. As he looked at her, Gomes thought Marcia was very good at what she did. At about 5'2", golden brown with a very short Afro and always impeccably dressed, Marcia kept her distance from everyone while never being impolite. Contrary to her predecessor in that position, Marcia was not interested in socializing with the staff or knowing anything particularly personal. Which was why her question to him took him by surprise that morning.

"Good morning, David. I hope that you had a good weekend. How does it feel to have Pamela around?"

Gomes stopped in mid-step and looked at her twice to make sure she was not playing with him in some way, but her face—and particularly her eyes—seemed sincere. Gomes walked over and leaned against the desk.

"I appreciate your asking. To tell you the truth, it's fantastic having her around, and my only regret is that after Labor Day we have to return to only seeing each other on weekends. She's an amazing person."

A phone call came in and Blake held up her finger to signal that she had to answer it. Gomes began to step away, but she signaled that he should remain.

"You are most lucky, David," she said after transferring the call. "I don't know Pamela, but I can tell that the two of you are quite a couple. Count your blessings. I got out of a horrible situation, which brought me here. I can only hope that I can connect with someone—" She stopped when the phone rang again. David remained in place.

"I hope," she continued after handling the call, "that I can connect with someone that gives me the glow that you always have when you come through those doors on Monday morning." For the first time she gave him what felt like a sincere smile.

Gomes thanked her, wondering as he turned toward his desk what had gotten into Blake. As he took a step he realized, through a reflection in the glass, that there were people in the conference room. He saw Jacqueline sitting at the table speaking with a woman he could not identify. All he could see was that she was white, with long black hair, and of indeterminate age.

"Who's in there with the boss?" Gomes asked Blake.

"Jacqueline's interviewing this girl for an internship. She showed up, apparently not far from being out of school. I don't know anything about her other than her name: Mariana Alvares."

Gomes went to his desk and reviewed a memo for additional documents that Jacqueline sent him regarding the future of the paper. He had taken Pamela's advice and prepared a memo for

Jacqueline suggesting that she start to think through her own vision for the paper.

His phone rang.

"David, I'm in the conference room. Would you have a moment to join me?" asked Jacqueline.

"Be right there, boss," he responded and hung up.

Gomes grabbed his pad and went to the conference room. He knocked on the door as he entered, holding a hot cup of coffee. Jacqueline and the unknown woman were sitting across from one another. Gomes sat beside Jacqueline and took a sip of his coffee.

"David, I would like to introduce you to Mariana Alvares. Mariana is from Cambridge and is recently out of school. She is interested in pursuing journalism. She is looking for an internship and I think that we have come to an agreement. I told her about the different projects we are pursuing here, and she was quite fascinated by your shipyard story." Jacqueline looked from Alvares to Gomes.

Alvares appeared to be in her early 20s, jet black hair with light green eyes. Her skin indicated either a suntan or a little African or Indian blood, Gomes could not tell, but assuming that she was Portuguese, any number of ethnic mixtures were possible. She was dressed neatly but casually, wearing blue jeans and a light blue sleeveless blouse. Gomes thought the young woman was not inappropriately dressed, but someone coming for an internship interview might wear something more formal.

"Actually, I'm from *East* Cambridge, Mister Gomes. People from my neighborhood like to make that distinction," she offered in a serious voice, though breaking into a mischievous grin.

"I came to the Cape to rethink my life. I have a job as a waitress, and I'm prepared to do some housecleaning if the waitress job dries up. But I have time to work with your paper. Miz Reynaud has been explaining the work of the different writers here and I was struck by the story that you are working on about shipyards. I've had a couple of relatives who've worked at the Beth Steel shipyard in East Boston. Another at the Groton shipyard in Connecticut. They've all told me about the dangers, but I never really thought anything could be done about it. Miz Reynaud also told me about a story you're working on about the changing demographics of the Cape, something I'm *very* interested in given what's been happening in Cambridge," her last comment referring to the spreading gentrification afflicting the Greater Boston area.

Gomes liked her. She had energy and she seemed quite professional. A little long-winded, but that was okay.

"Miz Alvares, I'm going to need someone who's a good researcher. I assume that you've brought along a list of references?"

"Yes, Mister Gomes. I attended Lesley College in Cambridge. My folks didn't want me to go too far from home. In fact, they didn't want me to leave home, so I commuted. It's all in my resume."

This is someone ready to get to work, Gomes thought.

"Well, Miz Alvares, let me speak with the boss here and we'll get back to you. You're already living here?"

"Yes, Mister Gomes. I have a room here in Hyannis not far from the traffic circle near the Melody Tent," referring to the site for various performances in the summer. "A retiree who moved down here from Boston had a nice room in her house with its own bathroom. And I have a job as a waitress already," she answered, displaying reserved pride.

Alvares stood up, joined by Gomes and Reynaud. They shook hands, then Alvares left.

"What do you think, my David?"

"This could not come at a better time, boss. If her references check out, let's bring her on. Shit, even if her references don't check, I can use a good researcher to help me. Trying to understand all the background on shipyards is more than I bargained for. Doctor

Maeda mailed me information that I need to go over, but if Alvares were with me, it would really help."

"Excellent," Jacqueline responded with satisfaction. Still standing, she offered: "Make a few quick calls, David and, if people vouch for her, let's bring her on. If I can come up with a little extra money, I will offer her a stipend."

As Gomes headed back to his desk, in the back of his mind he found himself wondering about that old saying, *if something is too good to be true, it probably is.* But then again, he thought with an impish grin on his face, *don't look a gift horse in the mouth.*

9

Gomes called a couple of professors from Lesley College who both spoke highly of Alvares. They were convinced that she would be a good researcher. One of them, Professor Novick, was surprised to hear that Alvares was on the Cape, since she thought that Alvares was heading to Texas. In any case, Professor Novick was pleased to recommend her. That was all Gomes needed to call and arrange their first meeting.

"Mariana, let's start with basics. You are Mariana and I am David. No 'Mister' and 'Miz,' got it?"

Mariana nodded.

"Jacqueline is 'Miz Reynaud', however, until she tells you otherwise. She's my boss. She okayed a long time ago my calling her Jacqueline. You cannot call her 'Jacqueline until and unless she gives you permission. Got it?"

Mariana nodded.

"Okay, here's my telephone number at work and one for home. Call anytime you need me; I live here in Hyannis. Next, I need assignments completed on time and, as Jacqueline would say, with high quality. If you have *any* questions, don't make assumptions, just come and see me. Finally, we have a small staff, but everyone who works here is to be treated with the utmost respect. You don't have to like everyone, but this is a hell of a good team."

Mariana nodded, saying nothing.

"One more thing. You're going to be researching. I don't need you in the office every day. Yes, I want you to check in with me and give me updates, but you're probably going to need to be visiting libraries, making phone calls, reviewing material and things like that. You will be writing up memos to me summarizing the key material and anything that you think is of value to the story. There are a few spaces in the office for interns, but feel free to use my desk anytime you want, if I'm not here," he offered with a smile. "I have a great IBM typewriter here. Do you have a typewriter?"

"Yeah, an electric. It's not as good as an IBM but it works fine."

"Excellent. Do you have any questions so far?"

Mariana shook her head no.

"Let's start with this shipyard story. That's the one that I want you to focus on."

Gomes explained the background of the story, starting with the death of Pires and his investigation as it stood so far. He handed her a thick folder of material that Dr. Maeda had sent him on shipyards and the conditions of work. Mariana's eyes widened as she examined the size of the folder.

"I want you to start by going over this material and giving me a briefing. Then I want you to spin off from there and do some deeper background, including about the history of the Quincy shipyard, the union there, you know, the whole nine yards."

Mariana stood up and dropped her notebook in her bag.

"If you don't mind, I'll get started immediately. Can I hang out here rather than go back to my place? I can head straight from here to the restaurant where I waitress."

"Absolutely. This desk over here." He pointed towards one in the middle of the room. "That's open, stay as long as you want."

Gomes looked at Mariana as she deposited herself in the chair and got settled. *Damn, I'm lucky,* he thought, realizing that now he would have time to do some more interviews and get into the story. If Mariana proved as good as her former professors had suggested, this story would kick ass.

Just as she sat down, Gomes remembered something. "Mariana,

one more thing. Come with me a second."

Mariana got up and followed him into the lobby and to Marcia Blake's desk. Marcia was reading something but looked up as the two approached her.

"Marcia, allow me to introduce you to our new intern, Mariana Alvares. Mariana will be working with me on a few stories. I just wanted to make sure that the two of you met."

Marcia greeted Mariana formally and, typical for Marcia, suspiciously, though she offered a polite smile.

"Mariana, Marcia is the hub of this operation. She knows where everyone is at all times and how to reach us."

Gomes winked at Marcia as he and Mariana walked towards the door.

Marcia looked down at the floor. For the first time in a very long time, she felt like she really belonged.

10

Gomes sat at the table at *Carlo's*, a casual Italian restaurant on Main Street a couple of blocks away from *CIG* in the direction of West Yarmouth. It was known for exceptional food at reasonable prices, including lunch specials.

Gomes sprinkled pepper on the olive oil and dipped a slice of bread into it. He savored the flavor, nodding his head in enjoyment while he thought about his upcoming discussion with Jacqueline. She had requested they meet over lunch, something that rarely happened unless they both were feeling particularly relaxed. Feeling good but not particularly relaxed, he anxiously looked around for Jacqueline in between dips of bread. He was also anxious because he would have to explain to his parents why he would not be at the Gomes/Alves Labor Day reunion this year.

His parents had been hosting Labor Day events for years. Indeed, as long as he could remember. This year he and Pam decided that they needed to get away for the weekend. They were heading to New York City, planning to stay with a friend of David's from his military days. His friend had an apartment on the West Side of Manhattan, not far from where Pamela had lived on West 85th Street when she was working in the city. Gomes hoped that his parents would understand their absence. He and Pam needed some downtime for themselves.

Jacqueline came walking into the restaurant looking fabulous as ever. She always attracted attention and she always handled it well, including the occasional vulgar comment.

She wore her dark hair loosely and was dressed in a summery

yellow dress with light, vertical white stripes. She smiled at Gomes as she approached and seated herself, taking off her sunglasses and putting them on the table.

"Bonjour, Jacqueline. It's been a while since we've had a real lunch meeting. I've missed them."

"Bonjour, David. Indeed, it has been a while. There have been many things that I have missed. Time never seems to permit some of the more enjoyable parts of life." She picked up the menu.

When the waiter brought over water for Jacqueline, she ordered an antipasto and a glass of white wine. Gomes chose a vongole pasta and joined her with the white wine.

"David, I had the opportunity to review the memo that you sent me regarding the future of *CIG*. You raised an important matter about 'vision.' I wanted to meet with you today to discuss that, but also to get your assessment of the material that I sent."

She sipped the water, looking down at the table almost in shyness, but looked up as the waiter brought the two glasses of wine. Jacqueline and Gomes toasted, though for Gomes it felt like a formality.

"When I started the paper, I wanted a progressive voice on the Cape and Islands. I wanted to cover local events in a different way, but also provide commentary about national and global issues. But the resources to make inroads…well, they're not there.

"The news media is changing, David. I have been following developments across the United States. Papers are closing or merging. We are in competition with radio and television. It becomes harder and harder to sustain our papers. Many publishers don't want to admit it. We are all fighting for advertisers and the financial pressure on us is becoming more and more difficult to resist. The other part of this, which I haven't discussed with you, is that some advertisers want us to change our editorial policy."

"What do you mean by 'change our editorial policy'?"

"How should I put it? They want us to tone down our commentaries and become less...controversial."

Gomes felt as if he was turning red, a difficult act given his dark complexion. He was angry, not at Jacqueline, but at this situation.

She took a sip of wine and looked into his eyes.

"Therefore, even had I not been contacted by my friends in Quebec I would have to have given very serious thought to a different paper or a different arrangement with an existing paper."

"You think that it's inevitable that we shut down?"

"Not necessarily." She thanked the waiter as the food arrived. "We have been doing well and have an excellent reputation, but there are larger forces affecting our future."

They chatted about less important matters for a few minutes as they ate, though Gomes did not feel as hungry as he had when he first sat down.

"I realize, David, that my current vision for the paper is limited. I want to make sure that our staff are secure. And I suppose that I also want to see whether there's a way for us to make a mark in the world, recognizing that we simply do not and will not have the resources to expand."

Gomes forced himself to eat, twisting the linguine on his fork and slowly consuming it, permitting a little more time to think through how he wanted to respond.

"Jacqueline, given what you just said, and after reviewing the documents you shared with me, I'm not convinced that we can make enough cuts or shift our relationship with advertisers quickly enough or deep enough to address our financial situation. So given that, my recommendation is that you pursue discussions with the *Outlook*. The so-called consortium in southeastern Massachusetts does not have enough vision or leadership to make a breakthrough. They continue to think of themselves as a collection of little papers rather than really building something new. But the *Outlook* seems to want to do something different. We could be their Cape and Islands bureau, or a magazine supplement in southern Massachusetts. Who knows, but there are some possibilities."

Gomes stopped to eat another mouthful and to watch Jacqueline. She was sipping her wine and looking at him carefully.

"What else are you thinking?"

David looked down at what was left of his food and drank his remaining wine. The waiter looked towards David to see whether he wanted another glass, but David moved his hand over the glass.

"You and I have worked together for a long time, and we became very…close."

"David, we became *involved*. Speak directly."

Gomes was unprepared for this discussion and became unsettled. He found it difficult to look directly at Jacqueline, instead looking at a child playing with his mother sitting across the aisle.

"Alright, Jacqueline. 'Involved.' Despite how I felt, I was never sure how best to handle that. You were…you remain my friend. In fact, a long time ago you became one of my best friends. Yet you were and are my boss. I am very protective of you and want to make you proud." He stopped for a second and drank some water.

"After Pam and I broke up the relationship between you and me…intensified. We spent a hell of a lot of time together, both on the clock and off. But, at the end of the day, you were still my boss, and I could not figure out how to get around that basic fact, despite…despite my feelings."

Jacqueline looked away from him and out a window. She returned her attention to him, breathing deeply and slowly, her eyes focused on David's soul.

"You will always hold a special place for me, David." She looked at her watch, and then raised her head. Though she displayed no emotion, beneath the surface, a deep feeling was smoldering.

"David, thank you for joining me for lunch. I will pick up the tab, as they say. I need to get back to the office for a phone meeting. You have given me much to consider, and it feels as if you and I are on the same page." She signaled for the check, which was quickly brought to her.

Gomes watched Jacqueline pay the check. She touched his hand gently and nodded her head, then stood and walked away.

Gomes took another sip of water, wiped his mouth and stood up to leave. But he realized that he was not ready to return to the office, so he sat down and signaled to the waiter to order a coffee.

11

The following day as he drove into the parking lot of the shipbuilder's union in Quincy, Gomes reflected on his discussion with Mariana from earlier that morning. He was getting ready to go to New York City for Labor Day weekend and wanted to make sure that all her assignment was clearly laid out.

Mariana had reviewed the material from Dr. Maeda and was already doing additional research on shipyards, the history of the Quincy shipyard and the history of the shipbuilders' union. Gomes could not understand how a progressive national union in the 1930's turned into what seemed like a conservative force by the 1970's. He wondered whether this was just a problem in Quincy.

Mariana gave Gomes a preliminary report and promised more later.

Gomes never spent any time in Quincy. He thought of it, particularly in the aftermath of what was known as the "Boston Busing Crisis"—the desegregation of the Boston public schools—as one of several 'refugee towns' for white people who wanted to flee Boston and insert themselves into segregated suburbs. The white character of Quincy contrasted with a surprisingly integrated workforce in the shipyard, though Gomes did not have the details.

Looking at the building that housed the shipbuilders' union, the first word that came to mind was *archaic,* like something out of a different era. It was a two-story, wood-framed building that looked as if it had been a mansion or a small hotel from the 1940's. It looked old, but not decrepit, and sitting by itself across from the shipyard, it conveyed a sense of isolation or loneliness.

Gomes had an appointment with the union's president for noon and with one of the welding stewards for 1 pm. He had no idea how long the discussions would go.

The door to the union hall off the parking lot was locked. Gomes noticed a sign that directed visitors to walk up the stairs outside of the building to the main entrance.

Inside the hall, the air conditioning made the environment comfortable, a contrast with the heat outside. Behind an "L" shaped wooden counter a woman turned to Gomes and, with a high-pitched voice that could drive someone to suicide said, "Yes, may I help you?"

The voice reminded Gomes of nails scratching a chalkboard. The woman, probably in her late 40s, was slightly overweight and had the face of someone who had spent far too much time in the sun. By the way she wore her bleached blonde hair and tight, beige pant suit, Gomes could tell that this was someone who had memories of herself as a knockout; unfortunately, reality had not yet caught up with her.

She looked uncomfortable at the sight of Gomes, walking into the office carrying a blue sport jacket over his shoulder, wearing blue pants and a white shirt, his tie loose and top button open. Gomes was not sure whether her voice and look was a reaction to his race or just suspicion of him as an outsider. In either case, her voice and attitude conveyed her unease.

"Good afternoon," Gomes responded, attempting to be polite. "My name is David Gomes and I have an appointment with Mr. Ryan McIntyre."

"Is PRESIDENT McIntyre expecting you?" she asked, ignoring that Gomes had said he had an appointment.

"Yes, ma'am, I have an appointment for noon." He looked at the clock, which read 11:52 AM.

The woman, who had no I.D. badge, sighed and pointed to

some seats. A pale, stooped white man, probably in his 60s, came into the open office area and dropped some papers on the woman's desk, saying something quietly to her. He adjusted his eyeglasses and looked over at Gomes, then walked down the hall.

The woman, who appeared to serve as both receptionist and clerical worker, picked up the phone. When she ended the call, she walked back over to the counter, looking at Gomes as if he was an exhibit in a zoo.

"President McIntyre will see you in a few minutes."

Gomes nodded and sat back, looking around the office, wondering whether that had been McIntyre at her desk. The office felt like something out of a 1950's film that had never been redecorated since then. There were desks for three people behind the counter, but Gomes did not see three people working there. Sitting on the table to his right were a few magazines, including the publication of the national shipbuilders' union. There were also copies of *Time* and *Newsweek*, looking as if they had just been removed from a washing machine. When Gomes looked closer, he noticed that they were dated from the Spring.

Gomes glanced at the clock and then picked up the shipbuilders' magazine, wondering how long he would be kept waiting. He skimmed the magazine, immediately noticing that there was little of interest in its contents. There were stories about lobbying to get more US Navy work—rehabilitation and new construction—as well as stories about the leadership. He noticed an article about the Quincy shipyard that said little and did not convey a sense of the challenges working there. The article seemed to be more about the importance of restoring a domestic shipbuilding industry, the Quincy work being an example.

At 12:10 Gomes walked over to the charming receptionist.

"Excuse me," he started, his voice low, then noticing a nameplate that read "Sylvia Fontaine." He continued: "Excuse me,

Miz Fontaine. Do you have a sense of how long it will be until Mr. McIntyre can meet with me?"

Fontaine looked up from something she was working, face filled with annoyance. Her nostrils flared for a moment while she looked equally puzzled.

"President McIntyre will see you when he is ready...sir. He is wrapping up some work."

Gomes turned around, suppressing his frustration. Just as he was getting ready to sit down, a phone rang at Fontaine's desk.

"You can go in now...sir. Second door on the left. His name is on the door," she said while hanging up the phone, cutting her eyes while she did.

Gomes thanked her and proceeded down the short hall. The second door on the left had frosty glass on which was written "President Ryan McIntyre." The door was ajar. Gomes knocked and walked in.

Sitting at the table was a man in his 50's with a reddish face, graying hair and a thick gray and black mustache, almost a caricature of the labor union leader portrayed in the media. Though he was seated, Gomes could tell that he was tall and muscular, with a little extra weight that had joined him over the years. He took his glasses off but did not stand as Gomes entered.

"Sit down, Gomes," McIntyre said, pronouncing the name correctly but with little warmth. "Sorry to keep you waiting. So, you want to talk about that colored Portuguese guy that died a few weeks ago? Yeah, very sad."

"Thanks for seeing me, Mister McIntyre. Yeah, I wanted to speak with you about the *Cape Verdean* immigrant who fell to his death in July, but I also wanted to just speak with you about shipyards."

McIntyre ignored Gomes' correction of the identity of the deceased.

"Yeah, a real shame. Not sure what I can tell you. Did you speak with the Company?" When Gomes shook his head no, McIntyre continued. "I didn't figure they'd speak with you. So, I guess you're going to speak with the welding shop steward who looked into this, he can tell you more. Accidents happen in shipyards. This is not a place for sissies, Gomes. You've got to expect danger and know that it could happen any time. You can't walk around worried all the time."

McIntyre droned on as if he was giving a speech. In fact, it felt very much like a prepared speech. Gomes was struck by how defensive of the company he seemed to be, taking it for granted that people would get hurt and killed at the shipyard and that in many cases it was *their* fault.

"You know, Gomes, there was a crane operator who got killed here a while back," McIntyre continued, completely oblivious to Gomes having become disengaged. "The stupid son of a bitch picked up a load that was *way* too heavy for him. The crane toppled over and the guy was crushed when it fell. End of story. The idiot should've known that the damn load was too much, but he was in a hurry and…boom. Splat."

McIntyre made a sound, almost a chuckle, and then refocused on Gomes, who could not believe that this union president would place the blame for the death on the *crane operator* without some discussion about the pressures that the workers were obviously under to get their work done. Gomes was not even a shipyard worker and he knew the pressure.

"It's like war, Gomes. You ever been in a war?" he asked as if he was interrogating Gomes.

"Not exactly," Gomes responded.

"What the fuck does 'not exactly' mean?"

"It means," Gomes responded, taking a very deep breath and sitting forward, "that I was on the DMZ in Korea." Referring to the demilitarized zone separating North and South Korea.

McIntyre retreated into his chair for a moment, looking at his desk and then eying Gomes.

"Well, I was in a 'hot' war, Gomes. I was in Korea in nineteen-fifty. I volunteered to go. You go to war and you might get killed, that's the name of the game. You know that going in. It's sad if someone is killed but it happens. Well, the same is true in the shipyard. You know the name of the game when you enter those damn gates. You take the risks if you want the money. And the money is good!

"Damn, Gomes, you know they call shipyards the 'ass end of construction.' I've been a shipyard worker and in building construction ever since I got out of the military. It's risky and some people can't take it. I'm sick of hearing those faggots and communists complain. If they can't take it, they should get the fuck out of the shipyard!" McIntyre ended with his voice raised, almost hissing, his face turning red.

McIntyre sat back and pulled a cigar out of a drawer, lit it, and after taking a puff, moved his overflowing ashtray closer to him. Gomes closed his pad and put it in his bag.

"Thank you, Mr. McIntyre. I really appreciate your time, but I have to run to my next meeting with the steward, a Mr. Steve—"

"Carlotti, Gomes. Carlotti is a basically good guy, but he's too close to the Commies in the yard. In any case, he can tell you more."

Gomes stood and put out his hand to shake that of McIntyre. McIntyre looked at the hand as if he was being asked to handle a dead fish. He gave Gomes a weak shake, after which Gomes turned to exit.

"Don't let those communists fill your head with conspiracy theories, Gomes. You've been to the DMZ, you know how dangerous the Reds are!" McIntyre yelled as Gomes walked down the hall.

The Man Who Changed Colours

At the reception desk Gomes asked Ms. Fontaine if it would be okay to leave his car in the lot while he met with Mr. Carlotti. Fontaine had been watching Gomes as he walked past her and seemed annoyed by the question.

"Yes, since it's union business you can leave the car, but *don't* leave it all afternoon. This isn't a public parking lot!"

In his imagination, Gomes could see Fontaine wagging a finger at him like some overbearing teacher.

"Thank you, Miz Fontaine. I should be back in about an hour."

Fontaine turned back to her papers without another word.

12

The Club was at the end of a long block close to the main gate of the shipyard. Looking more like a bunker than a restaurant, it was a combination bar and cafeteria. Carlotti had told Gomes it was a hangout for the workers before going on and after going off shift.

Although it was two hours before the start of second shift, there were a few workers hanging out—a racially mixed group of blacks, whites and a couple of Latinos, some drinking, others eating, all but one talking.

Sitting alone was a thirty-something white guy, bald head with a thin mustache and beard, reading over something on a notepad. Dressed in white coveralls, a brown hardhat sitting beside him on an empty table, he seemed out of place with his serious demeanor.

"Mister Carlotti?" Gomes asked as he approached the man.

"Yeah, that's me. You must be David Gomes?"

"Yep, I'm Gomes. I just finished meeting with your union president."

Carlotti looked over Gomes' shoulder as if suddenly focusing on something or someone. He had dark eyes that contrasted with his complexion. Gomes reflexively turned around to see what Carlotti was looking at, but saw nothing noticeable.

"McIntyre's an asshole. The problem is that while the welders hate the bastard, he has solid support in some of the other trades, so, we're stuck with the son of a bitch. I'm sure he didn't offer you anything helpful."

Carlotti pushed aside an empty plate that had scraps of a submarine sandwich with tomato sauce on it. He drank some iced coffee and wiped his mouth off before continuing. Gomes offered an ironic smile in response, saying nothing.

"So, you want to know about the Pires death? Why is anyone from the Cape taking an interest in his case?"

"We cover a lot of things, Mister Carlotti, and not just on the Cape and Islands."   Carlotti nodded and drank more iced coffee.

"This is a dangerous, fuckin' place, Mister Gomes. I didn't really know Pires. I mean, I knew his name and saw him around. Him and these other Cape Verdeans came in around the same time a couple years back. I heard that he was a good worker, and I was surprised to hear about his death. You know, he was known for being careful. He didn't seem to do a lot of messing around or daydreaming, which I might add is easy to fall into here when you're doing the same fuckin' thing day-in and day-out."

"But others have fallen and, in some cases, died, right?"

"That's right. Mister Gomes, this place is a hellhole and the company doesn't give a shit. People are injured and they're told to come back the next day. Man, if you don't know your rights, they play you for a sucker. This guy fell a week or so before Pires. They had to take him to the hospital. I found out later that he was told to take one day off and go back to work! I mean the guy fell twenty feet and had a concussion and they tell him to take a day off and go back to work. Fortunately, he got better medical advice."

"So, what happened to Pires?"

"From what I can tell he was at his position, got up and either tripped or slipped over the side and down the hole. About fifteen feet. I looked into it. There weren't enough planks. There should have been planks beneath him so that if he fell it would only be a few feet. The company knew they'd fucked up. As soon as they found Pires, even before the medical team got there, the stage-builders were there putting up the planks the way they should've been from the beginning."

"Hey, Steve. I need to talk with you," came an angry voice from the front of the restaurant.

Gomes and Carlotti turned and saw a worker wearing military-style green coveralls approaching. Before Carlotti could say anything the worker nearly jumped at him.

"Carlotti. I thought you said we were going to hear from the company about my re-rate. Why are they jamming me? When's the union going to do something?"

"Bob, listen. I told you that I'd look into it. I did and I've gotten a run-around. I'm trying to figure out what's going on. Give me a minute to wrap up this meeting and I'll look for you."

Only at that moment did Bob seem to notice that Carlotti was speaking with Gomes. He looked over at Gomes curiously, knowing by the way that Gomes was dressed that he was not a shipyard worker.

"Oh, sorry…. yeah, excuse me mister. Okay, Steve, just get back to me. I'm starting to wonder whether I've not gotten it 'cause they're going to fire me or something." Bob turned around and walked back to join some other workers.

"My work is never done. These guys think that the 'union' is some big machine that can resolve everything for them, and they don't have to do a thing. But listen, I can't blame them. The Union's leadership, people like McIntyre, have taught the guys that lesson, so I guess you reap what you sow. As a result, we're getting our asses kicked by the company and a lot of our members wonder why. We're like an army that's been ordered to stand down!

"Listen, Gomes, I'm not sure what more I can offer. You told me that you'd been reading up on shipyards. Pires was just another number, man, and when his number was up, that was it. At least that's the way the company sees it."

Carlotti started to act as if their meeting was over, putting his pad into a pocket on his coveralls when something stopped him.

"Gomes, I'm assuming that the company bastards told you nothing, right?"

Gomes nodded.

Carlotti pulled his pad back out and wrote a name and number on a piece of paper, ripped it out and handed it to Gomes.

"Give this guy a call. His name is Jeff Tanner. He's the medic here. A 'physician's assistant' they call them. He's not a doctor but he's in charge of the clinic. Give him a call. Tell him I gave you his number, see what he'll tell you."

Looking through the window across the street, Carlotti added, "Have you ever been in a shipyard?" Gomes shook his head. "Okay, follow me."

Carlotti and Gomes got their things and headed out. When Bob looked surprised at their leaving, Carlotti signaled that he'd be right back. The two crossed the street, walked down a block to the main gate and approached a security guard.

"Lionel, hey man. Listen, this guy here's my guest. I want to give him a short tour of the yard. Would you give me a hardhat for him?"

"Gee, Steve, I mean, you know he's supposed to get clearance."

"Lionel, it'll just be for a few minutes. Just give him a fuckin' hat and a temporary badge for a minute, will you? We'll be back in, what, ten minutes. Okay?"

The guard, dressed in a dark blue uniform and a military cap, made a sour face and gave in. Gomes clipped a badge to his shirt and put on the hardhat and some safety glasses.

"Sorry I can't take you on the ships, Gomes, it's an experience that's hard to describe to a non-shipyard worker. Particularly when you look down from way up. By the way, don't look at the light that's created by the welding, it'll hurt your eyes. It's called a 'flash' and your eyes will start to burn. Also, keep those safety glasses on that Lionel gave you."

Gomes noticed that the safety glasses also functioned as sunglasses. The two of them stopped for a second near a long warehouse-looking building. Carlotti pointed out the ships under construction, some of the buildings, the huge cranes and a part of the yard that looked like a metal junk heap where various parts were being assembled.

"With all that metal, it's easy for an accident to happen. There are supposed to be safety meetings on every crew, but even when they happen, too many of the foremen don't take it seriously. And too many of the guys think that injury or death won't happen to them. You know—and you'll think that this is sick—there were two reactions after Pires died."

"Like what?"

"Well, the first one was shock and sadness. Some disbelief. A few days later there were jokes being told and stories about how it was his own fault. Amazing, Gomes. It's one way of dealing with the horror. Pretend that it's someone else's fault. So, the company fucks us and instead of fighting back, a lot of us go along with it, blaming ourselves!"

Carlotti made a U-turn and started heading back to the front gate. A woman passed the two and yelled hello to Carlotti.

"Many women working here?"

"Not a whole lot, and to be honest, most of them are better at what they do than the men. They fight to stay here and be respected. I don't know many who've left. On the other hand, I know a lot of dudes who decided that this was just not for them."

When they got to the gate, Gomes returned his equipment and thanked the guard. He turned to Carlotti.

"Thanks for all of this. I wish that I could've taken pictures. I want readers to know more than just about Pires. I want them to know about the conditions you guys are working under and what you're trying to do about it."

Carlotti stuck out his hand and gave Gomes a warm shake. Gomes thought this was a hell of a lot different from the McIntyre meeting.

"Listen, Gomes, I'm not sure that I was of much help. You get used to seeing these injuries, I hate to say. Anyway, when you're finished with that story, make sure we get it up here, the guys will want to read it. We need attention. Too many of our members who've been injured blame themselves. Too many who have been killed got scapegoated. If McIntyre had any balls, he'd speak up, but what can I say?"

Gomes thanked Carlotti and headed back to the union hall to get his car, just as Bob yelled at Carlotti demanding his attention.

13

Gomes was surprised when the caucus, otherwise known as Shipyard Workers United, had agreed not only to meet with him, but to meet him immediately prior to Labor Day weekend. He was able to arrange all his Quincy meetings on the same day, but the meeting with the caucus was going to be late afternoon, 4:30, after first shift, when a number of the caucus leaders were meeting at the home of one of their own in South Quincy.

With time to kill, Gomes drove to a *Dunkin Donuts* to get some coffee and do some writing. He did not know Quincy, only driving through it on his way to Boston any number of times. He found a *Dunkin Donuts* on Route 3A about a half mile from the shipyard. From the outside, it looked big enough to have booths where he could work.

Gomes pulled into the parking lot, found a space, turned off the ignition and sat in his car with the window open thinking for a moment. He wanted to make a few notes about his discussions with the union leaders while they were fresh in his mind before entering the *Dunkin Donuts*. Glancing around absent-mindedly, he noticed a payphone outside the coffee shop and looked at the paper with the number that Carlotti gave him. It was a work number for the medic. *Why not call him?* Gomes thought.

Gomes exited his car and walked over to the phone booth. As he did an older white couple walking into the *Dunkin Donuts* stared at him intensely with a wary look. Gomes returned their looks with a polite smile and a nod of the head as he approached the phone. He dialed the number and heard the phone ring.

"Clinic. May I help you?" A female voice answered.

"Yes, may I speak with Mr. Tanner? My name is David Gomes. Mr. Steve Carlotti suggested that I speak with him."

"Please hold," was all she said. Silence. Gomes stood at the phone booth and looked around at his environment, not absorbing very much. That same white couple exited the *Dunkin Donuts* carrying a bag and two cups of coffee. Again, they looked at him as if he was from outer space, *the 'creature from the Black Lagoon,'* Gomes thought as he watched them and awaited Tanner.

"Yes, this is Jeff Tanner. How may I help you?" The voice was strong and clear.

"Mister Tanner, Mister Carlotti suggested I speak with you. My name is David Gomes. I am with the *Cape & Islands Gazette.* I'm doing a story that was sparked by the tragic death of a Cape Verdean immigrant welder named Alberto Pires back in July. The story is about shipyards and the conditions—"

"Let me stop you right there, Mister Gomes. I'm not going to speak with ANY reporter about what happened to Pires or anyone else. I'm not going to speak about conditions in the shipyard. You can go to the office of the company president about such things. I'm sorry if Steve misled you. Have a nice day."

Click.

Damn, Gomes thought. It was not really a surprise, though Carlotti had raised Gomes' hopes that he might be able to get some inside information.

Gomes walked back to his car and sat in the driver's seat for a second to think, closing his eyes. *Should he try back again,* Gomes wondered. *Probably a waste of time.*

"Step out of the car…sir," stated a stern voice attached to a threatening image that Gomes saw when he turned to his left. Standing there with his left hand on his pistol was a very tall white man in a police uniform.

"Excuse me?" Gomes responded out of complete confusion, his eyes adjusting after having been closed momentarily.

"Get out of the car…sir…right now. Keep your hands where I can see them."

Remembering his training on how to interact with police should he ever be pulled over, Gomes told the officer everything that he was doing while he did it, slowly exiting the car. He moved slowly and kept his hands in view.

"Officer, can I ask what this is about? My identification is in my wallet. I'm a reporter for a newspaper in Hyannis."

"Keep your hands where I can see them…sir. Your car matches the description of one in a robbery. There was a black guy driving it. Some people here reported a strange black guy in the parking lot. What are you doing here, anyway? Show me the identification… *slowly*."

Gomes moved slowly, detailing every move as he made it, and offered his identification, feeling a cold fury that this was happening. But he also felt dread. Quincy was not known for having a large Black population and the Quincy Police were not part of the welcome wagon.

"I'm working on a story about shipyards. I just had a couple of meetings. I have some time to kill before my last meeting," regretting the use of the word "kill" as soon as he mouthed it.

The officer did not seem to be listening. He looked at the driver's license and the identification card that Gomes carried with him from the *CIG*. He walked back to his cruiser and got on his radio, periodically turning to look at Gomes.

Gomes felt his stomach tighten like a drum. At least the cop had not pulled his gun on him. Yet. *What the fuck?* Gomes kept thinking. *Sitting here in this parking lot, doing nothing and this shit happens.*

The officer approached him looking a little more relaxed and handed Gomes his identification.

"You're free to go," was all he said, turning around to enter his cruiser. Gomes stood paralyzed just watching as the officer pulled out of the lot and drove on.

A young, dark-haired white man, wearing a *Dunkin Donuts* uniform had come outside to watch the incident. As the officer drove off the employee stood there looking at Gomes, then turned on his heals and retreated into the store.

No apology from the cop, Gomes thought. *No explanation other than he looked like some other Black guy.*

Damn it to hell!!!

His stomach did not stop talking to him, even with the cop well out of site.

14

The caucus meeting was taking place in South Quincy not far from the South Shore Plaza shopping center. Gomes had looked at a map but it still took him some time to find the house.

The neighborhood was made up of maybe twenty single-family homes, most with small front yards. Gomes found the ranch-style home on a block with a mix of housing designs. There was a garage that could fit two cars. He saw one car in the driveway and others in front of the house. Apparently, the meeting had already started.

Gomes rang the doorbell. The door was answered by an Asian woman dressed in medical scrubs, her hair tied behind her. Gomes thought she might be a Filipina in her 20's, he could not tell for sure. Not that it mattered. She was looking very rushed while trying to be pleasant.

"Yes, hi. My name is David Gomes. I'm here for a meeting with the Shipyard Workers United. I was told to ask for Agnes Woodward. Is that you?"

"Agnes!" the woman yelled out, turning toward a hallway, "Someone here for you!" She then disappeared into another part of the house.

A white woman in her late 20's came towards the door. Wearing a t-shirt with worn jeans and what appeared to be burns on her pants, she possessed an engaging smile. Her brown hair was covered by a Boston Red Sox baseball cap on backwards.

"Mister Gomes, I'm so glad you were able to make it. I'm Agnes Woodward. I hope you had no trouble finding the place. Apologies for the way I'm dressed, we all headed over directly from the yard after first shift ended."

Before he could answer, the Asian woman came running out towards the door. She kissed Agnes on the cheek, saying, "See you tomorrow, sweetie. I may be home just in time to kiss you good-morning."

With that she was out and moving towards the garage.

"My roommate Rose is an RN at the hospital. Got called in late to fill in for some absent staff. Then, she has the graveyard shift! Terrible hours." Agnes stood by the door for a moment watching Rose drive off, then turned back towards Gomes.

"Come on back and meet the crew," she said smiling.

Agnes and Gomes walked into a family room with beautiful windows and plenty of light. There were glass doors to an outside porch. Behind the house Gomes could see the backyards of another row of homes. The Steely Dan album *Aja* was playing in the background. In the room were five other workers all dressed in work clothes, several with burn spots, particularly along the sleeves. There was a Black guy with a military hat and jacket, two other white women, a tall white guy, about 6'2", with a ponytail, and another guy of average height who looked Puerto Rican or Dominican, Gomes could not tell.

Agnes explained to Gomes on the phone that their caucus formed a couple of years ago in response to a pathetically conservative leadership of the union. Having met McIntyre, Gomes had an idea what Agnes meant. The caucus was pressuring the leadership to fight various company practices and to change the way the union functioned internally. From the minute that Shipyard Workers United surfaced, they were red-baited, gay-baited, and race-baited. Not to mention the sexual harassment that women faced, whether they were associated with the caucus or not. Despite all of that, the caucus persisted and forced the union's leadership on more than one occasion to do the right thing…despite themselves.

"Okay, team," said Agnes, "Mister Gomes is here to meet with us. Let's save the rest of our agenda so that we can help him out with his questions. Let's introduce ourselves."

The Black guy was Walter Jefferson, the white women were Connie Salerno and Karen Schwartz, the white guy was Michael Wellington, and the Latino gentleman was Ramon La Luz.

"Thanks so much for your time. Doctor Maeda told me about your caucus. I met with McIntyre and Carlotti today. I tried to speak with the company, but with no luck. I really need to better understand shipyards and what happened to Pires."

Agnes had disappeared for a moment but returned with water, iced tea and lemonade, the glasses already on the table. Everyone reached for the drink of their pleasure. The group then jumped in with one story after another about working conditions. Horror stories as well as funny stories. All but Wellington were welders; he was a pipe-fitter. They showed Gomes burns they received welding and discussed the sexual harassment that all the women experienced.

As the meeting started to return to order, Agnes intervened: "If the men at the yard knew about Rose and me…the hell that I'd have to put up with…they already call me a dyke."

Everyone looked at Agnes in silent support, all shaking their heads about the situation.

"What are you up to with this story, Mister Gomes?" a thirty-something, sun-glassed Jefferson asked with a raised eyebrow, conveying some level of skepticism.

"I want this to be an exposé, Mister Jefferson. I'm hoping that some other papers and maybe radio stations pick up on this and go deeper. From everything that I've learned in the last several weeks, when you shipbuilders go to work you end up playing with your lives, given the conditions you're operating in."

"Mister Gomes," interjected the thin and bearded La Luz with a soft Puerto Rican accent, "you don't know the half of it. Some of the chemicals that we're around don't affect us right away, but in twenty or forty years we could have all sorts of problems. And the company doesn't give a damn!"

The discussion remained lively. As it turned out, Agnes had known Pires.

"Very quiet guy, Mister Gomes. There's a woman on his crew named Alice Love who'd work with him a lot. She was there when he died, though I hear she was on break at the time. I asked Alice—after Pires died—about him. She said that the guy was very private. Didn't talk much. Could speak English fluently but just wouldn't engage in much conversation. We tried to get him into the caucus, but he would—politely—decline, saying he had other things to do and didn't want to get involved."

Karen Schwartz, a short woman with red hair and freckles, spoke up. "Mister Gomes, we know that Doctor Maeda gave you information. We put together additional information right here." Schwartz handed him a packet. "It has info on a number of things, such as the welding gases we're exposed to, some of the construction problems, and the hell faced by the sandblasters." She was referring to the workers who had to seal themselves completely—no matter the outside temperature—in order to sandblast various parts of the ships to clean them. "We hope you can use all of this. Something has to be done about the situation in the yard. People inside and outside the yard just take the whole situation for granted!"

Connie Salerno, dark hair, probably late 20's with the face of a smoker, had been quiet. She asked, "Mister Gomes, you said that you tried to speak with the company about Pires. What did they say? Who did you speak with?"

"Carlotti gave me the name and number for this guy in the clinic: Jeff Tanner."

"*WALLY!*" they yelled in unison and then broke into a fit of laughter. Gomes was completely puzzled.

Agnes explained as the laughter subsided.

"Mister Gomes, we laughed because Tanner is the spitting image of Wally Cox. You know, the comedian and actor. So, just about everyone at the yard calls him Wally. He used to hate it, but he's had to get used to it. Sorry if we confused you."

A bit flustered, Gomes continued his story as the room settled down. "Yeah, well, Tanner didn't want to speak with me. He even cut me off mid-sentence."

The group shook their heads.

"That's Tanner," offered Wellington, reaching for more lemonade. "A really decent guy who doesn't take *any* risks. I don't think any of us are surprised that he wouldn't speak with you."

The discussion kept going until Gomes looked at his watch and realized he had been there for well past an hour. He took loads of notes and knew that the caucus had other agenda items, so he moved to put his things away. He also hoped to get home to have dinner with Pam and pack for their weekend excursion to New York.

"May I use your phone to call Hyannis?" he asked Agnes.

"Certainly. There's a phone in the kitchen, feel free to use it."

Gomes excused himself to call Pamela as the group kept talking.

"Hey, love, if you haven't eaten yet and have no plans, I'll pick up some Chinese food on my way home so we're not rushed."

"That'd be great, David. I'm in the middle of a project anyway so that'd be a relief. I'll see you when you get here. I know that the traffic will be hell."

Gomes hung up and returned to the family room to say his good-byes. Agnes walked Gomes to the door and thanked him for coming to the meeting. He thanked her and said that he'd be back in touch.

"You know, Mister Gomes, I keep thinking about something that Carlotti said to me after Pires died. He said to me, 'Agnes, I swear I can't figure out how the hell Pires would've fallen.' He said that he would've had to have been really off balance and looking down the hole to have fallen because there really were enough boards for them to walk around and do the welding."

Gomes stood in the doorway. "What are you saying, Agnes? And, by the way, I wish that everyone would just call me David. I should've said something earlier."

"I'll tell the group, David," she said, smiling. "I don't know what I'm saying, and I don't know what Carlotti was thinking. But, you know, this guy that fell a week or two before Pires? Well, he was standing on this one board held by stiffeners. There was nothing securing the board. He apparently lost balance. There was nothing like that with Pires. With no indication of drugs or alcohol, that was one hell of a mishap. David."

Gomes had no response for Agnes. Workers get killed at work all the time and it is rarely reported. He'd probably never know the truth, and it was highly unlikely that anyone would ever come forward with more detailed information. Particularly after his call with Tanner, he was feeling pessimistic.

15

Their Labor Day trip to New York City was fabulous. Though technically a visit with Gomes' friend, it really was a mini-vacation for Pamela and David. They had to make do, given that money was tight and they could not take a real vacation this year. Maybe when Pam was out of school, but not before then. That said, David's friend gave them plenty of space so they could do what they wanted, which ended up being a lot of walking through Manhattan, time in Central Park, as well as some partying at night. Nothing remarkable, except the time together was, itself, remarkable. It was *their* time. Both David and Pamela needed a break from the intensity of their lives.

It was difficult missing the Gomes-Alves Labor Day reunion, but David felt like his parents and other family members really needed to learn to accept that he and Pam had their own lives. What's more, the reunions were changing each year. Some relatives had died, others had moved out of the area. Even the political discussions, such as around the Cape Verdean independence struggle against Portugal that had been a recurring theme of earlier reunions, receded. Gomes was not sure if that was the result of Guinea-Bissau and Cape Verde gaining their independence from Portugal or whether there was some other change underway among Cape Verdean Americans.

Something else seemed to be playing out. The Gomes-Alves reunions had been both a family gathering and a cultural gathering. Specifically, a *Cape Verdean* cultural gathering. David noticed that many of his younger cousins were having a different sort of identity challenge than David had known growing up. When David was young, the big challenge was recognizing that one was *not* white and *not* Portuguese, a point of major contention within the extended family. It was about both Black pride *and* Cape Verdean pride.

Many younger people in the family were ambivalent about their Cape Verdean-ness. They either saw themselves as Black or, in some cases, tried to pass as white. This was playing out in the family reunions in terms of who attended, who did not, and who brought whom. This certainly was not across the board. Particularly among relatives in New Bedford, there was an almost defiant pride in their Cape Verdean heritage. David thought he might want to write something about this someday.

The good news, however, was that now that David and Pamela were married, Pamela was fully accepted in the family, though that did not stop some of the older family members from still making side comments about her dark skin, even if, in some cases, they were the same color.

The Tuesday after Labor Day, Gomes was back in the office by 9 am. Jacqueline was flexible with reporting hours after three-day weekends, allowing the staff to come in a little late unless there was some urgency. Gomes never abused that policy and, on this day, came in on the early side to finish his article on Pires and the shipyards.

Mariana had left David plenty of material and a detailed memo. That, plus his own notes and research were more than enough to write the story he felt needed to be written. He hoped to have the article ready for the Tuesday edition of the paper, but it was just not ready. Instead, the *CIG* published a few Labor Day stories about workers, including union organizing efforts, the lives of workers, and the lives of contemporary deep-sea fishermen. It was all good, but it would have been even better if Gomes completed his piece on the shipyards. *Well,* he thought, *next week.*

Bill Fletcher Jr.

Gomes had just gotten off the phone with his mother, filling her in on the New York trip and checking on how the Gomes-Alves family outing had gone, when Mariana came into the office and approached his cubicle.

"Hey, David. Did you see my memos?"

"Great job, Mariana. More than enough here for my story."

"Did you get any new insights while you were in Quincy?" She sat down in the chair next to his desk, holding a notepad and a pen.

"Insights? Not exactly. The meetings filled out the picture, you could say. The one odd thing was something said by a caucus member and the welding steward. Both of them found it surprising that Pires would've fallen the way that he did."

Mariana looked at him quizzically, moving her hair away from her eyes.

"You mean like it *wasn't* an *accident?*" she asked, as if an electrical charge had gone through her body.

"No, not that. I think more like shipyards are very dangerous places and there are usual ways that people get injured or killed. This happened to not be one of them."

Mariana sat back nodding her head affirmatively. "Yeah, that's what it seems after the research I did." She put away her notebook. "Well, listen, I have to take off and do a few things before my job starts. When do you want me to start working on my next assignment?"

"Let me complete this story. I should have it done by tomorrow. After the editing it should be ready to run next week, so you and I can start talking maybe..." he paused looking at his calendar, "Thursday or Friday. Does that work?"

She got up and bid him farewell, looking excited, almost bouncing. As Gomes watched her leave, he thought to himself that she might have a great future in journalism. She had just the right sort of energy and was a hell of a researcher.

16

"Dying to Work" proved to be a hit article for *CIG*. The responses kept coming in. Gomes sent copies of the paper to the Shipyard Workers United and to the shipbuilder's union. Readers were immediately grabbed when they saw the face of the late Alberto Pires on the front page of the paper, the picture copied from his identification badge and the years of his birth and death listed right below his picture. Gomes even got a call from Tommy Lopes, the cousin of Pires, applauding the article and telling Gomes that he had no idea about the danger of shipyards.

Dr. Maeda was elated by the article and tried to get the story in broader circulation. Gomes called union president McIntyre but never received a return call. Carlotti called, and so did the leadership of the caucus, both praising his story. Carlotti told Gomes that McIntyre told the union leadership that this sort of article was bad for business and might hurt the company's ability to get more work. Carlotti had a few choice words for McIntyre, one ending with the letters "Y-O-U".

Gomes had to move on to his next stories. He and Mariana met at the end of the prior week as planned and discussed several possibilities. Speaking with the Shipyard Workers United gave him an idea for a story on the challenges Vietnam veterans on the Cape and Islands were up against returning to the USA: finding jobs, families, etc. It turned out there were quite a number of Vietnam Vets among the shipyard workers.

Mariana jumped at the idea of the Vietnam veteran story and they agreed on a research strategy to help pin down the topic. She, too, was excited about the response to the Pires story and was delighted any time Gomes had a new piece of feedback to share with her. He was delighted to have her on board.

On Friday Pam was on her way back from Boston. Gomes had just about wrapped things up for the day and saw no reason to stay late. If he got home before Pam, he would fix one of his spaghetti dinners with his famous tomato and anchovy sauce that Pam and many others loved so much. He had put some wine in the refrigerator before heading into work just in case. He thought about dinner and Pam as he took his tie off, turned off his typewriter and began to put a few folders in the drawer.

The phone rang. It was Marcia Blake. *Damn,* he thought, *I figured that I could get out of here!*

"David, I'm sorry to bother you but there's a caller on the line who wants to speak with you. They don't want to leave their name. What do you want to do?"

Over the years Gomes received all sorts of calls from people who did not want to leave names. Sometimes they were tips, other times they wanted to attack him for something that he wrote, and on a few occasions there were threats. Nothing ever came of it, but he took all the calls seriously.

"Thanks, Marcia. Please put the call through."

Gomes hung up and waited for the phone to ring. As soon as it did, he picked up the receiver.

"This is Gomes."

"Mister Gomes, you and I met, or I should say we spoke a few weeks ago when you called me at work." Gomes tried to remember the voice. Suddenly it clicked.

"Mister Ta—"

"I don't think that we need names, Mister Gomes. At least, we don't need to discuss them. I saw your article about Pires. Good work except for one thing."

"What's that, Mister X?" Gomes asked half-jokingly.

"It wasn't an accident, Mister Gomes. It was murder."

"Excuse me?" responded Gomes, stunned.

"My conscience has been bothering me ever since you called. It was one thing for me to not say anything after the incident, but when you started looking into it, it just became too much. My wife insisted that I call you."

Gomes was not sure what to say. He was sure it was Tanner's voice, though they only spoke briefly when he called the shipyard's clinic.

"I need more information, Mister X. Can we meet?"

Gomes could hear noise in the background. Tanner was calling from a payphone near a busy road. The man said nothing for a moment, leading Gomes to think that Tanner had abandoned the phone.

"I tell you what, Mister Gomes. Meet me this Monday at, let's say, 5 pm at the Quincy Center 'T' station on the Red Line. Sit on the departure side. That won't be hard to figure out since it is the first and last stop. We'll sit there and have a brief chat. Have a good weekend, Mister Gomes."

******

Gomes was almost finished preparing dinner when Pamela got home. Their faces brightened as they hugged each other.

Gomes gave her a kiss on her neck, which always tickled her, literally and figuratively. She carried her bags into their bedroom and took a few minutes to get unpacked and settled. When she returned wearing a gray sweatsuit advertising Boston University, Gomes presented her with a glass of wine. They toasted and sipped their wine. Gomes resumed preparing his spaghetti sauce, raising a spoon to taste it. He added a few chopped anchovies into the mix and stirred.

Pamela had a lot to tell Gomes about her week in Boston. School was going well, and she even found the time to get involved in some community work that focused on the disappearance and murder of Black women, crimes that received scant attention by Boston's finest. A community organization called "CRISIS" recently formed and was trying to raise awareness about the situation. Led by black women, it was making its mark and, in the process, shaking up some of the older male leadership in Boston's Black community.

When it was his turn, Gomes told her the latest on the future of the paper and the discussions with *Outlook*. He then switched gears.

"So, babe, I got this call today from the medic at the shipyard. I felt like I was in an episode of *The Rockford Files*. He didn't want me to use his name and he was very careful about what he said. But here's the punchline: he said that Pires had been murdered."

Pamela put her wine down and sat up straight. *"Murdered?"*

"Yep. He and I are going to meet on Monday in Quincy. He set up this elaborate meet, but I'm going to go through with it. He sounded scared."

"Who would murder the guy? And why wouldn't this come out earlier?"

"All good questions, sweetness. I have no answers. I feel like I've been thrown a curve."

Pamela turned towards Gomes with a serious face. "And besides that, how was the play Missus Lincoln?"

They both broke into a laugh and sat down for dinner. They did not discuss the Pires case again, but it loomed in the background for the rest of the evening. Pam could tell every time that she looked at David that a storm was brewing.

17

"What do you mean, *murdered*?" Mariana almost shouted.

"That's what this guy said. Please don't ask me who he was, but he was an inside contact, and he wants to talk to me."

Mariana paced around the conference room.

"Murdered?! Damn!!! Do you think that this contact of yours is some sort of nut?"

"No. I think that he is very serious, but whether he's accurate, only time will tell." Gomes immediately recognized that he should not have indicated the gender of the informant, Mariana did not need to know a lot of detail. It would protect her in case this whole thing went bad.

"When do you meet?"

"Today, late afternoon. And before you say anything, no, you *cannot* come along. I have to do this solo."

Mariana smirked, getting ready to respond. Gomes held up his right hand to signal there would be no debate on the issue. She retreated, looking uneasy and disappointed.

"Alright, I got it. If you run into trouble, call my landlord. She's a darling. I don't get casual calls at her place, so she'll know that it's important."

"Thanks, Mariana. I'll keep that in mind."

******

The ride was not bad going north against traffic on Route 3, so Gomes was able to relax, having gotten to Quincy Center a little more than thirty minutes early. He parked his car, walked over to a coffee shop near the station and bought a cup of coffee. Yeah, it would keep him up, but he also needed to be fully awake for the drive back to Hyannis.

At 4:55 pm Gomes entered the "T" station, paid, and went through the turn-style. The station was busy with rush hour commuters heading north and others returning from a day in Boston or farther north. He had to give it to Tanner, the meeting place wasn't a bad idea. Jim Rockford would have been proud.

Gomes looked around for "Wally Cox" but saw no one who fit the description. Many people were moving towards the platform, others were moving away. Suddenly, Gomes saw a face. It was a man sitting on a bench reading the paper with his legs crossed. Gomes approached him to get a closer look.

"Good afternoon, Mister Gomes," said a voice from behind him.

Gomes turned around and looked at the face of 'Wally Cox,' otherwise known as Jeff Tanner. He turned back to look at the man who was sitting down, but the fellow had vanished.

"What a coincidence that there would be someone looking like me here today. Oh, well. Let's grab a seat and keep this brief."

Walking over to a bench that cleared as a northbound train left the station, they sat down next to one another, but Tanner did not look at him. He sat, crossed his legs, and looked out at the crowd. The northbound platform was beginning to fill up again as another train was directed to that side of the station.

Tanner did not await any questions. He moved his right hand to his chin.

"When I was called about the accident I went over right away. There were some welders and cleaners standing near the hatch. I climbed in and saw the body. I checked quickly and determined that he was quite dead, with no chance of resuscitation. There were a few workers standing around me, but I told them to move away and give me some breathing space."

Another train came into the station, its brakes screeching. Passengers exited, heading to their various destinations. Tanner stopped talking until the train pulled away.

"Pires had clearly fallen, but his injuries were more complicated than a simple fall. Someone had broken his neck and made it look like it was an accident."

"How would you know that, Mister…"

"Because I was in the 'Nam and I know something about death," Tanner responded. "I know what's an accident, and I know what's intentional. Your friend Pires was murdered."

Turning toward Gomes, Tanner added, "I looked around the compartment where he fell, and on the wall was a circle with two blue lightning symbols."

Tanner looked at Gomes as if that piece of information should mean something to Gomes.

"The *Blue Lightning Society*. They're a group of white racists who formed during the Boston busing mess. These are guys who would love to yell 'Heil Hitler' if given the chance. They're the sorts of bastards my father fought against in the War."

"I'm not familiar with them. Why's that symbol important?"

"Because they're known to leave that symbol after they create some…mischief. Like the Ku Klux Klan leaving burning crosses. These are bastards who hate colored people, hate immigrants— unless the immigrants come from Ireland or Italy—and really get their rocks off fucking with people they think they can bully."

"So, you think it was the Blue Lightning Society that pulled off the murder?"

"I honestly don't know, but it was one hell of a coincidence that this would show up just as this guy was killed."

As another northbound train pulled out of the station with a whine, the platform temporarily cleared.

"After you discovered that Pires had been murdered and saw

the symbol, what did you do?"

Tanner put a toothpick in his mouth while watching another train move onto the northbound track.

"I...told my boss that I thought that there was something strange about the Pires death. I didn't mention Blue Lightning, even though I know that they operate in the yard. My boss reviewed my findings and decided that I was overstating the case—those were his words—and that it was clear that Pires *could have* fallen to his death.

"I tried to explain to the asshole that of course it was *possible* he had fallen to his death, but the circumstances as I found them indicated, at least to me, that Pires had been murdered. But he wouldn't listen. He wouldn't bring in the cops. And he told me to leave it alone. So, I left it alone for as long as I could."

The crowd was building up and for some reason the doors to the northbound train were not open. When they finally opened there was a mad rush for seats.

"That's about all I can tell you. My name stays out of this, of course. If you mention my name, I will deny it and I will accuse you of having harassed the shit out of me for your story. Got it?"

They looked at each other and nodded. Tanner rose and headed for the northbound train with the ease and elegance of a professional dancer. He entered the subway train car and turned towards Gomes just as the doors closed, a blank expression on his face.

18

The rush hour traffic south on Route 3 was brutal, but Gomes did not think about it as he was completely absorbed in rehashing the discussion with Tanner. He hadn't decided what conclusions to draw, but decided he needed to get to a pay phone.

Gomes pulled off on Route 139 and looked for a gas station where there might be a payphone. He quickly found one, pulled in and parked near the phone. A white mechanic came out of the garage and watched Gomes. He was chewing something: gum or tobacco, Gomes could not tell. The mechanic stood, leaning against the door to the station office, staring at Gomes, studying his every move. Gomes ignored him, except with the 'third eye' that racial minorities rely on in order to survive, particularly in areas that were 'melanin deficient.' His recent experience with the Quincy police had this upper most in his mind.

Gomes pulled a paper with various phone numbers out of his pocket and found the one he needed. He dialed and the phone rang.

"Agnes? This is David Gomes. I'm sorry to bother you but I need a little assistance."

"No bother, David. What's up?"

"Agnes, have you ever heard of 'Blue Lightning'? Some right-wing group."

"Sure. They're a bunch of racist assholes. They have a few members in the shipyard. Why you asking?"

"Well, their name surfaced as I was looking into the Pires case and I'm trying to put all the pieces together."

"I thought that Pires' death was an accident. I haven't heard Blue Lightning was into killing people." Agnes sounded perplexed. And concerned.

"No, don't jump to conclusions. I'm not sure they have anything to do with the Pires story, but I'm trying to find out what I can about them."

Agnes was silent for a moment.

"Listen, David, there's a guy I know in the yard. Good guy. Irish immigrant. Lives in Dorchester. You know, in Boston. He knows these Blue Lightning characters. He's got an interesting history. Let me give him a call. If he wants to chat with you, I'll see what I can arrange. Does that work?"

Gomes agreed, left his telephone numbers, thanked her, and returned to his car. As he got back into his car, he asked himself, *Am I on a wild goose chase? Is this gonna be another dead-end story?*

19

At 9 pm while reading a novel, Gomes received a phone call.

"Hello," Gomes answered, somewhat unfocused.

"David, this is Agnes. Is it okay to talk?"

Gomes came to attention. "Yeah, it's fine. What's up?"

"Well, I contacted my friend from the yard. He can meet you on Friday after first shift. There's a bar on Quincy Shore Drive called *Derry by the Sea*. Get there around 4 pm. Will that work?"

"Yeah, that's great. What's his name?"

"Eddie O'Hare. He'll know who you are. If there are any problems, get back to me before Friday morning, I should see him in the Yard on first shift."

"All set. Thanks very much."

Another trip to Quincy, he thought, shaking his head. He felt exhausted already, and now he had to go back into hostile territory.

******

Tuesday morning Gomes entered his office dressed in a well-fitting black suit, white shirt and red silk tie. Jacqueline wanted him at the table during the first meeting with the *Boston Outlook*.

At 10:30 am two representatives from the *Outlook* entered the *CIG*. Marcia, also dressed for the occasion in a light brown full-length dress and a thin attractive necklace, escorted the representatives to the conference room, where they left their things. Then she took them on a tour around the headquarters, introducing them to staff along the way. A few minutes later they were joined by Jacqueline and Gomes, who had decided to make a subtly late entrance.

The meeting was an opening round of talks. There were memos back and forth, but this meeting was meant to move the discussions further. The talk focused on the background of the two institutions, their goals and respective directions.

At 12:30 pm the meeting broke for lunch. Jacqueline and Marcia arranged to have food brought in. Everyone raced to any free phone they could find to check on phone messages and return important calls. At 1 pm, lunch of tasty sandwiches and sodas was served in the conference room. The mood was quite relaxed.

Which was why Gomes had to get a few minutes of Jacqueline's time. Despite the way that the meeting was progressing, Gomes was having a hell of a time maintaining his concentration. The two of them stepped out of the conference room.

"Boss, I'm sorry, but I don't think that I'm of any assistance to you. I'm not focused on this. There's been this strange development in the Pires story, and I keep finding myself thinking about it."

"I could tell there was something on your mind. No worries, David. It is helpful to have you in the meeting. More than anything else I need you to flag if something is going wrong or if there is something that I need to address. I was not expecting you to speak up, to be honest."

Jacqueline kissed him on his cheek and returned to the conference room. Gomes stood still for a second. They had been secluded, so he was not concerned about being seen, but that kiss seemed to come out of nowhere. It was not inappropriate exactly, but it was a surprise. He did not want to overthink it, so he took a deep breath and returned to the conference room.

As the meeting resumed, Gomes forced himself to concentrate, but the thought kept breaking in: *'Why the hell would someone want to kill Pires-the-gardener?'* It just did not make sense, unless this was a random racist murder. He wished that the meeting with O'Hare was tomorrow rather than Friday. He made notes on the pad about the investigation instead of anything that concerned the current negotiations with the *Outlook*.

20

"Mariana, I want you to do some research on a right-wing group called the Blue Lightening Society, or something like that. They're here in Massachusetts. They seem to be based in Boston."

"Is this a new story, David?"

"Maybe yes, maybe no. It may have something to do with the Pires death, but I'm not sure. I have another meeting in Quincy with a contact who may be able to fill in some pieces. In the meantime, please look into this, okay?"

"Okay, chief," she said with a straight face, Gomes looking up to see whether she was teasing him. "A shipyard worker, David?"

"Yep. This outfit may have been active in the shipyard. I don't know whether there's any connection but there are some odd pieces to this story."

"So, this could've been a racial killing?"

"Don't get ahead of yourself. We don't know for a fact that he was murdered. It's possible that this racist group did this intentionally or that things went too far. Or, that they had nothing at all to do with it."

"But didn't you say that this guy Pires was quiet and didn't create any stir?"

"When did that ever stop racists? You need to study up on your American history and look into lynchings, Mariana. Look up a young man named Emmett Till."

Mariana turned red and stared at the floor in embarrassment, but Gomes did not belabor the point or apologize. He did not mean to embarrass her, but sometimes the naivete of white people pushed him over the edge, even someone who was young and well-intentioned.

******

Friday did not come soon enough. Mariana found out a little about Blue Lightning, but it only touched the surface. It was started by white Vietnam War veterans who returned to the States furious that their government had not allowed them to commit full genocide. That was not quite the way the veterans framed it, but it was close. The vets believed they were held back from doing what was necessary to win, reminding Gomes of many veterans of World War I in Europe who morphed into fascists.

At first Blue Lightning was almost a club, but when busing to achieve school desegregation was implemented in Boston in 1974, they found a new purpose. They became part of the fascist wing of the white anti-busing movement and pushed for a broader right-wing agenda that went beyond matters of busing. This resulted in attacks on racial minorities, as well as on gays and lesbians, demonstrating that their agenda had nothing to do with school desegregation.

But how would they have gotten involved in killing Pires? Mariana asked David that question, again, after providing him with a preliminary report. He had no answer, but he did thank her for the report, which would help him in his meeting with O'Hare.

21

Derry by the Sea was a club across from Quincy Bay, near Wollaston Beach. There were not many establishments there, though during the warmer months there were a few food stands for people at the beach. Gomes drove into the club's parking lot at 4:05 pm.

Gomes opened the wooden door and walked in. The club had a wide window looking out on Quincy Shore Drive and the beach, providing a lot of natural light and a view of the sea.

When Gomes took a look around it was clear why Agnes was not worried about O'Hare finding him. There was not one other person in the bar with any degree of African, Asian, Latin American, or Native American blood in the room, at least from what he could tell. The bar was not full, which made his entrance even more noticeable. Nearly everyone in the room stopped talking and looked at him as he came in. Most of those in the bar were men.

"Are ya in the right place, my friend?" came a voice with a slight Irish accent to Gomes' left.

Gomes turned and saw a man wearing an apron picking up some glasses and moving towards the counter.

"Yeah, thanks. I'm here to meet someone."

Slight murmurs around the bar.

A man was sitting to Gomes' right ignoring the whole thing, reading a book, smoking a cigarette, and drinking a beer. A couple of the women who first noticed him returned to their discussion. Another woman smiled at Gomes fondly but said nothing.

"You're probably in the wrong place, lad," said another

man who appeared out of nowhere. He was built like a wrestler, probably in his 30's, dressed in a blue work shirt, stitched onto it the letters of a company, "QPR". "We don't get many of your kind in this establishment. We're very particular, you know. No offense intended."

"No offense taken. I was told to meet someone here so, since he appears not to be here at the moment, how about you leave me alone and let me get a beer and relax, okay? I'll just wait for him to show up."

"I think that the owner of this here establishment believes that it's unlikely ya would be meeting someone here, lad. And I think that we'd be all happy if ya just moved on. Ya get me meaning there, lad?"

Gomes concluded that he was going to have to rethink spending time in Quincy. The busing crisis showed that Malcolm X was absolutely correct: the problem in the USA was not the South. The South, Malcolm said, was anything south of the Canadian border. *Why do these white Quincy folks keep fucking with me*, he asked himself?

Gomes looked at his watch.

"I got your meaning," he said, walking over to a table near the window behind the man reading the book.

Mr. QPR pursued him to his table. "You don't seem to understand, lad," he said again, this time putting his hand out to grab Gomes by the left shoulder.

Bad move.

The next thing that Mr. QPR knew, he was being held with his arm behind him and Gomes' other arm pressing against his larynx.

Gomes whispered into Mr. 'QPR's' ear. "I want to be left alone. I'm not interested in dating your sister or daughter. I'm not interested in moving next door to your racist ass. Just leave me the fuck alone. Got it, *lad*?"

Gomes pushed the man away, the latter shaking his arm and rubbing his throat. He looked over at a couple of other men in the room, who rose in sync, the three of them approaching Gomes.

As Mr. QPR approached, the man who had been reading the book took his right hand and grabbed the fellow in the crotch. QPR screamed. The other two men immediately stopped advancing.

"I think that the gentleman behind me asked to be left alone. Did I hear him right, buddy?" the man said with an Irish brogue.

"Yeah, yeah," responded Mr. QPR in obvious agony, standing on his toes, paralyzed, looking as if he was going to burst.

"So, let's get this straight. The three of you are going to leave this gentleman alone. You know I regularly visit this establishment, and I think that you really don't want to piss me off. Am I right about that, my friend?"

The bartender signaled to everyone that they calm down. He yelled out, "Look, I think we had a misunderstanding. No harm."

The man released QPR's crotch and the victim limped away towards the restroom, looking over his shoulder at Gomes. The Good Samaritan then turned to Gomes. "Good afternoon, Mister Gomes. My name is Eddie O'Hare. Sorry about the difficulties."

"*Difficulties?!*" Gomes responded incredulously. "You were just going to sit there while I got my ass kicked?"

Once Gomes joined O'Hare at his table, the two men continued their discussion. "But you didn't. Besides, I had to see what sort of person ya are. People are interesting, Mister Gomes, and you need to see them under pressure. I saw ya under pressure and, to be honest, I'm impressed.

Before Gomes could respond, O'Hare went on, "From what I'm told, you want information that could put me in serious danger. I need to know whether it's worth my taking risks." He took a sip of his beer and licked his lips.

Gomes finally smiled, nodding his head affirmatively. He took a look at O'Hare. The man was probably in his late 30's, a tad over six feet, with short, dark hair and dark eyes that, along with his eyebrows, presented a look of melancholy. He was thin without being skinny, black eyeglasses and appeared to have not shaved for a couple of days. He was wearing shipyard coveralls with several burns in the cloth. His face was quite clean.

"Can I order you a drink?" O'Hare asked, extending his hand to shake. "I suppose I owe you that, having scared the shit out of you," he said chuckling.

"Thanks, Mister O'Hare, but the drinks are on me. I appreciate your time," returning the shake.

O'Hare signaled for the bartender and they both ordered. The bartender was uncomfortable, not looking at Gomes, but now coming across as polite, in contrast with his earlier behavior. He took the order and left.

"I'm Eddie, Mister Gomes, and if it's okay with you, you're David, alright?"

"Absolutely."

"So, you want to know about the Blue Lightning boys. Why?"

As the bartender delivered their beers, Gomes thought about how much to say to O'Hare. About partial truths and full lies. But there was something about O'Hare that left Gomes feeling like he needed to play this one straight ahead. So, he laid out what he had heard about a possible murder.

O'Hare listened intently, periodically looking around the room to see what the other guests were doing. He would then return his gaze to Gomes, never looking outside. When Gomes finished speaking, O'Hare shook his head.

"Davey," he launched in, "These guys play at organization. They like to think of themselves as a sort of underground military unit. The Irish among them glamorize the Provos and the INLA, but these guys are just a bunch of racist bullies. They don't know their asses from a hole in the ground."

Gomes did not know a great deal about the struggle in Northern Ireland that had evolved into what was politely called a "low-intensity war." The minority Catholic, or nationalist community in Northern Ireland, had been fighting for their rights as well as for unification with southern Ireland, only to be violently repressed by the Protestants, or Loyalist community, who had the support of the British.

Gomes stared at O'Hare. O'Hare took another sip of his beer, staring back.

"Alright, Davey, I tell you what. Let me ask around. I think that you're barking up the wrong tree, but who knows, right? I'll call you after I do some checking."

The bartender came over and they asked for water but no more beer.

"Where you from, Eddie?"

"I was born in a place called South Armagh, which you've probably never heard of. It's not far from the border with the twenty-six counties. I moved to Belfast and was there for a while before it came to be necessary, my friend, that I vacate the premises."

O'Hare grinned but his eyes did not smile. Gomes was not sure what to do with that.

"You were involved in the struggle, Eddie?"

The bartender returned with the water. They both thanked him. The bartender stood there for a moment.

"Eddie," the bartender started, "I want to apologize to you and your friend here. You know, we didn't know he was a friend of yours, and ya know that we're sort of particular about people coming here."

The bartender only glanced at Gomes and did not offer an apology. O'Hare said nothing, but looked over at Gomes, who answered, "We're okay."

"You heard what the gentleman said, Larry. Just be more careful the next time. My friend here is very particular about the establishments that *he* visits. Do you get my meaning?"

Larry nodded his head and went back to the bar, where two women were setting up shop and looking to order. Larry changed his demeanor and suddenly became gregarious.

"I come here, Davey, maybe once a week or once every other week. It's where I can think. Sometimes I bring people here, other times it's just me. I can't figure Irish Americans, Davey. In the north of Ireland and in Britain, we're treated like shit by the Brits and the Loyalists. When I came to your country I walked through the streets and the way that the Blacks are treated is almost identical to the way that we're treated at home. You'd think that people could see that. But instead of joining hands, Irish Americans more often than not act like the Loyalists back home except when it comes to discussing Ireland itself!"

"That's because when they come here, Eddie, they become 'white people,'" Gomes responded, raising his figures in air quotes.

O'Hare's eyes widened as he raised his glass to Gomes.

"Indeed, Davey. Indeed!"

They touched glasses and sipped their water.

"Tell me about your life, Eddie, if you don't mind," asked Gomes.

"Only if in return, you tell me about yours." With a promise from Gomes, O'Hare went on. "My family was quite poor. Very early we all understood the politics of the north of Ireland. My father had been in the IRA back in the 1950's and..."

An hour later Gomes and O'Hare were still sitting at the table, having decided to have another round of beers. Gomes learned more about the Irish freedom struggle than he could ever have imagined, better understanding the split in Sinn Fein and the Irish Republican Army and the later growth of the Irish Republican

Socialist Party and their military wing, the Irish National Liberation Army. Gomes was only able to tell O'Hare a little about his life before he had to reluctantly tell O'Hare that he needed to get home. As agreed, Gomes picked up the tab and O'Hare promised that he would get back to Gomes, regardless of what he found out about Blue Lightning.

Gomes stopped at the restroom before leaving. He had a long drive. O'Hare was still sitting where he had been, returning to his book as Gomes headed towards the door.

"Excuse me, sir," said a female voice.

Gomes turned and saw the face of the woman who had smiled at him earlier. Her voice was deep and pleasant, she had long, blond hair nearly to her waist, and was dressed in a short, light blue dress displaying the curves of her body. Gomes looked at her then quickly looked around the room, noticing that some of the men were watching him carefully.

"I'm sorry about the way that you were greeted earlier. I hope that it doesn't stop you from coming here. I come by every so often and maybe we could...talk sometime."

Suddenly thinking, *this woman is going to get me killed,* he politely thanked her and excused himself, keenly aware that he was being watched all the way back to his car. O'Hare watched the crowd just to make sure that there were no disturbances.

Gomes made it back to his car safely and, with all deliberate speed, headed home.

22

Pamela could not control herself when Gomes told her what happened. She was somewhat annoyed that he came home so late, but when he told her what happened at the bar, and particularly the last episode with the white woman, she was at first horrified, only to erupt into laughter.

When she stopped laughing, Gomes tried to be serious.

"This story is damned complicated, Pam. O'Hare doesn't think that it is the group of racists, so maybe the medic was wrong and it *was* an accident."

"Or maybe, David, there's another culprit. Are you going to keep going with this?"

"I really don't know, sweetness. This is starting to feel like one of those Russian dolls, where you open it up and there's another one and then you open that one up and there's another one...and so on and so forth."

The conversation wound down, but both David and Pamela were winding up. Having not been together for several days, they found it difficult to keep their hands off one another. Pam grabbed David by his hand and pulled him towards the bedroom.

******

Saturday morning Gomes met his old friend Vinnie Amato for breakfast. Gomes and Amato had been friends since their teen years, and while Gomes went into journalism, Amato, a tall, generally well-dressed man with a face made for politics—or television—went into law enforcement, becoming a detective and currently, a prosecutor in Barnstable County. The two had significant political differences—Gomes moving left, Amato moving to the right—but they had been able to retain their friendship over the years…for the most part.

The two old friends did not see as much of one another as they once did, so their periodic Saturday morning breakfasts were important.   This particular morning they met at an International House of Pancakes on the edge of Hyannis.

"Mister Prosecutor, how the hell are you doing?" greeted Gomes.

"Not bad, distinguished writer!" the surprisingly casually dressed Amato responded with a laugh. There was no laughter in Amato's eyes, however. Gomes noticed this but made no comment.

The two traded jabs, then ordered coffee. When the waitress returned, they ordered breakfast, then caught up on gossip and events. Gomes told Amato about the discussions on the future of the paper and then went into the Pires story. Surprisingly, Amato asked him little about either. He seemed distracted, looking at Gomes but not quite seeing him. When their breakfast of pancakes and sausages arrived, they continued their banter, but something about Amato seemed unfocused.

"What's up, Vinnie? I can tell when you've got something on your mind."

Finished with his breakfast, Amato was sipping his coffee, playing with a toothpick.

"I think that we're going to break up, Gomes," he finally said with a low and sad voice. Gomes knew that his friend was referring to his marriage. "We've just been living different lives, my friend, and it's like we don't know each other anymore."

Amato was having a difficult time looking at Gomes. He looked at the table, glanced quickly at Gomes, then turned his gaze to the room.

"Don't say it, Gomes. I know. You've been trying to get me to see for years that there was something wrong with my marriage. I know. I don't know what the hell to do about it."

Gomes sat silently sipping his coffee.

"So, what are you going to do, Vinnie?

Amato finished his coffee and finally looked directly at Gomes.

"I'm a Catholic, Gomes, just like you. I can't divorce her without a blow-up in my family. Plus, there's the kids to think about. I should have realized that she had things that she wanted to do with her life and that I had a leash around her. I thought... man, I thought for so long that she was just the dutiful wife, but it was all an act. I don't blame her, Gomes, she was acting as much for herself as she was for me. I don't know what the hell I'll do."

Amato signaled for more coffee. The waitress walked over and filled his cup, looking at Amato's face as she poured. Something in the way that she frowned showed concern for Amato. When she walked away, she turned to look back at Amato. The man never seemed to notice.

The discussion did not yield any resolution. Looking out the window of the IHOP, Amato mumbled a few barely audible comments about what he, maybe, should have done in the past. But he was not looking for advice. Suddenly Amato switched gears and started talking baseball. His energy level returned and he grew animated, except, once again, there was no excitement in his eyes. Then he switched gears yet again.

"Listen, Gomes, you know that we're good friends and I read all of your columns, but don't you think it's time for you to tone down some of this 'race' stuff for a while? Don't you think people are getting tired of hearing all this rhetoric about race and discrimination? Isn't it time to put this behind us? I just feel like..."

Gomes tuned out. He sat looking at Amato, periodically nodding his head. Gomes finished his coffee and offered a few words, struggling to contain his frustration. For some time, he had watched his friend move slowly to the political right. It wasn't just Amato's defense of almost anything and everything the police did. It was deeper, resulting in the two of them talking past one another. What troubled Gomes at the moment, though, was Amato clearly trying to deflect real discussion about his marriage.

Gomes looked at his watch.

"Listen, Vinnie, I've got to take off. Nothing personal. I know you're glad that Dukakis didn't get the Democratic nomination for Governor. I get that. And I know that you think too many of us have our hands out, but let me make you an offer. Let's take a ride someday soon and go take a look at poverty, and then let's talk about handouts. Let's also take a visit—together—to Fenway Park and see the Red Sox, and you can determine whether it's a comfortable environment for people who look like me."

Amato turned red and looked uncomfortable.

"Sorry, Gomes, about going on and on. I didn't mean to bend your ear so much. It's just…" but he didn't finish.

The two old friends split the bill, left a healthy tip, and stood to leave.

"Vinnie," Gomes said as Amato was leaving, forcing him to stop and turn around. "Listen, man, if you want to talk…I mean, if you ever want to talk about what's happening with you and Connie…you know, just call, okay?"

Amato offered a half smile and then, to Gomes' surprise, gave him a hug.

"Thanks, brother." Amato turned back to the door and headed out to his car.

Gomes watched Amato walk to his car and found himself thinking that it was not just Amato's marriage that had come undone. The friendship that the two of them shared for years was also fraying. What gnawed at Gomes was that he was not sure what, if anything, to do about it.

******

Gomes looked at Pamela, awaiting a reply to his report on his breakfast with Amato. She looked pained, periodically turning her head to the floor when Gomes relayed the conversation about Amato's marriage.

"One of the things that you told me, David, when we got back together, was that you did *not* want a relationship, let alone a marriage, like Vinnie's. You remember that?"

Gomes nodded his head, his face drawn in anguish.

"I just didn't know what to tell the guy. I've been feeling for a long time that the two of them need to go their separate ways. This whole 'I can't divorce because I'm Catholic' is b.s. He knows that. It's just an excuse."

Pamela had nothing more to say. She was not standing in judgment; she just knew that anything that she said would be something David had already considered or had already communicated to Amato. The two of them had had numerous discussions of Amato's dysfunctional marriage. It reminded her of what she went through deciding to get back with David after they had gone their separate ways. She insisted that their relationship be a partnership based on honesty. She wanted to know whether he was truly ready to commit. She also wanted to know about Jacqueline, but about that, she never asked.

And about Jacqueline, Gomes never said a word.

23

The Green Derby was located just north of Fields Corner on Dorchester Avenue, in the Dorchester section of Boston. It was a regular watering hole for a local clientele from the white section of Dorchester. There were two pool tables towards the back, along with a bar and tables where patrons could eat and drink. Plaques and pictures from Ireland were set along the wooden walls of the establishment. With little outside light coming through high windows, *The Green Derby* had this strange appearance. The large room, bathed in artificial light, had the atmosphere of a Vegas casino, where you lose any sense of time. By 6:30 pm it was busy and generally remained so 'til closing.

Jimmy Scanlon and Jackie Nellis came walking in around 7:30 pm, loud and joking as ever and headed over to the bar to order a couple of beers. Both married, they spent as little time at home as they could, leaving their spouses to take care of the kids. Their philosophy was simple: they brought home the bacon, their wives cooked it. The bacon came from working construction or in the Quincy shipyard.

They were sometimes called "Fat & Skinny" because Scanlon had a hell of a beer belly and Nellis was as thin as a weed, reminding you of the old Laurel & Hardy comedy team. They went everywhere together, including into periodic fights that they seemed to love.

Nellis looked around the bar and saw Eddie O'Hare at one of the pool tables shooting pool by himself. Nellis and Scanlon picked up their beers, walked over to the table and pulled up a couple of stools. They sat for a moment watching O'Hare concentrate on his next shot.

Crack.

O'Hare's targeted ball went right into the pocket. No surprise, O'Hare was a brilliant player. He regularly won and in fact, always seemed to win when he played for money—which he did only on rare occasions. He relaxed when he shot pool by himself, testing various shots, pushing himself again and again.

"Good evening, boys," O'Hare said as he walked around the table strategizing his next shot. "Thanks for joining me."

"Ya said it was important, Eddie," Scanlon said, watching the master at his work.

O'Hare glanced over at the two of them but refocused on the balls on the table.

"Something's come to my attention," he said, lowering his voice. "You know that Cape Verdean guy that got killed in the shipyard back in July?"

Crack. O'Hare carried out a combination shot to the side pocket.

"Yeah, I remember when the nigger got killed. Dumb fuck probably wasn't paying attention," said Nellis, smiling as if he was describing a circus act gone bad.

Crack. The six ball went into the corner pocket seemingly at the speed of light.

"I've told you before, cut that 'nigger' shit, unless you want me to put this stick up your ass," O'Hare said without once looking at Nellis, who turned red and repositioned himself on the stool as if to burrow in.

"Anyway, what's the emergency, Eddie?" Scanlon asked, trying to change the subject and the feel of the moment.

Crack. Another bank shot into the other side pocket. O'Hare walked around the table.

"Well, boys, the word on the street—or maybe I should say

the word in the 'ard—is that it wasn't an accident at all, but it was murder, and your little outfit was behind the killing. I just thought that you should know. That's all."

Out of the corner of his eyes O'Hare saw Scanlon and Nellis freeze as he lined up another shot.

"What the fuck you talking about, Eddie?" replied Nellis, his eyes twitching from nerves, with Scanlon starting to say the same thing at the same time.

"Just what I said. The symbol from your 'club' was found at the site where the guy was killed. There's some thinking that the guy was murdered."

"Where the hell did you hear that, Eddie?" Scanlon almost yelled, some of the nearby customers turning to look at him.

Crack. O'Hare knocked the five ball into the corner pocket and then turned to face Fat & Skinny.

"You don't need to know that, boys. What you *do* need to know is that if your group of happy soldiers was behind this, you're probably going to have hell to pay, but not because I'm going to snitch on you." He returned to focusing on the table.

Scanlon and Nellis looked at each other. Without saying another word, Nellis took off and went to a payphone near the restrooms. O'Hare walked around the table exploring different potential shots.

Crack. Scanlon shook at the sound and looked around nervously as he watched for his buddy to return.

Nellis came running back.

"Nah, Eddie, it wasn't us. I knew that it wasn't but I just needed to make sure that no one went rogue. But, nah, we're not looking for any trouble with that nig…that Black social club in the shipyard or with anyone else." said Nellis, a line of perspiration running down his face.

These stupid amateurs, thought O'Hare. *I lay this shit out and they go make a call in the same location where the three of us are meeting. If they had brains, they'd be dangerous!*

"But listen, Eddie, one of our friends in the Society wants to talk with you about this so that we can, you know, get to the bottom of what's happening and who's trying to set us up. So, it shouldn't take a long time, if, you know, you just come with us."

O'Hare faced the two of them and held his Q-stick, applying chalk to the tip. His eyes went back and forth between the stick and the two gentlemen standing in front of him.

"If you boys think I'm going anywhere with you this evening, you've lost your minds. And if you think I can be taken against my will, you underestimate my friends. You wouldn't think that I'd come to this meeting with you two guys unprepared, would you?"

Scanlon and Nellis looked around the room, peering at different faces. There was no way to tell whether O'Hare was pulling their legs or whether he had friends in the club.

"I'm telling you this shit because it's a warning. I don't like your group and I don't like your ideas. I don't like the way that you play with fire and you bully people. But I think that you're being *played* right now and I don't know why. So, boys, we're just going to leave it at that, aren't we?" He blew on the tip of the Q-stick while eying the two men.

"Ah, yeah, Eddie, no problem. We'll explain it. Maybe some time we can all meet, you know, have a beer, and clear this up, but we get it," Nellis said with a shiver in his voice.

O'Hare nodded his head and turned his back on Fat and Skinny.

Crack. Eight ball in the corner pocket. O'Hare smiled, as did several others watching the master at work, while Fat & Skinny hurried away.

24

When Gomes walked into *Derry by the Sea* he felt like he was in a time-warp. It looked like the same people who were there the first time he visited were still there, almost all positioned in the same places. Even the attractive and flirtatious white woman was there, brightening up when she saw Gomes enter, giving him a smile and mouthing 'hello' in a most inviting manner. The only thing that seemed different were the outfits everyone wore. A low murmur in the room stopped briefly when Gomes entered.

Very carefully Gomes nodded at the woman and the bartender and proceeded over to the table that O'Hare was occupying. He was reading *The Autobiography of Malcolm X*. Gomes could not believe this guy.

"This is the second time I've read this book, Davey," O'Hare said as Gomes sat down. "I cannot get over how much this reminds me of what we lived and *live* through in what you call Northern Ireland. We were never slaves, Davey, but the Brits made a point of treating us as an inferior race, a fact that many of my Irish American sisters and brothers seem to forget. And the Brits weren't joking when they used the term 'inferior race,' by the way. In any case, listen, thanks for coming up to meet me."

Gomes got comfortable in his chair and signaled to the bartender for two beers. O'Hare nodded his appreciation as he closed the book and put it aside.

"So, Eddie, you said that you had some information. I'm anxious to hear about it."

"The playpen warriors don't seem to be behind this, Davey," he said, looking over at the woman who had eyes for Gomes. Gomes followed O'Hare's line of sight, noticing that the woman at the bar was looking in his direction. Gomes returned his focus to O'Hare.

Gomes opened his mouth to ask O'Hare something when Eddie held his right index finger up.

"Davey, let me switch gears for a quick second. That lady over at the bar seems to have the hots for you. Be careful, my friend. She's someone who likes to play with fire. I don't think that she intends to create problems, but, well, just be careful. She's a regular, and from what I hear, well, don't take this the wrong way, she has a 'thing' for Black men."

"I appreciate the advice Eddie, but don't worry. Nothing, and I mean *nothing* is going to happen between me and her." Gomes replied, his face deadly serious. "But listen, tell me more about these racists."

The beers arrived, along with some peanuts brought by the bartender. The two toasted, the bartender smiling disingenuously as he returned to the bar.

O'Hare described his discussion with 'Fat' & 'Skinny' and how their reactions convinced him that nothing was afoot.

"I think that I could tell, my friend. They were much too scared. They like to show off, but they aren't going to take real risks. No, Davey, I think that this is a dead end. Sorry to tell you that."

The woman at the bar was trying to get Gomes' attention, periodically looking over and playing with one of her earrings, but Gomes continued to ignore her. She even walked by him on her way to the restroom, smiling as she passed. In return, he gave her a polite but distant smile.

Gomes was preoccupied with what had and had not happened in the shipyard. O'Hare watched him, saying nothing, until Gomes broke the silence.

"If they weren't behind this, what the hell was that Blue

Lightning symbol doing there?"

"I don't know, Davey, I'm just telling you that I don't think that it was them. Let's play this out here. Two cleaners showed up in the compartment where Pires was found dead. That's the story, right?"

Gomes nodded his head and took another sip of his beer.

"This woman, what's her name, *Alice Love,* showed up later, after the body was found. So, that lets her off the hook since a number of people saw her leave the work area *after* Pires went on break."

Gomes nodded his head again.

"No one else was seen and that hatch was the only way in or out. Hmm…" O'Hare looked out the window at the Bay.

"So," Gomes started, "the murderer must have been one or both of the cleaners, right? I have their names; I got them from Carlotti. One of them is Cape Verdean and the other is a Black American. But look, it just doesn't make sense. Could they be that incompetent as killers that they hung around long enough for people to see them? Or, my friend, was this just an accident? Maybe an accident that the cleaners were involved with?"

O'Hare looked back and forth between Gomes and the Bay.

"I don't know what to tell you. Maybe they were the killers or maybe there was an accident in that hole and they don't want to 'fess up to it. Unless you can come up with a motive, this road has just come to its end."

"Yeah, I hear you, man. You know, this may be one of those situations where we are just stuck. After all of this, there may be no story here."

Gomes looked up from his drink and over at the bar. The woman was alternating between looking at her friends and looking at Gomes, giving Gomes an uneasy feeling, despite how attractive she was with her tight skirt and low-cut blouse. *What was she thinking,* he pondered? Gomes shook his head and refocused.

"Let me make two toasts, Davey," said O'Hare with a strong voice and holding his mug of beer over the table towards Gomes. "First, to your uncovering the mystery behind the death of Pires!"

They raised their mugs and took their respective swigs.

"Let me make the second toast, Eddie," Gomes said after savoring his beer. "To a united and socialist Ireland!!"

O'Hare broke into a huge grin and again they raised their mugs.

"Now, Davey, how about those Red Sox..." O'Hare offered, and they both broke into laughter.

"Actually, Eddie, how about you tell me more about Northern Ireland and your escapades there. You seem to be a man of mystery, if you get my meaning?"

O'Hare broke into an even bigger grin.

"Well then, my friend, let's start with a little discussion of the Irish Republican Socialist Party and we'll see where we end..."

They never got to a discussion of the Red Sox, let alone Pires. And despite the fascinating discussion of Irish politics, a little voice in Gomes' head kept asking the same question: *could this really have been an accident? After all, how could a killer have gotten out of a compartment without being seen when there was only one exit?*

25

Gomes sat at his desk on Friday afternoon trying to concentrate on two unrelated matters. The first was a strange call he received from the editor of the *Taunton Register*, a small local paper. The editor was very cautious, but eventually got to the point. He was calling on behalf of the consortium of papers exploring the idea of a new publication. This was the group that Jacqueline had mentioned to Gomes some weeks earlier. The editor was concerned that Jacqueline was not sufficiently engaged with the group and wanted Gomes to put pressure on her to join forces. Gomes listened respectfully but made no commitment.

The second thought had to do with Pamela. Sitting there looking at her picture on his desk, he was conscious of how much he missed her during the week. Even though he would see her *that* evening when she returned from Boston, the commuting was putting pressure on their relationship. There were things that both of them wanted to do, but the long-distance work and their respective careers were getting in the way. It was not as if he had a solution other than to be patient and to look forward to Pamela graduating…unless he was ready relocate to Boston and start afresh. He sometimes considered that latter option but was not sure he was ready to give everything up on the Cape.

He was getting no writing accomplished, twisting his pen with his fingers when his office phone rang.

"David," started Marcia, "I'm sorry to bother you this late on a Friday, but there's a gentleman here who asked if he could speak with you. His name is Rodrigo Cunha. He knows that it's late and that he doesn't have an appointment, but he's hoping that you have time to meet with him."

"Did he to say what this is about, Marcia?"

"No. But he looks pretty normal, if that means anything," she said with a smile in her purposely lowered voice.

"Okay, show him to the conference room and tell him that I'll be right out."

He picked up his pad, tucked his pen behind his ear and headed to the conference room.

The man was just sitting down as Gomes approached the conference room. By his name and appearance, Gomes thought Mr. Cunha might be Portuguese—as opposed to Cape Verdean or Brazilian—with light brown, almost blonde hair. He was suntanned and well-built, probably in his 30s. To some he would look like a surfer, but there was something about this guy, perhaps weather-beaten, maybe something else, that conveyed a very different path in life.

"Mister Cunha, I'm David Gomes," he said, entering the conference room and shutting the door. "What can I do for you?"

"Mister Gomes," he started with a distinct Portuguese accent. "I am sorry to bother you late on a Friday, but I just get off work. My English is so-so, Mister Gomes. My apologies."

"Not a problem, Mister Cunha, because your English is certainly better than my Portuguese." Gomes sat down and opened his pad.

Cunha opened a copy of the *CIG*. The issue with the picture of Pires on the cover.

"Mister Gomes, this an interesting article. Sad about this guy dying. This is the guy who died in the shipyard, Mister Gomes?" he pointed toward the picture of Pires.

"Yes," Gomes answered, sadly and perplexed. "Yes, that's Alberto Pires who died in the shipyard. Why?"

Cunha kept looking at the picture. He started shaking his head from left to right and back.

"No, Mister Gomes, this not some Alberto Pires. No. Davi Rodrigues. That is a picture of *Davi Rodrigues*."

Puzzled, Gomes sat for a few seconds rubbing his chin, fingers going through his short beard.

"Senhor Cunha," Gomes offered, "with all respect, I think that you have the wrong person. This man, Alberto Pires, worked at the Quincy shipyard and had identification. He has relatives here in the United States who attest for him. You must be mistaken."

Cunha slowly looked up and straight into Gomes' eyes. The man's voice started with a rumble that made Gomes think of a volcano getting ready to explode. "Mister Gomes, I knew this man. I saw him several times a week. His name was Sargent Davi Rodrigues, and he was in the Portuguese Army, attached to a unit of the P.I.D.E., or by that time it was the DGS, in Cape Verde. We had many names for him. He was sometimes called 'o camaleão', the "chameleon" if your Portuguese is not so good," he offered almost graciously.

Stunned, Gomes wrote down this information on his pad.

"But he was also known as 'o homem que mudou de cor,' '*the man who changed colors*'."

Gomes stared at Cunha, the only sound in the conference room the distant hum of traffic on West Main Street.

26

"Have you ever heard of Tarrafal, Mister Gomes?" Cunha asked, sipping some water Gomes brought him. The two men had remained in the conference room, the sound of traffic on Main Street picking up.

"Yes, it was some sort of concentration camp that the Portuguese set up in Cape Verde for political prisoners, wasn't it?" Gomes responded, no longer focused on getting home for the evening.

"Yes, Mister Gomes. You know history! It was the location for Salazar to put his political prisoners, but also prisoners from the colonial wars.

"The security was most strong, Mister Gomes. I was in the Portuguese Army in Cape Verde. I was in logistics, driving people and equipment from the docks and from the airfield to the prison. Tarrafal, it was known as the *'camp of the slow death,'* Mister Gomes. Salazar modeled this on the Nazi concentration camps."

Cunha stopped for a second. He looked at the picture of Pires, then shifted his eyes, looking out the conference room window, as if in a dream.

"Rodrigues was a mystery man, Mister Gomes. One day you would see him in the uniform of the Portuguese Army and the next day he would be in a wagon with prisoners looking dirty and messy. I did not know what to make of this and it was not something that soldiers wanted to discuss. We would see him and not say anything. Our superiors would say that we should stay out of the…way…out of the business of the secret police.

"But we started hearing stories, most confirmed after the

April Revolution in 1974. Rodrigues had been *both* an interrogator and spy. When he wore his Portuguese Army uniform, he was an interrogator. But he would change and look like an ordinary prisoner and use that as a way of getting information out of other prisoners who did not know who he was.

"He was cruel, Mister Gomes. *Very* cruel." Cunha was shaking slightly as he uttered those words. Gomes could not tell whether it was anger or nerves.

Gomes felt as if his world had shattered. Through his article he worked to build up sympathy for Pires, along with countless other shipyard workers, and now this guy was telling him that Pires had been a member of the Portuguese version of the Gestapo!

"How do I know that what you're telling me is the truth, Mister Cunha? What are you doing here on Cape Cod, anyway?"

Cunha looked up, seemingly surprised by the sound in Gomes' voice, a sorrowful frown on his face.

"I was involved in the April Revolution that overthrew the fascists. Rodrigues and a number of the other fascists took off as soon as there was word of the Revolution. I never saw him again. I returned to Portugal, but the revolution came apart and, eventually, I came to the United States to start over. I work here in Hyannis on the docks. I repair boats. If you want to check me out, you can: Hyannis Marine Services is the company where I work."

Cunha folded up the newspaper and tucked it in his pocket. "How do you know that I tell you the truth?" he continued. "Well Mister Gomes, you don't. You can look into it, but I'm not sure, unless you talk with someone who was in Tallafal, that you will get a straight answer. And even then, there remains fear.

"One thing, Mister Gomes. Keep my name out of this. The fascists were defeated, at least this time, but they did not disappear. And your country…did not play a good role in Portugal in 1974 or in the colonies, Mister Gomes. So, I must be careful."

Before rising to leave, Cunha leaned across the table and handed Gomes a piece of paper with his telephone number on it. "You know where to find me, Mister Gomes, but as I said, keep my name out of this."

Cunha pivoted towards the door to the conference room, aiming to leave.

"One second, Mister Cunha," Gomes said with some urgency, rising from his chair. "Why are you telling me all of this? I may never be able to verify your story. You must know that. Why did you come here today?"

Cunha stopped, turned and with a tight face and in a deep voice responded, "I saw what this man did, Mister Gomes. He was a demon. I read your story and I know that he seems to be a nice, peaceful man. You need to be asking how this torturer got to the United States and why. He was…"

Cunha did not finish the sentence. He shook his head, exited the conference room and walked out of the office, leaving Gomes feeling as if he was standing in the middle of a stadium alone and naked.

27

"And that's what he said," Gomes said, closing off the story to Pamela.

Wayne Shorter's album *Native Dancer* played in the background as Gomes and Pamela exchanged glances. He looked into Pam's eyes over the rim of his glass of wine to see what sort of reaction she would give.

"Who've you told about this, David?"

"Jacqueline, Mariana, and now, you," he responded, putting his glass on the table.

They had not eaten dinner and it was after 8 pm. When Pamela got home and after embracing, Gomes jumped right in with the story about Cunha. They sat down over drinks while he walked through what he had been told.

"You really like Mariana, David," Pamela either stated or asked, Gomes was not sure. She stared at Gomes.

"She's been very reliable and very helpful with this story. I'm going to need some more of her research assistance. And, of course I had to say something to Jacqueline."

"Of course," Pamela responded in a matter-of-fact way, putting her glass of wine on the table, looking between the table and Gomes.

"What's wrong?"

Pam said nothing at first, studying her glass of wine.

"You are a very trusting person, my love. I think that you need to be more careful. You don't really know Mariana. And Jacqueline, well…"

"Look, Pam, I didn't give away government secrets. This guy may have destroyed my story. I needed to say something, didn't I?"

"Whatever," she responded casually and with a shrug, appearing to dismiss his response.

"On a separate note, my parents have invited us over for dinner on Sunday, if that's okay with you?" Gomes was suddenly feeling tense with the way that the conversation had moved.

"Sure, David. I can go to Boston Monday morning instead of Sunday night." She had a wrinkle in her forehead displaying concern. "If what this guy Cunha said is true, then this is a whole new ballgame, David. This could be anything. Yeah, it could still have been an accident, but it might have been something else."

"Like a hit," Gomes replied as a statement and not a question.

"Like a hit, my love. Like a hit."

The phone rang. Pamela leaned over and picked up the receiver. In a low voice she offered greetings and then turned the phone over to Gomes.

"It's Mariana, babe," she said quietly, no expression on her face as the phone changed hands.

"Not a problem," Gomes said into the phone, after thanking Pamela. "No, I understand that you were rushing, and I appreciate your taking the time to hear the outlines of what happened… Yeah, that's right. So, listen, I need you to do some of that excellent research that you've done for me. I need some more background on the Portuguese P.I.D.E. and that concentration camp in Cape Verde that they used, you know…yeah, Tallafal. That's right. You think that you can get me something later this week? Thanks, Mariana. I owe you."

Gomes handed the phone back to Pamela, who hung it up.

"You're going ahead with this story, David?" she asked.

"I don't think I have much of a choice. If what Cunha said is true, I may have written an interesting story about Pires, but it may have been fiction. In the meantime, I'm going to check out Cunha and see whether he's the real deal. This may be nothing more than a wild goose chase."

"Let's put together some dinner," Pamela said as she stood up and walked towards the kitchen, looking at the floor. Gomes stood and joined her. He could tell by her walk and what she was not saying that she was worried.

As they entered the kitchen *Native Dancer* came to an end.

28

Gomes looked forward to dinner with his parents on Sunday. He enjoyed his parents, though he was finding it difficult to watch them age. Not that they were becoming more difficult, but to hear them discuss what they would do upon retirement was jolting. He wondered if it reminded him of his own aging.

Joining them for dinner would be David's Uncle Al and Aunt Flora. Uncle Al and Aunt Flora were progressive and engaging, and always supportive of David in his writing. They had both been especially helpful some years ago when David investigated the murder of Osterville construction contractor T.J. Smith. Aunt Flora was a long-time activist, including in the labor movement. They were both involved in supporting the movement for the independence of Guinea-Bissau and Cape Verde.

As their car pulled into the driveway, David found himself thinking about Uncle Al and Aunt Flora's children, Al, Jr. and Ricardo (though everyone called him Ricky). Although both of David's cousins were raised in a loving home, they had fallen into troubled lives. As a result, they often went unmentioned during family discussions.

David's mother Helena always seemed to know when David and Pamela pulled into the driveway and was there to open the door and embrace them. A woman with golden-brown skin, slightly graying brown hair, and standing about 5'2", she had a commanding presence, whether speaking or silent. She and David's father, who David glimpsed as he and Pamela walked into the house, were both wearing aprons as they were preparing dinner.

David's father, Joaquin "Jack" Gomes, had a personality that complemented that of his wife. Where David's mother was warm and affectionate, Jack, a tall, coffee-colored, good looking and quietly serious man, could be distant, except with immediate family. Always cordial and polite, he was slow to engage new people and had a high bar when it came to trust.

Uncle Al and Aunt Flora were in the dining room of the one floor home, helping with set up while also watching a baseball game on television. With the same coloring as his father Jack, and both in excellent health, they were each very different from David's own parents. While Jack tended to be distant, Al was gregarious and always the life of the party. And Aunt Flora, who always looked out for her husband, could be soft spoken while at the same time incisive with her commentary.

"Nephew!" yelled out Uncle Al. "And the beautiful Pamela. How are you both doing?"

There was something in Uncle Al's voice that always put a smile on David's face. The warmth and caring, but also a sense of humor mixed with optimism. Aunt Flora came over and embraced David and Pamela, giving them both kisses. Uncle Al and Aunt Flora had always been supportive of David's relationship with Pamela, even when some other extended family members had been less engaging. Their love for Pamela was sincere.

Dinner this evening was simple, though tasty. Fish and potatoes, along with salad, and excellent *pudim de queijo* (cheese pudding) for dessert. The six of them ate and drank. They were chatting about this or that when Aunt Flora abruptly shifted in her chair, and shifted the subject.

"We heard from Al, Junior," she said firmly, out of nowhere.

Everyone turned toward her except Uncle Al, who was nursing a Narragansett beer held in his right hand.

"Is he okay?" David's mom, Helena, asked.

"Yes, yes. He and Cynthia are doing well, though the situation in the Philippines remains very dangerous for both of them," Aunt Flora replied. Uncle Al said nothing, staring at the beer can as if he was reading its small print.

Al, Jr. was drafted into the Army and deployed to Vietnam. The experience shook him and made his hatred for what the United States was doing in Vietnam so intense that when his two years of service were up, he never returned to the USA. Instead, he relocated to the Philippines and ending up on the island of Panay, where he became a teacher. There he met the woman he eventually married, Cynthia Luna, who was also a teacher. Though Al, Jr. indicated in his letters to his parents that he wanted to lead a quiet life, it soon became clear that that was not meant to be. He and his wife appeared to have gotten involved in the movement against Philippine dictator Ferdinand Marcos, although neither Uncle Al nor Aunt Flora were clear as to how involved they were.

"They're doing well. They seem to be working hard and keep putting off having children," Aunt Flora said with a sigh.

Uncle Al excused himself from the table and went to the restroom. Discussions about both of his sons, particularly Al, Jr. were very difficult for him. He could not accept that his pride and joy—Al, Jr.—refused to even visit the USA.

"How's Ricky?" Jack asked, shifting the subject, though this topic brought its own complications.

Aunt Flora shook her head with a smile. "Oh, you know Ricky, Jack. Can never decide what he wants to do when he grows up. Making trouble but always there when we need him."

Aunt Flora's smile reflected her deep attachment to her youngest son. She was very protective of him, despite the fact that Ricky was a semi-thug. He was someone who "got things done." Nothing violent as far as the family could tell, but he skirted the line between legal and illegal. Brilliant at math as a student, Ricky had joined the military, where he picked up some bad habits. He returned to civilian life with an idea to get rich through scheming. Aunt Flora adored her youngest, but she never excused him. In fact, she never made life too easy for him.

Uncle Al returned to the dinner table, his eyes slightly red.

"Pamela, how's school?" Al asked, as if nothing had happened.

"To be honest, Uncle Al, I'm sick of it. I hate commuting, though I do love the students that I have. I'm looking forward to graduating."

"And then what?" Al asked.

"And then, I hope to teach. Well, I want to teach, plus do some other things. Working for that magazine was great, but I think I want to try my hand at some other projects, like filmmaking. I haven't mentioned this to anyone, but I want to make a documentary about Cape Verdeans in America. I don't know where I'll get the funding, but I'm already looking. It may be a hard sell, though."

"Why?" asked Aunt Flora.

"Because we're Black," she responded, using the first-person plural even though, technically, she was not Cape Verdean. "But also because documentaries are hard to fund unless you are a celebrity filmmaker or know someone who will fund you. Maybe if I made a Blaxploitation film, I could get some backers, but that's not my direction."

"What about approaching Horace Silver?" Helena asked, referring to the distinguished Cape Verdean jazz pianist known internationally for his piece *Song for My Father,* among other compositions.

"Oh, I'll approach him, but my guess is that he is probably regularly hit up for money. That said, he might be able to help if he is inspired by this project. Maybe he'd even do the music!"

David was just about to put a spoonful of his dessert in his mouth when Uncle Al turned to him.

"Alright, nephew, how close are you to receiving your first Pulitzer Prize?"

Everyone chuckled, though they all felt immense pride in David's writing. David put the pudding down before he could consume it, looking into his uncle's deep, black eyes.

"Uncle Al, my career is at something of a crossroads. The paper is in financial trouble and, partly due to that, my boss is thinking about selling the paper or maybe merging with someone, and she has asked for my help. I have very mixed feelings about the entire situation."

While the family had great respect for Jacqueline and liked her as a person, over the years there had been an ambivalence about her relationship with David. It was never discussed, but there was a certain questioning look that would appear on the faces of his parents as well as uncle and aunt, a tension, or a forced smile whenever Jacqueline's name was spoken. When Pam and David broke up, David had brought Jacqueline to a few family gatherings. While she was well received and treated politely, David's family did not know what to make of the relationship: was it more than friendship? David never discussed this implied question.

"Tell them the rest, David," Pam said, softly putting her hand on his hand.

"Well," David started, clearing his throat, "you know that story that I wrote about the shipyard worker who fell to his death? Well, it may not have been an accident and, the guy may not have been who he claimed to have been."

As David told the story, with each line there was a growing unease on the faces of his relatives. No one interrupted him and no questions were asked until he finished his narrative. Everyone seemed frozen in their seats and frozen in time.

"And this Cunha is reliable, son?" asked Jack, his wrinkled

forehead, displaying worry.

"I've already started to check him out, Dad. I should know more later this week, but, yes, his employer is real. He's employed there and I know at least one person who knows the guy, though not very well. But Dad, I have to tell you, I can feel in my gut that what the guy said was true. I mean, you should have been there to hear his voice as he told me the story. You don't make this stuff up."

In a quiet voice Aunt Flora asked: "David, why are you going to pursue this? This sounds very dangerous. If the shipyard guy is who this Portuguese soldier says, then, good riddance, God forgive me for saying. I don't see where anything is gained by you digging into this."

Uncle Al sitting beside her nodded vigorously.

"What do you think about this, Pamela?" asked Al who always treated Pamela with tremendous respect and wanted to know her opinion on everything.

"You remember the Tavares/Da Silva case, Uncle Al? Need I say more?" Pamela was referencing the 1970 murder case involving the construction contractor T.J. Smith and David's dogged approach to finding the answers.

Aunt Flora shook her head in frustration and looked at the ceiling. "My Lord, David. Some doors don't need to be opened!" The sound of her words rang in the house.

Jack got up to start cleaning off the table while Helen sat quietly, her eyes looking at the remaining silverware on the table. Pamela joined in the cleanup.

"I'm not sure what to tell you all. There's a story here and I have to figure it out. Maybe it will go nowhere, maybe not, but it's not only my job, it's also my reputation."

There was silence except for the sound of the dishes being rinsed and placed in the dishwasher and the television playing low in the background. David began thinking that this might be the appropriate time to head home when his mother spoke.

"Marcelino is getting remarried," she announced.

"You've got to be kidding," replied Al with a laugh. "What is this, wife number twelve?"

Everyone laughed about both the historical antipathy between Al and Marcelino and the fact that Al was basically right. For what seemed like the umpteenth time, Marcelino, David's mother's brother, despite his alleged Catholicism, had fallen in love and was marrying. The atmosphere immediately broke, just like the humidity after a New England thunderstorm.

But all was *not* right with the world.

29

The Tuesday following the family dinner, David was returning to his office after a brief lunch at a Chinese restaurant on Main Street in Hyannis. He found himself lost in thought as he walked back, mulling over a story about cranberry bog workers, many of whom had historically been Cape Verdean, though a surprising number had been Nordics. The conditions of work were abysmal and yet, in the annals of working-class history, very little was written about them. David stumbled across some old-timers who had worked in the bogs and soon built a relationship with them as he started to craft a story.

POW!!

Gomes heard what sounded like a motorcycle backfiring and at the same time the sound of a bullet passing in front of him and hitting the wood frame around the entry to a store. Gomes dropped to the ground, his military training kicking in. He heard the sound of a motorcycle take off at high-speed heading west on Main Street.

If this had been summer, there would have been a crowd, but it was autumn so there were fewer people on the street. Nevertheless, a small circle of people gathered around Gomes asking him what happened and whether he was okay. Gomes thanked them, looked around, then went to a payphone a half block away to call the police.

It did not take long for a police car to show up, it must have been nearby. Its siren was blaring as it approached, shutting down when they were nearly fifty feet away. Their blinking lights remained on.

Gomes did not recognize the officers, but he explained what

happened as they took notes. Gomes and the two officers walked back to where the shooting took place to inspect the area. They found the location of the bullet that had entered the wood frame and made a call on their radio to get crime scene investigators out to review the site. When they had no further questions, they released David to return to his office, but told him that a detective would drop by later in the afternoon to get a more detailed statement.

Shaken, Gomes returned to his office. He planned on saying nothing until after speaking with the detective, but that plan was thwarted when Marcia greeted him.

"David, it seems like half of Hyannis has been calling. You were *shot*?" she asked, standing as if she wanted to give David a hug.

"Shot *at*, Marcia...*shot at*. I'm okay but badly shaken, if you want to know the truth." Gomes tried smiling but only produced a smirk.

Shaking slightly, Gomes headed to his desk before he had to answer any further questions. He did not quite make it.

"*David!*"

Gomes turned and looked into Jacqueline's fiery eyes.

"Okay, boss, before you say anything, yes, it's true, I was shot *at* on Main Street. I think that it was someone on a motorcycle or something. One shot, a clean miss. But, yes, I must have been the target."

Jacqueline turned towards her desk with Gomes following. The conversation was far from over. Gomes sat down across from her. Jacqueline, wearing a beige dress with a necklace holding an amber pendent, crossed her legs and arms, looking at Gomes as if preparing to interrogate him.

"Is this about the shipyard?" she asked. Her voice was steady but just above a murmur.

Gomes wanted to compliment her on how she was dressed but realized that this would not be the time for such remarks.

"Unless someone has an issue with me writing about cranberry bogs, my guess is that it is. None of my stories are particularly controversial, and there is nothing else going on in my life that would invite an attempt on my well-being."

Gomes went on to minimize the threat and to emphasize the importance of his completing the Pires story.

"I am going to surprise you, David. I am sure that you were expecting me to tell you to drop your investigation. While I would love to do that, I know that it would make *no* difference. If anything, and I can see it in your eyes, you will become more insistent on finding out what was really behind the possible murder of that shipyard worker and who was shooting at you."

Gomes was surprised. He opened his mouth to reply when Jacqueline's phone rang. She answered, nodded, stared at Gomes, and then told Gomes that a Detective Griffin was in the conference room waiting to interview him about the shooting. Gomes thanked her, rose from his chair, and proceeded to the meeting.

30

Most of the lights in the house were kept off, which spoke to his mood more than anything else. Evenings during the week were quiet and lonely with Pamela away in Boston. Rarely did Gomes feel like cooking, so he had frozen dinners or picked something up. This particular evening was no different. He heated up some New England clam chowder and made a small salad.

What really preoccupied his thoughts was whether and what to tell Pam about the shooting. He did not want to alarm her and he did not want her lecturing him. So, he needed to say something quickly and decisively.

He sat in his living room under the table light and picked up the phone to call Pam, visualizing the phone ringing in her studio apartment in the Allston-Brighton section of Boston. On the third ring she answered.

"Hey, babe. Before anyone else tells you, let me. There was a shooting today. Someone tried to shoot me, but they missed. I'm okay. The shooter got away, but the cops are looking for them."

There was silence on the other end, though Gomes could hear traffic in the background.

"You were shot?" she asked, with a quiet intensity.

"*Shot at*, love. Shot *at*. They shot and missed. I'm okay, but I wanted you to know."

"You're damned right I needed to know. What are the police saying?"

For the next fifteen minutes Gomes explained and re-explained what happened and what the police said. He preempted her by saying that he guessed that it had to do with the shipyard story, but he was not sure how or why. Pamela then asked whether Jacqueline was taking him off the story.

"I told Jacqueline that I wanted to continue with this story," he answered, telling Pamela the truth, but not exactly the whole truth.

Pamela sighed, sounding like air slowly leaving a balloon. She asked him to be careful and wondered aloud whether he needed to apply to carry a gun.

"If I carry a gun, Pamela, I might kill someone!" he said, laughing, though Pamela did not join him. "No, baby, in my line of work carrying a gun would not work too well. There're too many people that get angry with me and, truth be told, there's too many I get angry with!

"But in all seriousness, the fact that someone would try to take me out raises a question of whether the Pires death was not only more than an accident but more than a one-on-one matter. In other words, are there others involved?"

There was silence on Pamela's end. Gomes heard a car honk in the distance. Gomes tried to shift the conversation, asking her about her day and about school. Though Pamela answered, there was no enthusiasm in her voice and she largely spoke in monosyllables. Gomes could not take the tension and sadness on Pamela's part, so he pretended to have work to do.

"David, is this story *that* important?" she suddenly asked.

"I don't know how important or unimportant it is. But right now someone has decided to make it personal."

Silence.

"Good night, my love."

Pamela hung up without a word of good-bye.

Gomes knew trouble was brewing.

31

"So, you're really not going to tell me about this informant, David?" Mariana was sitting across the desk from Gomes, preparing to head to her waitressing job.

"No can do, Mariana. Sorry. It's for your protection and that of the informant. This guy doesn't want anything traced back to him."

"But you think that he's for real, right?"

"Yeah, I do. I did some checking and he's the real thing. Look, I don't have confirmation of his story, but I believe it. So, tell me, what have you come across?"

Moving hair away from her face, Mariana put a memo down in front of Gomes along with photocopies of several articles from books and periodicals.

"When you get a chance, please take a read. That prison camp was what your informant said. Political prisoners and prisoners of war were placed there. The prison was closed at one point due to international outrage but then re-opened. Of course, after the coup in Portugal and the independence of Cape Verde and Guinea-Bissau, the camp was closed for good."

Gomes sat looking over Mariana's shoulder so intensely that Mariana turned to see what he was peering at. There was nothing there.

"So, this apparent Cape Verdean collaborator who worked at the concentration camp somehow makes it to the US of A. He goes to work at the Quincy shipyard and seems to lead a pretty dull life. If that is all true, then we must assume that his supposed aunt was in on this. Right?"

Mariana nodded her head 'yes,' making a note in her pad. "What about his cousin who he was living with?" asked Mariana.

"Nah, I didn't get the sense that he had any idea of who Pires was other than what his aunt told him. He was *far* too open in our talk. He never seemed to be hiding anything. In a funny way, he seemed as confused about Pires as we are."

Gomes doodled on his notepad, lost in thought.

"Anything else, boss?" Mariana asked, resigning herself to not getting an answer. "I need to head off to the restaurant."

As if coming out of a trance, Gomes shook his head 'no.' He thanked her for her work. As she walked away, Gomes turned toward the material that she had produced for him. Shutting out the rest of the world, he focused on her report and on the photocopies.

On her way out of the office, Mariana stopped at Marcia's desk.

"Marcia, sorry to bother you, but I wanted to ask you something." She waited patiently while Marcia looked through some notes in response to her question. Mariana nodded and thanked her, heading off to work. She looked back towards Gomes who seemed to be completely lost in thought.

32

Rosa Macedo did not want to speak with Gomes. That much was obvious from the tone of her voice when David called. She kept making excuses about how busy she was and how complicated life had become. Gomes was nothing less than persistent, telling her that he was going to be in the New Bedford area anyway, and that he would only need a few minutes of her time. She finally relented, insisting that she would not have more than thirty minutes to spend speaking to him and, once again, she had nothing more to add.

When Gomes showed up at the Macedo doorstep, part of him anticipated that she would be a no-show. How often that had happened to him when he was supposed to interview someone for a story!

This time, upon ringing the bell, the door was opened almost immediately and a surprisingly relaxed Rosa Macedo invited him inside.

Macedo offered him a seat in the living room and apologized that she had nothing outside of water to offer Gomes. Gomes graciously declined and reaffirmed that he would not take up much of her time.

"Before we get started, Mister Gomes, I have a quick call to make. A gentleman friend of mine is taking me to dinner, so I promised him that I would call when you arrived so that he could plan accordingly. Forgive me for a moment." She exited the living room carrying her phone with its long cord.

Gomes heard her voice but could not make out the words. She was off the phone in a matter of seconds, after which she returned to the living room and sat across from Gomes, nodding her head for him to proceed as she lit a cigarette. Macedo, wearing a purple skirt and a sweater-blouse a shade lighter, crossed her legs awaiting his first question.

"Missus Macedo, I'm doing a follow-up on the story that I did about your relative, Pires. I hope you saw my story?"

Macedo nodded her head affirmatively with a slight and polite smile.

"How much did you know about Alberto's life before he came to the USA?"

"Very little, Mister Gomes. Just that a relative said that he was living in the Azores and had a job possibility at the shipyard," she said with a slight shrug, deeply inhaling the cigarette smoke.

"You know, at the shipyard there were sometimes difficulties for Blacks and immigrants. Did Pires ever say anything about having trouble with anyone?"

"He wasn't 'Black' Mister Gomes. He was Portuguese, from Cape Verde. He spoke good English. He didn't have any trouble with anyone as far as I could tell. If he had, his cousin Tommy would've said something to me and, you know, maybe we would've found him another job."

Macedo was far calmer than she had been the first time that Gomes had met her, though the emotion in her voice in asserting that Pires had not been "Black" was off-putting. Then again, Gomes was used to that among some Cape Verdeans. Her calmness was odd, particularly given how reluctant she had been to have a meeting in the first place.

"So, Pires never mentioned any enemies or anything?"

"What's going on, Mister Gomes?" she asked, incredulous. "I thought that he was killed in an accident. That's what you said in that great article that you wrote."

Not sure whether she was being sarcastic, Gomes ignored her tone.

"Yes, Missus Macedo, that's what I think. But I'm covering all bases because of stories that I heard about problems that... immigrants and others had at the shipyard. It could've been an accident, but one where someone was asleep at the switch and not being careful. You know?"

Macedo shrugged her shoulders and took another puff of her cigarette.

Gomes felt uneasy, not sure where to take the discussion. He got ready to stand up and leave.

"Mister Gomes, when you were last here you seemed very interested in my family. I found some letters from my father after you left that I thought might interest you. Let me get them and you can take a look."

While Macedo stood to leave, Gomes sat there taken aback, hoping that it had not shown on his face. She had been resistant to meeting with him, had little more to say about Pires, and was now going to show him some personal letters. He looked at his watch and noticed that his 'thirty minutes' were just about up. At that moment Macedo returned.

"Here you go, Mister Gomes. Take a look. If there's material that you could use for your story about our family, I can copy them and mail them to you. But you can take a look."

"I don't want to hold you, Missus Macedo. I can come back some other time and look."

"No, Mister Gomes, please, take a look. I have a few more minutes."

Reluctantly Gomes took the letters and began reading them. They were in chronological order and seemed to be in relatively good condition. The letters were postmarked from different parts of the world. Each letter combined expressions of love and loneliness with a sort of travelogue of her father's journeys. Gomes found himself enthralled by the letters.

The phone rang. Gomes looked at his watch as Macedo went to answer it. He realized that he had now been at Macedo's for nearly an hour.

"My gentleman friend had told me that he was going to be delayed, so I didn't worry about time. But that was him calling and he's on his way. Are there any of those letters that are helpful, Mister Gomes?"

"The letters are quite amazing and descriptive, Missus Macedo. Let me mull them over and get back to you. I might want to read them all and develop a different story. I'm not sure that they will help me with the Pires situation, but they could make a story in and of themselves."

Macedo thanked him for reading them, smiling proudly. She told him how personal they were and how much it meant to her that her father had regularly written the family while he was overseas.

Gomes thanked Macedo and headed for his car. He sat there for a moment thinking, half-noticing a man across the street working on a car, his head under the elevated hood looking at the engine.

Gomes looked at his watch and decided that he would visit his uncle and aunt. He had a few things to ask them.

33

Had they not been relatives, Gomes would have called in advance, but dropping by to visit family was fine, even with no notice.

Uncle Al and Aunt Flora lived off of Acushnet Avenue in New Bedford, not far from the Bay Village housing projects. They lived in their small one-family home for years and always made it comfortable and welcoming.

David rang the doorbell to the brown, two-story home, hearing his Uncle's voice in the background as he approached the door.

"Nephew!" Al exclaimed. "Did I miss something? Did your aunt forget to tell me that you were dropping by? We just had an early dinner, but we have plenty left over if you want to join us."

David walked in, shook his uncle's hand. "No, Uncle Al, I just want to speak with you and Aunt Flora for a moment. I'm sorry I didn't call in advance."

Aunt Flora came out of the dining room and smiled at David.

"You know that it's no problem, David. Come on in, we're just wrapping up dinner. You sure you don't want something to eat? I can heat something up. Or if you want some coffee or tea?"

David gladly accepted the offer of coffee, sitting down at the table where the dishes had mostly been cleared away. His uncle and aunt looked at David awaiting whatever he wanted to ask or tell them.

"I just came from the home of Rosa Macedo. Do you know her?"

Al looked down at the floor shaking his head in obvious

disgust. Aunt Flora rolled her eyes and folded her arms.

"Of course, we know her. That Portuguese wanna-be. Lord, that woman loves to be with her Portuguese friends and that thug boyfriend of hers! For goodness sake!" Aunt Flora spoke with a tone of total revulsion, as if she was getting ready to spit.

Gomes explained to them more about the story and her supposed relationship to Pires. Uncle Al got up to get David the coffee he'd requested. Gomes ended by telling them about his visit earlier that evening and the odd response that he received.

"She was born bad, nephew," Uncle Al said as he walked back into the room with the coffee. "She trashed anything good. I mean she trashed our PAIGC support work," referring to their backing of the liberation movement that fought Portuguese colonialism in Guinea-Bissau and Cape Verde, "and she was always going after the Black Panthers, copping to the argument that the Panthers were terrorists and troublemakers. If I never run into her again it will be too soon."

Aunt Flora said nothing, just looking at David as if she was awaiting something.

"I guess that I really came over here to ask you about the discussion at my folks' place. The two of you were very down on my doing this story about Pires and looking into it. Why? You have always supported me in the past."

Uncle Al got out of his chair and walked back into the kitchen, this time to start washing dishes, curiously leaving Aunt Flora alone with David.

"We still support you, David and always will! Your Uncle and I worry about you, though. That's all," she said with warmth and a smile. "We remember when you put your life on the line to do that story about Little Tony back in '70. You could have…" she turned away from him to look at a picture on the wall, leaving the sentence unfinished.

"David," she continued, though still looking at the picture, "you have stumbled into something that may be nothing or may be something dangerous. We heard about the attempt on your life. Maybe we weren't supposed to hear anything and maybe it has nothing to do with this story. Be that as it may, your uncle and I see no point in you pursuing it. You don't know whether this Pires was who he said he was or whether he was a collaborator with the Portuguese. If he was a collaborator, good riddance, whether it was an accident or…on purpose. I have no idea. But I don't see where you gain anything pursuing this."

"It's my job, *titia*," Gomes said, using the Kriolu word for "aunt." "You know that. You know that I have to get to the bottom of a story."

Uncle Al seemed to have disengaged. David was unsure whether it reflected how deeply emotional Uncle Al could be, rarely wanting to express his feelings publicly. This evening he worked away at the dishes while Aunt Flora turned back to the picture.

"Just be careful, David. Just be careful," she said, walking over and kissing David on the forehead and then heading to the kitchen.

I guess that's my signal to leave, he thought. *But why couldn't Uncle Al sit here with us and talk?*

Gomes politely excused himself, bringing the empty coffee cup into the kitchen and putting it into the sink. His uncle and aunt hugged him, but these were hugs of sadness rather than affection. He could almost feel their frustration in not being able to convince him to drop the story. He was equally frustrated at being unable to convince them that he had to see this through to the end. He felt deflated, steadily losing energy as he prepared to leave.

Heading back to his car, David looked back at his uncle and aunt's home, but they were not looking out at him through either the door or the windows. He entered his car, made a U-turn, and proceeded back to Route 195 and home.

34

Gomes decided to take the Bourne Bridge over the Cape Cod Canal. Since there was not a lot of traffic, he figured that he would head to Route 6 once on the other side rather than drive along the west side of the canal and then cross the Sagamore Bridge.

Gomes shifted gears and reduced his speed to about 40mph, keeping pace with the traffic, driving with his windows up and the radio off. It was a good time to think.

As Gomes reached the downhill side of the bridge, he put his foot on the clutch to downshift.

KA-POW!!!!

His foot on the clutch went right down to the floor. He moved his right foot over to the brakes to decelerate. Something was wrong, his foot was pushing the brake pedal deeper and farther than it should normally go and the car was not slowing down.

Gomes looked in front of him and saw the brake lights of cars approaching the traffic circle at the base of the bridge. Hoping that the problem was the master cylinder, Gomes kept pumping the brakes, but nothing happened, the car only slowed slightly, which all but guaranteed he would collide with one of those cars in front of him or one already in the traffic circle.

Gomes pulled the emergency brake, but it was jammed. *This was not going to end well*, he thought, approaching the traffic circle.

Suddenly the car directly in front of him made it into the circle and nothing was imminently approaching him. Using the momentum of the car—and thank God he could still steer the vehicle—he stayed in the right lane of the traffic circle, gradually slowing as the car went slightly uphill, and pulled into the gas station on the traffic circle. Unable to stop, he drove right past the gas pumps and only stopped when his car hit a wall next to the air hose pump. Rattled but okay, Gomes turned off the ignition and disengaged the keys.

Two gas station attendants came running over to the car to check on Gomes. He thanked them, but waved them off, wondering what had just happened and thanking God for seatbelts. The station attendants kept looking back at Gomes as they returned to the station.

Gomes went to the payphone after looking over the damage done to the front of his car. It was not terrible and it could have been a hell of a lot worse. Though Gomes had AAA coverage for his car, he instinctively called his father's service station. His father was already home, but Paul Woods, Jack's long-time second in command, answered the phone and promised to get a tow truck out to the traffic circle asap.

Gomes stood by his car breathing deeply, waiting for the tow truck. Fortunately, he did not have to wait long, though he had enough time to go to the coffee shop next to the gas station and get some very strong coffee. The station attendants came back out and spoke with Gomes while he was drinking the coffee. They started looking over the car while he explained what happened.

Paul Woods drove up with the tow truck as the gas attendants were looking over the car. Paul wasn't going to trust the safety of the owner's son to someone else. That was just the sort of guy that Paul was. He took a quick look at the car, then hooked it up to the tow truck and headed to Mashpee. Gomes rode with Woods in the passenger seat, detailing the whole set of events. Woods, a burly man in his 40s from Maine, asked him about the brakes. Gomes thought it over and admitted that on Route 195 the brakes had seemed a little softer than usual, but he hadn't thought much about it since he didn't have to use them much on the highway. But none of that explained what happened to the clutch. Woods kept looking down the dark road.

"I'll drop you by your folks' place and then drop the car off. Tomorrow we'll get back to you about what happened, but given what you said, this may take some time to repair. Listen, David, let me tell you, from what I can see, you were lucky as hell that you didn't find yourself in the middle of a crash."

"No shit, Dick Tracy," Gomes responded with a smile.

Paul got on the CB radio and contacted the station, telling them to call Jack in advance of their arrival. He signed off and kept driving into the dark back to Mashpee.

35

After Paul dropped him off at his parents' home, Gomes explained the situation to them and then borrowed his mother's car to get home. On his way out of the house his mother echoed her in-laws in suggesting it was time for David to pull back from this story.

The following day David received a call at work from his father. "Dad, thanks for calling. Did you find out anything?"

"We're going over the car now, son," Jack said, the sound of cars driving by the station in the background. "You got a minute? I want to fill you in. If you don't, we can talk later."

"No, Dad, now is good. What's up?"

"Well, to be blunt, I wish I could tell you that you have the worst luck in the world, but I'd be lying. Someone is trying to kill you. Well, you know that someone is trying to kill you because someone shot *at* you, but what I mean is that someone seriously played with your car."

David could hear something in his father's voice. Maybe it was the way that he exhaled after completing his point. Jack usually controlled his emotions tightly, but when his voice cracked at one point, David knew his father was more than nervous.

Jack explained to David that someone sabotaged his clutch cable. The brakes were also sabotaged in such a way that it would have taken some time for the brake fluid to leak out.

Silence.

"Dad, is it at all possible that this really was bad luck?"

David heard a car horn sound as it went by the gas station.

There was also the noise of an air gun and men laughing.

"Let me answer that this way, son. I don't want either of us to be kidding the other. Look, this can all be repaired. I'll take care of the labor costs, but I need you to pay for the parts. The main thing is that I *am* damn sure that…someone was sending a signal… actually, they were sending more than a signal, David."

Silence again, except the sound of cars in the background going through the Mashpee traffic circle.

"Son…is this story important enough for you to take these risks? Have you spoken with your boss about this?"

"I think it's important, Dad, though to be honest, I have no idea what's really going on. And, yes, I've spoken with my boss. Listen, let me head on and check in with you and Mom later. Thanks so much, Dad. Don't worry; I'll be okay. And, of course I will pick up whatever the costs are. I just appreciate you and your team. Love you, Dad."

Rarely did David ever tell his father that he loved him, despite the fact that he did. Deeply. He knew that his father was worried, and he knew there was nothing that he could do to calm him. He also knew that he had not fully answered his father's question.

Gomes realized he needed to speak with Jacqueline. He left his desk and headed to see her. As he walked past the front door on his way to his boss's desk, he nearly ran into Mariana entering the office.

"Good morning, boss-man," she said, greeting him with a warm smile, though looking surprised to see him. "I wanted to stop in and check on any new developments."

It must have been the look on his face because Mariana's bright smile and mischievous look disappeared immediately.

"What's wrong, David?" she asked with new seriousness.

"It looks like there was another attempt on my life. Someone messed with my car and I nearly had an accident…I could have been killed. Fortune favored me and I was able to avoid a big problem."

"Did you report it to the police?" she asked, studying Gomes' eyes as she spoke.

"I'm getting ready to, now that I know that it was likely an attempted murder. I wanted to tell Jacqueline first."

"What happened?"

As Gomes explained the details of his eventful evening, Mariana shook her head in disbelief.

"It could have happened either when I was at Macedo's or my uncle and aunt's place. Someone could have followed me to either place. Because Macedo was acting so strangely, I'm inclined to believe that it was at her place."

"You mean that she set you up?"

"Yeah, but I'm not sure why. Even if she helped to get Pires into the country under false pretenses, there's little way for me to prove it unless I go to the Immigration and Naturalization Service and seek an inquiry, and that would be a hell of a reason to try to kill me. After all, I'm trying to figure out who killed her supposed nephew! Of course, there's no reason that someone associated with my aunt and uncle would sabotage my car."

"I figured that you were going to see Macedo, David, but I didn't want to push it. I was going to offer to go with you as company, if you wanted someone along for the ride."

Gomes gave her a polite smile, not quite sure how to interpret her belated offer.

"Now what, David?"

"Now I tell the boss and we'll see how *she* responds." Gomes told Mariana he would get back with her later when he could figure out their next steps.

Upon returning to his desk he found Jacqueline was still not at hers, so he pivoted and headed to the receptionist.

"Marcia, have you seen the boss?"

Marcia held up her finger signaling him to hold on while she resolved a call, then turned to David. "Yes, David, she's upstairs working on something. I don't think she'll object to you dropping in, but it's probably best for me to check."

Gomes nodded and waited for clearance to proceed upstairs. A moment later Marcia pointed upstairs.

The stairs to Jacqueline's apartment were entered through a door that looked like it was for a closet. The staff knew about the stairs, but no one used them unless Jacqueline invited them up for a meeting. Both doors had locks on them.

Gomes opened the door to walk up, noticing after he let the door closed behind him that the door at the top of the stairs was slightly ajar. He walked up to her apartment.

Jacqueline's apartment, always neat and attractive, seemed like an entirely different world from the office on the first floor. There were beautiful prints and paintings on the wall and a light pink wall paint that worked wonders when the sunlight entered the rooms.

Jacqueline was sitting at her kitchen table with a phone attached to a long extension cord resting on the table next to her. She looked up with a smile. "Bonjour, my David. What can I do for you?"

"Bonjour yourself, boss. I need to speak with you about something, though I'm sorry to bother you, you look busy."

Jacqueline shifted positions and pointed to the chair across from her. She stood up, walking over to the stove to heat some water for their ritual tea. David noticed that she was dressed casually as if not planning on coming downstairs. She was wearing black jeans and a plain white button-down blouse, a red half scarf tied with a bow around her neck.

"Busy...oui...but never too busy to speak with my best journalist," she offered while she moved around the stove preparing the tea.

Gomes waited for her to return to the table while the water in the kettle heated.

"Let me get straight to the point, Jacqueline." Gomes said, looking into her black eyes. "There was another attempt on my life. Last night, on my way home from New Bedford."

Gomes explained the story, waiting for Jacqueline to blow up, but she didn't. She listened quietly, asking him questions while making a few notes.

"What do you plan on doing?" she asked, directly.

"I'm not sure, to be honest. My family wants me to drop this story. I haven't told Pam yet and I can only imagine what she will say. I wanted to chat with you."

As the kettle started whistling, Jacqueline rose to fix the tea. She put the tea bags in the cups and turned towards Gomes.

"David, I learned a long time ago, especially after the TJ Smith case, that there is no point warning you of danger. There is little to be gained by trying to pull you off of a story since you will dismiss the concern and proceed on."

Gomes was surprised by this response. There was no anger in her voice. No resentment. Nor was it dismissive. The word that best described her tone was *'dispassionate.'* It was as if she had just told him the Sun would be rising the next morning: *that matter-of-fact.*

Jacqueline returned her attention to the tea and prepared both cups with milk and sugar, which was how she always drank her tea. She walked back to the table with both cups, placing one in front of Gomes.

"You decided a long time ago that your mission in life was to follow through on a story to the end. I would not say that you are cavalier, but you *want* to take risks in order to get a story. The fact that it frequently scares me to death does not seem to matter to you. I have come to accept that you are who *you are.*"

She blew gently on her cup. "Do I want you to drop this story?

Of course! Could I order you to stop? Of course! But I know that you will simply not rest until you get to the bottom of what is going on."

They removed their teabags and stirred their cups, each taking a glance at the other, and then sipped their tea.

"Ironically, if no one had tried to kill me—twice—I probably would have dropped this story. It's an odd story and I probably would have left it alone. But then someone had to go about trying to kill me. That has not made me happy."

They both smiled, sipping their tea in silence.

Putting down her cup, Jacqueline said: "I know. I know because I know you. I probably know you better than anyone, including, if you will allow me, your own wife. Therefore, let's get down to business and talk through this story."

Jacqueline picked up a notepad, flipped to a fresh page and began writing notes as Gomes spoke. They spent an hour discussing possible angles, scenarios, and directions to go in the story. When Jacqueline put her pen down Gomes could tell that the meeting was nearly over.

"You have a problem, David. You have no way of proving that the death of Pires was a murder. You have no way of identifying who is attempting to kill you or whether this is a case of mistaken identity. You cannot explain why Rosa Macedo would have been as reluctant to meet you and then turn so hospitable. Yes, you can speculate, but speculation does not make for a story. So, tell me, my David, how do you propose to answer any of these riddles?"

Gomes felt as if he was a collapsing balloon. Jacqueline was correct in her observations and questions. As much as he did not want to admit it, he probably should drop the story.

But he knew deep down that the story was never going to drop him.

36

Gomes arrived home late, as he normally did during the week when his wife was in Boston. He grabbed a beer and called Pamela. He figured she would be back in her apartment.

Pamela answered on the second ring.

"Hey, lover-girl," he greeted. "Have time to talk with a lonely husband?"

"Let me think on that," she responded. "Well, if you insist." They both chuckled.

Before Gomes could tell Pamela about the attempt on his life, Pamela started discussing school and a particular challenge she was having with one of her students who could not decide whether she wanted to complete school or go into a life of activism. The student was feeling guilty about her work in the arts, irrespective of the encouragement that Pamela offered. David listened, knowing that there was little he could offer by way of advice. Pamela had dealt with many of those same demons and she continued to with respect to her students. More than anything else, he knew she needed to talk things through in developing a plan.

When Pamela finished, Gomes told her his story about the near catastrophic accident. He tried to keep his voice even.

"So, my love, I didn't want to call you last night because...well, I just didn't want you to worry."

Pamela said nothing. Occasionally Gomes could hear a car driving near her apartment.

Pamela cleared her throat.

"So, you were set up?" she asked.

"Yeah, it appears so."

"Does Jacqueline know?"

"Yeah, I met with her this afternoon. She…well, she basically thinks that I need to do what I need to do."

Silence. Gomes could hear almost nothing in the background except a distant voice, probably from the street.

"You have a smart boss and a very good friend, David," she finally said. "Yes, if you want to know, I'm worried about you and I wish that I could convince you to drop this, but I know, just like Jacqueline knows, you are so damned hard-headed that there is no convincing you to drop this story. Yes, of course I will support you, but VERY reluctantly, David. This is a weird story, I understand why you might want to get to the bottom of it."

"But, baby," he responded, "I probably *am* going to drop it. I have too little to go on, you know, except, yeah, someone is trying to kill me."

"But why haven't they *succeeded*, David?"

Startled by the question, he did not know how to answer.

"Think about it, sweetie. Two failed attempts on your life. Yes, both could have resulted in your death. The incident last night probably wouldn't have killed you even if everything went wrong. You could've gotten banged up, for sure, but I don't know. Why not just *kill* you outright? Why not someone come up to you in Fairhaven or New Bedford and…*bang?* You remember back in 1970 when someone fired a shotgun at you. Their intent had not been to scare you but to take you out. You see what I mean? Obviously, I wouldn't want something to happen to you, but it *is* strange that this would go down this way."

Gomes had to confess that he hadn't thought about it that way. He had attributed it to good luck on his part, but could it be something else?

37

The warm days of summer were well in the past as October was approaching November. The nights were getting cooler and the absence of vacationers on the Cape often made for lonely, sometimes desolate-looking streets.

Gomes was at his desk on a Wednesday afternoon when the phone rang.

"David," said Marcia, "I have an officer from the Barnstable County Police on the line asking to speak with you. Do you have a moment?"

"Sure, put them through, thanks." He hung up to await the call. The phone rang.

"David Gomes, here."

"Mister Gomes, my name is Detective Rachael Schwartz from the Barnstable County Police. Sorry to bother you, but I'm hoping that you can help me. Do you have a few minutes?"

"Certainly, detective. What can I do for you?"

Through the phone line Gomes heard a couple of people speaking in the background while he awaited the detective's response.

"Ah, Mister Gomes, does the name Rodrigo Cunha ring a bell?" The detective pronounced it KOON-Ha, as opposed to KOO-nya.

"Cunha?" he replied, thinking for a moment and then proceeding carefully. "A few weeks ago, a guy named Cunha came by our office to speak with me about an article that I wrote. I believe that his name was Rodrigo. Why, detective? What did he do?"

"Do, Mister Gomes? He died. Actually, Mister Gomes, he was

killed. His body was found in the Bass River."

As Gomes sat straight up, a thought flared in David's mind.

"Bass River? I just read an article about a drowning victim in the Bass River. The article said that they had no identity on the victim. Is this the same guy?"

"Yeah, Mister Gomes, same guy. The article should never have been published. This was no drowning victim. Someone got ahead of themselves in writing that piece."

Gomes sat at his desk saying nothing, his mind spinning.

"Mister Gomes, would you mind dropping by the substation in Dennis so we can chat? You may be able to help us."

"Sure, detective. I can be there in about…an hour, if that works for you?" Gomes looked at his watch.

"That's very generous of you, Mister Gomes. Yeah, that should work. I'll meet you here."

Gomes slowly put the phone back in the cradle while mulling over how to handle this and what to say to the detective. This may be a situation where Gomes would have to follow an approach he had used successfully over the years: tell the truth; but not *necessarily* the whole truth.

Gomes drove out Route 28, encountering little traffic at that time of the day. Upon sighting the Bass River bridge, he felt a shudder go through his body as he approached the site of Cunha's death. Crossing the bridge, he looked to his left and right at the river, almost expecting to see the man's body floating.

After that it was less than a quarter mile until Gomes saw the small shopping mall on his left that housed the police substation. He pulled up in front of the building, noticing a woman standing outside smoking a cigarette. She looked to be in her 40s, brown hair, 5'5" or so, athletic looking, and wearing sunglasses. She did not seem to notice or chose to ignore Gomes as he parked. She paced in front of the substation which looked like a small shop in the mall. Gomes assumed that this was Schwartz.

As he got out of the car, the woman threw the cigarette away and looked at Gomes. Her face changed from a cold seriousness to a warm smile.

"Mister Gomes, I presume?" she asked as he closed and locked the car door.

"Yes, Detective Schwartz?" he responded with a smile.

"Thanks so much for coming out here. You mind walking, Mister Gomes? I hate this damned office."

"Sounds fine, detective."

The two of them walked down towards the Bass River along a sidewalk next to Route 28. Schwartz initially spoke about the mall, but not about the case. Gomes felt like he was on a first date. She was charming and engaging, so much so that Gomes nearly forgot the reason for this visit. She joked about being located in the shopping mall, some of the characters she had seen, but also about being close to the Bass River and how much she loved taking her daily walks down to the bridge.

"Detective, what happened with Cunha?"

"Sorry, I guess that I've been mis-pronouncing his name. I grew up outside of Washington, DC, and still don't always get the pronunciation right of these Portuguese names." Schwartz was embarrassed, her eyes looking upwards as if for forgiveness from the Creator of all things.

Gomes waited for her to continue, but she just kept walking in silence.

As they approached the Bass River bridge, Schwartz pointed toward her left, down river.

"Some kids found his body on the rocks on the Dennis side of the river. We were lucky they found him because he could have drifted out into the Sound. Blunt force trauma killed him, but he was worked over prior to death. No, Mister Gomes, it was no accident."

"So, how can I help?"

"You met Cunha. What did he want?"

"He read my piece about the death of a Cape Verdean immigrant who worked up at the Quincy shipyard. He was struck by the story. He knew about shipyards from Portugal. He didn't stay very long. That was the first and last time that I saw him."

When they got to the Bass River bridge, they walked about a third of the way out on the northside of the bridge and stopped. Schwartz leaned against the rail and looked up-river. Beneath her there were a couple of kayakers paddling and several people sitting on the bank of the river on both the Yarmouth and Dennis sides. The way that Schwartz was leaning and looking out made her appear more of a tourist than a detective.

"His body came from somewhere up-river," she said, pointing north. "It's all very odd. Cunha's girlfriend says that he told her he received a call from a Miz Nancy McMichael who lives in an expensive house on the Yarmouth side of the river, about a mile north. McMichael allegedly called Cunha to get his help repairing the motor on a boat of hers. Cunha would freelance from time to time."

Schwartz stopped and lit another cigarette, taking her sweet time and looking relaxed.

"There's only one problem, Mister Gomes." She slowly turned to look directly at Gomes. "Nancy McMichael is out of town. In fact, she is out of the country, in Britain. She's been out of town for two weeks and is not anticipated back for another three. She is a divorcee and lives in a very nice home. By herself. We got this information from a neighbor who watches the house when she's out of town. And the neighbor had no idea what we were talking about when we mentioned Cunha."

Schwartz looked at Gomes' face carefully, then returned her gaze to the river.

"Detective, I have a number of questions, but the most important is this: how did you come across my name? How am I involved in any of this?"

"Well, Mister Gomes," she said, looking down at the river, "apparently a few weeks back Cunha came home and told his girlfriend that he had met you…I guess visited you…and that you seemed like a decent guy, but he was worried that he had told you too much. His girlfriend did not get out of him what he told you. She was clear, though, that Cunha did not fear *you* but, I guess, feared that something that he told you would get out."

Schwartz took a drag on the cigarette, blew the smoke out and turned to face Gomes again.

"So, Mister Gomes, what did Cunha have to say that was so important? And, by the way, what does any of this have to do with the recent attempts on YOUR life?"

Gomes was stunned by the turn of events. He knew he had to think quickly. He also knew that Schwartz, while appearing so casual was quite shrewd.

He could not play any games with her.

"Cunha appreciated the story, as I told you. But he told me that Pires—the guy that was killed in the shipyard—was using an alias and that he had another name."

"How did he know that?" she asked, looking intensely at Gomes, taking another drag on the cigarette.

"He had seen him in the Portuguese military during the colonial wars. He had not seen him since, but he said that the guy had a different name. And, before you ask, I don't remember the name, but I have it written down in my office."

Schwartz looked at him for a moment and then turned back toward the river, throwing the cigarette butt into the water.

"Who, besides your wife, did you tell about Cunha?" she asked.

"How did you know—"

Before he could complete his question she pointed towards his wedding ring. He nodded his head and smiled.

"I told my boss, Jacqueline Reynaud. But I did not tell either Pam—my wife—or Jacqueline, Cunha's name. I just told them about the incident. It was all sort of peculiar."

He remembered that he had mentioned the meeting to Mariana, but he had not mentioned Cunha's name and decided to leave it alone.

"Interesting," she said with a smile, turning back towards Gomes. "So, this guy appears out of nowhere, mentions that the person you wrote about may not have been who he claimed to be, there are attempts on your life—yes, I know about all that— and you see no possible connection???"

"Detective, Cunha told me about the *possibility* that Pires could have been someone else. That did not matter since my story was about the dangers of shipyards and the focus was on the death of this Cape Verdean immigrant who'd come here for work. I wasn't doing a story on illegal immigrants or people who slipped past INS or veterans of the Portuguese colonial wars. Yes, it was interesting and curious, but that's a different story. I just took it for granted that Pires was killed in an accident. The story was not about trying to get to the bottom of his death."

Schwartz studied Gomes' face. She smiled and shrugged her shoulders.

"Let's head back." She took out another cigarette, then put it back. "I've got to kick these."

They walked a few feet in silence. "Listen, Mister Gomes, please get back to me with the name that Cunha gave you. Also… well, let me put it this way. You seem to be an intelligent person. You may think that you can handle this situation on your own or that for some other reason you don't want me to know the whole story, but…well, Mister Gomes, I may look young, but I'm not wet behind the ears, if you get my meaning?"

Schwartz was looking straight ahead as they walked back towards the police substation, and while Schwartz did look young, she was clearly not a kid.

No, detective, Gomes thought, *you are definitely not wet behind the ears. My guess is that you saw right through me. I really wish that I could trust you because you are right. This is way into uncharted territory.*

38

Gomes sat at his desk the next morning making notes to himself. When Mariana dropped in, he thought about telling her about Cunha's death but decided to leave it alone. He did not want to complicate her life if the police decided to pull her in for questioning. She left to continue her research.

At 11:20 am his phone rang.

"David," said Marcia, "I have a Mister James Connolly on the phone for you. He says that he only has a minute but needs to speak with you."

"Connolly" was the name of a famous Irish socialist and nationalist but also the name O'Hare said he would use if and when he needed to call.

"Put the call through," he said, hanging up and awaiting the connection. The phone rang.

"Jim!" Gomes greeted, "What can I do you for?"

"David, my friend. I figured it out. I've been stumped since you and I spoke, but I think that I figured out how someone can be at two places at the same time…and there's no magic at all! Listen, can you meet me in Quincy tomorrow after work? Say, about four fifteen or so at the entrance to the Quincy Center 'T' station?"

Knowing that O'Hare was on a 30-minute lunch break, Gomes wasted no time going to his calendar to check his schedule.

"Yep, that works. See you then!" he said and hung up.

With a mischievous smile on his face, he wondered what the hell was O'Hare talking about.

*****

Gomes found street parking near Quincy Center. He arrived at 4:00 pm, got out of his car and put coins into the meter to cover him for 90 minutes. He figured that would be enough time. With his leather jacket and a black scarf around his neck, he walked over towards the station, a cool, damp breeze blowing.

Gomes took his time. Fortunately, the weather was not yet frigid, the sun passing in and out of the clouds. Gomes headed toward the entrance to the 'T'. As he found out when he went to meet "Wally" some months back, the Quincy Center 'T' station could be very crowded at rush hour, so Gomes wanted to position himself to make sure he did not miss O'Hare.

"Good afternoon, Mister Gomes," he heard from behind him.

Turning, he saw the smiling face of Ed O'Hare, dressed in shipyard coveralls, over which he had a blue jacket and a black military cap.

"I just got here myself. Listen, let's go to this coffee shop about a block from here, I've got a story for you."

With O'Hare in the lead, they crossed the street, walking away from the station and back in the direction of Gomes' car. They took a turn at the corner and walked a little more than a half block, entering the doors of *Quincy Coffee & Pastries,* the smell of fresh coffee filling the air.

The establishment offered take-out, but there were several tables and one booth. O'Hare smiled at the woman behind the cash register and headed to the booth. She gave him a nod and a smile. Gomes could not get over the network that O'Hare seemed to have.

The same woman, who apparently doubled as cashier and waitress, came over and took their orders for two coffees and two donuts. Though friendly, she did not engage in any conversation. Brown hair worn largely under a cap, freckles, and a reddish complexion—probably a smoker, Gomes thought—she might have been in her early 30s. She and O'Hare clearly knew one another, but how deeply was unclear. After she took their order and retreated behind the counter, O'Hare withdrew a piece of paper from his pants pocket and put it on the table. He opened up his jacket and sat forward in his chair.

"David, I could not get over the sense that I was missing something after we last met. It felt like there was an itch I couldn't scratch. How, I asked myself, could someone have carried out a murder when there was only *one way in*? Right? That's the obvious question."

Gomes nodded in agreement.

O'Hare opened the paper, revealing a handwritten diagram. It looked like a pyramid or a trapezoid of some sort. O'Hare pulled out a pen to use as a pointer.

"This, my friend, is a side view of the compartment where Pires and Alice Love worked. It's broad at the bottom where they entered through this hatch here." He pointed with his pen to an area where it read "hatch." "And then, it narrows towards the top, up here." He said moving his pen. "That's at the top of the compartment, and it was the level where Pires was when he fell. As you see, I put lines in here for the planks."

"What's this over here on the left side that looks like a cone or something?" Gomes asked.

"Ah, my friend, here's where it all gets interesting. The workers go in and out of the hatch. Right? But about midway up there is an opening into the neighboring compartment. It is NOT a hatch at all. All of this area will ultimately be flooded with water. The hole is for the water…the ballast…when the ship has been completed. But the hole *is* passable by a person during construction. You would just have to crawl through."

"This cone is a hole, O'Hare?" Gomes asked.

"Sort of. Let me tell you. I have been working on the same sort of tanker and, for curiosity's sake I was walking around and went to the comparable compartment on my ship. I took a quick look inside the compartment. *Presto!* I found this connecting hole. It goes from one compartment to another.

"Here's my guess. No one, and I mean *no one*, thought about this hole because no one uses it. My guess is that some cans were put up there so that no one stopped to think about the hole. Cans are always left all over these compartments, no one thinks twice about them. You would not notice it if there were cans there and you weren't looking for it. You'd simply assume that there was only one way in and one way out."

O'Hare sat there looking very pleased with himself, smiling like the Cheshire cat.

"So, if I may ask, what's in this other compartment?"

"It's just another compartment, David. But that means given the state of the ship that Pires was building at that time in July, there was more than likely either some workers on that side or a way to get in. When I looked at my ship, I saw lights running through. You know, when the work is finished, they don't immediately get rid of the string of lights in the compartment."

"So, let me get this right. You're telling me that there *was* another entrance into the compartment where Pires was killed?"

"That's *exactly* what I'm telling you, my friend. The problem is that any number of people could've gotten in, particularly since it was breaktime." He ended the sentence with a shrug.

Gomes looked at the diagram. The waitress brought over the coffee and donuts. Gomes ignored his donut and went right for the coffee.

"So," Gomes said, "it's at least possible that one of the three people who discovered the body could have killed him and then returned to the scene of the crime but from a different direction?"

"Yes, Davey, that's right. Now, of course, it could've been someone else. But if you eliminate the Blue Lightning folks, it's really unclear who would've either had a motive or ability to kill Pires. And let's be clear, there's no indication that those cleaners, or even Love, had any motive at all to kill Pires."

"It would seem so," said Gomes.

O'Hare held his index finger up. "*And*...let's eliminate the Blue Lightning boys. I have kept asking around and I just don't think that it works. They were seriously afraid of a retaliation, as best as I can tell. There's no percentage in it for them. They're bullies, not soldiers."

Gomes studied the diagram as if he was reading a map. He looked up and broke off a piece of the donut, then took a sip of the coffee. "This," he said slowly, "changes everything, O'Hare."

"Maybe yes and maybe no. It would be tight, but any of the three of them *could* have pulled this off."

"Then, Edward my friend, I guess I'm going to have to interview them and see whether I can come up with something. In the meantime, I need to get to my car and make it back to Hyannis before dawn," he said with a grin.

The two toasted one another with their remaining coffee, paid the bill, and headed to their respective cars.

39

"David, this may work as a crime drama on television, but I don't think this story is coming together, at least the way that you seem to think that it is."

Gomes sat in front of Jacqueline feeling that he was being berated by the teacher. He tried to explain the various dynamics of the story, at least as he was able to put them together. There were still significant missing pieces.

Gomes realized that the deeper problem was not his failure to be convincing, but that Jacqueline was terribly distracted. He could see it written all over her face.

"What's wrong, Jacqueline?" he finally asked in the near sound-proof conference room.

She looked up from her notepad.

"You're not there for me, David. You haven't been for a while. You are the most important person to me…in this office and I have trusted you with everything. But we are at a fateful moment, and you are missing in action."

"Well, boss, I have to confess to being preoccupied with figuring out who's trying to kill me. But you know it's nothing personal," he said in as light a tone as possible, hoping to get her to smile.

It didn't work.

"Yes, I know that you have your story. But we are at a critical moment in negotiations with the *Outlook* and I need you engaged!"

"Alright, let me try to reorganize my time so that I can spend more working on this possible merger or whatever it is that you're calling it."

"Merci, David," she said standing up, emphasizing her French pronunciation of his name, *Da-veed*. She left the room without another word.

Truth be told, Gomes was not sure he could be of use to Jacqueline. He had nothing against the *Outlook* and the possibility of a new relationship. The people that he had met seemed fine to him. But, at the end of the day he wasn't sure that was the direction that he, personally, wanted to go.

His unease started with a side discussion after one of the negotiating sessions between the two papers. During a break one of the *Outlook* editors had struck up a conversation with Gomes. It was going well until the editor offered an insight.

"Mister Gomes—David, if you'll allow me—you do some fine work. I and others have read many of your pieces and we like your writing and your thoroughness."

Gomes smiled, accepting the compliment.

"If this arrangement between our papers goes forward, however, we will need something different from you in the future. You are passionate, David, but we need you to spend more time understanding both sides. You go on 'crusades'; we need you to be more objective.

"I hope you understand that I'm not criticizing you?"

Gomes smiled and said he appreciated the honesty. As he explained to Jacqueline later, it felt as if they wanted *part* of him but did not want all of him. How could he do the progressive journalism that was central to his identity if they were going to demand what *they* called 'objectivity'? In other words, no firm positions.

Pamela understood immediately. She also understood that David did not take this personally. Neither of them was sure whether this editor spoke for the paper or was just offering his own opinion. Gomes was surprised that Jacqueline seemed unphased by the entire conversation. He expected some act of solidarity, but all she could seem to muster was to say, "They'll have to get to know you, my David. Don't worry, things will work out."

Gomes understood that whether this merger succeeded or failed, his relationship with Jacqueline had changed, and it could not be resolved by his simply spending more time on the negotiations. Jacqueline was slowly disengaging. He could see it in the way she interacted with staff and with him. It was in her eyes and in her face, and it left Gomes feeling very much on his own.

40

"Given this situation, Mariana, I think my first step will be to interview the three people who were the first ones on the scene of the accident."

Mariana reached out to Gomes and put her hand on his arm. "David, if you think that this might be a murder, you need to be careful. There have already been two attempts on your life."

"Thanks, I get that. But I need to start somewhere. Among other things, I need to figure out who is trying to kill me, and I need to get that stopped in whatever way that I can. Truth be told, Mariana, I think that it's too late for me to put a hold on this story."

She let go of his arm. "How can I help?"

"You can set up appointment for me. If they hear from you with your wonderful voice rather than me, they may be more willing to meet.

Mariana smiled at the compliment. Gomes continued, "I know that Alice Love lives in New Bedford. One of the cleaners, his name is Ivandro Dias, he lives in New Bedford. See if you can coordinate my meeting with him and Love. The other cleaner is in Taunton. Marcus Williams. I got telephone numbers for them from the shop steward at the Yard."

He handed her a paper with the names and numbers. "I will want an hour with each. Can you put that together?"

"Sure. When do you want to meet them?"

"As soon as I can. We're approaching holiday season and people start getting busy, so I'd like to take care of this sooner rather than later."

"Okay, boss. I'll call them from work, if that's okay with you?"
"Of course! Just keep me posted."

******

Gomes straightened his tie and walked towards the conference room. The negotiations were to be held today in the *CIG* offices. There was nothing that he could do to get out of them.

Leading the team from the *Outlook* was Paul Murray, a mid-50s New Englander, pale skin, with short greying hair and a thick, grey mustache. Were it not for the hair, he'd pass for someone who was ten or fifteen years younger, looking like he had been a college athlete many decades earlier.

Also on the team were Sylvia Mott and James Silverman. Mott and Silverman were not only younger than Murray but were clearly in subordinate roles, frequently appearing to be unable to speak. Mott and Silverman were always conservatively dressed but looked as if they would be far more comfortable in tennis outfits, whereas Murray was impeccable in his suits. He *made* the suits.

Their entire team was white, and unapologetically so.

Jacqueline, David, and Carmen Romano were the team from *CIG*. Carmen was a masterful CPA who always provided Jacqueline with an accurate financial picture of the paper. From the Dominican Republic, with light brown skin, a short Afro, and wearing a grey business suit, at first glance Carmen appeared all business. But when they all went out to dinner for a holiday celebration one day, Gomes was surprised to see she had one hell of a sense of humor. He could not believe the way she seemed to switch between two different personalities. Gomes thought she could make an excellent standup comedian should she ever desire to change careers.

After pleasantries, they got to business.

"Jacqueline, as I understand it, the proposal that we seem to be centering around would involve *CIG* joining our family and becoming the Cape and Islands branch of the paper as a weekend supplement."

"Yes, that is correct, at the general level, Paul. You saw our proposal regarding structure, personnel, and resources? Are we on the same page?"

Gomes had reviewed all the material and was familiar with the proposed arrangements. He was still unsure as to what he thought.

"We read your proposal, Jacqueline," replied Murray with a smile and nod, looking at his two colleagues, neither of whom made any facial change. "I think that it is fair to say that we are on a similar page."

Murray handed out a three-page, stapled memo, the last page containing columns with numbers and dollar signs. The *CIG* team looked at it as Murray started to speak.

"We propose to change very little of your operation. We are impressed with your work and how you have used resources. That said, when you depart, Jacqueline, we will place an interim manager in charge to help with the transition. Since there will be an adjustment to the culture of the *Outlook,* we want to keep you on with a retainer for one year during the transition." Murray looked at Jacqueline, who was still reading the memo.

"In consultation with your leadership team, we shall do an assessment of the staff. We will also have to decide whether this building makes the most sense or whether we should think of another site, though I must confess that I very much enjoy these surroundings.

"The biggest change will be that we will want to deploy new staff here to gain experience and get used to digging up stories as opposed to having stories fall into their laps. We may want to put one person each on Martha's Vineyard and Nantucket; we are not yet sure."

Gomes looked up from the memo.

"So, we become the *farm team* for the *Outlook?*" he asked, but with no sarcasm in his voice and, hopefully, none showing on his face.

176

"Maybe a Triple A Minor League team, David. We want the new staff to get experience. Expanding out of Boston brings with it new challenges, including competing with other local papers such as the *Cape Cod Times* and the papers on the other side of the Canal."

Murray was as smooth as good cognac. But Gomes was still not sure the arrangement was going to work, at least for himself. He always assumed that should Jacqueline depart he would have a chance of taking hold of the reigns. Murray was not making any promises. In fact, he was being cagey.

Jacqueline looked over at David, but he kept his eyes on Murray, saying, "Understood, Paul. And from what I see here, you will put the resources into keeping us properly staffed, at least for year one."

"Correct, David. We want to make sure this will work, and we are not sure what this will mean, resource wise. *CIG* has been able to sustain itself through advertising. It clearly worked…for a while. But you started to have difficulties sustaining advertisers and gaining significant new ones. Keep in mind that should we upscale the paper, there are greater costs involved."

Gomes was getting ready to reply when he happened to see Marcia signaling him from outside the conference room. He excused himself and went to see what was up.

"David, I'm so sorry to bother you. Mariana is on the phone. She was able to connect with the guy from Taunton. She said you would know what that meant. He wasn't working today and is home and said that you could drop by later if you wanted to talk. She's working on getting to the other two people, but they're still at work."

"Thanks, Marcia. And thanks for the interruption. Please tell her to go ahead with the arrangements."

Looking concerned, she responded, "Are things going badly in there, David?"

"No, I think that they're going okay. It's just…it's just that I'm not very focused on what's going on. I keep thinking about this story I've been working on."

Nodding her head, she replied: "Yeah, I hear that. I guess that you're thinking about the two attempts on your life?"

Gomes nodded his head, smiled and returned to the conference room.

41

In many ways Taunton was quaint, but in other ways it was a sad, depressing town. A feeling that often accompanied a drive through southeastern Massachusetts. The region suffered from what would soon be called deindustrialization. The industries that had built New England into a manufacturing powerhouse were disappearing as they relocated to the South in search of less expensive, non-union workers. Abandoned factories littered the landscape and families migrated in search of work…if they could find any.

The house Gomes pulled up to sat no more than two blocks away from one such closed factory. From his car Gomes could see a faded "for sale" sign on the walls of the factory and a rusted metal fence that encircled the building. There was no sign of life. Or hope.

The house was a dull white and three floors. On the front porch there were two chairs and a table. Comparing this house with other houses close by, Gomes was impressed with how Williams kept it up. Several other homes looked as if they were going the way of the deserted factory, needing paint or repairs on broken gutters or windows.

Gomes rang the bell and was greeted by a man who looked like he was in his late 40s, standing about 5'10", very dark skin and a broad nose and bright teeth that Gomes could see clearly when a smile was offered.

"Mister Williams?" asked Gomes.

"Yes, sir, Mister Gomes. If it were a warm day I'd say let's sit out on the porch, but I think you'd better come inside, if you don't mind."

Gomes entered the house and took off his jacket, looking around. The house was quite old, probably from the 1920s, but in good condition. Walking into the living room, Gomes saw twin pictures of President John Kennedy and Rev. Martin Luther King, Jr. next to one another. Williams pointed toward the couch for Gomes to seat himself. Williams sat across from him in a lounge chair.

"Thanks for seeing me, Mister Williams. I just wanted to ask you more about the day that you and Mister Dias discovered the body of Mister Pires."

"Would you like some coffee or water, Mister Gomes...you know, before we get started? My wife taught me to be the proper host."

"I'll take some coffee if it's no bother, Mister Williams?"

Williams rose and, yelling from the kitchen, asked how Gomes wanted the coffee. Black with a spoon of sugar, Gomes replied. Williams returned carrying two cups of steaming coffee.

"A very nice place you have here, Mister Williams," Gomes offered sincerely.

"I love this place, Mister Gomes, though it's not the same since my wife died. She taught me how to take care of this place. The house has her spirit inside it, if you know what I mean, Mister Gomes."

"I'm sorry to hear of your loss."

Williams nodded his head, took a sip of the coffee but continued to look into the cup.

"We were the same age. Been together since high school, believe it or not. That's a picture of her right behind you, Mister Gomes."

Gomes turned and looked at the picture of a young woman, probably in her 20s, with sparkling eyes and light-brown skin.

"The Lord called her home about eighteen months ago. Very sudden. She had been in great shape... I could not keep from

180

hugging her every day we were together."

A small tear appeared under Williams' eye.

"But I was blessed to have had her at all, Mister Gomes. Some people...actually a whole lot of people, are not that lucky." The man's wistful grin turned serious. "But you want to hear about Pires. Well, there's not much to tell. Me and Dias were told by our foreman, this white guy named Rogers, to go through compartments on that side of the ship around the hole where the company's going to put those big LNG spheres," referring to liquified natural gas containers.

"You know, we had just finished cleaning up in another part of the ship and had relaxed for a moment, hiding out toward the bow. Rogers saw us and thought we needed more work to do," Williams offered with a smirk. "So we went over to that compartment. Dias went in first — we would sort of alternate who would go in first — and I was just putting my right leg through the hatch when Dias yelled something in Portuguese that I think was like 'Oh, shit.' He told me to get my ass in there.

"When I got in, I saw the body. Dias was bent over trying to see whether the guy was alive. Pires was lying on top of a blower. His head was at this strange angle, and he was bleeding. I took off to get help. When I got back that woman welder Alice was standing outside the compartment. She was looking around, I think looking to see when they would bring the crane to get the body off the ship. I don't know.

"Next thing I know, the medic shows up. You know, *Wally*. He told us Pires was dead. We helped get the body onto the stretcher and the crane took it out of the hole. That's about it, Mister Gomes."

Gomes looked up from notes. "Did you see anyone else enter or leave the compartment, Mister Williams?"

"No. There was no one around when we got there."

The two of them chatted for a while about shipyards, the union representing the workers, and the various dangers. Gomes soon realized that he had run out of questions to ask, but he was still glad to have made this connection. He started to put his pad and pen away.

"You know, Mister Gomes, it was just damned peculiar about that accident. Look, shipyards aren't safe. Some of the time the stage builders don't put things together the right way or completely, but in this compartment…well, it was a hell of an aim for that guy to fall that way."

Gomes stopped to look at Williams.

"What do you mean, Mister Williams, by 'aim'?"

"Oh, I'm probably using the wrong word. It's just that, well, this guy fell right through the opening between the planks. Nose-dived. I would've thought that his head might have hit one of the planks higher up and caught him there or something."

"Yeah, Mister Williams, I've wondered the same thing. Thanks so much for your time and for the coffee. And, again, I'm sorry about your late wife. I can tell that you still very much love her. I understand that kind of love."

Williams stood up and shook hands with a face of fondness and gratitude, saying, "Mister Gomes, before you leave…well, hold on a second. I want to give you something."

Gomes stood near the door perplexed by Williams' statement. In any case, he waited patiently, looking around the room while Williams hurried off to another part of the house. When Williams returned, he held something in his hand.

"Mister Gomes, this may sound strange, but, you know, when we cleaned up the compartment after they removed Pires' body I stumbled across this. Alice never mentioned losing anything so I figured that it must have been from Pires."

Gomes stared at the neck chain and the crucifix that it held, taking it carefully from Williams.

"Mister Gomes, I didn't bother giving it to lost and found. I figured that his relatives might want it, you know? And, hey, it's not likely that I'm getting to the Cape any time soon, so I was hoping that you might take it to his relative that he was staying with?"

Williams focused on Gomes' eyes, looked away, and then down at his shoes.

"Sure, Mister Williams. I'll get it to his cousin. He doesn't live that far from where I stay. I'll get it to the family."

Williams smiled, shaking Gomes' hand again. Gomes excused himself, headed to the car and back to the Cape.

42

The following day Gomes got to the office at 8:30 am and found Marcia already there, drinking coffee and reading through something.

"Good morning, Mister Gomes," she said, smiling in a way that was growing familiar, warm and sincere.

"Miz Blake, how do you do on this cold but beautiful morning?"

"I could not sleep, David, and decided to get up, come here and get some work done. To tell you the truth, I think I'm sort of anxious, you know, wondering about the future of this place, given all these negotiations with the *Outlook*."

Gomes stopped for a minute, looked down at the floor and then over at Marcia.

"Yeah, Marcia, I get it. I think that we're all trying to figure things out about the future. The only thing that we know for sure is that things are going to change…big time."

"Oh, by the way, David, Mariana left you a message with the night service. I wrote it down. Here it is."

Gomes thanked her and took the message. To his surprise it confirmed that Love and Dias were open to an interview. They would do it that Saturday with Dias at 1 pm and Love at 2. They suggested a sandwich shop near a club called The Bomb Shelter in New Bedford.

While Gomes liked to keep his Saturdays open for Pam, he had no choice but to do these meetings. He thanked Marcia for the note, looked up and nearly ran into Jacqueline.

"Good morning, boss."

"Bonjour, David. Ca va bien?" she offered, smiling. "We should debrief the meeting with the *Outlook*. If you are free today, this would be good."

They agreed to meet in an hour, which would allow Gomes time to get settled.

******

"Are we on the right track, David?" Jacqueline asked.

It probably took Gomes too long to reply, based on Jacqueline's tense facial expression.

"For the most part, boss, yes, but I have some concerns," he said, sitting down at her kitchen table. "Yes, I think the outlines are fine. I must confess it bothers me that they didn't even consider me to run the operation. It's clear they will be reorganizing us— including our mission—under the new leadership. So, I guess all I can say is that I will wait and see."

"David, I told them I wanted *you* to be in charge. I told them I was going to step out of the way. They didn't want me to step down and go back to Quebec. I thought I had convinced them that you should take over and they would offer assistance. They…seemed to have changed their minds."

"Boss, I will work with you through this whole process. My guess is there won't be a real place for me in the new operation. Look, I'm sure they'll be polite. I'm sure they will listen to my suggestions, but at the end of the day I think they want to make sure that someone less 'radical' than me is in charge. You've heard them."

Jacqueline did not argue. She did not debate him. She got up from the table and went to the kitchen to get some water. She drank the water and stood at the sink looking at nothing, then put the glass in the sink.

Gomes stood up and walked over to Jacqueline., Embracing her affectionately, he said, "Thanks, boss. You've been great. I don't hold any of this against you. You did what you could, but you had to move on. You have your life. I respect that."

Gomes stood a moment, hands in his pockets. "Listen, I'm going to head back downstairs."

Jacqueline said nothing. As he walked downstairs he felt as if his life was moving in an unpredictable direction.

"David! There you are!"

Startled, he recognized Mariana's voice as he walked into the lobby.

"I wanted to get by here to make sure you got my message and to check in with you about your meeting with Marcus Williams."

Marcia made a face after overhearing Mariana's words. Gomes could read her mind: *Does this girl think that I can't deliver messages?* he knew she was saying to herself.

"I was just in with Jacqueline. Come on over to my desk, I'll fill you in."

Gomes and Mariana sat down to discuss his meeting with Williams. She asked a few questions to get a picture of whether the meeting was worth it.

"Yeah," said Gomes, "it was worth the trip. I think that he was really stunned by the death. He didn't have many new facts, but he was as stunned as I was that Pires could have fallen the way he did.

"In any case, so we have the two meetings for Saturday, right?"

"Yep. They're all set, David. They both told me they have nothing to add to what they have already said, but when I told them that you were buying them lunch, they agreed to meet."

Gomes' mouth dropped, followed by his breaking into a serious laugh.

"Okay, if that's what it takes, so be it."

43

The stress of a long-distance relationship was grinding Gomes down. The lonely nights between weekends together got to him. Working on weekends was especially difficult, knowing he was giving up time for their relationship. The stress led to arguments or sarcastic comments that were completely unhelpful (and for which both would later apologize).

Gomes thought of this repeatedly while on Route 195 heading to a meeting on Acushnet Avenue in New Bedford. A nice breakfast and lunch place, Gomes wasn't sure whether it offered dinner. When he walked in at 12:50 pm on Saturday, there seemed to be a lot of people in the cafe.

"Sit wherever you want, brother," said a 20-something brown-skinned woman with a large Afro, blue-jean bell-bottoms and an apron over a white blouse.

Gomes looked around to see whether Dias was there. He did not know Dias, any more than he knew Williams or Love. He had been given a general description and Mariana had given them a description of Gomes. Though some of the customers looked at Gomes, none looked like the right candidate.

Spotting a nearby table, Gomes cut a beeline over to it. The waitress Gomes had earlier seen came over and took his order for coffee and water while he looked at the menu.

The door to the café opened and two men entered, one resembling the description of Dias. Gomes stood and signaled to them. They proceeded over to his table.

"Mister Dias?" Gomes asked.

The Man Who Changed Colours

The shorter of the two men, who looked like a wrestler with strong arms, a bald head and light, almost yellow skin, looked at Gomes.

"I Ivandro Dias. This, David Fernandes. My good friend," Dias stated in halting English, pointing at the tall, light brown man standing to his right, wearing a black sweater under what looked like a well-insulated jacket for the Pawtucket Red Sox, a Minor League team from Rhode Island.

"Hello, Mister Gomes. Yes, I'm David Fernandes. Ivandro asked me to come along as his, sort of, interpreter. His English is better than he thinks but, you know, he's a little insecure about it. I hope that you don't mind?"

Fernandes was very polite, almost sheepish in his approach. Gomes appreciated his being there. His own Portuguese and Kriolu would not have been enough to make it through this interview. The three of them sat down, as the waitress came over.

While Fernandes looked at the menu, Dias ordered coffee and a turkey sandwich. Fernandes decided on the same, telling Gomes that he would cover his own costs, but Gomes declined the offer and thanked Fernandes for being there. Gomes decided to stay with coffee.

"Mister Dias, I spoke with Mister Williams, but I would like to know, in your own words, what happened in July at the shipyard on the day of Mister Pires' death."

Dias nodded his head up and down, took a sip of water, and then spoke, looking back and forth between Gomes and Fernandes. Fernandes interpreted.

"He says that he and Williams were told to check out this compartment to figure out what was needed inside. When he went inside, he saw the body," Fernandes explained.

"Was there anyone else around, Mister Dias?" Gomes asked.

Fernandes interpreted: "No one but him and Williams. Alice Love showed up later."

"What did you see when you walked into the compartment?"

As Fernandes interpreted, the waitress brought their lunch and coffee. Dias jumped at the sandwich as if he had not eaten in years. He looked over at Fernandes and spoke to him, with food in his mouth.

"He said that the body was on top of a blower. His neck was broken. His face was scratched. There was blood on the blower. It was ugly. Dias has seen death before, but he was still startled."

Fernandes and Dias both devoured their food. Gomes thought about his questions.

"What do you mean by scratches on his face?" Gomes asked.

Fernandes and Dias looked at each other as the question was translated.

"It looked like someone had grabbed his face," Fernandes said, interpreting Dias's comments.

Dias asked Gomes, through Fernandes, some questions about his family, how long they had been in the United States, whether he had ever been to Cape Verde and why he cared about this story. Gomes chuckled, feeling as if *he* was being interviewed rather than being the interviewer. Dias looked at Gomes very seriously.

Gomes relaxed and answered. "Mister Dias," he said shifting gears, "why did you come to the United States?"

Dias did not wait for the interpretation. He started speaking to Fernandes.

"Ivandro fought in Guinea-Bissau during the war. He was caught by the Portuguese but escaped and made it to Conakry. He was redeployed and fought for the rest of the war. He went back to Cape Verde but there was not enough work, so, he got a job here."

"Are you planning on returning to Cape Verde?" Gomes asked.

Again, without waiting for the translation, Dias responded via Fernandes.

"He said 'Of course!' He just wants to make some money so

that he can return home and start a business. He doesn't like it here and he misses Cape Verde."

Dias nodded his head and finished his lunch, sipping his coffee. He then said something to Fernandes.

"Ivandro says that Pires was a strange one. He didn't like to talk about his life in Cape Verde or the Azores. He didn't like to talk much at all. Ivandro couldn't figure him out."

"Did Pires have any friends in the shipyard?" Gomes asked.

Dias sat there for a moment sipping his coffee as if he had not heard the question. He then turned toward Fernandes.

"Ivandro said he could not think of anyone Pires was friendly with except, maybe, the white guys that he rode with in the carpool."

Fernandes and Dias thanked Gomes and started to get up to leave. Gomes looked at his watch and saw that it was 1:50 pm. When the door to the café opened he looked up and saw a Black woman entering. She looked around and quickly shut the door behind her. Probably 5'5", she was dressed casually with jeans and a UMASS sweatshirt beneath a black, wool overcoat. She removed a purple beret from her head as some of the customers pushed by her to leave the cafe.

That must be Alice Love, Gomes thought. He signaled her when he caught her eye and she proceeded over to his table.

Dias looked at Love and grunted something that sounded like "hello." Fernandes did not seem to know her, introducing himself and extending his hand. She accepted it.

Leaning over toward Fernandes, Dias said something that was more than a murmur but not a full voice. Gomes could tell that Dias was saying something in Portuguese or Kriolu, but he could not make it all out. He did, however, hear Dias say what sounded like "cadela," or "bitch."

Had Gomes not been looking at Love, he would have failed to

see her reaction—a swift, intense look of ferocious hatred as soon as Dias made his remark. And just as suddenly she focused away from Dias and approached Gomes.

Although Dias chuckled after making his remark, Fernandes did not return the smile. He looked embarrassed and quickly moved to get his coat on and leave the restaurant, Dias following in his wake.

"Mister Gomes, I'm Alice Love."

44

Inviting Alice to join him, Gomes said, "Miz Love, thank you for meeting with me. You obviously know Mister Dias, I see."

As she sat down Gomes looked at her more carefully. Alice had very dark straight hair and eyebrows that reminded Gomes of a Vulcan from Star Trek. Her brown skin looked golden, as if he was looking at a sunset. Love seemed to have little make-up on and the only jewelry she wore was an unassuming neck chain with a Cross. There was something about her radiating self-confidence and, simultaneously, humility.

"Yeah, I know the asshole. Mister Gomes, one thing that women face in the shipyard is that there are some guys who, if they can't get inside your pants, write you off as a 'bitch' or worse. I made it clear to Dias some time ago that I wasn't interested in his drunken self. He's been a royal pain in the ass ever since."

'Bitch,' Gomes thought. *She knew exactly what Dias was saying! No wonder her reaction was what it was.*

"I hear you," he replied. "Let me ask you about the day of Mister Pires's death. Would you mind telling me what happened?"

Love looked at Gomes carefully and then walked through the story that Gomes already knew. He made a few notes. She indicated she had gone on break, gotten some coffee, took her time returning to the compartment and then saw Dias, with Williams later joining them.

"Was there anything going on with Pires prior to your leaving the compartment that led you to believe he might have been ill or something?"

"No, he was fine. He was another asshole, but he was fine. If he'd been sick, I would've gotten him to the clinic. I have no idea what happened to him."

When the waitress came over, Love ordered coffee and French Fries. .

The two of them chatted about working conditions at the shipyard. She had little to say about Pires and the death, assuring him that by the time she had gotten to the compartment, he was dead.

"What sort of relationship did you have with him? What kind of person was he?"

Love did not immediately answer. The coffee and French Fries arrived, and she covered the fries in catsup and hot sauce. She played around with a few fries for a moment.

"*Relationship*?" She laughed. "Our foreman, Richie LeBlanc, seemed to think that me and Pires worked well together. I guess that we did, at least in some ways. He was a very hard worker and a damned good welder. A perfectionist, I'd say. But on a personal level, he was an asshole.

"You know, Dias wanted a piece of ass. He was clear on that. Pires, well he was sort of funny…and I don't mean 'ha-ha' funny. I mean, strange. He was sort of old generation, despite his age. He really didn't believe that women should be working in jobs like in shipyards. I mean, this guy was not old, but he had the mind of an old man. I had to force the bastard to accept that I could do the work. Eventually, I guess, he accepted it, but he didn't like it."

She ate a few fries and took a sip of water.

"You from New Bedford, Miz Love?"

There was this odd look in her eyes, almost as if she was refocusing.

"I grew up on the Cape. In Sandwich. My father was from New Bedford, but I grew up there."

Gomes could not interpret the look. Embarrassed? Angry?

"You went to UMASS?" he commented, pointing to her sweatshirt from the University of Massachusetts.

"I started at UMASS-Amherst but didn't finish. I should've. I was too impatient or something. A great school but maybe I just wasn't ready. That's the way that I've been most of my life—impatient. Looking for quick results."

Gomes was curious about who she really was.

"So, you never went back to the Cape?"

"No fuckin' way, Mister Gomes. When I was out of there, *I was out of there*. I mean, I know that you're from the Cape, so don't take this personally, but I'm not interested in going back there."

She had cleaned her plate of the fries and finished her coffee. She was sipping the water.

"Look, Mister Gomes, I told your assistant that I really didn't have much to say. It's not like I'm hiding anything. I just didn't see anything. I'm sorry the bastard is dead but that's about it."

Gomes thanked her and stood when she got up to leave, shaking her hand. She seemed to be quite taken by how polite Gomes was, lowering her gaze while shaking his hand. There was no flirtation, it was strictly business.

Gomes packed up and paid the bill, thanking the waitress for her patience. He searched his pocket to see how many coins he had and went to the phone booth near the restrooms. Depositing the coins, he dialed a number and waited.

"Hello," answered a woman with a very musical voice.

"Graciela, this is David. I'm sorry to bother you on a Saturday but do you have a few minutes?"

"Of course, David," she responded, her voice growing friendly. "Where are you? I hear all of this noise in the background."

"Sorry. I'm on the road. Just interviewed someone for a story. How you been doing? It's been a while."

Graciela Monteiro was a long-time friend—and former girlfriend—of David. More importantly, she was an outstanding reporter with the *New Bedford Tribune* newspaper. David and Graciela would speak about once every week, the romance replaced by a solid friendship. Graciela and Pamela were not best friends, but they were friendly and comfortable with one another and comfortable with Graciela's relationship with Gomes.

"David, it's good to hear from you. Things are fine. Work is work, but I can't complain. What's up?"

"Well, before we get into that, how's Tommy doing?"

Tommy was Graciela's brother. A Vietnam veteran, Tommy Monteiro had never been able to readjust to civilian life. As opposed to Uncle Al's son who just decided not to return to the States, Tommy returned but could find no peace and no stability. He was in and out of jobs.

"Thanks for asking, David. Yeah, he's got a job. Living in Wareham by himself. I only talk with him every so often. I really appreciate your always asking about him. I've given him some of the advice that you've shared with me. There are some groups of Vietnam vets that I think would really be of help to him, but I've got to get him out of his shell."

"But it's up to him, Graciela. You and your mom have tried to be there for him. I hope he'll listen to you."

"Of course you're right, David," she said with a sigh, a touch of sadness in her voice.

"Graciela, I need your help. I need some information on a shipyard worker who lives in New Bedford. Her name is Alice Love. I don't have a full address; I do have a phone number for her. I believe that she lives on South 6th. She grew up in Sandwich, on the Cape." He read off the phone number.

"I'm writing this down, David. Listen, is she in any sort of legal trouble? Weren't you working on some industrial accident?"

"As far as I know she hasn't done anything and, yes, I did a story on the death of a shipyard worker. To tell you the truth, Graciela, I'm not sure what's happening, but there's something about this sister that leads me to believe there's more going on than meets the eye."

There was silence on the line; David assumed that Graciela might be writing something.

"Okay, David. I've got the information. This may take me a few days, but I'll try to find out what I can."

"Graciela, that's all I can ask. Thanks so much. Best to Tommy."

45

In the days since his visit to New Bedford it felt as if events were flying by at light speed. Gomes heard nothing from Graciela Monteiro and there were no developments on his story, but there were developments on the future of *CIG*.

The Monday when he got back in the office, he, Carmen (the CIG accountant), and Jacqueline drove to Boston in what turned out to be the finalization of the negotiations with the *Outlook*. There had been phone calls between Jacqueline and Murray prior to the meeting, so the outstanding issues were settled.

The meeting did not last long. The two teams met, reviewed the final agreement, signed it, and then had a champagne toast. There were no further issues to discuss. Gomes put on the appropriate smile for the occasion and hid his deep unease from everyone.

The ride back to Hyannis was surprisingly somber. Each of the three of them seemed to be engaged in their own thoughts, only occasionally opening up to the other two.

"When do you expect us to feel the change?" David asked as they crossed the Sagamore Bridge and he looked to the left in the direction of Provincetown, out over Cape Cod Bay.

Jacqueline was sitting in the backseat while David drove, with Carmen in the passenger seat. When Jacqueline did not immediately respond, Gomes assumed that she was lost in thought.

"I don't know, David," she suddenly said. "Boston will be moving someone down to the Cape soon. I don't know the name of the person yet. When they get here there will be a management team meeting with them to map out the plans for moving forward."

Jacqueline returned to silence and Carmen looked over at Gomes with a blank expression on her face. Gomes got ready to ask a follow up question but decided to drop the matter.

******

"May I have EVERYONE'S attention?"

Jacqueline had called everyone together in the conference room. She asked Marcia to put the nightline on so that they wouldn't be interrupted by phone calls.

Standing next to Carmen, she tapped on her glass.

Some people were still entering the room, including family members of staff and close friends. Gomes was standing towards the rear, near the door. He did not do well in crowds, and there was something about this moment where he felt the need for space.

"For months we've been speaking about a possible merger with the *Boston Outlook*. I can proudly say that the agreement has been signed. It is a good agreement, and this is a great advance for the *Cape & Islands Gazette* family!"

Clapping ensued. There was real excitement in the room.

"I will send around a memo later today with a summary of the key points about our agreement. The bottom line is that in joining *Outlook*, we become their Cape and Islands component. We will publish on Fridays, Saturdays and Sundays from May through October, and Fridays during the rest of the year UNLESS demand changes."

Paula Price, a freelance writer who lived in Falmouth and did a lot of work with *CIG*, raised her hand.

"Jacqueline, I guess the obvious question is what will this mean for all of us and how quickly will things change? Sorry. I'm not trying to be selfish in asking."

"I appreciate the question, Paula. The agreement calls for *Outlook* to send us a person they call a 'transition director.' They will work with me to oversee the operation here and begin the process of transformation. Part of that transformation will involve an organizational assessment. Given the plans that Boston has, it is highly unlikely that anyone will be let go. If anything, in the coming months, we may need to staff up, but not immediately."

Jacqueline looked around for other hands. She saw the hand of Terry Romano, an excellent staff writer for the paper.

"Jacqueline, I feel a bit uncomfortable asking this but…well, how long will you be around, and does all of this mean the *Outlook* puts someone permanently in charge of our operation…someone who hasn't been in the trenches with us here on the Cape?"

A few people looked at Gomes, who continued to stand in the back sipping some coffee. Jacqueline made eye contact with Gomes; he stared back with no expression.

"Terry, let me start with the easy part. I have no formal end date. I plan on working that out with Boston. It might be sooner, or it might be months from now. I don't have a specific date when I must be back in Quebec.

"As to structure…there have been no decisions made about the final structure. The transition director will make an assessment and make recommendations to Boston. I am sure they will consider any input we wish to offer.

"*Tout le monde*, let's celebrate this new step for our paper and the influence *we* will have on a much larger publication!"

Champagne was opened and passed around. Gomes smiled, grabbed a glass and returned to his desk, putting his feet up on the desk. He listened to the voices coming from the conference room, but his mind was elsewhere.

******

Leaving the office, Gomes felt a little tipsy. He thought, *maybe I shouldn't have had two glasses of champagne!*

Regardless, the deed was done and there was no point in hanging around the office. Feeling for his car keys, he felt some plastic in his pants and realized it was the bag containing the chain that Mr. Williams gave him to return to Pires' family. He had been carrying it around, intending to drop it off at Lopes' place. Looking at his watch while putting the plastic bag into his jacket, he concluded that Lopes was more than likely home, so he could stop there before proceeding to his own house.

Gomes wondered whether he should call first, then decided to just drop by, it would only be for a minute.

Gomes pulled into Lopes' driveway and parked right behind a black Chevy Impala. Before Gomes could lock the car door Lopes was standing in front of him.

"Hey, Gomes. What's happening?" Lopes said, a smile on his face, sticking out his right hand to shake.

"Lopes, I'm doing okay. Listen, sorry to drop in like this but I have something to give you and I kept forgetting to get over here."

Lopes frowned slightly, with a look of curiosity, waiting to have the surprise revealed. Gomes moved his left hand around in his jacket's pocket, feeling for the chain.

"Here you go, Lopes. One of the cleaners found it in the compartment where your cousin died. He asked that I return it to the family, so I wanted to get it to you."

Lopes took the plastic bag with the chain, almost reluctantly, and stared at it. He then turned his head to Gomes.

"What's this, Gomes?"

"The cleaner figured it was your cousin's, since no one ever asked for it. I remembered seeing the Crucifix in his room and just figured that this was his."

Lopes shook his head no.

"Gomes, my cousin wasn't particularly religious. He went to church every so often, but I can't remember him ever going to confession. Yeah, he had that crucifix in his room, but that was more cultural than anything else. And, I don't remember ever seeing a cross around his neck."

Gomes moved his right hand to his face and tugged on his beard. "Sorry to have put you out, Lopes. I just figured…well, you know."

"No problem, Gomes. Maybe that cleaner should have taken it to the lost and found at the shipyard. Let me tell you, the day that he was killed, my cousin wasn't wearing anything like that when he headed to work."

Gomes looked at the chain as Lopes returned it to his hand. *Oh, well,* he thought, *so much for good intentions.* He'd have to return the chain.

Every time he thought he had an answer, up popped another question.

46

A message was sitting on Gomes' desk when he returned from visiting Lopes. It had no time stamp. "Call Graciela Monteiro." The number was for her office line.

"Graciela, this is David returning your call."

"Hey, David. The word on the street is that *CIG* went in with the *Boston Outlook*. True?"

"Yep. Beginning of a new era, Graciela. And who the hell knows what will happen."

"So, what does it mean for you, good looking?" she asked with concern in her voice.

"I don't know, to be honest. In the immediate, nothing. But long-term, I'm not sure."

"I thought you would be taking over if and when Jacqueline left?"

"Yeah, but she's not just leaving. The paper is being taken over by another outfit. That's what makes things difficult."

"Ah, I see what you mean."

"Yeah, anyway, were you able to come up with anything concerning Alice Love?" he asked, appreciating Graciela's ongoing concern for him.

"It's an interesting story, David. Alice is the youngest of three girls in the Love family. The family's name, though, didn't start off as Love. Her father, Joseph, was born with the name Lubrano. He got married, changed the family name, moved to Sandwich, entered the 'white world,' and had little to do with the rest of his family.

"Here's where it gets *more* interesting. Joseph Lubrano—who became Joseph *Love*—was very light-skinned, with straight hair. He married a woman, Valeria, who became Valerie, also very light-skinned. Well, they had two girls. They were both light-skinned and could have passed for anything. Joseph really wanted a son, so they tried again. Out came Alice and, as you could see, there was no way that she could pass for white."

"For sure."

"David, as they say, this put a cramp into Joseph's and Valerie's plans. They had moved to Sandwich and tried submerging into a white world. From what I can figure, the white folks assumed that the Loves were white. Until Alice was born. Then things became complicated. Alice's life was rough, but I don't have a lot of details. I mainly got this from a family friend of Alice's once I was able to get some of the basic background."

"Why did Alice move to New Bedford, Graciela? Do you have any idea?"

"She wanted to get away from her family. She was treated as the ugly duckling. Alice has an uncle here…Denildo Lubrano. People know him as Denny. Runs a club in New Bedford called the Unity Club. Used to be the Brava Club, but he got some political consciousness and decided that he needed to reach out to all Cape Verdeans."

"Is he a leftist of some sort?"

"No. I guess that you'd say he has some progressive political inclinations but he's not political. He also sort of works both sides of the law, but nothing serious. He looks out after Alice, though. From what I can tell, she has nothing to do with her parents or siblings."

"So, Alice Love is Cape Verdean! She let something slip when I met her and that's what started me down this road."

"Is that important, David?"

"More than you can imagine, Graciela. More than you can imagine."

"David, what the hell is going on? This is sounding *very* mysterious."

"Graciela, I can't go into details, I'm really sorry. Nothing personal. I'm working a hunch that started to eat at me recently and I don't want to get anyone into any trouble. But what you told me really helps. Thanks, babe. Let me run and I'll definitely keep you posted."

They said bye and disconnected. Gomes realized that he was going to have to play his hunch out and that it was going to be risky.

Very risky.

47

Gomes invited Mariana over to his house that Saturday morning. He wanted to engage her and Pam in thinking through next steps.

Gomes worried that with snow falling Friday evening it might make the roads impassable. In the end there was not much snow, and Saturday morning turned out to be both beautiful and cold, with the roads a little messy, mainly slush.

As they finished their breakfast, Gomes moved from general chatting to the challenges in front of him with the Pires story. He took them through the facts as he had them and advanced some theories.

"So, that's the gist of it," he said, concluding his summary.

Pam sat back and sipped her coffee, frowning with worry. Mariana, in contrast, was very animated, full of energy and ready to talk.

"What difference does it make that Alice Love is Cape Verdean?" Mariana said with some frustration.

"I'm not sure that it makes any difference, but we now know that she is Cape Verdean, that she disliked the guy she worked with, that there was another way to get into the compartment where she and Pires worked, and that her initial alibi may no longer hold. I'm convinced that she is either behind this or knows more than she's ready to admit."

"It seems weak, my love," Pamela offered, putting her coffee cup on the table. "It's an interesting possibility but nothing clearly ties her to the murder. According to you there were enough people who saw her wandering around the shipyard."

Gomes stood up from the table and took his plate into the kitchen to start washing dishes.

"I know, Pam," he said from the kitchen, raising his voice slightly. "I know. Look, I think that I have to push her. My gut says she knows more than she's saying and I'm not going to find out unless I can put some pressure on her. I've got to get a handle on not only who killed Pires but who's trying to take *me* out. This is my only lead. The two cleaners just don't fit. And there's no one else in the shipyard who seemed to have an ax to grind with Pires." He dropped a spoon on the drain board. "You should have seen her when we met. She was much too cool for this. Both Williams and Dias were shaken by the death, and Dias has been in a war!"

Gomes returned to the dining room and picked up the plates and silverware, leaving their glasses in case they wanted more to drink.

Pamela said, "David, let's go to the cops with this story. That detective that you met with over by the Bass River, you seemed to feel good about her. Maybe she can put all of this together with the killing of Cunha and the attacks on you. I don't see how you can do this yourself. As you always say, you're *not* a detective! And this is very, very dangerous."

"Who the hell is Cunha?" Mariana asked, squinting her eyes.

Pamela looked at David in astonishment. "You never told her about Cunha?"

David's complexion was changing as he stumbled around to figure out how to respond.

"My apologies, Mariana, I was trying to keep you out of this." He reminded her of the meeting that he had with someone who raised questions about Pires. That was Cunha, and Cunha was murdered.

"Now, Mariana, do you see why I think David should go to the cops?" Pam crossed her arms as if to say that her point had been proven.

"I don't agree," Mariana with a hard edge to her voice. "You bring in the cops and we'll never figure out what's really going on. They'll want to know why David didn't fill them in from the beginning. And once you go to the cops, whoever is behind this *and* behind coming after you is going to go underground."

Pamela sat there, astonished, her eyes wide open as if she was ready to lunge out of the chair. "How would *you* know, Mariana?" said Pamela, raising her voice. "We're talking about my husband. You're proposing that David takes a *big* risk."

"Hold on, everyone," Gomes said, stepping away from the dishes in the sink and returning to the dining room, his hands still wet. "Both of you are making strong points. And I know that you both care.

"Here's my thought. I want to get Alice Love in a safe place where I can push her on a few things. I want to know more about her because I'm *convinced* she is somehow in the middle of all of this. Look, she's cool…and I mean cool. I can tell she's used to walking around with a shield. Not a chip on her shoulder but a shield. I think I can crack that shield."

Pam picked up the coffee cup, left the room and headed to the kitchen, where she poured out the remaining coffee and put the cup in the sink. Without missing a beat, she headed to their bedroom and closed the door. There was no slam, but it was clear to Gomes and Mariana that she was not a happy camper. Mariana looked at Gomes, but he shrugged and walked into the kitchen to finish washing the dishes. Mariana followed him and picked up a towel to dry the dishes.

"Mariana, I want you to get me any information on the Unity Club, you know, the place that Alice Love's uncle runs. I need the address and anything else that might be useful to know."

Gomes handed her a plate to dry.

"I'm going to interview Alice, again, but this time I want to do it at the Unity Club. I want her to be comfortable. That way she may drop her guard. And I want to do it before Christmas. We've got about two more weeks."

Gomes handed her another plate and then went to work on the coffee mugs.

"David, do you want me to come with you for the interview?"

Gomes looked over at her for a second, then back at the mug he was rinsing.

"Thanks, Mariana, but I'll be okay. I'm going to call her, this time. If you call her, she might feel comfortable putting us off. I need to speak with her. If you can just get me the information about the Unity Club, that should be enough."

Gomes started washing the silverware, then rinsed it off and handed the pieces to Mariana.

"Is…is Pam going to be okay?"

Gomes did not say anything. The only sound was the water rinsing the silverware.

"Yeah, she'll be okay. Truth be told, Jacqueline, Pamela, my parents and an uncle and aunt of mine have wanted me to drop this story. I'm not sure I was even conscious of this 'til the other day when Jacqueline made the announcement about *CIG* being taken over by the *Boston Outlook*. This may be my *last* major story for the paper. I think there's a better than even chance that I'll need to move on."

"Is the story worth your life?"

Gomes and Mariana turned and saw Pamela standing there glaring at him. He prepared to respond but stopped, realizing that what he was going to say would come off as dismissive.

"I don't know, Pam."

Pamela watched while Gomes finished washing and Mariana completed the drying. The only sound was that of the dishes and silverware being put away. Mariana pressed her lips together tightly, looking nervous. *I guess that she's worried about me too,* Gomes thought.

"I need to get going," Mariana stated with false joy. "This is Saturday, I'm needed for lunch and dinner at the restaurant. I'll get on these questions right away and call you with what I come up with." She proceeded to the door, walking carefully past Pamela, at least an arm's length away.

"Thanks. And thanks for coming by. Hey, how'd you get here in the first place? You don't have a car."

"A friend lent me his."

"Ah, okay. Well, listen, drive carefully. The snow out there—"

"David, I drove here, remember? Yes, I'll be careful."

Gomes looked a little embarrassed, shifting his footing while displaying a sheepish grin.

"Of course. Okay, let's talk later."

He walked her to the door and she was soon on her way. Gomes turned around and saw Pamela sitting in the kitchen staring, off into space.

Gomes returned to the living room and picked up his address book, looking through it until he found the number he needed. He dog-eared the page and put the address book into his pocket.

"I need to go out for a minute. I want to think about all of this, and I want to think about your concerns. I want you to know that I heard you."

Pam sat there not replying, instead twisting a paper towel until it snapped.

Gomes put on his coat and headed out to his car. He drove to Route 28 and headed in the direction of Mashpee, but pulled over at the first payphone that he could find. He exited the car and went to the phone. Putting coins into the slot, he dialed the number and waited for it to ring.

"Hey, yeah, it's your friend on the Cape…Yeah, I'm doing well…Listen, I may need some help. You have time to meet this week? I don't think that it will take long…Yeah, that works. Thanks. I owe you."

He hung up the phone and listened to the coins drop into the box. He could feel a chill in his bones, knowing that matters were definitely coming to a head.

48

As he drove down Route 6 in New Bedford approaching the Unity Club, Gomes reflected on his conversation with Alice Love. He had called hoping to convince her to meet with him one final time. She was reluctant but became curious when he suggested meeting at the Unity Club. He also emphasized loose ends that he was trying to address before writing his final story on the shipyard and Pires. Ultimately, she agreed.

The Unity Club was near the border between New Bedford and North Dartmouth. The building was not much to look at: two floors, drab exterior, no sign. It resembled a fortification, with a solid-looking door and high, round windows like portholes on a ship. Not a welcoming look. Gomes searched for a parking space and found one a block away.

Gomes expected a place that was either rustic or gaudy. When he opened the door to the club it turned out to be neither. It was well laid out, the recorded jazz music of McCoy Tyner playing through speakers mounted high on the walls. Upon entering and to the left was an "L" shaped bar with eight stools around it. To the right were booths, while in the middle of the room there were tables with comfortable looking chairs.

This was not a place for dancing, this was an establishment where people met, chatted, dated, maybe even conspired, but did not dance. Above the mirror behind the bar and on the wall to the right were chalk boards advertising light food, but from what Gomes could tell, this was mainly a meeting and drinking establishment.

The Man Who Changed Colours

On his left Gomes saw a door leading to stairs going up to the second floor. His cousin Ricky had been told that the first floor was open to everyone, the second floor was a private space for Unity Club members. There was a large, bald, light-brown man sitting on a chair near the door to the second floor, apparently protecting the entrance. In his 20's, he wore a knit pull-over cap partially covering his bald head and a heavy gray wool sweater. He had a toothpick in his mouth that he was working.

Alice Love was sitting in the second booth against the right-hand wall. She was dressed almost identically to what she wore at their first meeting, the only difference was a sweatshirt saying "Montreal," displaying a *fleur de lis*. Her eyes caught his as he approached her booth, unbuttoning his coat. There was no warmth in her look, only a recognition.

The club was not very busy, only a dozen customers in the place, with three people at the bar. A black couple was sitting with shot glasses in front of them, the man running his mouth, the woman looking bored. A white man sat alone drinking a beer and reading *Sports Illustrated*. The other people in the club were in booths, most discussion muffled with an occasional laugh or chuckle. All the colors of the rainbow seemed to be represented among the clientele.

"Good afternoon, Miz Love. Thanks for joining me," Gomes said, sitting down, trying to sound as pleasant and non-threatening as possible.

"You know, Mister Gomes, I had the sense that you weren't giving me much in the way of a choice." Love had an unfriendly look in her eyes, her right eyebrow raised.

A waitress came over and took their orders, Love ordering a boilermaker, Gomes stuck with a ginger ale and a slice of lemon. After ordering, Love sat in silence, Gomes getting the feeling that she was energizing her 'force-field.'

"You had a choice, Miz Love, and I appreciate your choosing to meet with me."

"Listen, Mister Gomes, why this place? Why did you pick *this place* to meet?"

Gomes looked around as if inspecting the establishment. The waitress came over with their drinks in the meantime. They toasted, though for Love it was clearly half-hearted.

"Simple. Because this is *your* uncle's place," he said, following her eyes as she quickly looked to her right at the bartender who Gomes assumed was Denildo Lubrano, according to the description he had been given. "I figured you might feel a little relaxed here. Was I wrong?"

For the first time since meeting her she offered a sincere smile. "Touché, Mister Gomes, you did some homework. Point number one for your side." She held the shot of whiskey up and took a sip, followed by a sip of the beer.

"Miz Love, there are a number of things that I don't really understand. Maybe you can help me. Let's start—"

The door opened and a couple entered the club laughing. The man looked white, probably Portuguese, or maybe a light-skinned Cape Verdean. He was dressed entirely in black: a turtleneck, wool pants, a full-length leather coat and a sailor's cap. He and the woman looked as if they were preparing to go out on the town. What caught Gomes' attention was the woman, with her white headwrap over her brown skin, a blue pantsuit worn with a white blouse and blue jacket, leather boots and bright red lipstick. After removing her black wool coat, she leaned into her partner, sharing a few intimate words. They sat at a table in the middle of the club to the left of Gomes but slightly closer to the rear of the club.

The loud and joyous couple caught everyone's attention. Once everyone in the club adjusted to their presence, they went back to their respective conversations and Gomes returned his gaze to Love.

"Miz Love, it's pretty clear that Pires was murdered. The intent may not have been to murder him, maybe manslaughter, or a fight that got out of control. But the real deal is that he was pulled down from his position, his face scratched in the process. Scratched enough to bleed. That's pretty odd. It's not something that a man would tend to do, even if pulling someone down."

Love rolled the shot glass between her fingers as Gomes continued.

"Then we have the question of how this could've been pulled off in the first place. It turns out that there was another opening into your compartment. An opening that was covered by cans so that no one would stop and think about anyone entering any way other than the main opening. Once I discovered that, the mystery was gone. You, for example, could have gone on break, circled around, entered through that neighboring compartment, carried out the murder and then…poof…out of there."

Gomes took a sip of his ginger ale and watched her, having taken a chance that he was right about the cans. She was as cool as a cucumber, not giving anything away…except for a nervous tick in her left eyelid.

"You're reaching, Mister Gomes. Plenty of people saw me walking around the yard."

"Indeed they did. But there is one more little thing."

"And that is, Mister Gomes?"

"The chain."

The eyes of the otherwise cool April Love widened.

"You see Miz Love, a cleaner by the name of Williams found a chain with a crucifix on the floor of the compartment where Pires fell to his death. I didn't think anything about it at first since I assumed that the broken chain belonged to Pires and somehow snapped off during this fall. But then I remembered noticing *your* chain and crucifix when we first met—a crucifix almost identical to the one that you're wearing now. While I believe in coincidences, this is a hell of one, and it doesn't pass the smell test." Gomes hoped that he had not overplayed his hand.

"Are you planning on turning me in?" she asked with a self-confident, almost smug look on her face, her earlier shock vanishing as she finished off the whiskey and turned her attention to the beer. "At best, Mister Gomes, you have circumstantial evidence."

"I'm not—"

The loud, flamboyant couple started laughing and teasing each other, distracting Gomes. The woman reached across the table, touching the man's left arm and rubbing it romantically.

"I'm not intending on turning anyone in, Miz Love," Gomes replied, refocusing on Alice Love. "I'm trying to figure out why Pires was killed and, frankly, who the hell is trying to kill *me*?"

There it was: something about her eyes. When he mentioned that someone was trying to kill him, she seemed to come to attention, straightening herself in her seat. That was interesting. She put the beer down.

"Someone is trying to…kill *you*, Mister Gomes? You're kidding." She shifted in her seat and smirked as if to dismiss his comment as unbelievable, but she did not fool Gomes.

"Miz Love, there have been two attempts on my life, and they all happened once I started to investigate the Pires death which now I can call the Pires *killing*."

Love looked over at her uncle, who had been watching the two of them since Gomes had sat down, all the time polishing some glasses. His facial expression was that of concern, though he made no move from behind the bar, periodically joking with his security person sitting by the door.

"So, Miz Love, are you going to come clean with me? I'm not interested in dropping a dime on you, but I need to know what the hell is going on. I want to know why *you* placed the symbol of the Blue Lightning in your compartment. Was it all about shifting blame? If—"

At the table next to Gomes and Love the well-dressed couple had shifted from all fun and games to arguing, and they were getting louder.

"Mister Gomes, are you crazy enough to think I would admit to murder? Did you think that in arranging to meet me at my uncle's club I would break down and tell you what you wanted to hear? You've been watching too many re-reruns of *Perry Mason*. What would be my motive? I mean, Mister Gomes, I know that you're supposed to be a good reporter but—"

The couple had gotten inappropriately loud, other customers noticing the exchange, a combination of disgust and irritation on their faces. Lubrano looked over at his bouncer, nodded his head and pointed at the couple. The bouncer got out of his chair and walked over to the couple, approaching them cautiously, with no air of hostility.

Gomes was watching this while trying to get Love to finish her point. He was mentally concluding that she was correct, he had thrown the dice, probably deluding himself into believing that he could get Love to even partially acknowledge that she had been involved in the Pires killing. The dice had turned up snake eyes.

"Excuse me," Gomes heard the bouncer say to the couple in a low and respectful voice, "but would the two of you keep your voices down a little? You're just a bit too loud."

"Who the fuck do you think you are?" the woman said to the bouncer, shaking her head and pointing her finger at him, her voice laced with hostility.

"Madam, my boss is just asking for you to keep your voices down. Nothing personal."

Gomes watched this in wonder. Why was this situation escalating? Were these people high? Love seemed to also be

216

perplexed at what was underway.

"Excuse me, buddy," said the man, slowly standing up. "I came in here to relax and not for you to harass my girlfriend here. I want you to get out of our faces and let us drink in peace."

The bouncer opened his mouth to reply when the woman slammed her fist into his crotch, forcing him back against another table.

What transpired next lasted only seconds, but Gomes felt as if he was watching it unfold in slow motion.

The male partner of the couple put his right hand inside his coat—which he had never taken off—and pulled out what later turned out to be an AMT Hardballer .45 semi-automatic pistol. Instead of pointing it at the wounded bouncer, which was Gomes' initial assumption, in the next nanoseconds he looked over and pointed the pistol at Love's head. At the same time his female partner also stood and turned towards Lubrano who had moved from behind the bar and was approaching the couple. She pulled a gun out of her pocketbook. Gomes and Love were frozen in position.

Pow! Pow!

The shots came from neither the man's gun nor the woman's, but from another location. Gomes and Love saw the man thrown backwards and down and the woman thrown against a table, a bullet in her head. They both lay motionless.

Gomes looked up and over towards the bar, noticing that the white man who had been sitting at the bar was now standing, holding a pistol in his right hand. He put a handkerchief around his mouth and was wearing sunglasses.

Nobody moved. Gomes was not sure that anyone breathed, let alone tried to move.

There was an eerie silence except from the bouncer, who lay on the floor moaning in pain. The white man at the bar quickly walked over to the two bodies, grabbed their pistols and checked the bodies. Apparently satisfied that they were dead, he put his right index finger across his lips to encourage silence and backed out of the establishment, making quick eye contact with Gomes. Gomes barely nodded his head, silently thanking Eddie O'Hare for demonstrating that he was indeed an excellent soldier and marksman. O'Hare refocused his eyes on Lubrano, making sure that *he* did not go for a gun. Lubrano moved not an inch. A few seconds later O'Hare was out the door. A few seconds after that Gomes heard two shots and then, silence.

Lubrano ran over to his bouncer to check on him and yelled for someone to call the police and request an ambulance. He then looked up at Gomes.

"What the fuck happened? Who was that white guy at the bar?" he asked Gomes with ferocity, showing his teeth.

Gomes looked at Love, who was shaken, but also angry as hell, then he turned back to Lubrano.

"*WHO* was that guy? I'd say that was the person who saved the life of *your* niece, and maybe your *ass*. If I were you, I'd get my story together before the police arrive."

49

"If I've told you once, detective, I've told you a thousand times, I don't know who the hell that gunman was. I don't know who the assassins were either! I'd never seen them before. Two of them came into the club and sat near me and Miz Love and, well, you know the rest. In fact, detective, who the hell were they anyway?"

Gomes received no answer. The discussion between Gomes and Detective Sorvino had been going on for an hour at police headquarters on 128 Union Street in New Bedford. When the police arrived at the Unity Club they did an on-the-spot examination, sent for the detectives and the crime scene unit and held everyone temporarily in place. The officers on the scene took initial statements.

Detective Peter Sorvino, in his late thirties, a thin but nevertheless imposing figure with piercing eyes, a sharp nose and dark features, took the lead. He separately interviewed Alice Love, Denny Lubrano, the bouncer—whose name Gomes never caught—and Gomes. The last time that Gomes saw Love, she was being walked into an interrogation room, visibly shaken. Gomes thought about how shaken *he* was. It had all happened so quickly.

"Alright, Gomes, so let me get this right. There have been two attempts on your life since you started in with this story about this guy killed in the shipyard, right?"

"Yes, detective, his name was Pires. He was killed in an accident and I've been investigating it ever since."

Sorvino pulled up a chair, looking Gomes in the face.

"So, you go to this club to interview another shipyard worker. The club happens to be owned by the shipyard worker's uncle. These people appear out of nowhere and they attempt to kill you. This other white guy decides to play good Samaritan and takes out the two assassins, then goes outside and whacks their get-away driver. That's your story?"

Gomes did not report that the male assassin had first aimed at Alice Love. *That* piece of information could complicate matters, since Gomes was not interested in revealing too much information about his growing suspicions. The fact that there had been two attempts on his life was on the record, so this would all be consistent…sort of.

"Yes, detective, that's what I'm saying and I'm sticking to it. All that I can guess is that this was one hell of a coincidence."

"How the fuck could this be a coincidence, Gomes?"

"Hear me out, detective. There have been two attempts on my life. Someone seems to know where I'm going to be at key moments. So, I came down to New Bedford to do a follow up interview with this worker. The assassins came in. I can only assume that the gunman who took them out had been *independently* after *them* for whatever reason. He had his opportunity, and, *bam!*"

Gomes folded his arms across his chest, feeling proud of his fairy tale.

"You're telling me that this gunman knew where these folks were going to be? You, Lubrano and Love all said that your savior got to the club before you arrived!"

"Yeah, that's right. My guess is, the gunman got information on the assassins the same way the assassins got information on where *I'd* be. There was a leak somewhere which, in this case, was to my advantage."

"To your advantage my ass," sounded off Sorvino. The

detective was incredulous and looked the part, moving his hands through his hair and then closing the file on the table. Without another word he stood and left the interrogation room, leaving Gomes to sit looking at his reflection in the two-way mirror.

50

As Gomes walked down the hall of the police station toward the waiting area, he wondered what Alice Love and Denny Lubrano had said. Exhausted from the interrogation, he felt like he needed to go to a bar and have a drink, but the better course would be to get to his car and head back to Hyannis and Pamela.

"*Sobrinho,*" Gomes heard, gazing up and refocusing.

"Nephew," came his Aunt Flora's voice again, this time in English.

"*Titia,*" Gomes replied. "What are you doing here?"

"New Bedford is a small town, David, the word quickly spread about the shootout at the Unity Club. When your name was mentioned, I rushed down here right away. Are you okay?"

Aunt Flora stood in front of him as radiant as ever, but with a look of deep concern on her face reflected in a frown accentuating lines on her forehead.

"Yes, Aunt Flora, I'm fine. Just a grueling afternoon with New Bedford's 'finest' following an experience I shall *never* forget."

"A good friend of mine called me about the shooting. I checked with the police and found out that you were fine. I called your folks, *and* Pamela, so, don't worry about any of that."

The two of them walked towards the exit, buttoning their coats in preparation for the cold.

"You have to tell me what happened, David," Flora insisted.

"Let me process it, Titia, and then call you and Uncle Al later."

Flora looked at him for a moment as if examining a patient. "Let's talk. You're not ready to go home yet, I can see it in your face."

Gomes admitted to himself that she was probably right. The more he thought about it the more he realized that in driving home he would be preoccupied by this latest near-fatal situation. Being an inattentive driver could result in a disaster. He suddenly became aware that he was shaking, as if he were standing outside in below zero weather without a coat.

"There's a coffee shop I like over in North Dartmouth when I really need to get away and not run into people I know. Let's go there. I don't have a car, I took a cab over here when I got the news. You up for a drive?"

Gomes nodded his head, and they went to his car. As he approached it, he saw that Alice Love and her uncle were also leaving the police headquarters. Gomes excused himself for a moment and walked over to them.

As they approached, Lubrano gave him a cold stare. Love, on the other hand, had an inquisitive and warm look in her eyes.

"Miz Love," he said, ignoring Lubrano, "I hope you're okay."

"Yes, Mister Gomes," she replied, with a kindness in her voice he had never heard from her. She reached out and took his hand. "I want to thank you for whatever you did to protect us. I have never been that close to death before. When I was looking at that gun barrel…" Her voice drifted off.

"As I told you both, I didn't arrange for the protection. We were lucky."

"Sure, Mister Gomes…Sure…I hear you…and my uncle hears you, too, right Uncle?"

Lubrano nodded slowly, not relaxing or changing his facial expression.

Looking at both Love and Lubrano, Gomes asked, "I'm assuming that you both told the police that the gun was pointed towards me, as we agreed?"

"*Yes,*" they said simultaneously.

"Good. That's for the best. We don't need to open up Pandora's Box."

"I'm afraid Mister Gomes that the box has already been opened," replied Love's uncle.

"Indeed, Mister Lubrano. Now we have to confront the demons that are emerging."

Love surprised Gomes with a warm hug. Gomes shook Lubrano's hand, then headed back to his aunt waiting by the car.

51

Gomes used the ride to debrief the entire experience with his aunt. As always, she was an amazing listener, asking the right questions at the right time, but otherwise paying attention to his every word.

"So, you did *not* tell the police that the gun was first aimed at Miz Love?" she asked with some surprise and emphasis, turning towards Gomes as they drove.

"No, Titia, I saw no purpose in getting her further involved. I'm convinced that she killed Pires but, and I know that this will sound odd, she's not a murderer. There's something going on here that I'm not getting."

Flora said nothing, just nodded her head in apparent understanding.

The coffee shop was on a short block in a mainly residential neighborhood, located next to a hardware store and a small grocery store. Gomes could tell that it was a mainly white area, but Flora seemed to not be concerned with their safety.

They found a parking space near the coffee shop, parked and entered. The woman at the cash register gave Flora a welcoming hug. Gomes found a table and sat down while his aunt and the café owner (as it turned out) chatted. Flora and David ordered coffees which were delivered with a pastry for the two of them to share.

"This is going to kill your appetite, Titia," Gomes noted, knowing that she and Uncle Al should be eating soon.

"Not to worry, David. This is a little ritual. These pastries are excellent and not too filling."

They tasted the pastry, making faces of joy as the lemon filling tickled their senses. Gomes started to relax and appreciated his aunt taking this time with him. But as he looked at her, something was changing in her face. It seemed to be tightening, the relaxed and warm look slowly disappearing like a ripple on a lake. Her beautiful brown skin was always very smooth, but there was something new in her appearance.

"Aunt Flora, I imagine that you're waiting for me to acknowledge that what you and Uncle Al said was correct. That I should have dropped this story because of the danger connected with it. Well, I guess you were both right but, you know, I'm a journalist and have to follow things through."

"David," she responded holding both of his hands firmly and speaking with a low voice, "we are *way* beyond that at the moment. What's the expression? 'The horse is out of the barn.' It's not only out of the barn, it's off the ranch. David, you have stumbled into something that your Uncle and I were hoping you would avoid. Now the stakes are much higher, and the danger is…well, the danger is on a different scale."

Gomes was so stunned that he withdrew his hands from Flora's, placing them in his lap. Flora finished her coffee, ignoring his withdrawal. She put the cup down and looked into David's eyes.

"David, what I'm going to say to you must stay between us and, of course, your uncle. Understood? Not even discussed with your parents."

Gomes nodded affirmatively. Cautiously.

"Yes, your guess was correct. Alice killed Pires. We told her to stay away from him and not touch him, but she broke down and… decided to take matters into her own hands."

"Who's 'we', Titia?"

"Well, let's just call it 'the Committee.' There are some Cape

Verdeans in the area who became active in supporting independence for Cape Verde and other progressive issues. We're not public, for a variety of reasons."

Gomes didn't know what to make of this. He felt like he was entering another world.

"You mean the PAIGC Support Committee?" he said, referring to a coalition set up to support the liberation struggle in Guinea-Bissau and Cape Verde.

"No, David. Something different. Maybe we'll talk about that some other time."

"Titia, I'm going to need you to explain what you're getting at."

Flora looked over at the waitress and nodded her head. The woman brought over more coffee for them.

Flora tapped her fingers on the table.

"There are things that you need to know and things that you *don't* need to know. Here's what I feel that I can say. Alice is a wonderful person. She developed a friendship with another Cape Verdean welder there named Moreno Rosario. An immigrant. A former political prisoner. He claimed to have been a member of the PCP. You know, the Portuguese Communist Party. But it's hard to say whether that was true or not. We do know that he was imprisoned at Tarrafal. He told Alice that he'd been in Portugal, active with the PCP, and imprisoned by the PIDE. He and Alice became close while at the shipyard.

"But Moreno was a little 'off.' He drank and was not always working on all cylinders. Was it the result of being tortured in prison? Who knows? The PIDE was brutal. But according to Alice when Moreno was at work, he was focused."

She sat for a moment holding her coffee cup and then continued.

"Alice and Moreno met while they were both on second shift. They would talk a lot and he never hit on her. They both got moved to first shift at the same time. One day at work Moreno told her that he'd seen a ghost. She figured that he was sort of out of it or drunk, but he was neither. He didn't want to talk about it, but Alice forced him to talk.

"Moreno claimed to have seen the man that you know of as Pires. He could not believe it. He had last seen him in the prison in Cape Verde when he was using a different name, but he'd not seen him since the end of Portuguese rule. He had been an interrogator. Moreno followed Pires around the shipyard at different points just to confirm that it was him. He told Alice all about him and asked her what he should do."

Flora became silent.

"What happened?"

"Alice didn't believe him. The guy would make up stories, but he insisted that this was the same guy he knew in prison. He told Alice that he could tell by Pires's walk. Pires didn't seem to remember him. In any case, Alice's opinion changed when Moreno was killed in a car accident in Scituate. He was returning home from a store and was the victim of a hit and run. Well, Alice was beside herself. She became convinced that he'd been murdered. The rest of us weren't so sure and wanted to check into it. Alice decided not to wait for a verdict."

"Aunt Flora, when there were attempts on my life, I thought that whoever killed Pires didn't want me to get to the bottom of the story. But after speaking with Alice, and certainly after the incident today, it became clear that something else was going on."

Flora wagged a finger at Gomes. "This is why I said you were *way* beyond whether your uncle or I wanted you off the story. We were trying to protect Alice. Yes, we wanted you off the story, but not in the way that you had thought.

"After the Portuguese Revolution in 1974, a number of unsavory characters started to surface in the area. We uncovered information that these right-wing Portuguese were operating in southern New England in an organized fashion. Their organization was called the Front for the Liberation of the Azores. They are a right-wing secessionist movement, *and*, a criminal organization."

"Unbelievable, titia."

"Later we stumbled across something else. Something more ominous. We don't know much about it, only that it is known as the *Organização do Exército Secreto Português*. The Portuguese Secret Army Organization, or OESP for short. They borrowed the name of that French fascist group from the time of the Algerian Revolution. We have only the rough outlines of who they are. What we *do* know is that their local leader, and probably their principal leader on the East Coast, is a guy named Carlos Souza. He owns a package store in New Bedford, on County Street."

Flora sat for a moment looking out the plate glass window of the store.

"We know they function like a military outfit and a criminal gang, and they are ruthless. My guess is they pursued you, pushing you to find out who killed Pires. They sized you up correctly, David. They knew that attempts on your life would inspire you rather than scare you. Pires was either one of their people or an ally, we don't know for sure. When they concluded that Alice had killed Pires, they decided to eliminate both of you."

Gomes was overwhelmed with this information. He had a thousand questions and he had none. He suddenly realized that he was staring at his aunt without seeing her.

"You were lucky today, *sobrinho*. In fact, you and Alice were *very* lucky. The man who saved your life was a godsend. But I need to know *nothing* more about that."

Gomes was about to ask a question when Flora held up her hand to stop him.

"Alice is leaving town. For good. You need to do the same.

Let me be clear, David. You caught those thugs off guard. The first attempts on your life were aimed at prodding you to investigate this case. What happened today was different. The next time you will not be so lucky. You need to make sure that you and Pam are off the Cape while we see whether things cool down. The one advantage you have over Alice is that journalists aren't supposed to get touched. It's bad luck, they say. Let's hope that the OESP knows that."

Flora suggested they leave the cafe. They stood, David paid for the coffee and pastry and they headed for the car. Gomes wanted to ask his aunt a question, but the words stuck in his throat. They drove to her house in silence.

"Keep your eyes open, David," she said, exiting the car. "You bloodied their noses today, which took them by surprise, but…"

Gomes thanked Flora and headed to Route 195 and home. At one point he would have said 'the safety of home,' but nothing felt safe anymore.

52

Though it was Saturday, it was also a few days before Christmas, which meant the traffic would be unpredictable. Although Gomes was making good time returning to the Cape, his anxiety was still killing him.

He crossed the Bourne Bridge, having a flashback to his near accident a few weeks prior. Driving along the Canal, he saw a sign for a skating rink and entered the parking lot in search of a pay phone. There were two outside the main entrance to the rink, so he parked and approached the phone.

At the sound of the dial-tone, he hit zero followed by a 413 number for Western Massachusetts.

"Operator, I would like to make a collect call to 'Dana Andrews' from 'Edward Robinson.' Thank you, operator, I'll wait."

Gomes waited and listened to the phone ring. When heavy male voice answered the phone, the Operator asked for Dana Andrews.

"Operator, Dana Andrews doesn't live here but if Mister Robinson calls back in, let's say, forty-five minutes, I should have a number where he can be reached."

Gomes thanked both the operator and the voice on the other end of the phone. He returned to his car and headed back onto the road hoping to get to Hyannis on time.

Turning off Route 6 onto Route 132, he headed toward the Barnstable County Airport. He made a right turn into the parking lot at a shopping center and spotted a bank of five payphones. Gomes parked, turned off the engine and waited in the car as it grew cooler. Regularly checking his watch, he got out of the car with three minutes remaining on the forty-five minutes waiting time and headed to the payphones. He stood next to the phone farthest to the left.

And waited.

At exactly forty-five minutes after his call to Dana Andrews the phone rang. Gomes picked it up in the middle of the first ring.

"Hey, man, thanks for calling me back," said a cold and nervous Gomes.

"Hey, buddy, it's been a little while. Why the cryptic call?" answered Hank Matthews, one of David's dearest friends. For years, Hank had owned and operated a hobby shop on Main Street in Hyannis. After reconnecting with the love of his life—and with considerable encouragement from Gomes—he up and moved to Northampton, Massachusetts, where, true to form, he opened another hobby shop. And got married.

"I'm in deep trouble, man. I need the sort of insight that only you can bring to the table."

Hank had a background that he never discussed, though occasionally hinted at. He admitted to having been in the military, but he clearly had a greater level of involvement, something like Special Forces or one of the intelligence agencies. He appeared to have gained deep experience in covert operations. Hank and Gomes were deeply loyal to one another, and Hank had offered wise counsel over the years.

As per an earlier agreement between Matthews and Gomes, neither of them mentioned any names. Gomes went into detail on his situation. They had both brought along enough coins to prolong the conversation.

"This is what we need to do," stated Hank after hearing his friend's summary. "First, I'm going to call you back tomorrow at, let's say, 5 pm. I will not be calling from a payphone, but it will be safe, so we can talk for a while, if necessary. I'm going to make arrangements for you to hold up somewhere for a little while."

"That's great."

"Second, tell your wonderful spouse the whole nine yards on this. And tell her that when she returns to Boston—I assume that she is still in graduate school— she needs to stay there until she hears from me. Tell her that you will be out of communication for a while. Understood?"

His teeth chattering from the cold, and nerves, Gomes said, "Got it, man. Listen, have you ever heard of this OESP?"

"I know a few bits and pieces. The advice you received about getting out of town makes sense. Give your spouse a kiss for me. Tell her I miss her and that my spouse sends her best...to both of you."

They hung up. Gomes hurried back to his car, started it and pumped up the heat.

53

Pam was in the living room laying on the couch with the television on, but not paying it much attention.

When David walked into the house, he expected she was going to grab him but, instead, she remained on the couch, saying nothing.

"Hi, babe. Aunt Flora told me that she called you. After I left the police station I spent some time with her."

"Glad you were able to find the time to get home. Have you eaten anything?"

Gomes felt as if he had just been slapped. He walked into the kitchen, opened the fridge and grabbed two beers. He walked back into the living room, placed a beer next to Pam and sat down. He took a long sip of his beer and looked over at Pam, who had not touched hers.

"I'm not sure where to start. After the 'incident' I was taken to the police headquarters and interrogated. Then I went to meet with Aunt Flora. We discussed the whole situation. On the way home I called Hank through a secure arrangement that we put together some time ago in case of emergencies."

Getting no response, he added, "I'm sorry I couldn't call you earlier. I needed to find out what was going on and who was trying to kill me. Things played out more dangerously than I had expected."

Pamela sat quietly. She did not open the beer, just fingered it as if she was going to peel it apart. She looked at Gomes with the most serious gaze he had ever seen, leaving him feeling as if a laser had been fired at his eyes. He could almost feel the pain.

"*MORE DANGEROUSLY THAN YOU EXPECTED??!!* This morning, Mister *DAVID SMARTASS GOMES*, you left the house as if it was just any other day. You told me that you were doing this interview and that you needed to push this Alice Love. *But* you didn't tell me that you were putting your life on the line. In fact, I had asked you whether this story is worth *your life*. You obviously knew this was going to be dangerous because you arranged for some backup!"

"Pam, I don't know—"

"David, stop right there! Just stop *RIGHT THE HELL THERE!*" Her voice was loud and shrill. She held her right hand up with the palm pointed at Gomes. "Don't play me for a fool, David. Don't tell me that you don't know who the gunman was who saved your damned life. Please…don't treat me like an idiot. I'm not going to ask you who it was, but you clearly knew the person. You can tell others until the cows come home that you don't know who that person was, but don't lay that shit on me."

Gomes sat back in the chair, feeling like he had taken a shotgun blast in the chest. Looking at Pam, he took another long drink of his beer.

"David, I thought that you and I had an *understanding*. Maybe your brain has gotten foggy, so let me clarify what we agreed to. You and I are a partnership. I did *not* come along for the ride. I am *not* your assistant or muse. I am *not* someone to be entertained and protected as if I am a baby in a carriage. I *am* your wife and partner. We are in this together. I am *not* someone to be sheltered. *Got it?*"

Before Gomes could open his mouth, she went on, "If you thought that we signed up for some sort of *other* relationship, let's put that on the table right now and figure out what to do. I expect honesty, I expect directness, I expect collaboration. An attack on you is an attack on *us,* and I'm not simply collateral damage. Got it??

"So, MISTER DAVID GOMES, the *love of my life and 'partner in crime,'* you and I are going to take a deep breath and we're going to start this entire damn story over from the very beginning. We *are* going to discuss how you ended up in a shootout at the O-K Corral. *And,* we're going to discuss what we need to do. I'm sure that Hank has some serious suggestions and we're going to factor all of that into *our* next steps. Got it, or do I have to draw you pictures?"

Pam grabbed the beer, opened it with force and took a deep drink. She slowly sat back in the couch looking deep into her husband's eyes.

"I got it," he said, his voice low, eyes looking at the floor to break from her gaze. "Alright, then. The best way to do this is to explain why I went to New Bedford on this trip and what I discovered."

Pamela took another drink of beer and seemed to relax. Slightly.

"Well, maybe we should start with the visit I had from Cunha. The plot thickened with what he revealed. It turns out…"

54

Pam and Gomes sat in the living room into the early morning hours discussing the entire story. Periodically Pam interrupted him to ask a question, but Gomes mainly laid out the story as if he was laying out a case. They took very few breaks.

Gomes was drained from the day and from this exchange with Pam but knew that she was going to be the person who would determine when the discussion ended.

"Hank's correct," she finally said. "We both need to get out of here for a while. I was planning on driving to Boston tomorrow night anyway. You and Jacqueline need to have a talk, and you need to warn Mariana about what happened so that she can watch out."

"Good. Good."

"You could forward our mail to your folks, they can pay the bills. I can send them the money. You're going to have to explain this to them, in either case."

"Yeah, I know. I'm going to do it today. But I can't tell them everything that I discussed with you or what I went over with Aunt Flora."

"I understand. Well, let's get a little sleep and take a few steps tomorrow."

They hugged with concern but not a lot of energy. Gomes was embarrassed by the entire situation as well as deeply worried for Pam's safety. After reading her husband the riot act she was confident he heard her concerns. But something was bothering her that had nothing to do with David. Something she could not identify, like an itch that she could not reach to scratch.

******

David's visit with his parents was painful. They were not only worried about Pam and him, but they felt that he had been cavalier towards the whole story and the concerns of his family. David tried explaining what he was doing, why he could not tell everyone more, and his obligations as a journalist. They reached an impasse that was only broken when his mother declared David clearly understood the gravity of the situation and that she was confident he was preparing to take the proper steps.

David's father got up, his face tight, and went to the garage to check the tire pressure on his cars. The door slammed when he entered the garage. Realizing that the discussion was over, David kissed his mother on the cheek and headed home. He felt a dull ache in his mid-section and a tightness in his body that would not let go. The pain was made all the worse knowing he would be unable to share the Christmas holiday with them. He hoped the absence from family would not be permanent.

When Gomes returned home, Pam was working on her lessons plans for the coming week, the television on with a football game in the background. This was the final week of classes. She and David decided they would celebrate their holidays separately and discussed how to explain that to everyone. David would tell the family about the shootout in New Bedford and say he had decided to take some private time cross-country skiing and hiking. The most difficult part was being away from the Cape over the holidays and for who knew how long.

Noticing that 5 pm was approaching, Gomes bid good-bye to Pamela, telling her that he would be back for dinner. To his surprise she stood up, put her arms around him and gave him a passionate kiss. He loved her full, wonderful lips. They held each other so tightly Gomes was afraid they would break each other's ribs.

"I'm going to Boston tomorrow morning very early. I need another night with you, here, in our home. I can't leave tonight."

"I wanted to ask you to stay but thought it would be irresponsible. Listen, I'm going to take this call from Hank, then get back here. Do you want me to pick up some food or do you want me to cook?"

"Neither. I'm making some good minestrone soup and garlic bread. Just come home with an appetite."

55

"Hey, man. Right on time *again*," said Gomes, picking up the receiver on the payphone in the same shopping center as the day before.

"How you doing, David?" Hank asked, the background quieter than the call the previous day. In fact, Gomes could hear nothing in the background.

"Not sure how to answer that, my friend. Scared, angry…and *very* sad. Realizing that I'm not going to be around family for the holidays, and especially not wake up next to Pam on Christmas… well, it's taken the wind from my sails."

When Hank did not immediately reply, Gomes wondered whether the connection had been broken.

"Well, my friend, for the next few weeks you're going to live a very different life. You have a couple of options. One, you can come out here. There's a place that I can hook up for you to stay in. Two, you can find yourself a place. If you go with option two, it has to be a place that's off of the radar screen. Some place where no one would look for you."

"Look, man, I appreciate you more than you'll ever know. Let me find a place. I have a few ideas. I don't want to bring trouble any closer to you than I have to."

"If you find your own place, make sure to bring extra cash, things to read and work on. Bring some music, you know the routine. I'm going to start making inquiries tomorrow about that Portuguese group. In the meantime, you *must* keep in mind that no one, and I repeat NO ONE, can have a clue where you're going to

240

be. If you must say anything, just say that you need time off to be by yourself and figure things out. Understood?"

"Yeah, I got it."

"One final thing. While you're away, I'll have a friend of mine check in on your house every so often. You don't have to do anything. Just lock it up. That's all."

"When will I know that it's time to head back home?"

"I want you to call me once a week. Ask for 'Mike Caine.' If it's okay to return home, I'll reply by saying 'Mike Caine isn't here right now but he should be home soon.' If it's not okay, then I'll just say 'Mike Caine isn't here and I'm not sure when I'll be hearing from him.' But don't start calling me right away. Give me a couple of weeks."

"All right. If I run into problems finding a place I'll get back to you and maybe head your way, but that's only a last resort. Will that be okay?"

"No problem. Listen, you've probably stunned these fascists. That gives you a little time. But don't take it easy, at least not yet."

"Don't worry, I won't."

Gomes hung up, headed back to his car and returned home. His stomach was tied into knots.

He didn't expect to see any improvement for some time.

56

Gomes called Jacqueline Sunday night to give her a heads-up about the crisis and his need to speak with her. She told him that he could come over if he wanted, but he said he needed some rest and they should speak Monday morning. This was the truth, though not the whole truth. He needed the evening to be with Pamela.

With no interruptions.

*****

On Monday morning Gomes went to the post office and arranged to have his mail temporarily forwarded to his parents' home. From there he went to the bank and withdrew cash to cover what he expected would be his living costs (mainly eating) over the next several weeks. He then headed to the *CIG* office for his meeting with Jacqueline. He still was not sure where he would be staying, but he knew that he needed to get out of town quickly.

Marcia's face changed when Gomes entered the building. She took her headset off and literally reached out to him.

"Is it true what they said about the gunfight?"

"Yes," he said quietly, approaching her station. "It was *crazy*, Marcia, like something out of a movie. While it was happening I was too stunned to be scared, but when it was all over…well, it took me a while to recover. The New Bedford police didn't help either, but that's a different story."

"Jacqueline's upstairs working. She's been doing a lot of that recently, by the way. She said that I should send you upstairs as soon as you arrived."

Gomes thanked Marcia and headed upstairs, not bothering to

go to his desk.

"Hey, boss," he said, opening the door into her apartment.

"'Hey, *boss*'? You nearly get yourself *killed* and you say 'hey, *boss*'?" She looked at him with fire in her eyes.

"Alright, alright. I got my ass kicked from one part of the Cape to the other by Pamela and my parents. If you want to join in, you can, and I'll just bend over. Or you can listen to what I have to say."

Jacqueline stood up, folded her arms and began pacing, not saying a word.

Gomes seated himself and encouraged Jacqueline to sit down. He then walked her through everything that took place on Saturday.

"So, listen, boss. There are some things that I would rather not tell you because I want you to be able to say that you did not know, if you are ever asked. And I don't want someone to ever pressure you into telling something that might compromise me or someone else."

Her posture changed from anger and worry to something else. She pulled a pad of paper closer to her and started doodling on the top page with her pen as he spoke, not looking up at Gomes.

"I need to get out of town for a few weeks. I need to find a place to go where no one will be looking for me. I need to also find out something more about the people behind the New Bedford shootout and behind the attempts on my life."

"You're telling me that it was *not* Alice Love that was behind the attempts on your life?"

"No, it was a group of Portuguese fascists and, based on the information shared with me, they were using those attempts on my life to goad me into finding out who killed Pires. Once I discovered it, or at least discovered it to their satisfaction, they were finished with me… and, with Alice Love."

Jacqueline put the pad and pen down. "David, we are in a new and complicated situation with the paper. For all intents and purposes, *CIG* has ceased to exist, though we will continue to publish under that name for a few more months. Tomorrow the transition director arrives. I've met him a couple of times but don't really know him. His name is Arthur Franklin. He and I are supposed to navigate the ship together. We'll see how long that lasts." Jacqueline raised her eyebrows, skeptical about what she had just said.

"What are you telling me?"

"Once upon a time if you asked for several weeks off to 'disappear' I would and could authorize that in a second. Now... well, I must explain things to Franklin and make sure that he and I are on the same page because the reality is, if Boston doesn't like it, they are the ones who hold the veto. I can make the case, but that's it."

Gomes sat looking through his datebook. Suddenly he sat up.

"Back date it," he said matter-of-factly. "Put together a memo approving my request for time off dated *prior* to the merger agreement. Tell Boston that I'd been thinking about taking some time off anyway, but after this incident I decided that I needed time off right now. Say the decision was made prior to the agreement and that you're holding to it."

"Oui, that should work. But Franklin will probably have a lot to say about how you spend your time when you return from your 'vacation.' By the way, where are you going in case we need to reach you?"

"Well, that's an interesting question. I don't know. I have to find a place, quickly. Maybe I'll find a motel somewhere. Since this is off-season, I can probably get a deal. But it has to be somewhere no one will look."

"I have a better idea." Jacqueline stood up. "Why don't you stay at my place in Wellfleet? You know the place. It's out of the way and there should be no one around. Plus, even if there are, they won't know you...remember you."

'Remember you' was an interesting addition to the sentence. Yes, he had been there many times, but that was several years back.

"I can't ask that of you! I don't want you to get into any... difficulties."

"It is not a problem. In fact, I *insist*." She went to her desk and pulled out some keys.

"Do you remember how to get there? The house will be cold, but the heat and hot water work and the electricity is on, I keep it available in case I need to get away. The phone, however, is dead since I only connect it in the late spring or when I've lent the place out."

Gomes said, "That won't be a problem, I won't be on the phone. It's a great place, that I remember."

Jacqueline gave a slight smile and looked at the floor for a moment before turning her eyes back to Gomes.

"Yes...a nice place...Then it is settled. You should go pack and buy food. Everything else that you need should be there. And here." She leaned over to write something on a piece of paper, standing up when she finished. "Here is the address and a reminder of the directions off Route 6. It is easy to find. There's a garage where you can put your car and, as you remember, there is great space where you can walk. If it snows, there are shovels in the garage."

Jacqueline looked at David carefully with her last sentence. Gomes accepted the keys and thanked her.

"Listen, I'll do this, but you can't say anything to anyone about this. If anyone asks, just tell them that I went to Vermont for skiing and hiking. Tell them that I needed to clear my head."

"*Bien sur*. That is how it shall be done. Have you told Mariana about what happened on Saturday? She needs to know. She may need to be careful!"

"I'll check with Marcia to see whether Mariana has dropped by or when she should be in."

Gomes had a terrible feeling that he was saying 'good-bye' to Jacqueline, not in the sense that he would never see her again, more that he would never see the *same* Jacqueline again now that the paper had been sold. He wanted to give her a hug and kiss good-bye but did not want that misunderstood.

Returning downstairs, Gomes walked over to Marcia's station.

"Marcia, a question. Have you heard from Mariana today? I figured she would've left me a message by now."

"No, David, no word. Sorry."

Gomes headed back toward his desk, concerned to have not heard from his assistant.

"DAVID!" yelled Marcia, waving an envelope in her hand.

Gomes turned on his heels and returned to Marcia's workstation.

"I'm so sorry. With all the excitement and worry about you I completely forgot that this envelope was left for you. I found it in the mail drop when I arrived this morning."

Thanking Marcia, Gomes accepted the envelope. Only his name was written on it. He walked back to his desk and opened the envelope.

Dear David: I'm sorry that I cannot deliver this to you in person. My boyfriend got a job in Colorado and we need to head there asap. His new employer wants him there right away. I am so sorry to do this to you. I have to go with him. Thanks for the opportunity.

--Mariana

Gomes was stunned. He did not know that Mariana had a boyfriend. And one that she would follow to Colorado?

He went to the copy machine, made a copy of the note and left it on Jacqueline's desk with a note that he had just received it.

Gomes went through his desk, putting together everything that he would need while on the road. Looking around the office, he did not feel up to saying good-bye to anyone except Marcia.

"Listen, Marcia, I'm going to be on the road for a while. If people are looking for me, just tell them that I'm taking some time off and will get back to them. I may call in but don't assume that I will. Take good care of the boss, will you?"

As Marcia lightly touched his arm, Gomes could see tears in her eyes. He turned and headed out the door, to what future he could not imagine.

57

After leaving the *CIG* office, Gomes decided to make a quick stop on his way to Wellfleet. He drove to the traffic circle near *Aunt Betty's Pond* and followed Scudder Road, turning off onto a small side street. He found the house number and pulled in front.

It was a two-story home, small and cute. White and grey, with a front yard that was probably quite beautiful in the warmer months, Gomes stepped to the front door and rang the bell.

The front door was opened by an older woman, pale complexion, wearing a light brown wool dress, long-sleeved, and a sweater around her shoulders.

"Missus Kearny, I'm David Gomes. We met some time ago when Mariana first moved in."

The woman smiled and opened the storm door.

"Oh, Mister Gomes, yes, I remember you. Please come in. It's cold out there," speaking with a melodic voice.

Thanking her, Gomes stepped into the house. Kearny led him to a small living room in the front and offered him a seat.

"Missus Kearny, I came about Mariana. I got to the office today and there was a note from her saying that she was leaving and going to Colorado. I just wanted to make sure that everything was alright."

"Oh, Mister Gomes, I'm so sorry. She never told you? It seems it was a very sudden decision. I was surprised myself.

"Friday evening, she came home early from the restaurant. She told me that she had been seeing this guy for a while and that he just got a job in Denver. He wanted her to move out there with him and he was driving down from Boston to pick her up. She was surprised by this but decided to do it. She called it an 'adventure.'"

"Well, Missus Kearny, when did she leave?"

"Saturday morning. Late morning. I remember that her boyfriend got here around ten-thirty. She was packed…you know, she didn't have much here…and off they went."

Gomes stood for a moment, scratching his chin. It was so odd that she would leave without calling him. To just leave a note was very impersonal.

"You know, Mister Gomes, I had no idea that Mariana had a boyfriend. She would stop by to have tea with me occasionally, and we would talk about a lot of things. Even about men," Kearny said with a light blush. "But she never mentioned having a serious relationship with a boy."

"What was the man who picked her up like, Missus Kearny?"

"Very handsome, not very tall. Very black hair. But the thing that I most noticed, Mister Gomes, and this may sound strange, was that he was not particularly friendly. And I don't mean just towards me. You know, you'd figure that a guy coming down to pick up his girl to travel across country would be excited and a little romantic. Maybe a kiss here or there. No, he didn't act like that. Guess I'm an old romantic, but he acted more like a mover than a boyfriend. In fact, I've met some movers who have been more friendly than he was!"

"Did you get the sense that she was being forced to do something against her will?"

"Heaven's no, Mister Gomes. It was just so…business like."

"Did you catch his name?"

"Only his first name, Mister Gomes. Paolo. That's all that I got. I'm so sorry she didn't tell you that she was leaving. That seems so unlike her to be that rude, even if it was a surprise to her."

"Did they have some sort of truck or trailer for all of their things? I'd assume that this guy Paolo picked up her things from Cambridge."

"Now that you mention it, no, there was only the two of them and a car. No trailer or truck. She packed her things and off they went."

Gomes thanked her and headed back to his car. There was no reason Mariana shouldn't have called him Saturday morning to say good-bye. In any case, he had more to worry about than the rudeness of an intern. He needed to get out of town in one piece.

58

Once Gomes finished packing and loading his car, he checked the house to see if there was anything he'd forgotten. He left the water dripping in the faucets and the heat set just high enough so the pipes would not freeze. Checking the security of all doors and windows and picking up the remaining garbage, he exited the house and went to his car. He packed plenty of books, pens and typing paper. Jacqueline told him that she had a good electric typewriter at the house, so he would not need to bring one along.

Gomes headed out of Hyannis, regularly checking his rearview mirror to ensure he was not being followed. Approaching Route 6, he decided to head west toward the Sagamore Bridge rather than towards Wellfleet. Entering Route 6 at a high rate of speed, he drove to the first exit, Route 149, turned off and crossed over Route 6 to reenter the highway going in the opposite direction *towards* Wellfleet.

With each move Gomes kept checking his mirror. It did not appear that he was being pursued.

About a half-mile past the Orleans traffic circle on Route 6, Gomes pulled into a *Cape Food & Health* store to do some shopping. Jacqueline had told him what was already in the house, but he would have to get food and drink.

Gomes returned to his car with several bags of frozen food, orange juice, coffee, tea, pasta (and sauce), fruit, ginger ale and an assortment of miscellaneous items. Looking around, he saw no one and nothing that looked suspicious. Off-season and close to noon, the masses were not out shopping.

After loading the car, he locked it and went to a coffee shop next to the food store, where he picked up a coffee-to-go. He proceeded on to Wellfleet, sipping the coffee and listening to nothing except the sound of the engine and the occasional car traveling in the opposite direction.

As one travels farther out on the Cape in the direction of Provincetown it becomes more and more of a summer rental setting. For Gomes, the 'real' Cape was from Yarmouth west to the Canal. Though he loved the Cape as a whole, *this* area became particularly deserted in the off-season, while no less beautiful, making it an ideal area to hideout.

There was something eerie about driving towards Wellfleet. Gomes found himself thinking about a similar drive he had taken seven years earlier around the same time of the year, only on that trip he had a companion who had a gun pointed at him the entire trip. In this case, the trip was solo. And voluntary.

When Gomes saw the "Welcome to Wellfleet" sign he began looking for his first landmark. Within a mile he saw on his right an old, family-owned motel that was shaped like a partial "U". He made a right-turn and drove about a half mile down—in the opposite direction of Wellfleet Center—until he saw what looked like a green archway to a small road. There were no signs, only a couple of mailboxes with numbers on the boxes, but no names. He took a right turn onto a gravel road and into a forested area that within fifty feet forked. Gomes paused the car. The road to the right went towards what he could see was the outlines of a house. The road to the left seemed to go deeper into the forested area. Gomes went to the left.

Proceeding slowly over the gravel, Gomes found himself thinking about what it might be like to find oneself stuck here during a snowstorm. He wasn't worried at the moment, since he had plenty of supplies, but he knew he would have to give daily attention to the weather forecast.

The road ended at a Cape-grey colored house, two stories with an attached garage. Looking at the porch on the left that faced trees, Gomes remembered there was a pond beyond the trees. He drove slowly up to the garage and shut the car off.

When he got out of the car he was immediately struck by the silence. He could hear the wind blowing through the trees and bushes and, periodically, the sound of an animal, but that was it. He heard no cars and no people. He opened the house, did a smell test to make sure there was no gas leaking, and then unpacked the car. After that he opened the garage door and drove the car in. There was plenty of room, even with the gardening supplies and a woman's bicycle. He closed and locked the garage door.

Gomes did an outside inspection of the house, followed by an internal one. There was a beautiful living area with a couch facing a sliding glass window-door looking out towards the porch and the pond. To the right of the living area was a hallway heading towards the back of the house; to the right of the hallway, a den with bookshelves with books and ornaments and a staircase to the second floor.

Gomes walked down the hallway, passing a dining area on his left that opened onto the kitchen. One could also walk straight through the living area into the dining room and on into the kitchen. Off the kitchen there was a coat closet and a door to the basement.

Gomes went into the basement where, as Jacqueline had informed him, he found a shotgun and cartridges. He looked at the shotgun and the box of buckshot and slugs. Ensuring that the safety was on, he took the gun and the ammo upstairs and placed it near the staircase. He wanted that gun near him at all times.

Gomes had been surprised when Jacqueline told him about the shotgun, but then she reminded him that she grew up around guns, though she was not a fanatic the way "You Americans are about your guns," she insisted. She also informed him that she had a legal permit for the gun.

Gomes surveyed the kitchen. He propped one of the chairs up against the rear door in such a way that, even if someone was able to unlock the door from the outside, they would not be able to open it without breaking the glass.

Just a precaution, Gomes thought.

Gomes went upstairs to the guest bedroom. Jacqueline said he could use the main bedroom, which was to the left of the stairs, but he refused. That was a corner room, with one set of windows that faced the front of the house and another that faced the pond. The guest bedroom had a window that faced the pond. There was a nice, full restroom to the right of the stairs. He dropped his things in the guest bedroom and went back downstairs.

Gomes took a deep, weary breath and grabbed a beer from the refrigerator. Sitting in the living room and looking out at the beautiful, cold day, he thought, *Today is the first day of my exile. Let's hope that it remains this quiet.*

He took a sip and listened to the silence, punctuated periodically by a mournful wind calling to the leafless trees.

<u>59</u>

After a sound night's sleep, Gomes prepared a light breakfast. Chewing the toast, he pulled out a piece of paper and started crafting a daily schedule. He knew that in the absence of a schedule he would become unhinged, particularly with no one there as company. After all, this was no vacation.

As the coffee cooled, he made notes. *Get up; exercise; eat; listen to the news; go for a walk (weather permitting); write/read; lunch; exercise; go for a walk; write/read; prepare dinner; write/read/watch television; sleep.* And on Saturdays, *clean.* Making note that there would be no garbage pickup, he decided to periodically drive out looking for garbage cans or large bins where he could deposit the garbage, being careful to minimize his use of disposable items in order to reduce such trips.

As his exile began, Gomes largely kept to the schedule. He made a note to call Hank once a week from different payphones in Eastham, Wellfleet, and Truro. Hank promised he would call Pam on his behalf, though Gomes sneaked in a few brief calls to her when he was distant from Jacqueline's house. He knew he should not be making such calls, but he needed to hear her voice; needed to break the isolation.

In years past, Gomes spent considerable time at Jacqueline's Wellfleet home. When Pam and David broke up in 1971, Gomes and Jacqueline became intimate, spending many weekends at Jacqueline's home. He loved this house. Over the years Jacqueline put considerable work into it, including building the garage. As a result, each day he now spent at Jacqueline's house felt like a weird

255

combination of being in a relaxed home and being under house arrest.

His walks took him farther than Hank would have recommended. He discovered paths in the woods that took him around the pond and onto the property of various neighbors. From what he could tell, no one was residing in any of these houses, at least at the moment. Carrying binoculars from the house, he surveyed the area, infrequently seeing anyone, and usually only at a great distance.

Christmas was especially difficult. Gomes had the television on all day just to have some background noise. He decided to make a spaghetti dinner, since he was tired of the frozen dinners. He also violated 'curfew' to find a payphone and call Pam. They spoke for only a few minutes.

Each day he kept to his routine, but each day was a challenge. He kept thinking about the OESP. About whether there was something that he had ignored and about how to get out from under this messy situation. He found himself thinking about Jacqueline and the paper...but especially Jacqueline. Every time that he looked around the house, he had a memory of times past. Feelings about Jacqueline that he thought had been settled arose, creating a level of discomfort that he was not prepared to address. He tried to brush them off, blaming his emotional state on loneliness.

New Year's Eve and New Year's Day were no better for Gomes, pushing him into depression. He sat up late and watched television on New Year's Eve, arose late on New Year's Day and drove to a payphone on the Truro/Provincetown line, where he called Pam. They spoke for only a few minutes, then he returned to the house, stopping for fuel along the way.

Driving up to the house, he was surprised to see a car in the driveway to the left of the garage. Momentarily frightened, he stopped his car, keeping his foot on the brake, only to realize that the car was Jacqueline's. *What the hell is Jacqueline doing here on New Year's Day? Or any day, for that matter? Is there an emergency?*

Gomes pulled up in front of the garage and turned the engine off. He ran to the house and entered, immediately hit by the wonderful smell of turkey roasting and potatoes boiling in a pot.

"Jacqueline?"

Coming into full view from the kitchen was Jacqueline, wearing an apron over casual clothes.

"*Oui, monsieur. Bonne annee!*" came her reply over the sound of the fan running in the kitchen above the stove.

Gomes almost charged down the hall.

"What the hell—"

He did not have a chance to finish. Jacqueline leaned over and gave him a kiss on his cheek. Gomes was stopped in his tracks.

"Jacqueline…what are you doing here? This is *very* dangerous for you *and* me. I'm trying to keep those fascists as confused about my location as possible."

Jacqueline seemed not to be paying attention to Gomes, focusing instead on the greens that she was preparing.

"I simply could not imagine you by yourself on another holiday. I had some friends over last night and we cooked a feast. I was sure—knowing something about your culinary expertise—that you have not had a good dinner in some time. So, I packed up some leftovers plus these greens, and here we are. *And,* before you say anything else, I took precautions coming here, including alternating between Route 6 and 6A. I stopped once just to check whether I was being followed."

Gomes was exasperated, pacing the kitchen trying to figure out what to say. Tongue-tied, he returned to his car and put it in the garage, then stood outside for a few moments before reentering the house.

******

Jacqueline smiled, thinking of David's response to her surprise visit. While he was out of the house, she reflected on her decision to come for this visit. The decision to come to Wellfleet had not been impetuous. From the moment that she offered Gomes the safety of her Wellfleet home, she found herself wondering whether she should come to visit him.

When she awoke that New Year's morning, she decided to go to Wellfleet. Though she kept looking into her rearview mirror to ascertain whether she was being followed, she was really preoccupied, thinking about David and their complicated relationship.

Ever since she and David had broken up she had done her best to hide her feelings for him. She smiled for a moment, thinking that she seemed to have carried it off very well. Everyone knew that she and David had been close, and they may have speculated that something had been going on, but no one ever asked. And even after the breakup, when her heart was sinking, she did not give away how deeply she had come to feel about David Gomes.

While driving to Wellfleet she thought that this might be a moment where she could finally tell David how she had felt. She was not trying to restart the relationship, that train had left the station. But she might be able to explain that her leaving *CIG* was brought about by a convergence of factors, him being one of them. She did not want David to feel that his leaving her to return to Pamela had resulted in her wanting to leave town. That would be unfair. And untrue.

More than anything, she wanted to get *him* to talk. Their split had not been explosive, though very sad. It did not happen suddenly either. She felt a distancing between them and could not put her finger on the source of it. When he told her that the relationship needed to end, it was not a surprise, but it deeply hurt.

In any case, following the split they never discussed what had happened. This led Jacqueline to hold in her feelings. She knew that holding this all in was far from healthy.

This could be an interesting visit.

******

When Gomes returned to the kitchen, he saw an open bottle of red wine sitting on the kitchen table.

"Let it breathe for a moment, my David, and then join me for a New Year's Toast, oui?"

Gomes reluctantly accepted the situation and poured two glasses of wine. Jacqueline picked up both glasses, giving him one, and they toasted. For some reason he burst out laughing. Jacqueline looked at him with surprise and then joined in the laughter.

60

The two of them sat in the living area looking outside, then at one another. *The wine was good*, thought Gomes. He was not sure what he felt about Jacqueline's presence, but he knew that the break from solitude was most welcome, even though it was reckless for her to be with him. Anyway, there was nothing that he could do about it now.

They caught up on world affairs and then, inevitably, discussed what might happen to *CIG*. They went over Gomes' story and the dangers involved.

Taking a break, they went for a long walk around the pond and out towards the ocean. Walking in silence, for Gomes it was a head clearing experience. When they returned to the house he made coffee and they sat back, relaxed, and continued to discuss life.

Having decided that they would have an early dinner so Jacqueline could drive home before it got too late, Gomes set the table as the sun was going down. Jacqueline lit two candles in the dining room and they had what Gomes acknowledged several times as a marvelous meal. It did not taste or feel like leftovers. Come to think of it, he remembered the food the day after a feast seemed to almost always be better than on the day of the feast.

******

With the dishes cleaned and the remaining food put away, Jacqueline and Gomes sat down in the living area. The window shades were open and it was very dark outside. The lights in the living area were out, the only light coming from the dining room. There was no sign of civilization outside. No lights from neighboring houses.

No lights at all.

"You better head back before it gets too late. You shouldn't have any trouble with traffic."

Jacqueline took a sip of their after-dinner cognac.

"I brought along an overnight bag just in case. It's late, I'm tired. I can get a good night's sleep and head back tomorrow mid-morning."

Gomes raised his eyebrows but said nothing. He stood up and closed the shades, self-conscious of being a possible target if there was someone outside. More immediately, he just did not like people being able to look in on him, even though it appeared they were isolated.

Jacqueline excused herself and went upstairs. Gomes sat back on the couch and realized that a lot of the tension that he had been feeling since he got to this house had evaporated during this one day. He took a sip of the cognac and closed his eyes for a moment. When he opened them, Jacqueline was sitting on a chair to his right facing him.

"David...I feel like there are many things that need to be said between us. I have put this off and, to be honest, I never thought that I would bring this up. But we are in a unique situation. It is unlikely that we will be interrupted, and we will probably never have another moment like this one.

"You asked me about what was motivating the sale of the paper. Everything that I told you was true. What I was about to tell you when we had lunch that day was an underlying issue."

Jacqueline stopped and sat silently for a moment. She looked towards the shades as if she could stare right through them.

"David, I have never gotten over our relationship. I have tried and I think that I've put on a great face. You and I have worked well together, but I realize that my feelings for you are very deep.

In fact, coming here and looking around, I find myself thinking about trips that you and I made here together and the time that we spent…" She did not complete the sentence.

Gomes had hoped that this conversation would never happen. It was filled with landmines.

"Yes," she continued, "I accepted when you broke it off and I did my best to work with you and not have my feelings get in the way. I must admit that I also hoped that you would someday return to me. So, I put my life on hold without ever being conscious that I was doing just that. Then came the financial crunch for the paper, and the requests from my comrades in Quebec to return home. It all came together. Even if my feelings for you had not been… lingering…I would still have had to face facts.

"I needed…I need to move on with my life."

Though Gomes had never wanted to have this discussion, he had prepared for it.

"Jacqueline. When Pam and I broke up, back in '71, I was unsure what I wanted to do with my life. You and I had been close, we enjoyed working together, we seemed to like each other and, to be honest, I found you—*find you*—gorgeous. The relationship that we started was great. And my feelings deepened. It was comfortable, except for one thing I will get to. We could speak with each other about just about anything. And the intimacy was…well, it was *amazing*."

He stopped for a moment, looking at her face to see how his comments were registering. There had been a slight blush when he mentioned their intimacy, but no larger response that he could see.

"But there was one thing, and later two. *You were my boss.* You never held this over me. It never came up when we were 'off the clock,' so, this is not a criticism. But it hovered in the background like an apparition, and I could not shake it. It affected how we both dealt with the outside world.

"Jacqueline, had we not been working together, it would have been a different matter…and I am not sure where we would be today, to be honest."

Gomes stopped to take another sip of the cognac, feeling the warmth of it going down his throat. Jacqueline was looking at him carefully with her dark eyes. No tears, no anger, but a face that nevertheless was displaying a growing emotion, her head held at a slight angle.

"Yes…the other matter was Pam. The work thing was always in the background, and I could not figure a way out of it unless I quit. But I didn't want to give up working with you and working for *CIG*, and I didn't want to give up on you. So, I kept suppressing my concerns. And then I stumbled back into Pam."

Jacqueline nodded her head slightly, her eyes focused on the floor. Gomes looked at her, then looked away.

"Yes, Jacqueline, I loved you. Damn it, truth be told, I still do. But I could not see where things were going, and when Pam reentered my life, well, she was like a different person. Or maybe we were both different. But something changed for me. I could not explain this to you, other than the whole work thing. And I was torn up inside. I did not want you to think that I was simply dumping you…you know…that you were some sort of interim pleasure. It wasn't anything like that, but how could I explain to you that Pamela was my soulmate?"

Now it was Jacqueline's turn to sip her cognac and reposition herself in the chair, like a hand entering a glove. She said nothing but looked back and forth between the cognac and Gomes, folding her legs under her.

"And it was not that I am white?"

"Not at all. Of course, I am not one of those stupid people who claim to be color blind. I was aware that you are Quebecois and white. But you have never treated me as if my being Black…my

263

being Cape Verdean…is the starting point. And, more importantly, you are fiercely anti-racist in your approaches. No, my returning to Pamela was not about race."

Jacqueline nodded her head and took another sip of the cognac.

"I understood your love for Pam, David. I was happy for you and sad for me. I hoped that it was a temporary reconnection, but, well…yes, I understood."

She stood up abruptly and walked into the kitchen. Gomes heard her washing her glass and then walking back to the living area. She remained standing.

"David, this was a wonderful day. I needed this day, and it was great to not have the pressure of other meetings. I think that I will go to bed now. Let's have breakfast tomorrow and then I will travel home. Maybe we can get away with not setting an alarm to awaken? Thank you for the discussion."

The conversation had ended too abruptly. Gomes thought he might have pushed the envelope too far.

"Absolutely. You go ahead up. I'll be going to bed soon as well." He tried to control his voice so as to not to respond to the sudden end to their conversation.

As Jacqueline walked upstairs, Gomes went to wash his glass and put it away. He wrapped up the trash and figured he would dump it somewhere in the morning after Jacqueline left. He heard the water running and the toilet flushing upstairs as he tidied up, then went upstairs.

Gomes used the restroom to prepare for bed, washing his face, brushing his teeth, and then decided to take a hot shower. When he exited the restroom, towel around his waist, he noticed that the light was off in Jacqueline's room, the door closed. He entered his room, put on his underwear and a night shirt and got into bed. He was asleep before his head hit the pillow.

61

Gomes was in the middle of a dream about being on a trip to California when he heard a creaking sound in the floor. He opened his eyes and turned towards the door. Jacqueline was standing in the room wearing a short, sexy nightgown. She slowly moved toward to him.

Gomes was perplexed. He was trying to figure out whether he was dreaming, but when Jacqueline got closer, he could smell her perfume and felt her weight as she sat on the bed.

She put her right index finger over his lips. He shifted in the bed, backing away, but she moved closer, unbuttoning her nightgown. She brought her mouth to his and kissed him tenderly. Deeply.

Gomes was torn between desire and terror. This was not what he wanted.

Or was it?

Grasping her head, he pulled her away. He saw the passion in her eyes that had once brought him to the heights of ecstasy, but this time he had to deny his own desires

"I'm sorry, Jacqueline. Truly sorry. I can't do this. As much as I want you; as much as I love you, I can't do this to Pamela. I'm sorry."

She stared at him for what seemed ages. Then she stood up, her head held high, shoulders back. She buttoned her nightgown and silently slipped away.

Gomes lay back, closed his eyes and hoped it was all a dream.
******

Why he awoke, he would never be sure. Listening to the

stillness, he heard something outside, as if a branch on the ground had cracked.

Beneath someone's foot.

Getting silently out of bed, he went to the window and looked outside. He saw nothing but darkness.

There! Another noise in the back of the house. It sounded as if someone was trying to open the lock on the kitchen door. He ran back into his room and put on his socks, pants, a sweatshirt, and sneakers, then he silently walked to the room where Jacqueline was sleeping.

"Jacqueline," he whispered, his hand near her mouth, "wake up."

She came out of the sleep confused. He pulled his hand away from her mouth.

"Someone is outside," he whispered. "Not sure how many, but I hear it. They're trying to get in. I'm taking the shotgun downstairs. I need you to get up and get dressed—quietly. When you hear the sound of something falling over, flip on the lights over the stairs and duck. I might also yell 'Now!' Just keep listening. Don't show yourself under any conditions. If something happens to me, barricade yourself in your room and stay away from the windows. Got it?"

Jacqueline nodded, coming fully awake. Gomes left the room with the loaded shotgun on safety. Quietly he went to the stairs. He had practiced walking down the stairs many times since he had arrived, finding the creaks in the steps so he could avoid them if he had to go down in the dark.

The sound in the back of the house was gone. Maybe the chair routine had worked. The intruder would have to break the glass, and that would make far too much noise. But then Gomes heard someone walking out near the porch. Had this been summer

Gomes would have heard nothing, but in the middle of winter, the frozen ground and frozen grass were a natural warning system.

He tried to place himself into the mind of the intruder. They had tried the back door, which made sense, it was farther from the bedrooms and probably easier to break, but they encountered an obstacle. The intruder would look for other ways to enter the house, the most obvious being the front door rather than forcing any windows. They would have to be careful not to awaken Gomes—had Gomes been asleep.

Gomes positioned himself behind the couch with a clear line of sight on the front door. He placed the shotgun on the living room table and clicked the safety off.

He waited, listening carefully, his heart pounding and, despite the coolness of the house, perspiration coming down his face.

There it was, thought Gomes. A sound toward the front of the house. The intruder was trying to avoid making noise. Gomes listened to the storm door opening and the doorknob being tried, unsuccessfully.

Gomes heard the intruder picking the lock. *This guy's good,* Gomes thought. A click and the door slowly opened. Despite the darkness, Gomes could see the intruder was holding a pistol in his hand. The bare outlines of a figure slipped through.

The intruder looked around, getting his bearings. Seeing the nightlight on the second floor, he slowly approached the stairs.

Gomes looked around the room. He saw a baseball in a glass holder on the living room table. He remembered that he and Jacqueline had gone to a Minor League game of the Pawtucket Red Sox, where a batter had hit a foul ball right into his hands. The player had autographed the ball and given it to Jacqueline.

Gomes took the ball and tossed it over his shoulders. It hit the wall and bounced. In the silence of the house, the noise could have awakened the dead.

The lights suddenly went on. The intruder fired his pistol toward the sound of the baseball. The shot made a muffled thump, telling Gomes the man was using a silencer.

Another shot hit the wall at the top of the stairs, Gomes prayed it missed Jacqueline. Then, *BANG!*

The explosive sound was the last thing the would-be assassin ever heard. The shotgun blast hit him midbody, blowing him off his feet and forcing him against a wall, where he collapsed. Gomes walked over to the body, kicked the pistol away and checked to ensure that the intruder was dead.

"Jacqueline! You can come downstairs now, he's dead."

Dressed in jeans and a sweater, Jacqueline came downstairs, slowly at first, looking around. She walked quickly over to Gomes and hugged him tightly.

"You have to get out of here," she said to Gomes. "They were obviously out to get you."

Gomes looked at the blood spreading across the floor.

"Listen," Gomes said, holding her tight. "We're going to have to move fast. *You* need to pack your things, clean up your room so that it does not appear that anyone was staying there, and get home as fast as you can without getting pulled over for speeding. If the two of us are here when the cops show up, it will raise too many questions for either of us to answer."

As Jacqueline stepped back he looked into her eyes, making sure that she was clear about what he was raising.

"Jacqueline, I mean it. You need to get out of here. Someone may have seen me here over these weeks. If the cops start asking questions and you claim that you were here alone, it might get ugly. So, you get home and expect that the police will call you. You can even tell them that you came up here today but returned home. Got it?"

She nodded her head and headed upstairs. Gomes bent down

to check, again, that the intruder was dead.

When Jacqueline came back downstairs, she had everything packed.

"Okay, so they will call you. Act surprised. You will probably need to drive back here later this morning. Sorry. But you can't be here when the cops show up. I'll follow you out and get to a payphone and call the cops. I'll bring them here and stall them as long as I can so you can get home."

Gomes walked her to her car, carrying a few of her things. When she opened the car door, she gave him a warm and passionate kiss on the lips but said nothing. He threw her things onto the backseat of the car.

Gomes went to the garage and got his car. By the time he made a U-turn and pulled out, Jacqueline was long gone.

Driving slowly through the dark lane to the main road, Gomes looked to see whether there was any indication of the assassin's car. When he reached the main road and made a left to head towards Route 6, he saw the vehicle pulled onto a grassy embankment. Gomes did not stop.

It was pitch black except for an occasional streetlight. Gomes realized that he had no idea what time it was. His watch indicated that it was well after three in the morning. *Damn,* he thought.

It suddenly occurred to him that there might be a payphone at the motel that had been his landmark. He made a U-turn and headed back, entering the motel parking lot. The motel looked closed for the night, with only a nightlight on in the office. Spying a phone on the wall near the motel's office, Gomes pulled in, got out of the car and went to the phone.

The dime made a little tinkle as it dropped into the phone.

"Yes, I would like to report a killing."

62

"Officer Hawkins, I explained that to you. Yes, I had the permission of the owner to be here. No, I have no idea who the intruder was."

Gomes had been sitting in Jacqueline's house for over an hour. The police had taken a full 15 minutes to arrive at the motel, during which time Gomes had an encounter with the motel owner who inquired—with a gun pointed towards Gomes—why this Black man was standing in front of the motel at 3:30 am. Gomes explained that he was waiting for the cops. The skeptical motel owner was about to call the police when a patrol car with lights flashing turned into the parking lot, not daring to run his siren in the middle of the night.

Gomes led Officer Hawkins to Jacqueline's house. It did not take long for a crime scene investigation unit to show up. While Gomes was trying to answer questions, two other officers surveyed the scene, examined the body, looked for bullet holes and took photographs.

Gomes was running on adrenaline but getting more and more exhausted. Every so often he felt as if he was drifting off to sleep in the middle of a conversation. He had to force himself to stay alert. He looked up and saw an ambulance arrive at the same time as a Barnstable County Police cruiser. Officer Hawkins also noticed and breathed a sigh of relief. This had been Hawkins' first killing, and Gomes could tell that he was uneasy about how to proceed.

The emergency medical personnel entered the house carrying a stretcher, and approached the crime scene investigators. Next entered Detective Rachael Schwartz. Schwartz was wearing a grey parka, a black knit cap and black boots. Looking around the house, she made eye contact with Gomes, offered a slight smile, and walked over to him.

"Detective, you look like you haven't had your first cup of coffee."

"Mister Gomes, I feel like hell. If you're offering some coffee, I'm first in line!"

"I'll take care of that right now. Officer Hawkins, would you like a coffee?"

Hawkins looked at Gomes with surprise. Stumbling with his words he said, "Well, yeah, Mister Gomes, that would be very gracious of you."

Gomes walked into the kitchen and turned on the stove to boil some water. Schwartz followed him in, taking off her coat and putting it over a chair. Gomes pulled out a coffee filter and some coffee and then grabbed three cups. He watched the water patiently, waiting for it to boil.

"Well, Mister Gomes, it seems like death is following you all over New England."

"It seems that way, Detective," Gomes replied, looking at the flame under the kettle.

Schwartz watched him. Hawkins seemed uncomfortable.

"Has the owner of this home been notified about this attack?" Schwartz asked Hawkins.

"Ah, well," said Hawkins, "I was waiting for you, Detective. I wanted to make sure that I didn't create some sort of problem. And, after all, it is *really early* in the morning. I figured we could call later in the morning. You know, I wouldn't want to scare her."

Schwartz looked at Hawkins as if the man had an IQ of ten. *"Scare her?* The woman's house was just hit by an assassin! I think this might be a good time to call her. Maybe before your coffee is ready?"

"Sure, sure thing. It's just, this house doesn't have a working telephone line so…" he mumbled the rest of his answer.

Gomes said, "Officer, why not radio your station and ask someone to call her?" He grabbed a paper towel, wrote down Jacqueline's number and turned it over to Hawkins, who thanked him and hustled to his car. Gomes looked at his watch, hoping Jacqueline had made it home in time.

Gomes slowly poured the boiling water into the glass coffeemaker, watching the fragrant brown liquid drip through the coffee grounds.

"Mister Gomes, why don't we take this from the beginning?"

As the coffee dripped, Gomes started off describing why he came to this house, getting Jacqueline's permission, Jacqueline visiting for the day, and the events that morning. Schwartz listened carefully. Seeing that the coffee was ready, she stepped toward the pot, but Gomes stopped her and poured cups for her and Hawkins, who had just returned.

"Ah, Detective," said Hawkins, "we reached her. She was shocked and said that she would head up here first thing in the morning. She said that she didn't trust herself to drive at the moment, she needed to sleep some more so she didn't fall asleep at the wheel. She asked about Mister Gomes, here. Said that, yes, she'd given him permission to be here."

"Thanks, Officer." Gomes finished with details of the attack.

"Mister Gomes, it's obvious that this was no ordinary B&E," Schwartz said. "This guy had a silencer on his pistol. He had no identification on him. There was a registration in the car, but the car was probably stolen. We've taken fingerprints, for what that will be worth. My guess is that if we do a *deep* search around where his car was found, we will find his wallet and identification hidden somewhere. But look, we may not be able to find it at all, this guy was a professional. He was clearly after you or Miz Reynaud, but the odds are that it was *you*."

Gomes blew on his cup of coffee. "Detective, I've now had four attempts on my life, although I think that the first two were threats. The last two were intended to take me out. You needn't say anything more. Yes, I'm scared to death, Detective."

Schwartz asked him additional questions, many repetitive. Hawkins sat in the living area, watching the crime scene personnel and the emergency medical personnel leave. It suddenly became strangely silent, though the lights from Hawkins' cruiser remained on.

"We're closing off the front of the house, but the rest of the house is useable. When Reynaud gets here, I'll need to speak with her."

"It sounded as if Hawkins was not sure when she'll arrive. Maybe you should go home and get some sleep and come back later this morning?"

"Gomes, the way I'm feeling now, if I go home, I probably am *not* returning!" she offered with a chuckle. "I've got a better idea. You go get some sleep, I'll send Hawkins home and I'll stay downstairs and kick my feet up until Miz Reynaud shows up."

Gomes thanked Schwartz, went upstairs and, despite having consumed the coffee, was asleep within minutes.

63

Jacqueline showed up at the Wellfleet house around 9:30 in the morning and was questioned by Detective Schwartz. As far as Schwartz was concerned—and Gomes could see this on her face—there was little that Jacqueline could add that was of any help. The detective assured Jacqueline that it was highly unlikely the intruder had been after her, but that she needed to take precautions. When Schwartz left, Gomes turned to Jacqueline with a questioning look.

"What now?" she asked.

"There will be an inquest. You should check with the detective about when this crime scene tape comes down. She's going to try to keep our names out of the news, but inevitably something will be mentioned about me. I need to reach Pam and tell her what happened."

Gomes saw no reaction on Jacqueline's face.

"I also need to reach a friend and see what he suggests. I can't keep running from these murderers."

Walking nervously around the kitchen, Jacqueline said, "You should go home. Or at least leave here. I'm going to survey the damage and then head home myself. The detective said they're going to have an officer drop by here while I am cleaning up, just to be on the safe side, but you need to figure out your next steps."

Gomes went upstairs to get his things. Jacqueline was walking through the house picking up trash with a broom and dustpan. Every so often she would stop and stare at the chalk outline of where the body had dropped.

As Gomes headed toward the rear door of the house, Jacqueline hurried to meet him.

"David, please be careful," she said softly, hugging him. "I'm sorry that this happened and I'm sorry if I...complicated things."

She hid her face from Gomes. He touched her chin and pulled her head up to face him.

"Things have always been complicated between us, Jacqueline. I think that we finally got things out in the open, even if it doesn't change the fundamentals. I think you and I are still good."

Jacqueline nodded her head in understanding, tears welling in her eyes.

As they walked to his car, Gomes handed her back the keys.

******

As his car approached the exit for Route 132 to Hyannis, Gomes thought about his next stop. First, the phone booth at the exit, it was time to call Hank.

64

Gomes picked up the payphone on the first ring.

"Thanks for being available," Gomes began.

"You sound really stressed. What happened?"

Gomes went through all the details, noticing as he spoke that there was dead silence in the background and he never once heard the cling of coins falling in a slot. Hank was calling from some place with a safe line, certainly not from home. Gomes, on the other hand, was standing outside freezing. Regardless of his trust in Hank, he decided to hold back on discussing anything about Jacqueline outside of what he he'd told the police. He didn't need any lectures about his relationship with Pamela.

"Okay then," Hank began, "this advances the clock, but it doesn't change the basics. First thing, I told you I've had an associate looking in on your house while you've been in Wellfleet. He's going to stay with you and Pam for a while. He won't get in the way. I trust him *implicitly*. Stay away from your house until 6 pm today. *Don't* go to work. Go to a bookstore or a library, or even a hobby shop." Hank chuckled with the hobby shop comment. "When you do return home, my associate will show up and say something very personal about me without mentioning my name, but something that you and few others would know. That will be the sign that he is legit."

Gomes unconsciously nodded his head. Steam left his mouth with every breath.

"Now, let me summarize what I've uncovered so you know what you're up against. First, nothing was sent to me in writing.

I was, however, permitted to take notes. Everything I was told supported the basic information that you have. I must say, for non-professionals, the people in New Bedford who gave you the information about the Portuguese group were quite good."

Coming from someone else, that last sentence might have sounded condescending, but from Hank it was high praise.

"The OESP was formed toward the beginning of the Caetano administration, after Salazar died. These fascists—and that's *exactly* what they are—were becoming increasingly worried that Portugal was going to pull out of their colonies. They didn't anticipate the 1974 Revolution, however. Their objective was to preserve the dictatorship and preserve the colonies.

"The OESP based itself in the Portuguese military and secret police. As it turns out, they were completely surprised by the Revolution. They attempted to mount a response, but failed. As a result, they started working to get some of the key fascists and other criminals out of Portugal before they were strung up."

"What bastards."

"To be sure. Did you read that Frederic Forsyth novel, *The Odessa File*? It's about a Nazi organization that smuggled Nazis out of Germany at the end of the war. OESP did the same thing."

Hank paused a moment to let the information sink in. "The CIA worked with them to get their people out of Portugal and out of the colonies. But the CIA also anticipated they might need the OESP to carry out a counter-revolution if things went too far to the Left in Portugal. As the Revolution weakened, the CIA was less interested in OESP.

"That said, the Company helped settle some of their crew in the US. They did the same with some of the Greek Junta that was ousted the same year, in seventy-four. In fact, they moved a Greek major who had done some clandestine work for them in Albania to New Bedford. His name is Alesandro Thanos. Does the name ring any sort of bell?"

Gomes thought for a second. "No."

"Just curious. Odd that they would move them both to New Bedford. In any case, once they got to the USA, OESP at first raised funds for projected military operations in Portugal, but that collapsed.

"So, like some of the anti-Castro Cubans down in Florida, they engaged in criminal behavior. Drugs, extortion, loansharking, smuggling. Something to raise money...and get rich. They became increasingly like the Cosa Nostra, in fact, leading to a sort of non-aggression pact with the Providence mob.

"Birds of a feather," said Gomes.

"Exactly. OESP is organized based on cells. Each cell has a captain, or *capitao*. The cells have territorial responsibilities, and they all report to the leader, in this case, Carlos Souza. Ex-PIDE. A vicious bastard, from what I hear. Runs the organization with a whip. His leadership is uncontested. About a year ago some ex-Portuguese military guy moved into the area and thought he should become the big cheese. He was found floating in the Bay. You should also know that OESP is *very well armed*."

This was fascinating, Gomes thought, but he was freezing his ass off.

"Do you have any information on the killers who attempted to take me and Alice out?" his teeth chattering.

"Nothing specific, except the guy killed in the club was definitely part of OESP. Beyond that, not sure. As best as I can tell, you have four options, none of them are good.

"Option one: go home and resume your life. You can operate on the assumption that since the OESP failed to kill you and Alice, and failed in the most recent attempt in Wellfleet, they will drop the matter, particularly since Alice has relocated and the cops are now involved.

"That sounds promising."

"It is, *but…* from what I've learned about the OESP, I expect they will track you down and try again."

"Yes, that sounds more likely."

"Option two: You do what Alice is doing: you relocate. Move South. Or West. Stay away indefinitely. But it's not just about moving, you'll have to assume a new identity. And you can forget about journalism."

"Wait a sec—"

"You and Pamela will have to become different people. Given her graduate schoolwork and what she wants to do, that would be rough, and I know it would be rough for you. And even if you do go that route, don't assume that the OESP won't find you. They might hire a professional hitman rather than deploying any more of their personnel."

Hank paused to let his words sink in. "Option three: you go to the police. This is probably what Jacqueline and others want you to do. I do not recommend it. The cops cannot protect you. And the cops in New Bedford may be infiltrated with OESP people. If you go to the police, I think that you're going to have to move anyway. I have absolutely no confidence that they will eliminate the problem."

Hank became silent. Again, Gomes heard nothing in the background.

"You said that there were four options, Hank. I'm waiting,"

"Option four: you allow associates of mine to eliminate the problem. The cost to you, financially, will be in the realm of supplies. The people I have in mind would do this *gratis* for personal reasons, one of which is that they owe me."

"Are you *joking*, Hank? Have you been watching *Three Days of the Condor* a few too many times? I'm not interested in starting a damn *war*. I don't want innocent people killed because they happen to be bystanders. Also, where would I get the money to finance such a thing?"

"I can advance the funds, you can pay me back over time. That way there would be no connection. My associates are professionals. They're highly experienced and can be relied upon to get this done. Plus, from what I can tell, the OESP overestimates their own strength, in part because they're so brutal."

"Hank, really...you've got to be kidding. If—"

"David, sorry to cut you off but you really don't get what you've stepped into. OESP is a quasi-military outfit. Alice took out one of their members or close allies, and then you bring in someone who whacks *three* of their people. Then you take out *another* one of their operatives. Come on there, buddy, let's get real."

"There's *got* to be another way, Hank. Once something like this gets going, who knows where it'll end?"

"If you can come up with another way, that's fine. It's your decision...well, yours *and* Pam's decision. I'm leaving the offer on the table."

"Christ! I'm not sure what Pam will think, but we'll talk it over."

Gomes thanked Hank and hung up the phone. He needed to reach Pam for a face-to-face talk, and he knew that was going to be brutal.

65

On the same day that Hank and Gomes were having their come to Jesus discussion about the future, Pamela was in Government Center in Boston wrapping up a meeting with a potential client for a photo shoot. Bracing for the cold and the wind, she headed to her car, conveniently parked not far from her meeting point.

Her next stop was Porter Square in North Cambridge, where she had a meeting scheduled with a friend from high school. She left Boston, and made her way across the river into the Lechmere section of Cambridge.

The moment she hit the neighborhood she found herself thinking that East Cambridge was not very welcoming to Black folks, so she needed to be careful. A second, unrelated thought, was about Mariana. She remembered that David's intern came from East Cambridge and had a fleeting thought to stop by Mariana's parents' home and just check on her. Like David, she was concerned with the way the young woman had left Hyannis and that she *might* have been forced to leave.

At a stop light Pam took her address book out of her purse. Pam remembered that she had written down Mariana's East Cambridge contact information in case there were problems and her folks needed to be notified. David never asked her to do this, but sometimes she had to do the thinking for the two of them.

Before the light changed, she found Mariana's address and home phone number. Yes, she did live on Cambridge Street. As Pam remembered, Mariana said something about living on the second floor of a three-decker. As the traffic started to move, she looked to her left for the addresses. Sure enough, based on the numbers, the house would be on the left side and she was getting closer, until… the numbers seemed to skip.

Assuming she had made a mistake, Pam pulled into an open space and parked. Leaving the car running, she checked the address in her book and then looked across the street. Something was wrong.

She turned off the car and got out, locked the door and proceeded to the corner, where she crossed the street. There was a delicatessen right in front of her on the corner.

Making a right turn when she reached the other side, she walked a few feet, looking at the numbers. They were too high.

Turning back toward her car, she glanced at the deli. On the door was the address she had been seeking.

None of this made sense, so she walked to each of the neighboring three houses and read the names on the mailboxes to see if she had written the address down incorrectly. There was no "Alvares" family on any of those houses. She even crossed the street to make sure.

Pam decided to go into the deli and see what she could find out. She looked around and, seeing nothing remarkable, decided to speak with the cashier to see whether he might know Mariana or her family. The man, a twenty-something, skinny with light brown hair and a thin moustache, wearing a sweatshirt with a Portuguese flag on it, was with another customer.

The phone rang. The cashier picked it up and barked, "Talk to me."

It was the way that he answered the phone that struck Pam. No "hello," no giving the name of the deli, just, "Talk to me." Not how one would expect someone at a store to answer the phone. She watched as the cashier kept the phone balanced near his ear, wrote something down and handled a customer, all at the same time.

Pam exited the store and looked for a payphone. She had plenty of change, so that would be no problem. She had to walk two blocks to find one. She knew the number by heart.

"*Cape & Islands Gazette/Boston Observer*, may I help you?" were the words of receptionist and administrator Marcia Blake.

"Marcia, this is Pamela. You know, David's wife. Listen, not to be rude, but is Jacqueline there? I need to speak with her as soon as possible. It's sort of urgent."

"Sure, Pamela. Hold on for a moment, would you?"

There was silence until Marcia returned to the line, asking Pamela to hold for the connection.

"Pamela, is everything alright?" Jacqueline asked cautiously, fearing that David had discussed Wellfleet with his wife.

"Yeah, Jacqueline, as far as I can tell. But listen, I need to ask you for a strange favor. I need you to call the number that Mariana gave David as being her family's home number. It's probably the number that you have for her. If a man answers, please engage him in a discussion. Tell him that you're looking for Mariana. Tell him that you're from the paper, that you wanted to send her a sort of bonus…whatever. But try to keep him on the line for a few minutes."

"When should I do this, Pam?"

"Give me…five minutes. If he answers and tries to get you off the line, try to keep him talking for a little while. Don't do anything suspicious. Then hang up. I'll call you after. Thanks. Here's the number."

Pam gave Jacqueline the number, hung up and walked back to the deli. As soon as she entered the store the cashier gave her a doubletake, then returned to the customer in front of him. Pam walked over to the refrigerated section and picked out a bottle of *Gatorade*. As she walked toward the counter the phone rang.

Even with another customer in front of Pam, she could hear one side of the conversation. The cashier was trying to be courteous, though he was abrupt. She heard him say things like, "I'll be sure to tell her," "I'm not sure when we'll hear from her," and "I'll tell the folks when they get home."

Pam paid for the *Gatorade* and left the store, proceeding back to the payphone, where she put in another call to Jacqueline.

"What is that famous line the astronaut on Apollo 13 said: 'Houston, we have a problem.' Jacqueline, I think that things just became more complicated."

66

Pamela's next call was to the friend she was going to meet in Porter Square. She called and asked that they meet a little later than planned, something had come up. Her friend was very accommodating, having nothing pressing to do that afternoon at her office.

Regularly overshadowed by its neighbor to the south, Lesley College is a small women's college north of Harvard University off of Massachusetts Avenue that specialized in education. Pamela had no trouble finding the school and made her first stop the administration building.

"Excuse me," Pamela said to a young Asian woman standing behind the counter in what appeared to be the central office. "I'm hoping that you can help me."

The woman, 5'3" in her mid-20s, with a white blouse and brownish/black skirt, walked over with a smile.

"Hi, I'm Pamela Peters. I'm a graduate student and teaching fellow over at B-U. I'm bringing on some interns and there's a young woman named Mariana Alvares who applied and informed me that she attended Lesley as an undergrad."

The young woman looked at Pamela pleasantly, waiting for her to finish and ask her question.

"I guess what I'm wondering is whether I can check on her references. I happened to be in the area—going up to Porter Square to meet someone—and had extra time, so I figured I'd just drop by here."

The young woman asked: "Do you have the names of any of

her references so that I can assist you?"

"As a matter of fact, I do. There was a professor, Doctor Deborah Novick, and a professor named Doctor Charles Everett. I just don't have any specific contact information for them," Pam offered, having obtained the names from Jacqueline when they had spoken.

"No problem, Miz Peters, this is easy. Doctor Everett took a teaching position in Minnesota at the end of the last school year. I can give you his new information, if you like. Doctor Novick has a temporary office in this building, her floor is being rehabbed. Let me call and see whether Doctor Novick is available."

While the administrative assistant was following up, Pamela walked around the office lost in thought, and worrying.

"Here we go," said the assistant with a cheerful tone. "This is the contact information for Doctor Everett. And Doctor Novick is free to see you now. Her temporary office is two-one-zero, right upstairs. You can exit here, go to the left and take the stairs up. You should have no problem finding her office."

Pamela thanked her and hurried to Novick's office. The door was open when she arrived, but Pamela knocked, gaining the professor's attention.

Doctor Novick was tall, in her forties, with short brown hair and glasses, wearing a non-descript pantsuit and her coat over her shoulders. She ushered Pam in with a welcoming smile.

"Thank you for seeing me, Doctor Novick," Pamela started.

"No problem at all. Please sit down and tell me how I can help you. Forgive me for wearing my coat, this temporary 'cave' can get a bit chilly." She lifted her glasses away from her eyes onto her forehead.

Pamela recreated the story about Mariana. She described what she needed in someone and said that Mariana had been an intern in Hyannis. Doctor Novick listened carefully.

"Over the summer I got a reference call from a gentleman on the Cape who worked for a small paper. I'm sorry that I don't remember his name. But as I told him, Mariana is outstanding. A great writer. Great follow through. I was surprised when this gentleman told me she wanted to intern with him on the Cape. The last I heard she was on her way to Texas to work for a year, and then enter a graduate program at the University of Texas at Austin."

Remembering what David had told her about the inquiry, Pamela said, "Interesting. She seemed to have enjoyed her work on the Cape, though she told me that it was a bit difficult being away from East Cambridge."

Novick raised her eyebrows, looking perplexed.

"East Cambridge? You must have misunderstood her. Mariana was from Malden," speaking of a suburb to the north of Boston. "And she wasn't so fond of Malden either. Felt that it was too small. She always wanted to move on."

"I suppose I misunderstood her," Pamela replied. "Maybe she was talking about a restaurant or something in East Cambridge."

Pamela thanked Novick for her time and headed downstairs. As she passed the reception counter, a thought came to her and she stepped up to the counter. The administrative assistant—Pamela could see that her name was May Kwan—looked surprised to see her again.

"Miz Kwan, forgive me for bothering you, but one more question. Do you happen to have yearbooks in your office? It occurred to me that in many yearbooks they tell you something about the graduates, their interests…you know, things like that."

"Certainly, Miz Peters. There's a library room two doors down on the left. If you go in there you'll see on the wall yearbook after yearbook."

Pamela thanked her and went to the room. She found the

yearbook for the class of 1978, pulled it off the shelf and looked through it. She was midway through the class of 1978 when she stopped, looking at the face of Mariana Alvares, only the name under it wasn't Alvares.

It was Fryda Nunes.

Pamela starred at the picture for a few moments and then turned the pages. She found pictures from different school athletic groups, societies, and organizations showing the *real* Mariana Alvares, as well as Fryda Nunes, the young woman who had presented herself to everyone on the Cape as Mariana.

Pamela decided to go back upstairs to Dr. Novick. When she arrived at the office, Novick looked up. Surprised at seeing Pamela again, Novick attempted a smile, shifting her glasses at the same time.

"Did you forget something, Miz Peters?"

"Doctor Novick, my apologies. Something just occurred to me. Mariana mentioned a friend of hers from her class, a young woman named Fryda Nunes. I was wondering about her and other peers of Mariana."

Novick's eyes widened.

"Mariana described Fryda as a 'friend'? I can't imagine that. Yes, they knew each other, but I would hardly describe them as friends."

Pamela eased over to the same chair she had been sitting on earlier and reseated herself.

"Miz Peters, to begin with, Mariana is politically on the Left. I don't know whether she is or has ever been in a leftist organization, but she is on the Left. Fryda was a conservative the entire time she was enrolled here. I saw her engage in a class debate about the impact of colonialism on the Third World. She took the position that colonialism had saved those populations. She used the Portuguese colonies as examples of where Europeans had 'uplifted' the native populations. I have no doubt Fryda believed that right wing crap."

"I'm not sure how I would have misunderstood."

"Mariana and Fryda would frequently clash. Some of it was probably personal, but it was mainly political. Fryda was Portuguese, from East Cambridge. She looked down on Mariana, mocking her for not being a 'real Portuguese.' I am baffled that Mariana would speak well of her."

Novick looked at Pamela curiously as if she smelled a rat. Pamela realized that she needed to say something quickly.

"She may have used the term loosely or I just made an assumption. I think that it may have been in the context of her saying that she did not hold things against people personally if there were political differences…that she could find good things in people. Something like that."

Novick appeared to relax and smiled, though she kept a skeptical look.

"That's possible. That sounds like Mariana. It sure doesn't sound like Fryda. It is true that Mariana did not hold any ill-will against others unless that person was cruel. But I wouldn't waste my time seeking out Fryda. I don't think she could help you understand Mariana."

Pamela thanked Novick, exited her office and the building. She had always had the sense that 'Mariana' was too good to be true, but she never guessed that the plot would play out this way.

Driving towards Porter Square and the meeting with her friend that she wished she could cancel, Pamela realized with the force of a strong gale that the fake Mariana must have been the leak in the operation.

Fryda was responsible for Cunha's murder.

And the murder attempt on David and Alice at the club.

No wonder she left town so abruptly.

67

Gomes tried to reach Pamela after speaking with Hank. Failing to reach her, he decided to kill time, as Hank had suggested, and went to lunch, then spent the lion's share of the afternoon in the Hyannis Library, leaving around 5 pm to have dinner out before returning home.

Gomes walked into his own house late that evening. After looking around for signs someone had entered the home, he turned up the heat and made a quick check to ensure that the pipes had not burst from the cold. The silence was eerie, but being back in his own place was a relief.

After unpacking he got on the phone to call his folks and catch up. They were relieved by his return. When he reached Pamela, he told her he was home, safe and sound, but that there had been another attempt on his life while away. Pamela wanted all the details, but Gomes told her that he would explain everything when she got home. The main thing was, he wanted her to know that for now, it was okay to be back in Hyannis.

Hanging up the phone, Gomes decided to make a quick trip to the store to restock the house. The trip ended up taking longer than Gomes planned, as he bought more food, beer and wine than he expected.

As Gomes was putting everything away, the doorbell rang, startling him. He was not expecting anyone. He looked through the peephole and saw a tall Black man he did not recognize. Gomes opened the door cautiously.

"Mister Gomes, I'm Hart. I've been watching your place while you were out of town. Our mutual friend's a great guy who rediscovered his lost love and, surprisingly, she was willing to take him back!"

That was apparently the code, since few people knew that Hank's wife had initially dumped him because he had been such an ass. Gomes opened the door and invited Hart in, giving him a chance to get a better look at the man.

Hart looked to be in his forties, with a graying Afro and milk chocolate skin. He was wearing navy blue construction worker coveralls. Over the coveralls Hart wore a Navy peacoat, a black scarf around his neck and a knit cap on his head.

"Mister Hart, I appreciate everything that you've done. Please take off your coat. Have a seat and relax."

"Just call me 'Hart' Mister Gomes. Just 'Hart.'"

"Then you can call me 'David' or 'Gomes.'"

Hart grunted and moved into the living room to take a seat.

"Mister Gomes," he started, ignoring David's request as to how he should be addressed, "I'm glad that we have some time to chat before your wife returns from Boston. Hank asked that I stay with you for a while. I work as a handyman and painter during the day. I leave early, usually by six thirty. I can sleep on your couch, if that's good for you, and I can leave my things in your extra room so they're out of the way."

"How long will you be with us?"

"Hard to say. We'll have to see how things play out. In terms of your security, you should know that I've set up some alarms around the house. You would not necessarily recognize them as alarms, but they will indicate where someone has been snooping. And if I am not here, I'll be checking when I return to see whether any of them were set off.

Seeing that Gomes was having trouble processing this news, Hard added, "I need you to go about your life. Just watch your back."

"Oh, what do we owe you for this, Hart?"

Hart looked at Gomes as if Gomes had just spoken Mandarin.

"Nothing, Mister Gomes. If you let me sleep here, that's fine. I'll check on my place. If anyone asks why I'm here you just tell them I'm doing some work on your house and that my own place is being redone," all said with a slight Southern drawl.

"But there's one thing that we need to discuss, Mister Gomes, and that's—"

The door opened and in walked Pamela with a huge grin. The grin quickly turned to puzzlement when she saw Hart.

"Pamela!" Gomes said, throwing his arms around her, while she embraced him lightly, looking at Hart. "You don't know how much I missed you. What the hell are you doing here on a Tuesday evening?"

Looking back and forth between Hart and Gomes, she replied: "How could you think that after telling me that there has been another attempt on your life I would have stayed in Boston? Everything that I need to do I can do here or on the phone. Excuse me, but, who is our guest, David?"

"My apologies, Pam. Please, I would like to introduce you to Mister Hart. He will be assisting us with security for a few weeks."

"Thank you, Mister Hart," she said, cautiously, looking at Hart as if to inspect him.

"Just Hart," he replied.

"Then call me Pam."

Hart nodded his head politely and mumbled something unintelligible.

"Please get yourself settled, dear. I'll go pick up some Chinese food for the three of us. Relax. Hart, you want to join me?"

Hart rose from his chair and the two of them left to get food.

As the door shut, Pamela reflected on what she had learned and what her husband had been through, thinking, *We must have stepped through the looking glass?*

68

While Hart ate his dinner, Pamela and Gomes were animated in describing their last several weeks. The main discussion was on the attempt on David's life. Hart looked back and forth between the two as if watching a tennis match. Finished eating, Hart said he had to review some papers and would do it in the room that David offered him. He cleaned his plate and went to the room, closing the door.

"Where were you when this happened, David?"

"I was in Wellfleet."

"I know, you told me that. What I mean is, *where* were you in Wellfleet?"

"At Jacqueline's summer place."

Silence.

"What were you doing *there?* I thought the idea was to go somewhere that would not be linked to you?"

"Hank offered me a place in Northampton, but it sounded like too much of a chore. Jacqueline offered me the place and I knew that it would be isolated, given we're not in the tourist season."

Pamela had finished eating and got up from the table to clean her plate, then walked around the room.

"Was she there with you...David?"

"She came up New Years to bring me a dinner and then went home. It was the night that the killer showed up."

"So, you go to the home of your ex-girlfriend and hang out with her? Then nearly get *killed*?!"

"I don't know how the killer found me. And Jacqueline was

only there for part of a day. It gave us time to…work things out about the paper. I better understand her position."

"*I bet you do,* David." Pam crossed her arms and straightened her back. "Are you reopening old ties?"

Gomes silently got up from the table and went to clean off his plate. He used this moment to try to figure out what he should say. Part of him wanted to tell her everything that happened, but he dreaded how she might respond if he told the whole truth.

"Pamela, when you and I reconnected, we both knew that, while apart, we had other relationships. I never asked you for any details and you never asked me. I'm going to break that agreement now.

"Jacqueline and I were very involved when you and I broke up. We had always been friendly, but when you and I split up, she and I…connected. But I was always troubled that she was my boss. And I was troubled that she was not…you."

Pamela gave him a hard stare as he sat back down at the table.

"When you and I reconnected I broke off the relationship with Jacqueline even before you and I returned to…*intimacy.* I knew that I wanted and needed you. Jacqueline understood that and continues to *understand* that. I will always have feelings for her. She has been an excellent boss and friend. Under other circumstances I might have pursued a relationship with her, but there were no other circumstances. There was the fact that she was my boss and there was the fact that you are…*you.*

"Jacqueline needs to leave the Cape. I also need to leave the Cape. But I need to leave the Cape *with you.* That became very clear to both of us in the course of her visit to Wellfleet."

Gomes reached out for her hand. "I'm not asking you about who you saw while we were apart. I just want you to understand… me. It might have been stupid for me to go to Wellfleet, but it seemed safe and reasonable at the time. I know that Jacqueline would not tell a soul where I was hiding out. And I want *you* to know that I have no desire to get back together with her. I could tell you that she means nothing to me, but you would know I wasn't being straight with you. The bottom line is that…you are my future."

Gomes knew that he could say no more. He was not going to argue out his conscience verbally. Nothing would be gained by discussing it further since there was no going back to Jacqueline. That ship had sailed.

Pamela took Gomes' hand. Holding it tightly, she said, "David, I know how the killer found you."

69

Shocked by his wife's words, Gomes sat and listened as Pamela explained about the phony Mariana, working her way through the details. He felt as if he had been a complete fool.

"I can't believe I got suckered," he finally said.

"Don't blame yourself, baby, she fooled everyone."

"But it's not just that she *fooled* us. Mariana must have been involved in Cunha's death. She must have found something on my desk, I let her use it when I was out. Damn!!"

Pam showed a flash of understanding. "I bet Fryda hung around the office. That's how she found out about Jacqueline's place in Wellfleet. She probably thought it would be a good hideout for you."

Pamela was about to add something when the door to Hart's room opened and out he peeked.

"Excuse me, Miz Peters," he said, coming out of the room. "I didn't mean to be listening in on your discussion, and I know that the two of you have a lot to discuss since you haven't seen each other for some time, but you're both missing the main issue."

Gomes and Pam looked at him quizzically, unsettled that he had been listening to their conversation. Pamela released David's hand and stood beside him.

Hart looked back and forth between the two of them. "The question is, what are you going to *do?* From what I can tell, the fascists dropped by here to check on your place while you were gone, though I don't know that for sure. And of course, they tried to kill you in Wellfleet. They're not going to forget you, Mister

Gomes. They'll be back. So…what do you want to do?"

As David and Pamela left the table to sit on the couch, Hart added: "Let me clarify the question. Our mutual friend told you, he—and I—think that you *had* four options. Those options are now down to two. Miz Peters, in case Mister Gomes didn't tell you, the options were: one, you return here and go on with your lives, assuming that the OESP will leave you alone. Two, you relocate and change your identities, since it's more likely the OESP is not going to give up. Three, go to the police and hope they give you protection. Four, you allow us to eliminate the problem."

Hart settled into a chair opposite the couple. "As of today, option one is gone. Option three, going to the police, is risky, they might not offer any protection or, as I'm sure that our mutual friend told you, they might have OESP members in their ranks. So, I think that's safe to say that you have only options two and four."

Pam's face tightened and her eyes widened as she thought through the implications of what she had heard. Hart looked very matter of fact, as if he had just commented on the likely contenders for the Major League titles in 1979. David stared at the floor, at a loss for words.

Pamela got up and walked toward the bedroom. David assumed she was angered by the discussion, but she came back a minute later with a folder. Sitting back on the couch beside David, she opened the folder and produced a notepad along with photocopies of a few articles.

"I got curious about the shootout, David, and since you were *incommunicado*, I decided to do a few things on my own. I didn't think you would mind." She gave Gomes a pointed stare and then turned to Hart, who sat forward in his chair, saying nothing.

"I called your *other* ex-girlfriend Graciela. at the *New Bedford Tribune* while I was in Boston." Pamela offered an ironic grin, poking at Gomes. "I told her that I needed to understand what happened in that shootout and wondered if she could help me by finding out pieces of information. She told me that the two of you had chatted about Alice Love, by the way.

"She's a good sister and she looked into what I asked. This is what she came up with." Pamela opened the pad and separated out a few articles.

"Of the three people killed that day, two were directly connected to the Souza organization, the OESP, though Graciela never mentioned the name of the group. The cops seem to look at them as something like a loose Portuguese criminal association; a kind of Portuguese mafia."

Pamela pointed at a line in one of the articles. "The guy killed in the club was one Salvador Carreira. Parents from the Madeira Islands; has a brother in the organization named Pedro. We'll come back to him in a second. The woman killed has no direct connection to the organization. The cops think that she was a contractor of sorts. Her name was Angela Boswell, out of Boston. She had many talents, including as a con artist and killer, though none of the murders associated with her were ever proven. The guy in the car was a former small-time car racer, believe it or not, named Tony Veiga, also connected with the organization."

Pamela stopped for a second and looked at the two men, who stared at her, completely engrossed.

"The police assume that Souza was behind the hit. He sent Carreira to take care of it and Carreira put together his own crew. Having Boswell there was a stroke of brilliance, it left everyone with their guard down. Had you not had assistance, David, they would have been successful.

"Carreira has a brother in the organization named Pedro, and *this* is why what Mister Hart raised is relevant."

"It's just 'Hart,'" Hart said in his low voice.

Pamela ignored him.

"Pedro Carreira and his brother have been involved in a number of criminal actions, some that they have gotten away with, others not. A couple of years ago they were *alleged* to have been involved in a murder-robbery of a fish cannery company called Poseidon Fisheries, Inc. It was ugly. The robbers came in to steal a payroll. Apparently, the chief accountant for the company was working late and wasn't supposed to have been there. The robbers killed him and took the loot. They also took a few other things and left the place a mess.

"Well, the guys were seen by this security guard making a get-away. The alleged robbers—the Carreira brothers—both had separate alibies. The security guard, who stuck to his eye-witness testimony, was the victim of an accident in the harbor. He ended up floating in the harbor and the case was dropped."

Pamela rose and grabbed a ginger ale while Hart and Gomes processed the new information. She sat down and looked at her notes again.

"Now, David, what you may find interesting—I certainly did— is that Pedro has a long-time girlfriend. *Rosa Macedo*. What did you tell me that your uncle and aunt said about her—that she was a Portuguese *'wanna-be'* or something like that? Well, yeah, she is."

Gomes said, "So you're telling me that Macedo has been tied with the OESP all along? You're saying that I'm responsible for the death of the brother of one of Souza's people at the shootout, making this not just political, but a blood feud."

Pamela said nothing. She just looked at David and then at Hart.

"Well, Mister Gomes, you've got a problem. These folks aren't going to forget you. This *is* personal."

"I think he's right, babe. Mister Hart's option four is startling, but I understand what he's saying. This is personal. We're in trouble. We're going to have to either disappear, or something is going to have to happen to these bastards."

Gomes got up and walked around the room. Hart added nothing. Neither did Pamela. Hart looked at Pam with a gentle smile to show his approval of her analysis.

"Alright," Gomes broke the silence. "We have to figure out a new option. I have an idea that may sound outright nuts, but I'll need help from my District Attorney friend Amato to pull it off. I'll also need your help on this, Pamela. You've already done a great job, but there's another place where you can make a real difference."

Gomes sat down and outlined what needed to be done. Hart and Pamela agreed it made sense, although Hart had reservations.

"Mister Gomes, even with this...even if everything comes together, I'm not convinced it will be enough."

"You might be right, Hart. But, let's try and see how it rolls."

Hart shrugged and went back to his room.

70

When Gomes entered the offices of what was now *CIG/Boston Outlook*, he was bombarded with questions about where he had been. His responses were evasive and he mentioned nothing about the latest attempt on his life.

He looked around and knew there was something different about the place. A nervous energy in the building.

After the initial excitement and questions, Marcia called Gomes over. "David, Jacqueline wants to meet with you and the transition director up in her apartment, this guy Arthur Franklin. I don't think you've met him, have you?"

"I haven't had the pleasure. Should I go upstairs now, Marcia?"

Blake pointed towards the door to the apartment in a way that suggested urgency.

Gomes proceeded upstairs, not even stopping at his desk. He knocked on Jacqueline's door and walked in.

The man standing there would not have fit into the old *CIG*. He wore an expensive grey suit, impeccably polished shoes, a white shirt and blue tie. A solid six feet, he looked to be in his late forties, with thick, black hair and graying sideburns. And he was white. Not that there weren't white people at *CIG*, they were just a different sort of white folk.

"Mister Franklin, I presume?" Gomes asked, walking through the door.

"Yes, Mister Gomes. I'm pleased to finally meet you. I've heard so much about you, particularly about these unfortunate attempts on your life. I understand there was another attempt just the other day, though Jacqueline indicated the police are trying to keep your name out of the paper, at least for now. I'm glad you are well and that we have finally met."

Reaching out a hand to shake, Franklin added, "I assume that you weren't hurt?"

"Not hurt, just shaken up and denied a full night of sleep," he responded with a chuckle that did not fool anyone. He found Franklin's use of the word "unfortunate" an interesting choice.

"Bonjour, David. I am pleased that you and Arthur have had a chance to finally meet," Jacqueline said, coming from the kitchen holding a tray with teacups, sugar and milk. She put the tray on the table and returned to the kitchen to get the pot of tea.

Gomes looked around and saw the several large boxes. There were empty spaces on the wall that were once adorned by paintings and pictures. Signs of transition. Recalling the New Year's night Jacqueline spent with him, Gomes fully understood what Jacqueline was doing.

"David, we wanted to fill you in on the transition," started Franklin after getting some tea. "Beginning immediately, I will want to go over your assignments with you. First, I want a complete report on the Pires story and how it evolved into a shootout at a bar in New Bedford and the attempt on your life in Wellfleet. I'm concerned about your safety, but I'm also concerned about any exposure for our paper. Please have a written report for me tomorrow morning."

Gomes looked over at Jacqueline, whose face had tightened, though she was trying to radiate a smile of assurance.

"Understood. I'll have it for you before ten tomorrow morning."

"Excellent." Franklin sipped some tea, then placed the cup down. "Now onto other business. For the short term, I want you to wrap up the Pires story. I don't want you to start with any new *major* stories, though I'm open to more limited ones."

As Franklin spoke, Gomes looked back and forth between Franklin, Jacqueline, and the teacup on the table. The discussion had shifted gears from a comfortable informality into the feel of a military operation.

"Boston thinks a lot of you, David. We want you to relocate to headquarters and take on new assignments in the main paper. We want you to do this sooner rather than later. We have sensed that you would prefer to take over the Cape and Islands operation after Jacqueline transitions back to Quebec, but we think that wouldn't be the best use of your talents and abilities."

As Gomes opened his mouth to speak, Franklin cut him off, saying, "But the primary reason for moving you is your safety. The attempts on your life must be taken very seriously, and not just by you. We think that it's in everyone's interest that you and your wife—Pamela, if I have her name correct—relocate and start fresh."

This was not the meeting that Gomes had been expecting. He sat taking in the implications of Franklin's words.

"Think about it over the next day or so and get back with us. If you are agreeable to this, we want to move quickly. In the meantime, we will be in discussions with the police about your safety."

After Franklin left, Jacqueline stood with Gomes in the doorway, saying, "I want to thank you for all that you have done for me and for this paper over the years. This is a unique opportunity for you. I hope you will give this offer *very* serious consideration." Jacqueline spoke with controlled emotion, barely looking at Gomes, sounding more like a spokesperson than someone with whom he had been so close.

Gomes sat back in the chair and finished his now lukewarm tea.

71

"Of course, I think we should do it!" Pamela said in the phone. "This is a tremendous opportunity for you, and I agree that this may help our safety. I won't be in B.U. forever, but my opportunities are much greater in Boston than if we stay on the Cape. And need I remind you that you were the one who was saying just the other day that you needed to leave the Cape?"

Pamela's excitement was contagious. Yes, his parents would have mixed feelings about their moving, but he and Pamela would both be stuck if they remained on the Cape, as much as they both loved the area. Plus, there were too many memories here that haunted him.

"Yeah, that's what I was thinking. But you know, Boston is a hard place to sink roots into. People are suspicious of outsiders. Some friends of mine have told me that it takes six or seven years to become accepted, at least in the Black community. And that civil war around busing doesn't make Boston the most hospitable place to move to."

"I get that David," Pamela replied, "and I know that we won't be going to any Red Sox games, at least any time soon. But the community will pull through, and we have some opportunities there that we both need to take advantage of. Hey, there's this Black state representative who's chosen to run for Mayor of Boston, so who knows what will happen!"

In some respects, there was no point discussing the move, Gomes understood that it *had to happen*. He recalled Franklin's comment, there was *no place for him in the new operation on the Cape*.

Gomes and Pamela signed off, wishing each other a good night and promising to speak the following evening. Gomes went over to reheat the food he prepared for himself and Hart, who was reading a copy of the socialist magazine *Monthly Review* that Gomes and Pamela had around the house.

"A few years back you couldn't have gotten me to read this left-wing stuff, but it's not bad. Leaves me with things to think about." Hart closed the magazine and put it down.

"You understand, Mister Gomes, this offer you got from your paper doesn't resolve the pickle you're in, right?" Hart looked at Gomes as if looking into his soul.

"I hadn't thought that far, Hart. They want to get me away from the Cape."

"That's noble of them, but they don't really understand what you're facing. They don't know about the OESP. They think that you're dealing with some street gang. I know they've spoken with the cops, and every so often a police car drives by here to check on you, but don't let that fool you, the danger hasn't evaporated."

"I know. And I know that you're pushing me towards war," Gomes said in a moody, angry manner, refusing to look at Hart.

"Not pushing you toward anything, Mister Gomes, just being real."

Hart finished eating and took his plate into the kitchen to wash it. Gomes felt embarrassed by his response but didn't apologize. Instead, he went to the telephone and dialed.

"Vinnie," Gomes said after Amato answered the phone, "listen, sorry to bother you."

"Never a bother, Gomes. What can I do you for?"

"I need to catch up with you. I've got a favor to ask, and I couldn't think of anyone better to speak with."

"Let's pull out our datebooks and figure out when and where, Gomes."

******

Amato met Gomes the following morning at *Emily's*, a breakfast and lunch place on Main Street where the two used to meet. Sometimes referenced as 'cops & contractors,' *Emily's* was a regular hang out for the locals. In the summer, tourists looking for a reasonable place to eat would stumble across the restaurant and become addicted to the place.

In the last few years Amato and Gomes met less and less. Changes in their lives left them less and less to discuss. But when they did meet at *Emily's* it generally raised their spirits. Amato was almost always there in advance of Gomes, regardless of what time his friend arrived. This Tuesday morning was no different.

"Mister D.A., how art thou?" Gomes asked as Amato stood up. They hugged each other.

"Not too bad, Gomes. Work has been intense." Amato sat back down, not mentioning anything about his family.

A young waitress came over to take their orders. *It seems like the waitresses are always young here*, Gomes thought, looking at the woman, a five foot, red-haired, freckled, probably twenty-something. Gomes and Amato both ordered fried eggs, bacon, potatoes, sausages, and coffee.

"Listen, Vinnie, thanks for meeting me this morning and going in late. Let me cut to the chase. I need some help."

Amato sipped his coffee as Gomes told his story, describing everything that led to the shootout in New Bedford.

Almost everything. As he told his friend about the attempt on his life in Wellfleet the food arrived.

"Yeah, I got a call about Wellfleet. You were lucky, Gomes. Detective Schwartz is going to sit on your name and Jacqueline's for the moment as the investigation goes forward. We don't want to make you too much of a celebrity, now."

Amato winked as he cut into the sausage and forked it and some eggs. "They may never find out who the assassin was. I just want you to know that. In any case, how can I help?" Amato filled his mouth with catsup-laden potatoes.

"Vinnie, the guy in the club who tried to kill me…he and his brother—the Carreiras—they almost certainly carried out a robbery and murder at a cannery and fishing company in New Bedford; a company called Poseidon Fisheries, Inc. A man was killed. The accountant. The Carreiras got away with it because they each had an alibi and the witness was killed."

"Classic defense tactic," said Amato.

"Vinnie, I need the full crime scene report. I need to know what was taken and what was not, where the body was found, you know, the whole nine yards."

Amato put his lips together and whistled. "Gomes, that's asking a lot. I mean, yeah, I have some connections in New Bedford, but, damn, why would you need that info?"

"It's better if I don't tell you why I need the info other than that it fits in with my story. If this whole situation blows up, I don't want you to have anything to do with it."

Amato was doodling with his pen, drawing on the paper place mat, not looking at Gomes.

"Alright, David, I'll see what I can do. No promises."

"That's all that I can ask, my friend." Gomes was getting ready to ask Amato about how things were with his marriage, but there was something in Amato's eyes that said such a conversation needed to go on hold for now.

72

Having made his decision, Gomes entered the *CIG* office the next morning and went upstairs to meet with Jacqueline. He saw that her apartment was becoming more cluttered. She was on her way out of town.

Jacqueline gave Gomes a hug and they sat down, though Jacqueline did not offer him any tea or coffee. There was a distance between them. They chatted for a few minutes and then he told her that he was going to accept the offer.

Jacqueline smiled and said, "I know that this move to Boston is the right decision for you. You will do great things."

Gomes noticed a tear in her eye.

"David, I am not going to apologize for the night in Wellfleet. What we shared that night convinced me, more than anything, that I need to leave the Cape. I thought that I had contained my feelings…for you…but I was wrong. I know that we have no future as a couple. But that night I needed to be able to say…to *feel* the good-bye to you in a way that…"

She did not end her sentence. David sat for a moment.

"David, I need to move on. That would be true even if the paper was in excellent shape. I am sorry if I created complications for you, but I am *not* going to apologize for our intimacy."

"Jacqueline, I almost think that it was inevitable. But that is why I had to say no, despite my feelings."

They sat and looked at one another in silence and sadness, a grief in their hearts.

"David, I will be leaving sooner than I expected. There is no role for me here." She raised her arms and pointed around the room. "This paper is no longer mine. It is a new project. I have a new mission that takes me back to Quebec. We...you and I...cannot be part of each other's lives. That is terribly sad, but it is the truth."

David tried to think of a quick come-back. Something optimistic that he could say to lighten the atmosphere, but he realized, as he opened his mouth to speak, that he had nothing to say. It had all been said.

And done.

******

When Gomes awoke on Friday morning, he was excited that Pamela would be returning home that evening. The house was silent, as usual. After exercising, Gomes walked out of his bedroom and headed to the bathroom to take a shower. To his surprise, sitting in the kitchen drinking tea, was Hart.

"You taking the day off, Hart?" Gomes asked, though Hart was dressed in his work coveralls, with a black shirt underneath.

"Not exactly. Take your shower and get dressed. There's something I need to discuss with you. Nothing urgent."

Gomes was showered and dressed in twenty minutes. When he walked out of his bedroom and headed to the kitchen to get some cereal for breakfast, Hart was still sitting there, drinking coffee.

"So, Hart, what's happening?" Gomes poured some milk over his cereal.

"Let's review the situation, Mister Gomes. We have to assume that the OESP is *not* going to let sleeping dogs lie. Option number one, you go on and resume your life, is dead in the water, if you'll forgive the expression."

Gomes finished off his cereal, got up and rinsed out the bowl. "What's left?"

Hart said, "I have to get into the field, Mister Gomes. I'll see you and your wife this evening and we'll talk this thing out."

Hart picked up his things and headed for the door, not looking back.

As he listened to the sound of Hart's car driving away, Gomes felt a powerful urge to pack a bag, jump in the car, meet Pamela in Boston and run away.

But he knew there was no place to hide.

73

On Friday evening Gomes returned home early from work, anxious to see Pamela. He looked around to see whether there were any suspicious cars in the neighborhood or strangers loitering about before entering the house.

Gomes changed his clothes, putting on jeans, sneakers and a sweatshirt, and pulled out a few items from work to review while he awaited his companions. These items included material from the Boston office to prepare him for his new responsibilities.

He heard the key in the door and the lock clicking, and was relieved to see Pamela. He hurried to the door and kissed her, then helped bring her things into the house.

They sat beside each other on the sofa and were just starting to go over their day when the doorbell rang. Gomes went to the door and opened it for Hart. Though Hart had a key, he always rang the bell unless he knew no one was home. *There was something about Hart*, Gomes thought. *Even after a day at work, everything always seemed in place.*

The unflappable man brought two large duffel bags in and set them down.

"I was just telling Pamela you wanted to discuss our plans, Hart," said Gomes. Hart suggested they talk over dinner and took his bags into the spare room.

Gomes went to work starting dinner while Pam went to change clothes. A few minutes later she reemerged, dressed casually in jeans, a black wool sweater, and house slippers, having removed the limited amount of makeup that she wore. She opened a bottle of red wine and poured out three glasses.

As they sat down at the dining table with their wine, Gomes saw that Pamela had a pad and photocopies spread out on the table.

"Gentlemen," she began, putting down her wine, "let *me* now lay out *my* report. Mister Hart, thank you for looking out for us. I just wanted to say, you are amazing."

Hart, who rarely exhibited any emotions, seemed to blush, seemingly caught by surprise.

"I looked into a few things. Poseidon Fisheries is the wholly owned subsidiary of a larger company called Poseidon, Inc. Incorporated in 1974. They have a cannery, fishing fleet, and more recently got into real estate in New Bedford and Fall River. It's unclear how they got their money. I asked a professor friend of mine at the BU Law School if he had someone who could investigate the company. They came up with a big question mark about them.

"They were founded in Boston by two Greek brothers. The man that was killed in the robbery was the godson of one of the brothers named Anthony Mavrakis and, according to a couple of articles I came across…" She pointed to the photocopies, "he was above reproach. One of the people interviewed for a story said that Mavrakis was a hard worker, but he did not stay late. He came to work early, before everyone else, because it worked best for his family's schedule. On that particular day he was behind in his work and needed to stay."

"Is this company mobbed up?" Gomes asked.

"It may be, David, but if so, it's being handled very well, and quietly."

"Who are the owners, Miz Peters?" Hart asked.

Pamela looked at her notes. "Damian and Alesandro Thanos," she replied, looking up and taking another sip of the wine.

"*Thanos!?*" Gomes asked, nearly shooting out of his chair.

Pamela nodded with surprise. "Yes, why?"

"That's the name of this guy that Hank mentioned. The CIA brought him over here after the Greek Junta fell in 1974. He was some sort of military person but worked for the Agency. Damn, this is odd as all get out!"

Gomes turned to Hart. "The Agency brings over the Thanos brothers *and* these Portuguese fascists and put them all in New Bedford. Interesting planning." Gomes raised his glass in a mock toast. "But I can't imagine that the OESP would have ripped off Thanos if they had known."

"That's a good assumption, Mister Gomes. I'm surprised that the Agency didn't tell both about the existence of the other. My guess is two different intelligence agencies were involved in this, and that's the reason behind this bizarre confusion."

"This is fascinating—" Gomes started to say, when the phone rang. Gomes answered it.

"Hello?"

"Gomes, this is Amato. Sorry to bother you on a Friday night. Listen, I have that information you wanted. You sounded like this was important, so I called in a favor. I can read you what I have, if you want?"

"Thanks, Vinnie. What if we come by your place in a few? It would be easier than my taking notes."

Silence.

"Mmm…okay. The wife is going out and I'm watching the kids. Sure. I guess. Drop by when you're ready."

Gomes thanked Amato and hung up the phone.

"Pamela, we need to take a ride. Hart, we'll be back in a while but there's no need for you to hang out here."

"I have nothing planned. I'll get some takeout and watch television."

"Pam, let's pick up some food on the way back. I need you on this visit."

74

The Amato family had a big four bedroom, two and half-bathroom house in West Yarmouth, about twenty minutes away from David and Pamela. This January evening there was little traffic and they got there in no time, pulling into the driveway next to a car that was running but no one in the driver's seat. It always drove David crazy when drivers would start their cars in the winter and leave them running; more fumes in the air and easy for someone to rip-off.

When they rang the bell David and Pamela could hear a television on in the background. The door swung open and Amato was standing there.

"My God!" he exclaimed with a tremendous Amato grin, "I got the dynamic duo!! Pamela, how the hell are you?"

Pamela and Amato hugged each other as he ushered them in. Right away Gomes sensed there was something off about the house. Perhaps the smell. Or perhaps how clean it was. Almost antiseptic. David's personal sensors were sounding off that this couple was in big trouble.

David and Pamela looked up as they heard Connie Amato walking down the stairs. The woman always was an enigma to David. She spoke very little and was near impossible to engage. He and Pam had seen Vincent and Connie together only three times, but it was never comfortable.

Once, after they had dinner together, Pamela asked whether there was anything that *ever* animated Connie. Gomes had no answer.

The woman walking down the stairs was Connie with a makeover. David always thought that the woman was attractive. Her dark features and olive skin reminded him of Jacqueline, though Jacqueline radiated a very different beauty. On this evening Connie was dressed to go out, with a form-fitting red dress, a sweater-jacket, heels, and an expensive looking necklace. She had cut her hair to shoulder length; normally she let it grow down to her waist.

There was something in her look tonight that was not about just going out. It was about going out to see *someone*. *This is worse than I thought,* Gomes thought, looking over at Pamela, who seemed to be reading his mind.

"Well, David and Pamela...how are you both? A long time."

"Connie, we're good. Sorry to bother you and the family."

"No bother. I'm heading out. You can have Vinnie to yourselves." She walked to the closet to get her coat.

"I'm picking up Sylvia first, Vincent," she said matter-of-factly, "and I'll see you in the wee hours."

Connie walked into the living room, where the children were watching television and said something that neither Gomes nor Pam could hear. Amato looked at Connie with a sad and depressed face.

"Let's go into the kitchen," Amato finally said.

As they walked into the kitchen and started to sit down, they heard the door closing, with no further good-bye from Connie.

"Can I get either of you something to drink? Alcohol, no alcohol? Your call."

"We're okay, Vinnie, we don't want to take up your time. We appreciate your seeing us," Pamela said.

"You're not taking up my time." He walked over to the cabinet to get a bottle of *Jack Daniels*. Pouring the whiskey, he seemed lost in thought. He put the glass down on the kitchen table and walked out, returning with an envelope. He handed the envelope to Gomes and sat down.

"I can't give you a copy of the formal report, but I thought it would be easier if I typed up the information so you didn't have to memorize everything."

David and Pamela examined the report. It confirmed everything that they had previously heard.

"Why would they kill the accountant, Amato?"

"The question for the ages, Gomes. Maybe they were surprised that he was there? Maybe they're just sick bastards? I don't know."

Pamela and David kept reading the report. *Bingo*, Gomes thought, but did not say.

Pamela asked, "Vincent, doesn't it seem odd that these guys would come in to steal the payroll and then decide to add these other things to the loot?"

Amato took a sip of the whiskey and nodded his head affirmatively. "Yeah, it's odd. It's odd as hell that they would take the time to grab anything other than the principal objective of the robbery. It's almost as if they wanted souvenirs. Maybe it's just that, you know, they wanted trophies."

Amato rolled the glass slowly between his hands. "You're sure you can't tell me what this is about, Gomes?"

"Sorry, Vinnie. It's for your protection. It's about my story and it's not illegal. That's what you need to know."

Amato took another sip of the whiskey. "So, I hear you might be moving to Boston."

Pamela and David looked at him in surprise, mouths dropping.

"Where'd you hear that, Amato?"

"My eyes and ears are everywhere, folks. You should know that. Is it true?"

Pamela and David looked at each other, then over at Amato, nursing his whiskey.

"Yeah, looks like we're moving. The paper offered me a great opportunity in the Boston headquarters. This seems to work well for us. Plus, with Pam in Boston and the opportunities that she can get, it makes for a great deal."

Amato offered a sad smile, turning his attention towards his whiskey, whirling the whiskey around in the glass.

"I think you're making the right decision. This place is too small for the two of you. In the meantime, you're going to have to watch your back. We don't know who that guy was in Wellfleet. We may never find out. But my guess is that he's connected with the gang in New Bedford."

Neither David nor Pamela seemed to know what to do with that statement. Before they could respond, Amato's phone rang. They overheard him tell the other person to hold on. He put his hand over the receiver.

"Folks, sorry, this is a work-related call, I've got to take it. I hope the information is useful."

"Amato, you're a gem. Thanks so much. Let's catch up later."

They excused themselves and put their coats back on, heading outside to their car.

"What do you think?" Pam asked as Gomes backed the car out of the driveway to head home.

"About what? The crime scene report or the fact that we're witnessing the marriage of one of my best friends come apart?"

Pamela noticed a tear slide down the side of David's face. He did not move to wipe it away.

75

When they returned, Hart was asleep on the couch with the television volume on low. Gomes did not really want to talk tonight in any case, he had things to think over. He and Pamela slipped into their bedroom and found themselves in each other's arms. They held each other for what seemed like hours, their caresses blossoming into unplanned, intense lovemaking. Afterwards they drifted off to sleep, a renewed sense of closeness between them.

For Gomes, the sleep was interrupted by periodic fear of those who sought to kill Pam and him. But also a different emotion. A sadness about his old friend, Amato, and a realization that there was nothing that he could do to help.

On Saturday, Gomes decided he needed some time to think. A cold day, logic should have kept him home in his warm abode. But he needed to get out to think. Had this been summertime, he would have gone to the beach to throw rocks into the water. Instead, he decided to take a ride.

Gomes desperately wanted Pamela to accompany him so that he could talk this all through, but he dared not ask her. He knew she had too much on her plate with schoolwork. He also knew if he asked her to accompany him, she would not hesitate. After doing his Saturday morning house cleaning, he told Pamela that he had to go out for a while. She assumed that he was going to the office.

Gomes had no particular destination, only a route. He knew he had to piece together a fifth option to address his quandary, and he wasn't going to stop until he got one. Driving down Route 6A, past some of the most beautiful sections of the Cape, a plan began to form. He drove along the Canal down to the Bourne Bridge traffic circle and then followed Route 28 towards Falmouth.

About two miles from Route 151 the plan came together in his head. He exited onto Route 151 and returned home.

Pamela was taking a nap and Hart was out. Gomes moved quietly around the house, then sat in the kitchen to compose his thoughts. *If* his plan came together, it just might get him out of this box.

The operative word was 'IF'.

******

Hart got back around 5 pm. Pamela was wide awake, working away. After Hart settled in, Gomes asked, "Hart, Pamela, have time for a chat? I want to run something by you two. It may sound crazy, but I think I've come up with *option number five.*"

The three gathered around the kitchen table.

Gomes said, "I took a long drive today and considered the options. I've come up with a fifth way."

For the next thirty minutes Gomes laid out his plan, Pamela and Hart listening carefully and making notes. When Gomes was finished, Hart walked over to boil water for tea.

"Mister Gomes, you've got quite an idea there. I think the logic basically works. A version of Mutually Assured Destruction. There's no guarantee it will work, but it's worth a shot. Except for one thing."

Gomes and Pamela looked at him in anticipation.

"If you're going to go this route, Mister Gomes, you'll need me and Pamela. You can't go into the lion's den without our support."

Pamela nodded her head vigorously. "I agree, babe. I know you want to protect us, but Hart and I aren't kids."

"But—" started Gomes.

"No, Mister Gomes, there really are no 'buts' on this one. Let me explain what we'll need to do. And let me add that I have already done some preliminary reconnaissance, so I'm not talking off the top of my head.

Hart looked down at his notes a moment. "I think that we can do it on Friday if you—Miz Peters—can take off from work and join us?"

Pamela nodded in agreement.

"Alright then. To do what you're suggesting, this is what will need to happen."

Hart laid out his addendum to David's plan. There were a couple of moments when David attempted to interrupt, but Hart would not permit it. He walked through his points.

When Hart was finished, Gomes said, "I can see the logic in your proposal, and I can't argue against it. It scares me, but it makes sense."

"Excellent. Then let me go to work on my preparations. And you better make sure that you have all of your ducks in a row, or we're all going to be in deep shit."

Characteristic of Hart, his look was glum. And deadly serious.

76

Having agreed to take the new position in Boston, the question was when he and Pam would be moving. Franklin, pleased by David's decision, suggested that in two weeks he start working five days a week in Boston, with the aim of relocating permanently. Everyone understood it would take time to sell their home and find new accommodations. In the meantime, Pam's place in Alston-Brighton would have to suffice.

This entire situation left Gomes uncomfortable. Since it was public that he was moving on, he felt less and less relevant to the *CIG* operation. He completed his assignments, including some promised articles and an op-ed, but he was not invited to meetings and he rarely saw Jacqueline. He felt as if he was becoming a ghost.

Had he not been preoccupied with the operation this coming Friday, he probably would have become unhinged. Everyone at the paper was polite, even friendly, asking where he might live in Boston, and then the conversation would drift off or simply end abruptly.

The clock was counting down to Friday.

******

Gomes was home early on Thursday afternoon. With little to do in the office, he returned to his place and spent the afternoon cleaning up. He thought about what he would take with him to Boston, but another thought kept intruding on his mind: *Would tomorrow's action work, or, would he find himself dead?*

Hart and Pamela arrived home within minutes of each other. Gomes had prepared a spicy spaghetti dinner, figuring they would meet over a meal. The smell of garlic bread toasting whet everyone's appetite. Gomes passed around glasses of red wine.

"So, let's go over everything," started Hart, a heap of spaghetti wound around his fork. "I'm heading out early tomorrow so I can be situated by nine-thirty."

Pamela asked if he had the vehicle.

"It's all taken care of, Miz Peters. I have a full description and the registration should be in the glove compartment."

Hart opened a small briefcase and pulled out two walkie-talkies. He turned them on to check their power, tested them and handed one to Pamela.

"Miz Peters, I'm 'Knight One.' You're 'Knight Two.' No names are to be used. I will signal you once I'm in position. From that moment on, you are to leave this on at all times. There is one of those earphones they have for transistor radios. You'll keep that in your ear, but you'll have to speak directly into the walkie-talkie. When you drop off Mister Gomes, you'll check in with me. You'll then drive around until I signal you.

Pamela carefully placed the walkie-talkie in her bag.

"Now, Mister Gomes, when you come outside after you've completed your work you will put your bag down on your *right* side and stretch as if you have been cramped in. If everything is okay, you shall pick up the bag with your *right* hand. If you suspect that there are *ANY* problems, you will stretch and then pick up the bag with your *left* hand. In any case, you will turn to the right after leaving the establishment and keep walking until Miz Peters connects with you. Understood?"

David and Pamela nodded in the affirmative.

Gomes said, "If all goes well, I should be out of there between forty-five minutes to an hour after entering."

"That makes sense," Hart replied. "If it doesn't go well, this could be a very brief meeting."

Under other circumstances, his statement could have provoked a chuckle.

"Miz Peters, you should drive around the area, but don't attract any attention. If there's a parking lot where you can sit, that's fine. I realize that it'll be cold, so it might be better to just keep driving and keep the heat pumped up. Bring a magazine or a book, though, in case you find some place to stop. But don't leave the car to sit in a restaurant or café. Be ready to move quickly. When you get the signal from me, you'll head to County Street, where you dropped off Mister Gomes, and you will continue down the street until you see him. You will then pick him up UNLESS I radio you about any problems. Then, you head back here.

"One more thing, folks. Dress warm, it's going to be a frigid night and one hell of a cold morning."

They each nodded at one another. Gomes walked over to the television and turned it on. They finished their dinner, the only sound that of the television. Nothing more needed to be said.

Nothing more could be said.

77

Hart had been right, it was frigid when Pamela and David got into the car Friday morning. Pamela had the walkie-talkie and David had his briefcase. They headed off the Cape to New Bedford for Souza's Package Store on County Street. According to information Hart obtained, Carlos Souza arrived at his store between ten and ten-thirty each morning, working out of an office in the back. Hart said that all meetings took place in that office and the word on the street was that Souza regularly checked it for 'bugs.'

******

At 9:30 am, a grey 1974 Chevrolet pickup truck with Massachusetts plates backed into the driveway of a light brown, nondescript, two floor private home across and down from Souza's Package Store. Anyone watching would have seen a man dressed in a heavy winter coat with a wool knit cap get out of the driver's side and go to the back of the truck. They might have noticed that he was wearing painter's pants and work boots, but it would have been difficult to make out his face, except to say that he was wearing sunglasses. From a distance they would have been unable to ascertain that he was Black.

The man walked to the rear of the truck, opened the tailgate, and pulled out a toolbox and a rolled tarp, laying them both on the ground carefully. He reentered the truck and put a nicely printed sign on the dashboard reading: "D&G Home Rehab / Crew Working Inside." He then walked to the front entrance of the house and rang the bell several times. Looking at his watch impatiently, he walked to the side of the house and rang a different doorbell. When no one responded he opened the storm door. The main wooden door was locked, but it was weak and insecure. The man looked around, put his right hand into his pocket and then moved his hand over to the door as if he had a key. He pushed the door and it opened easily. The man was inside.

Hart walked up the stairs to the entrance for the second-floor apartment. The only sounds he heard were the creaking of the house, the heat turning on and off, and the wind outside. When he got to the door for the second-floor apartment, he found it to be more secure. He went into his toolbox, pulled out something that looked like tweezers and went to work on the lock. In less than a minute he was in the apartment.

Hart walked through the cozy apartment to ensure that no one was there. The beds were made and the smell of burnt toast lingered in the air.

Everyone was gone.

Leaving the door open, Hart returned to his truck, picked up the tarp and carried it upstairs, making sure to close all the doors to the house. He carried the tarp over towards a window facing the street and put it on the floor gently, then he surveyed the house. There was a porch on the rear of the house, but no stairs down from it. There was a rope ladder near the door to the porch, a precaution in case of fire and an excellent escape route if someone was coming up the stairs.

Hart could not find a thermostat, concluding that the heat was controlled on the first floor by the probable landlord. The apartment was comfortable enough now, but since he was going to have to open a window, the temperature would drop. With that in mind he walked into the kitchen, inspected the oven, turned it on and left the door open to provide supplemental heat.

Returning to the living room, he looked at the window. There was a sheet of plastic covering the window, extra protection against the cold. He carefully removed the tape from the window's molding so that he could lift it up without ripping anything. That task completed, he opened the window and the storm window, not too high, looking out to see what sort of view he could get of Souza's Package Store. Satisfied that he would have a line of site, he closed the storm window and unfolded the tarp.

The M40 was a well-known and highly effective sniper rifle. Hart had considerable experience with it and treated it the way a scientist would treat their most important instrument. He moved some furniture around so that he could brace the rifle and then opened the stand. He attached and tested the scope, then reopened the storm window and positioned the rifle to have a clear view of the entrance to Souza's. It would be hard to hit a specific target inside the store because of the displays in the store windows. If need be, firing a round or two at one of those displays would serve as a distraction, and he could take out someone coming out of the store. He had a clear view of anyone entering or leaving the store.

Satisfied with his position, Hart pulled the rifle back and closed the storm window. Sitting in one of the chairs, he opened a coffee thermos and took a couple of sips. He then pulled out the walkie-talkie from his toolbox.

"Knight One to Knight Two, come in. Knight One to Knight Two, come in."

Silence.

"Knight One this is Knight Two, over," came Pamela's voice.

"Knight Two, I'm in position. All secure. What's your ETA? Over."

Silence.

"Knight One, ETA ten-thirty. Over."

"Copy that, Knight Two. See you soon. Out."

Now all he could do was wait. Well, almost. There was still one more task.

78

Pamela and David spoke very little on their way to New Bedford. Once the car's heater got up to speed, they felt more relaxed. When they heard from Hart they felt even better.

As they entered New Bedford and approached Souza's, Gomes turned towards Pamela. "Listen, babe, I have no idea how this is going to play out. This is the best option I could come up with. Keep your fingers crossed. I'm sorry for all of the stress that I've put you through recently."

Pamela looked in the rearview mirror for a sign that someone was following them.

"I'll drop you off, as planned." Her voice tight. "The weakness in this whole thing is that we're going to be out of communication with you while you're in there. They could do *anything*."

"Yeah, I know. But if there's no sign from me in an hour, Hart will call the Fire Department and report smoke from the package store. It's the best we can do."

"David, I know you don't want to hear this, but I still think option four was the best course."

"You're right, I don't want to hear it. I don't want to start a war!"

"David, my love, someone already started the war. The question is, who will win?"

Gomes chose not to reply, letting her words reverberate in his head.

One block from Souza's, Pamela pulled the car over and stopped. She grabbed David and kissed him passionately. As he opened the door to exit, she slapped him on his rear and yelled, "Break a leg!" David closed the door and she drove away.

"Knight One, this is Knight Two. The customer has been dropped off. Repeat. The customer has been dropped off. Over."

Silence.

"Knight Two, this is Knight One. I copy. Out."

It's the waiting that would kill you, she thought, coming to her first stop light. *No pun intended.*

79

David Gomes walked casually into Souza's. A young man in a black wool sweater was at the cash register reading the sports section of the paper. He was about 5'5", slim, with yellowish-white skin and an unkempt black beard There was no one else in the store.

The clerk eyed Gomes suspiciously. "May I help you?" the young man said, putting the paper down.

"I hope so. I'm here to meet Mister Souza."

The clerk almost came to attention in hearing Souza's name. He moved his left hand underneath the counter.

"Is Mister Souza expecting you?"

"I'd be very surprised if he was. Please tell him that Mister David Gomes from the *Cape & Islands Gazette* is here to speak with him, would you?"

The clerk picked up the phone, mumbling something Gomes couldn't make out. Gomes looked around the store, acting nonchalant.

A door at the rear of the store opened and a hulking, bald gentleman appeared. Gomes thought he looked like the monster from *The Thing* dressed up in a suit and tie.

The "Thing" held the door open and signaled to Gomes to enter.

Gomes walked through the door and entered a world that looked nothing like an office for a package store. It was a large room with a desk situated several feet in front of the door, plus a good-sized meeting table to the left of the desk. The floor was thickly carpeted and the walls, finished with fake wood, had pictures and flags mounted, along with trophies on stands near the walls.

Behind the desk and to the right was a small refrigerator. Seated at the desk was Souza. He was not a big man.

Souza signaled to the security person to check Gomes out. The "Thing" patted Gomes down, looking for weapons and listening devices. The security person shook his head at Souza.

Gomes used this moment to look Souza over. He estimated that his foe was probably in his late forties. Souza wore a tailored black suit with a red tie and a tie-clip with the flag of Portugal. The man looked like he walked off the screen of *The Godfather*.

"Mister Gomes, this is a *very* unexpected pleasure! Please sit down. Can I offer you anything to drink? Alcohol, coffee, soda? Name it."

"Thank you for seeing me, Mister Souza. A ginger ale would be great, even on a day as cold as this one!"

Souza swiveled his rolling chair to open the refrigerator, grabbing two ginger ales, passing one to Gomes. The security guard stood behind Gomes not making a sound. Souza held a can of ginger ale out for the security guard, but the guard declined. Souza returned it to the refrigerator.

"What can I do for you, Mister Gomes?" Souza had an expression of deep interest, moving his thick and calloused hands to his chin, stroking his well-groomed beard.

"Well, Mister Souza, I think that there has been a *misunderstanding* between us and I'm hoping to clear that up. I get the impression you think I'm somehow after you. I want to assure you that I bear you no ill will. I was investigating a story and suddenly some people started to try to kill me."

Pointing at Gomes but speaking to the security guard, Souza laughed.

"Hey, Rodrigo, you hear this guy? He thinks that there's a *misunderstanding* between us."

Sliding his chair closer to the desk, his laugh disappeared as quickly as it had appeared.

"Mister Gomes, there's no misunderstanding. Let's see." Souza held up a hand in a fist and one by one raised his fingers. "One. You started to investigate the murder of a friend of ours. Two. You led us to the killer. And three, you took out, what, three of my people at the club and another in Wellfleet. I don't think there's a misunderstanding, Mister Gomes. I would put it differently. I think we have a *problem*."

Gomes felt his stomach tighten. He did all that he could to show no fear.

"I wanted you to know, Mister Souza, that I have not provided the cops with any information. I have not mentioned your name. Neither have I have mentioned the name of your organization."

Gomes saw Souza's eyes widen in hearing the reference to organization. "I want a truce, Mister Souza. Nothing else."

"Tell me who took out my people and then *maybe* we can discuss a truce."

"I don't know who killed your associates at the club. I was as shocked as you were."

Gomes gave Souza a puppy dog look and tried to come off as perplexed as the next guy. It didn't work.

"Mister Gomes, don't play me for a fool. My people at the club were taken out by a professional. That professional was clearly working for you. You can sit there and look as innocent as you want, but I don't buy it. Although, I will give you two points for admitting you killed my man in Wellfleet."

Gomes heard the security guard chuckle.

Leaning back in his chair, Souza said, "Let me explain the situation to you. First, relax, you look nervous. Nothing's going to happen to you while you're at my establishment, I've had enough trouble with the cops."

Gomes felt his stomach relax a bit.

"Now, about our associate, Pires. We 'encouraged' you to get to the bottom of that, a little pressure through a fear for your life. It

331

worked! You led us to the killer...*Alice Love.*

"But then, *you* turned the tables on us, and *I* lost several good operatives. You could not have pulled this off by yourself. I want to know who your associates are. Tell us and I'll leave you alone." Souza leaned forward and stared hard into Gomes' eyes. "You try to play the tough guy, then one day out of nowhere you'll be the victim of a fatal accident. That's the deal, Mister Gomes."

Gomes opened his mouth to speak but was cut off. "There's no negotiation here. You can think on it overnight, but that's the deal."

Gomes finished off the ginger ale and looked at his watch.

"That's it, Mister Souza? That's your final answer? No negotiating room?"

Souza looked at Gomes as if he was examining a hamster on a wheel. Gomes, heard the "Thing" open the door. Gomes stood up to leave, shaking his head regretfully, exhibiting great disappointment.

"Too bad you wasted your time coming down here, it's such a cold day. Cold as the grave."

Gomes, stood up and looked at Souza, who had a cat-holding-the-canary look on his face. *Now,* Gomes thought, *time to shift gears.*

"Let me ask you something before I go." To Souza's astonishment, Gomes calmly sat back down.

"Couple of years ago two of your operatives robbed this place..." Gomes looked up at the ceiling as if trying to remember the name. "Poseidon Fisheries."

Souza picked up a pen in his right hand that he clicked...in, out, in, out, in...

"A real mess from what I hear. The accountant was killed. Tied up, mouth gagged, shot in the head. Twice." Gomes shook his head in disgust.

"I *read* about it," Souza replied with a low, angry voice. "No one was ever caught. My people had nothing to do with it."

"I'm sure, Mister Souza. I'm sure. Two people were identified. The Carreira brothers, who you know. A security guard saw them and saw their car. They were questioned, but before anything could happen, the security guard had an accident and ended up a floater. And the Carreira brothers both had alibis."

The smile returned to Souza's face. He sat back in his chair and clicked the pen: "Accidents happen, Gomes. All the time. And sometimes people are incorrectly identified. You're smart enough to know that."

Gomes heard the security guard behind him chuckle once again, reminding Gomes of a hyena.

"Indeed. Now, as I was saying, this robbery was messy. The robbers took the payroll and killed the accountant, a man by the name of Mavrakis. Then they did something strange. They stole some personal items. Money from the victim's wallet and an expensive watch. An Omega."

Souza glanced at his watch, the realization of where it came from slowly dawning on him.

"And they took this very unusual and beautiful Greek nautical clock."

Gomes saw a twitch in the corner of Souza's lip.

"A Greek nautical clock," Gomes repeated. "Well, that clock becomes very important in this story. It seems that one of the Carreira brothers—the one who is still with us—has this girlfriend named Rosa Macedo. I happened to visit Miz Macedo some months ago when I first started this story. I looked at her beautiful house and, lo and behold, what did I see there but this Greek nautical clock. A clock that stood out precisely because it was Greek, and everything else was either Portuguese or from the USA."

Souza sat stone-faced. As Gomes reached for his bag, the security guard moved forward, but Souza backed him off with the show of his right hand. Gomes pulled some photos out of his bag and handed them over to Souza.

"As you can see, the photos are of Miz Macedo's place, and right there—I circled it—is the clock. And by chance, Miz Macedo is standing right next to it. I asked her about the clock, and she told me that a 'gentleman friend' had given it to her as a present."

Souza studied the photos, then looked at Gomes and the security guard.

"Now," Gomes continue, "what the Carreira brothers did *not* realize—and my guess is that you didn't either—is that the accountant was not just a hardworking CPA but was also the godson of the principal owner, Alesandro Thanos. Thanos was grooming Mavrakis to take over the company and was devastated when Mavrakis was killed."

Souza was glued. That twitch was still going strong.

"Thanos, as it turns out, comes out of a similar field as you do. He was a major in the Greek Junta, until it collapsed back in seventy-four. He did some work for a US intelligence service, and as gratitude was resettled here in New Bedford when the Junta collapsed. He brought all sorts of funds that he and his brother had stolen over the years and launched their business, the fishery being part of it. Their operation, Mister Souza, is not altogether different from your OESP.

"From what I can tell, Thanos was willing to accept that his godson was killed by persons unknown, even though the Carreiras were identified. Given the alibis, he left it alone, but by all reports this remained a sensitive issue for him. My guess is that Mister Thanos would be deeply, deeply disturbed to find out that your organization carried out the robbery and killing, and that an item from his godson's office became a gift to the girlfriend of one of the killers."

Gomes held an innocent look on his face, adding, "Does this make sense, Mister Souza or am I just rambling?"

80

When Gomes finished his story, Souza looked like a volcano about to erupt, his face turning every shade of red.

"Listen, nigger, *you're* going to sit here and try to blackmail *ME*? Are you *serious*?"

"No blackmail at all, Mister Souza, and I'll ignore the insult. I'm only demonstrating that you and I have an interest in a truce and letting sleeping dogs lie. You leave me, my family, and friends alone, *and* you leave Alice Love alone and I will wrap up this story without any mention of the OESP, let alone the robbery and murder in connection with Poseidon. It's that simple."

Gomes went on to tell Souza that he had copies of all the photos, plus additional material. If something happened to him or someone he cared about, all the material would end up with the Thanos brothers. And the police.

"So, Mister Souza, shall we agree to leave well enough alone?"

Souza sat back in his chair rapidly clicking the pen. He was moving his eyes over his desk as if looking for something.

"How do I know you'll keep your end of this bargain, Gomes?" Souza asked, more calmly than Gomes expected.

"You don't. No more than I know that *you'll* keep your end of the bargain. Both of us will have to fear the consequences of a double cross."

Souza laid down the pen and placed his fingertips on the desk.

"Gomes, you're playing a dangerous game. But you're correct, neither of us has an interest in letting the cat out of the bag."

"Mister Souza, let's understand each other. We need to keep an open line between us. If there are any misunderstandings, rumors or anything else, we need to check with each other right away and not make any rash decisions. Agreed?"

Souza gazed at his desk, not making eye contact with Gomes, never looking at his bodyguard. He looked like a deflated balloon.

"Alright, Gomes. I think you're right. I don't like the feel of being boxed in, but I guess you know something about negotiations." Souza gave a chuckle that displayed no humor.

Souza sat back, an impish grin on his face. Gomes stood up, shook Souza's hand and turned towards the door. The guard looked at Souza, then opened the door.

Once outside the store, Gomes set down his suitcase, then picked it up in his right hand as they had rehearsed. *Things had gone well.* He started walking, looking over his shoulder to see if Pamela was driving up. Gomes walked four blocks when he heard a quick honk. Turning, he saw Pamela pulling the car over and opened the passenger door.

Gomes got inside and kissed Pamela. "Let's get the hell out of here, gorgeous, before that maniac changes his mind."

It did not take Pamela long to get the car onto Route 195 heading home.

81

Hart looked through his scope as Gomes left the store, keeping his eye focused on the entryway to the store.

"Knight One to Knight Two. Knight One to Knight Two. The customer is ready. Over."

Silence.

"Knight Two to Knight One. Message received. On my way. Over and out."

Hart moved the rifle around looking to see whether anyone followed Gomes. There were no moves.

"Knight Two to Knight One. Knight Two to Knight One. The customer is secure. Out."

Hart disassembled the rifle and wrapped it back into the tarp. He moved the furniture back into place and resealed the plastic over the window, then returned to the kitchen, turned the oven off and closed the oven door.

As he headed to the door, he took out his walkie-talkie. Twisting a knob, he switched channels.

"Knight One to Knight Three, come in. Knight One to Knight Three, come in."

Silence. Then, "Knight One this is Knight Three. Over."

"Knight Three, prepare for the inspection. Make sure that there is a full complement. Over."

"Knight One, copy your instructions. Will prepare for the inspection when there is a full complement. Over."

"Knight Three, thanks. Please confirm the inspection when completed."

"Copy that, Knight One. Out."

Hart placed the walkie-talkie back in his tool kit and took it down to the truck. He walked back upstairs and retrieved the tarp and brought that to the truck.

Hart looked around and saw that no one was watching him. He removed the sign, climbed into the driver's seat, started the truck, and took off. His first task was to get rid of the vehicle and then make his way back to the Cape. Then he'd be able to relax.

Maybe.

82

Almost as soon as the door closed on Gomes, Souza stood up and howled like a werewolf. Because the room was soundproof, he was not concerned anyone would hear. The security guard stood still and looked at Souza.

"That fuckin' nigger thinks he's outsmarted me. Rodrigo, we need to get each of the *capitao* here tonight. Get on the phone and get them here by seven-thirty. And I want YOU—Rodrigo—to take care of a special assignment. I need you to get your ass over to Pedro Carreira's and pick him and his Black bitch up. Get hold of them and then call me. I want to know what the fuck that guy was thinking giving that bitch the clock. And the watch!!! My god, I didn't know where that asshole got *this* watch. What the hell were they thinking?"

Rodrigo picked up the phone on the meeting table.

"Hold it, Rodrigo. I want to be clear. That *nigger* is not going to get away with this. I want people to understand that."

"Boss, what do we do about him dropping the dime on us?"

"We don't take him down right away. We have some groundwork we need to take care of. First we need to find out about these Thanos brothers, we don't need a war with the Greeks. If the Agency sees us going at each other, we'll be in deep shit. No, we must convince the Thanos brothers that *we* are not the problem. We need to make the Thanos brothers focus their anger on Gomes."

"How do we do that, boss?"

"I'm gonna go to the Thanos brothers and convince them we knew nothing about the robbery. That it was a rogue operation. To prove our sincerity, we sacrifice one of our own. We've got to get them to believe Gomes knew all of this but held it to use against us rather than doing the honorable thing and going to them with the information.

"Do we really have to sacrifice Pedro?"

"Pedro's history. He compromised us, he pays the price. He and his nigger bitch need to be sacrificed so we're not at war with the Greeks. We pull this off, we can take our time getting rid of Gomes."

Rodrigo picked up the phone and dialed the first number, a wide grin on his face.

83

At the same time that Hart was getting his rifle positioned in the apartment and Gomes was meeting with Souza, a truck pulled into the alley next to Souza's package store with a regular resupply of beer from the distributors. They pulled in front of a metal door covering the entrance to the store's basement.

"Alright, Mario" said the driver to his co-worker in the passenger seat, "I'll go in and get the door opened, you get the lift ready and start loading some boxes on the dolly. I'll get the basement door open."

"Got it, Chuck," Mario said, exiting the cab of the truck. Neither of the men paid much attention to a disheveled looking man on the other side of the alley warming his hands around a little fire in a trash-can. With all his layers of clothing, the man looked like a giant panda bear with sunglasses. He threw some tree branches and bits of lumber into the fire.

Chuck went around the corner to the main entrance, Mario went to the rear of the truck to unlatch the lift and open the truck's rear gate. He pulled himself up and into the rear of the truck and shifted one of the dollies to load it with boxes. He heard the sound of metal against metal as the basement door lock was released, then the sound of rusty metal as the door was opened.

Chuck and the store clerk appeared in the basement door, where they put down a ramp with rollers on the left side of the stairs. Mario shifted the leaver to slowly lower the lift with himself and the loaded dolly. The lift hit the ground with a soft thud.

"Okay, Mario, Sal and I have some paperwork to go through.

I'll join you in a few minutes."

Mario, standing there freezing, knew that Chuck would do anything to get out of work, particularly on a day as frigid as this one. He began transferring boxes from the dolly to the ramp, watching them ride the rollers into the basement. Once the dolly was free of boxes, he entered the basement, paying no attention to the panda bear standing by the barrel.

The panda bear turned his attention from Mario to the windows that opened on the ally, checking to be sure there was no one looking out. He contemplated putting something into the fire that would produce a little extra smoke to disguise his moves but decided against it. No point risking a call to the fire department.

He sauntered over to the truck and walked into the small space between the vehicle and the package store. Someone watching him might have assumed he was seeking a private place to relieve himself. But the panda bear—otherwise known as Alonzo Fleming—had other objectives. Standing near the edge of the truck, he listened carefully to the sounds coming from the basement. He heard shifting boxes, then, a voice yelling into the basement.

"Mario, come on up here, Sal made some coffee! Get a cup and then we can finish unloading together!"

"Comin' right up!"

Apparently unconcerned about theft, Mario shifted one more box and then headed up the staircase. This was Fleming's moment.

With a bag strapped over his shoulders, Fleming grabbed a box and carried it into the basement as if he were part of the crew. He moved quickly but quietly, hearing voices above him coming from the store. He placed the box beside others with the same brand, then surveyed the room to determine his best hiding place. He saw a space across the room near another set of stairs. Fleming guessed that those stairs went into Souza's office. Fleming moved over there, placed his bag on the floor and hid behind some boxes.

He heard a good deal of laughter from the men upstairs, then the sound of feet on the steps. The two men went back to work unloading the truck and stocking the boxes. The store employee— Fleming heard the other two refer to him as "Sal"— came downstairs and helped with some last-minute stocking, then and the three men headed upstairs, shutting the upstairs door behind them.

Once Fleming was satisfied that no one was going to return, he went to the bolted basement door to make sure he would have no trouble exiting. Seeing no potential problem, he returned to his hiding space and opened his bag. Pulling out a screwdriver and a flashlight, he began inspecting the basement, making mental notes. He pulled out his walkie-talkie and set it near his hiding spot. The volume was turned down so that he would know Hart was trying to reach by a blinking red light.

After walking through the basement, he determined placement and returned to his bag. He pulled out the first of two presents that would be delivered to Souza at the appropriate moment.

******

Hours later Fleming sat in his car, engine and heat on, watching the men enter the package store. Hart had been confident Souza would call a meeting of his team to deal with the problems Gomes had raised. Fleming's exit from the basement had gone unnoticed, the sound of the gate rising just enough for him to crawl out quieted by a healthy dose of lubricating oil. He could not relock the door, but it was shut, and it would not be obvious that it was unlocked unless someone looked closely.

When Fleming was sure the parade of visitors had ceased, he turned off his car's ignition and walked over to the package store. Looking in, he could see one man in the dimmed light. The man was pacing.

Fleming walked up to the door. The man inside, a large, hairy

343

brute who looked like a football player, approached the door. The burly man looked at Fleming and signaled for him to get away.

"I have something for Mister Souza!" Fleming yelled.

The guard kept signaling for Fleming to leave, but Fleming continued his demand to get something to Souza. The guard, looking completely frustrated, retreated into the store, put on his overcoat and returned, opening the door.

"What the fuck do you want? I told you we're closed!" The guard almost screaming.

"I'm sorry, sir, I was trying to tell you that I have a message for Mister Souza," he said, holding out an envelope with Souza's name typed on the outside.

"Who the hell are you? Who sent you?"

"My name is Frederick Olmsted. I was asked by a Mister Cabral to deliver this to Mister Souza's attention. He said that it was urgent. Would you please get this to him?"

The guard looked at the envelope skeptically, squeezing it to make sure that there was nothing besides a letter inside.

"Is this Cabral person expecting an answer?"

"No, sir. Mister Souza will know what to do."

Fleming walked off, with the guard scratching his head as he closed and locking the door.

The guard stood still for a moment trying to decide whether to interrupt the meeting. Since he had no idea how important this letter was, he decided to take a chance.

The guard entered Souza's office as the meeting was starting. The big man held up the letter for Souza to see. All those in the meeting turned towards the guard.

"Excuse me, Mister Souza, but this was just delivered, and the man said that it was really important."

"Bring it over here."

The guard walked over and handed Souza the note.

"Who the fuck is this from?"

"The guy called himself Olmsted and said that it was from a Mister Cabral."

"I know a million different Cabrals," Souza mumbled as he opened the letter. He pulled the letter out and read it.

Mr. Souza: You really should have trusted the deal rather than preparing to betray it.

The letter was unsigned.

Perplexed, he said to the guard: "What the hell is this about? Where is the guy who delivered this letter? I need to—"

Suddenly Souza stood up, wild-eyed. He looked at his men.

"Quick! We gotta, get the hell—"

Fleming was in his car a block away from the package store when he pushed a button. The brightness in his rearview mirror followed by the boom was all he needed to know.

He unwrapped a candy bar, took a bite, put the car in gear, and drove off. It wasn't long before the sounds of sirens began ringing through the area. He suspected that Hart and Hank would be more than pleased. And while there was nothing that Fleming could ever do to repay Hank for all that his friend had done for him, he felt an intense sense of satisfaction.

Another set of these fascist bastards gone to meet their maker. You can't take enough of them down.

84

David and Pamela went straight back to their place after the operation to continue packing. They had a meeting with a realtor later in the afternoon. By the time Hart showed up, everyone was drained, the adrenalin surge for the operation, gone. They ordered a pizza and bought some beer, the thought of cooking was simply too much. Over dinner they discussed what had happened.

"Hart, when the people return to their house, they're going to know that they were broken into."

"Yeah, they will…probably. But it will be a mystery to them. Their outside door will be broken. Well, they needed a new door and lock anyway. When they see that nothing was taken they will be left with a lot of questions, and no answers."

"What if someone tells the people in that house that they saw a truck?" asked Pamela.

"So what? Even with the best description, they'll come up zero. The truck wasn't mine. It will be found but there will be no fingerprints on it. We didn't have to exchange fire with anyone. So, it worked…for now."

Gomes gave Hart a squinted look, curious about his last statement but too tired to pursue.

No one had much energy, so the evening petered out. Hart agreed to spend another night at their place just in case something went wrong. David and Pamela retreated to their room. By the time they hit the sheets, they were out for the count.

******

Saturday morning everyone, including Hart, slept late. When

they finally got up, Gomes fixed an omelet, toast and coffee for everyone, Pamela returned to packing and cleaning up. Hart was busy getting his things together.

"Since you both are going to be heading to Boston, I guess this is pretty much good-bye," Hart said when they finally sat down to eat.

"Hart, you've been wonderful," Pamela said. "I don't know how we can return your generosity."

"Yeah, man, you were something. I hope we see you again, but under better circumstances. You know—"

The phone rang and Pamela ran over to get it. "David," she said to Gomes, "it's your cousin Ricky."

Gomes walked over to the phone, curious why Ricky would call this early in the morning or, for that matter, why he was calling at all. It was a rare event.

"Ricky, what's happening? Everything okay with you?"

"David, not sure whether you heard yet but…there was this explosion last night in New Bedford. It leveled this building."

"Is our family okay? Was anyone hurt?"

"No, David, it's not about us. I wouldn't even bother you except you mentioned to me a few weeks back about this Portuguese gangster named Souza who has this package store. Yeah, well, it was his joint. The place was leveled, cuz. It was closed for business but there was some sort of meeting going on. Everyone was killed, but nobody from the neighborhood was hurt. Fire Department said that it was a gas leak and that it could've been a hell of a lot worse. Anyway, I just wanted you to know."

Gomes slowly turned in the direction of Hart, who was finishing his eggs. Hart looked up, their eyes locking.

"Thanks for the call, Ricky," Gomes said and hung up.

"David, you look like you've just seen a ghost," Pamela said, staring at David's hardening face.

Hart raised his coffee mug and took a sip, calm and comfortable.

"So, you decided on option four after all, Hart."

"Is that a question or a statement, Mister Gomes?" Hart lowered the coffee mug, still looking relaxed.

"You tell me." Gomes shifted his body towards Pamela. "Pamela, there was an explosion last night. At the Souza Package Store. The place was closed but there was a meeting in the back, you know, where I met Souza. Everyone was killed. Ricky says that the word is that it was a gas leak."

Pamela turned toward Hart with a look of horror. "Hart, tell me you didn't do this. I thought that we'd all agreed on calling a truce. David worked out a deal with Souza. Why would you do this? Why, without even discussing it with us? We had an agreement!"

"You're assuming that anything was *done* and that I did it, Miz Peters." Hart looked calmly at her, leading her to look away. "Even if I did it, why would I admit it? But more to the point, your cousin, Mister Gomes, said that it was a gas leak. These things happen. And, Miz Peters, you were pretty clear that you would not have had any trouble with those fascists vanishing. So, it seems they're gone."

"Don't be coy, Hart. That's one hell of a coincidence that Souza and his team would all meet, the evening after I visited them, and they would be blown to pieces. That was not what we agreed to. And now the police will probably come looking for me, all those people killed. And innocent people could've been killed or hurt as well!"

Hart drained the last of his coffee and looked at Gomes, his expression never changing.

"You're a smart man, Mister Gomes. And, Miz Peters, you're just as smart. Your option five was very sharp. It didn't occur to me that there might be a way to pull the wool over the eyes of the OESP." He rose from the table and stood leaning against a counter, looking at Pamela and David.

"The problem is, you assumed that you had blocked all of Souza's moves. You assumed that you were dealing with someone rational. You assumed that Souza's anger wouldn't get the better of him. In sum, you assumed that you held the trump card."

"I know it wasn't fool proof," said Gome, but even so..."

"Try to understand this. I come from a different world. I'm not sorry they were killed in a *gas explosion*. After all, it was the intent of the OESP to kill the two of *you* in a gas explosion. No innocents were killed, so either God was looking out for everyone or the explosion was done in a way that there would be no collateral damage. Who knows?"

"You took an action without running it by us," said Gomes with growing anger, his hands balling.

Grinning softly, Hart replied: "Just like you didn't run by Miz Peters that you were bringing an assassin along when you went to meet Alice Love in New Bedford. An assassin who took out three people from Souza's operation."

Gomes opened his mouth to object.

"Please, Mister Gomes, let's be clear, the OESP was not going to settle for détente with you. This was a fascist military unit and a criminal gang, there was no way in hell they were going to allow a Black reporter—and I emphasize BLACK—to get the better of them. *No way.*

"As far as they were concerned, you were setting a very bad example from a business standpoint. Souza couldn't afford to come off weak in front of his organization. He couldn't have the reputation of having been stumped by a Black reporter who, by the way, was responsible for the death of four of his operatives. OESP is an organization of killers. *That's what they do.*"

"Yes, but—"

"Why the *hell* do you think Souza and his henchmen were

meeting there last night? For a *poker game*? Souza was *never* going to keep his end of the bargain.

"Never."

"I didn't—"

"Please, Mister Gomes, it's me you're talking to. No denials, no funny language. I get that you would no more admit you had anything to do with the termination of those operatives than I would about the explosion last night. I get that, but enough, alright?"

Gomes sat down, while Pamela remained standing. He looked at the floor, his anger turning into confusion and his energy slipping away.

"If you were going to take that step, you should've said something to us," Gomes offered in an unsteady voice.

"Really? First, *if* I had planned the explosion, you both would have tried to shoot the idea down. You know that! Second, *if* I had been responsible for the explosion, why would I want to implicate the two of you?"

"When the police come a calling, what the hell do we say?"

"Nothing," Hart said, his face softening. "Actually, you tell the truth, just not the whole truth. You went to meet Souza as part of your story. He denied any knowledge of Pires and could not explain why Pires came to the States. You then went home. Period! When the explosion happened, you were miles away, you don't know anything about it.

"Oh, and in case the issue of yours truly comes up, remember, I'm a handy man…a construction worker. I've been doing work on your place, nothing more."

"But what if they check into your past, Hart?"

"Let them look, Mister Gomes, they won't find squat." Hart walked to the kitchen to refill his coffee cup.

85

Relocating to Boston was delayed one week due to issues at the corporate level. With a reorganization going on, Gomes was told that he would be in the way and that it would not be a great entry. Despite his deepening discomfort at remaining at the Hyannis office—which was how he increasingly thought of the place—he stayed and helped with editing and researching stories that others would complete.

That Wednesday afternoon while sitting at his desk reviewing a well-written story concerning a zoning dispute, the phone rang. Marcia told him that Mr. Lopes was on the line and connected him.

"Mister Gomes, this is Lopes. You remember, the cousin of Alberto Pires?"

"Yeah, Lopes. Good to hear from you. What can I do for you?" Gomes leaned back in the chair, curious about what this might concern.

"Gomes, my aunt's gone. I mean, like, she's disappeared!"

Gomes sat forward in the chair. "When did this happen, Lopes?"

"The last time anyone saw her was this past Friday. She went to work as usual and left work a little early, saying she had a meeting. No one's seen her since and her mail has been building up at home. I called the cops and they got into the house but, nothing. No sign of her packing to go somewhere or what, just gone.

"Gomes, this is a long-shot but you spoke with her, do you know anything that could help? Or, maybe, could you look into this? I mean, you're a damn good reporter."

"Listen, Lopes, I appreciate the compliment but I really don't know anything. And besides, I'm being transferred to Boston, so I wouldn't be able to follow up on this sort of story. I'm really sorry, Lopes. I wish I could help you."

"Man oh man, I don't know what to do."

"Listen, she mentioned that she had a boyfriend. Have you called him?"

"That's the other crazy thing, Mister Gomes. I never met the guy, but some of her friends knew him. They tried reaching him, but he's not around either! I've got a bad feeling about this, Gomes. A really *bad* feeling."

"Lopes, there's a number of possibilities. They may have decided to split town together and elope. Maybe they'll be back in a few days. I think you were right to call the cops, but don't jump to conclusions."

"I guess so, Gomes. I just have a bad feeling about this," he said, sounding distant and worried as he hung up.

And so you should, Lopes, Gomes thought as he continued reading the draft. *And so you should.*

86

David Gomes sat at the table in his home office staring at the pages of the _Boston Globe_, lost in thought and not reading a word. His wife Pamela walked up behind him and draped her arms around his shoulders.

"Time to get writing, mister. I know you've got a million ideas about what you want to write about, but you seem to be second guessing yourself. Why don't you go write that novel you've been talking about?"

"Pam, I'm known for writing non-fiction, a novel would be a leap. I'm not even sure where to start."

"David, please. You have _so_ many stories to tell. Any one of them would be a good basis for a novel. Think for a second about some of the amazing people you've met in your investigations. You could use one of them as a jumping off point."

She kissed him on the top of his head. "Take the risk, lover, just start at the beginning," she said with a mischievous smile and walked back toward her office in their brownstone.

Gomes had just turned to the regional news from southeastern Massachusetts. Thinking about the advice that the love of his life had offered, he dropped the newspaper in the recycling box and turned on his desktop computer.

"What the hell," he mumbled as he opened a page for a new document.

Gomes would never read the article in the _Globe_. No one ever called him about it. It was sitting right there on the second page of the regional news—a small article that many people would skip over, but one that would have caught David's attention had he seen it.

In fact, it might have even helped him shape his novel.

Remains identified from a late 1970s missing person case

Mattapoisett, MA: The remains of one of two people found at a construction site for a new condominium have been partially identified as those of a Ms. Rosa Macedo, reported missing in January 1979. Macedo, then a resident of Fairhaven, MA, suddenly disappeared on her way home from work. The remains found with hers were those of an unidentified male. Curiously, there were also pieces of what police believe to have been an antique clock found in the makeshift grave. Local police were quoted as saying that the remains might never have been found had construction on a new condominium complex not been undertaken after the land was sold by the heirs of a wealthy, eccentric recluse. Police continue to investigate."

Acknowledgements

The Man Who Changed Colors is entirely a work of fiction. While there was a Quincy shipyard and that shipyard had a union, this is a fictional tale that uses the references as backdrops. Also, to my knowledge there was no Portuguese Secret Army Organization, though there probably was a similar organization with a different title. That said, any relationship to any individual or institution is purely coincidental.

The conceptualization of this story could not have happened had it not been for assistance that I received from Gloria Clark and Bruce Rose, both of whom helped me understand the city of New Bedford in the late 1970s. They were both exceptionally generous with their time and insight, and I owe them my gratitude.

I also received great support from screenwriter Mike Costa, who lived in both New Bedford and Cape Cod. This book could not have gotten off of the ground had it not also been for the assistance that I received from my dear friend Denise Perry, who read the first draft of the manuscript and offered critical suggestions. My old friend Jon Brandow helped me remember the shipyard days of the late 1970s, filling in critical blanks.

I was additionally assisted by my late cousin, Robert Hayden, Jr. who, unfortunately, passed away while my manuscript was being edited. Also let me thank Ricardo and Joao Rosa for their constant support of this project.

I cannot thank my publisher, Tim Sheard, enough for his excellent editing as well as continuous support for this project. Tim has believed in me, in this project...and in David Gomes!

As I noted in my first novel, *The Man Who Fell From the Sky*, conversations that I had with my wife, Dr. Candice Cason, and our daughter, Yasmin J.F. Braithwaite, Esq., started me down the road of writing these two novels. After I summarized the basic plot, Yasmin said—with the full agreement of her mother—"Dad, I think you have a story there…and maybe even two…" I took her at her word and wrote the first novel. After receiving surprising and humbling praise for *The Man Who Fell From the Sky*, I was encouraged to write a sequel. Remarkably, the outline of the story came to me quickly, as if it had been packaged and was awaiting a command to open.

I hasten to add that there is an additional reason to thank my daughter. She decided on her own that she wanted to be the final reader (and editor!) of this sequel. I was surprised when she made the offer and told her that she needed to work that out with my publisher, Timothy Sheard. She did just that and, presto, the manuscript became even better!! Thanks, counselor!

The Man Who Changed Colors takes place in 1978. Those of you who read my first book know that in 2004 David Gomes is alive and well. Thus, I was faced with the challenge of creating a mystery where the reader knows that, ultimately, the main character survives. This challenge forced me to construct a story where Gomes is trying to come to grips with several crises that he must address simultaneously. I am hoping that you, the reader, will enjoy and become engaged with how Gomes confronts the unsettling of what had once been a comfortable existence.

As with *The Man Who Fell From the Sky*, in writing this sequel I found myself thinking about my own experiences on Cape Cod, particularly as a child and teen-ager. I thought about the Daluz family, with whom my family developed an eternal bond, and I thought of my own family—mother, father and sister—who helped to make the Cape a magical experience for this boy from New York.

I hope that you enjoy *The Man Who Changed Colors*. ——
Bill Fletcher, Jr.

TITLES FROM HARD BALL PRESS

A Great Vision: A Militant Family's Journey Through the Twentieth Century, Richard March

The Activist Spirit: Toward a Radical Solidarity, Victor Narro

Caring: 1199 Nursing Home Workers Tell Their Story, Tim Sheard, ed.

Fight For Your Long Day, Classroom Edition, by Alex Kudera

I Just Got Elected, Now What? A New Union Officer's Handbook, Bill Barry

I Still Can't Fly: Confessions of a Lifelong Troublemaker, Kevin John Carroll (Winter 2018-19)

Love Dies – A Thriller, Timothy Sheard

The Man Who Fell From the Sky – Bill Fletcher Jr.

Murder of a Post Office Manager – A Legal Thriller, Paul Felton

New York Hustle: Pool Rooms, School Rooms and Street Corner, A Memoir, Stan Maron

A Pandemic Nurse's Diary, Nurse T with Timothy Sheard

Sixteen Tons – A Novel, Kevin Corley

Throw Out the Water – Sequel to Sixteen Tons, Kevin Corley

What Did You Learn at Work Today? The Forbidden Lessons of Labor Education, Helena Worthen

With Our Loving Hands: 1199 Nursing Home Workers Tell Their Story, Timothy Sheard, ed.

Winning Richmond: How a Progressive Alliance Won City Hall – Gayle McLaughlin

Woman Missing – A Mill Town Mystery, Linda Nordquist

THE LENNY MOSS MYSTERIES – TIMOTHY SHEARD

This Won't Hurt A Bit
Some Cuts Never Heal
A Race Against Death
Slim To None
No Place To Be Sick
A Bitter Pill
Someone Has To Die
One Foot in the Grave
All Bleeding Stops Eventually

Printed in Great Britain
by Amazon

41576687R00202